THE RISE OF
KYOSHI

降击神通

AVATAR
THE LAST AIRBENDER

THE RISE OF
KYOSHI

F. C. YEE with AVATAR CO-CREATOR
MICHAEL DANTE DIMARTINO

AMULET BOOKS · NEW YORK

Cataloging-in-Publication Data has been applied for and may be obtained from the Library of Congress.

ISBN 978-1-4197-3504-2
ISBN (B&N/Indigo edition) 978-1-4197-3991-0

Jacket illustrations by Jung Shan Chang
Book design by Hana Anouk Nakamura

Printed and bound in U.S.A.
10 9 8

ABRAMS The Art of Books
195 Broadway, New York, NY 10007
abramsbooks.com

FOREWORD

Any prequel story presents a unique challenge, never mind one set in a fictional canonical universe like that of *Avatar: The Last Airbender*. A common pitfall of prequels? Since the reader already knows how things eventually turn out, they are one step ahead of the hero. Done well, however, a prequel can expand and deepen a beloved fantasy world by exploring its history and characters in new ways. This is the case with *The Rise of Kyoshi*.

Readers familiar with the original Nickelodeon series might recall that Avatar Kyoshi was a legend, even among the impressive pantheon of Avatars. But how did she become a woman dedicated to fighting injustice throughout the world? And why was she so feared by her enemies? These were the questions left unexplored. In my first talks with F. C. Yee, we discussed a few possible plots but also asked ourselves: What kind of character is Kyoshi, what drives her, and what kind of events in her past could have caused her to develop into such a legendary figure?

I didn't envy Yee the challenge of tackling these questions. I knew he'd have to play within the conventions of an already-established world while simultaneously marking it with his own creative stamp. And the Avatar universe has no shortage of "must-haves." First, you must have an Avatar—the reincarnated being who holds the ability to manipulate, or *bend*, all four elements, who has a connection to the mysterious Spirit World, and who deals with conflicts among the Water Tribes, Earth Kingdom, Fire Nation, and Air Nomads. The Avatar can't do all this alone and thus must also have a core group of teachers and friends—a Team Avatar, as we like to call it. Political conflict is also a must: Whether it's a world war or a revolution, the Avatar inevitably ends up in the center of the fight before he or she is ready. And of course, there is never a shortage of epic bending battles.

Though all Avatars share certain rites of passage—such as mastering all four elements—each one must have a unique journey and face different personal and political challenges on their way to becoming a fully realized Avatar. In *The Rise of Kyoshi*, we meet a young woman so unlike the legend she is to become that we wonder how she could possibly transform into such a remarkable figure. She's not a great Earthbender. People don't even believe she's the Avatar at the start of the book—a great conceit on Yee's behalf, and one that provides the crux of the conflict for the entire novel.

Entrusting another writer with a world and characters that I helped create is always fraught with anxiety for me. In the wrong hands, it can be a disheartening experience. But when I read *The Rise of Kyoshi* for the first time, I was immediately drawn into the story and entranced by its intriguing new characters and backstory. I was eager to read on to find out how Kyoshi would overcome all the obstacles in her way (and Yee throws plenty of them in her path).

Working on this project with everyone involved has been a pleasure, and I couldn't be more excited about this incarnation of the Avatar universe.

Michael Dante DiMartino

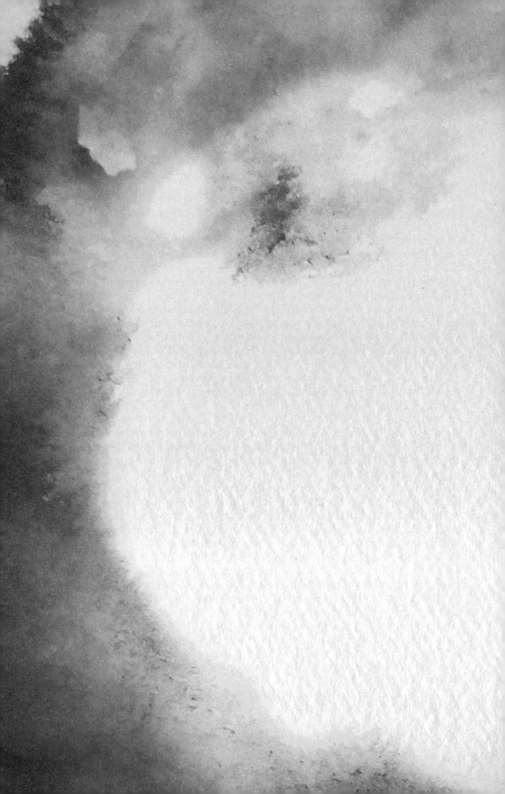

THE TEST

YOKOYA PORT was a town easy to overlook.

Situated on the edge of Whaletail Strait, it *could* have been a major restocking point for ships leaving one of the many harbors that supplied Omashu. But the strong, reliable prevailing winds made it too easy and cost-effective for southbound merchants to cruise right past it and reach Shimsom Big Island in a straight shot.

Jianzhu wondered if the locals knew or cared that ships laden with riches sailed tantalizingly close by, while they were stuck elbows-deep in the cavity of another elephant koi. Only a quirk of fate and weather kept piles of gold, spices, precious books, and scrolls from landing on their doorstep. Instead their lot was fish guts. A wealth of maws and gills.

The landward side was even less promising. The soil of the peninsula grew thin and rocky as it extended farther into the sea. It had disturbed Jianzhu to see crop fields so meager and balding as he'd rode through the countryside into town for the first time. The farmland lacked the wild, volcanic abundance of the Makapu Valley or the carefully ordered productivity of Ba Sing Se's Outer Ring, where growth bent to the exacting will of the king's planners. Here, a farmer would have to be grateful for whatever sustenance they could pull from the dirt.

The settlement lay at the intersection of three different nations—Earth, Air, and Water. And yet, none had ever laid much of a claim to it. The conflicts of the outside world had little impact on daily life for the Yokoyans.

To them, the ravages of the Yellow Neck uprising in the deep interior of the Earth Kingdom were a less interesting story than the wayward flying bison that had gotten loose from the Air Temple and knocked the thatching off a few roofs last week. Despite being seagoers, they probably couldn't name any of the dreaded pirate leaders carving up the eastern waters in open defiance of the Ba Sing Se navy.

All in all, Yokoya Port might as well not have been on the map. Which meant—for Jianzhu and Kelsang's desperate, sacrilegious little experiment—it was perfect.

Jianzhu trudged uphill in the wet, mucky snowfall, his neck prickling from the bundled straw cloak around his shoulders. He passed the wooden pillar that marked the spiritual center of this village without sparing it a glance. There was nothing on the sides or on top of it. It was just a bare log driven upright into the ground of a circular courtyard. It wasn't carved with any decorations, which seemed lazy for a town where nearly every adult had a working knowledge of carpentry.

There, the post grudgingly said to any nearby spirits. *Hope you're happy.*

Weathered houses lined the broad, eroded avenue, poking steeply into the air like spearpoints. His destination was the larger two-story meeting hall at the end. Kelsang had set up shop there yesterday, saying he needed as much floor space as possible for the test. He'd also claimed that the location enjoyed some auspicious wind currents, using the very solemn and holy method of licking his finger and holding it up in the air.

Whatever helped. Jianzhu sent a quick prayer to the Guardian of the Divine Log as he pulled off his snow boots, laid them on the porch, and ducked through the door curtains.

The interior of the hall was surprisingly large, with far corners draped in shadow and thick-planked walls cut from what must have been truly massive trees. The air smelled of resin. Ten very long, very faded yellow cloths stretched across the worn floorboards. A row of toys lay on each one, evenly spaced like a seedbed.

A bison whistle, a wicker ball, a misshapen blob that might have been a stuffed turtle duck, a coiled whalebone spring, one of those flappy drums that made noise as you spun it back and forth between your palms. The toys looked as worn and beaten as the outside of this building.

Kelsang knelt at the far end of the cloths. The Airbender monk was busy placing more knickknacks with a carefulness and precision that rivaled an acupuncturist setting their needles. As if it mattered whether the miniature boat sailed east or west. He stayed on his hands and knees, shuffling his great bulk sideways, his billowing orange robes and wiry black beard hanging so low they made another sweep over a floor that had already been scrubbed clean.

"I didn't know there were so many toys," Jianzhu said to his old friend. He spotted a large white marble that looked too close to the edge of the fabric and, with a graceful extension of his wrist, levitated it with earthbending in front of Kelsang. It hovered like a fly, waiting for his attention.

Kelsang didn't look up as he plucked the marble out of the air and put it right back where it had started. "There's thousands. I'd ask you to help, but you wouldn't do it right."

Jianzhu's head hurt at the statement. At this point they were well past *doing it right*. "How did you change Abbot Dorje's mind about giving you the relics?" he asked.

"The same way you convinced Lu Beifong to let us administer the Air Nomad test in the Earth Cycle," Kelsang said calmly as he re-centered a wooden top. "I didn't."

Like a certain friend of theirs from the Water Tribe always said, it was better to ask for forgiveness than wait for permission. And as far as Jianzhu was concerned, the time for waiting had long since passed.

When Avatar Kuruk, the keeper of balance and peace in the world, the bridge between spirits and humans, passed away at the ripe old age of thirty-three—*thirty-three! the only time Kuruk had ever been early for anything!*—it became the duty of his friends, his teachers, and other prominent benders to find the new Avatar, reincarnated into the next nation of the elemental cycle. Earth, Fire, Air, Water, and then Earth again, an order as unchanging as the seasons. A process stretching back nearly a thousand generations before Kuruk, and one that would hopefully continue for a thousand more.

Except this time, it wasn't working.

It had been seven years since Kuruk's death. Seven years of fruitless searching. Jianzhu had pored over every available record from the Four Nations, going back hundreds of years, and the hunt for the Avatar had never faltered like this in documented history.

No one knew why, though revered elders traded guesses behind closed doors. The world was impure and had been abandoned by the spirits. The Earth Kingdom lacked cohesion, or maybe it was the Water Tribes in the poles that needed to unify. The Airbenders had to come down from their mountains and get their hands dirty instead of preaching. The debate went on and on.

Jianzhu cared less about apportioning blame and more about the fact that he and Kelsang had let down their friend again. The only serious decree of Kuruk's before he'd departed from the living was that his closest companions find the next Avatar and do right by them. And so far they'd failed. Spectacularly.

Right now, there should have been a happy, burbling seven-year-old Earth Avatar in the care of their loving family, being watched over by a collection of the best, wisest benders of the world. A child in the midst of being prepared for the assumption of their duties at the age of sixteen. Instead there was only a gaping void that grew more dangerous by the day.

Jianzhu and the other masters did their best to keep the missing Avatar a secret, but it was no use. The cruel, the power-hungry, the lawless—people who normally had the most to fear from the Avatar—were starting to feel the scales shifting in their favor. Like sand sharks responding to the slightest vibrations on pure instinct, they tested their limits. Probed new grounds. Time was running out.

Kelsang finished setting up when the noon gongs struck. The sun was high enough to melt snow off the roof, and the dripping flow of water pattered on the ground like light rain. The silhouettes of villagers and their children queuing up for the test could be seen outside through the paper-screen windows. The air was full of excited chatter.

No more waiting, Jianzhu thought. *This happens now.*

Earth Avatars were traditionally identified by directional geomancy, a series of rituals designed to winnow through the largest and most populous of the Four Nations as efficiently as possible. Each time a special set of bone trigrams was cast and interpreted by the earthbending masters, half the Earth Kingdom was ruled out as the location of the newborn Avatar. Then from the remaining territory, another half, and then another half again. The possible locations kept shrinking until the searchers were brought to the doorstep of the Earth Avatar child.

It was a quick way to cover ground and entirely fitting to the earthbending state of mind. A question of logistics, simple to the point of being brutal. And it normally worked on the first try.

Jianzhu had been part of expeditions sent by the bones to barren fields, empty gem caverns below Ba Sing Se, a patch of the Si Wong Desert so dry that not even the Sandbenders bothered with it. Lu Beifong had read the trigrams, King Buro of Omashu gave it a shot, Neliao the Gardener took her turn. The masters worked their way down through the earthbending hierarchy until Jianzhu racked up his fair share of misses as well. His friendship with Kuruk bought him no special privileges when it came to the next Avatar.

After the last attempt had placed him on an iceberg in the North Pole with only turtle seals as potential candidates, Jianzhu became open to radical suggestions. A drunken commiseration with Kelsang spawned a promising new idea. If the ways of the Earth Kingdom weren't working, why not try another nation's method? After all, wasn't the Avatar, the only bender of all four elements, an honorary citizen of the entire world?

That was why the two of them were wiping their noses with tradition and trying the Air Nomad way of identifying the Avatar. Yokoya would be a practice run, a safe place far from the turmoil of land and sea where they could take notes and fix problems. If Yokoya went smoothly, they could convince their elders to expand the test farther throughout the Earth Kingdom.

The Air Nomads' method was simple, in theory. Out of the many toys laid out, only four belonged to Avatars of eras gone by. Each seven-year-old child of the village would be brought in and presented with the dazzling array of playthings. The one who was drawn to the four special toys in a remembrance of their past lives was the Avatar reborn. A process as elegant and harmonious as the Airbenders themselves.

In theory.

In practice, it was chaos. Pure and unhinged. It was a disaster the likes of which the Four Nations had never witnessed.

Jianzhu hadn't thought of what might happen after the children who failed the test were told to leave their selections behind and make room for the next candidate. The tears! The wailing, the screaming! Trying to get toys away from kids who had only moments before been promised they could have their pick? There was no force in existence stronger than a child's righteous fury at being robbed.

The parents were worse. Maybe Air Nomad caretakers handled the rejection of their young ones with grace and humility, but families in the other nations weren't made up of monks and nuns. Especially in the Earth Kingdom, where all bets were off once it came to blood ties. Villagers whom he'd shared friendly greetings with in the days leading up to the test became snarling canyon crawlers once they'd been told that their precious little Jae or Mirai was not in fact the most important child in the world, as they'd secretly known all along. More than a few swore up and down that they'd seen their offspring play with invisible spirits or bend earth and air at the same time.

Kelsang would push back gently. *"Are you sure your child wasn't earthbending during a normal breeze? Are you sure the baby wasn't simply . . . playing?"*

Some couldn't take a hint. Especially the village captain. As soon as they'd passed over her daughter—Aoma, or something—she'd given them a look of utter contempt and demanded to see a higher-ranking master.

Sorry, lady, Jianzhu thought after Kelsang spent nearly ten minutes talking her down. *We can't all be special.*

"For the last time, I'm not negotiating a salary with you!" Jianzhu shouted in the face of a particularly blunt farmer. "Being the Avatar is not a paid position!"

The stocky man shrugged. "Sounds like a waste of time then. I'll take my child and go."

Out of the corner of his eye, Jianzhu caught Kelsang frantically waving his hands, making a cut-off sign at the neck. The little girl had wandered over to the whirly flying toy that had once entertained an ancient Avatar and was staring at it intently.

Huh. They weren't intending to get a genuine result today. But picking the first item correctly was already improbable. Too improbable to risk stopping now.

"Okay," Jianzhu said. This would have to come out of his own pocket. "Fifty silvers a year if she's the Avatar."

"Sixty-five silvers a year if she's the Avatar and ten if she's not."

"WHY WOULD I PAY YOU IF SHE'S *NOT* THE AVATAR?" Jianzhu roared.

Kelsang coughed and thumped loudly on the floor. The girl had picked up the whirligig and was eying the drum. Two out of four correct. Out of thousands.

Holy *Shu*.

"I mean, of course," Jianzhu said quickly. "Deal."

They shook hands. It would be ironic, a prank worthy of Kuruk's sense of humor, to have his reincarnation be found as a result of a peasant's greed. And the very last child in line for testing, to boot. Jianzhu nearly chuckled.

Now the girl had the drum in her arms as well. She walked over to a stuffed hog monkey. Kelsang was beside himself with excitement, his neck threatening to burst through the wooden beads wrapped around it. Jianzhu felt lightheaded. Hope bashed against his ribcage, begging to be let out after so many years trapped inside.

The girl wound up her foot and stomped on the stuffed animal as hard as she could.

"Die!" she screamed in her tiny little treble. She ground it under her heel, the stitches audibly ripping.

The light went out of Kelsang's face. He looked like he'd witnessed a murder.

"Ten silvers," the farmer said.

"Get out," Jianzhu snapped.

"Come on, Suzu," the farmer called. "Let's get."

After wresting the other toys away from the Butcher of Hog Monkeys, he scooped the girl up and walked out the door, the whole escapade nothing but a business transaction. In doing so he nearly bowled over another child who'd been spying on the proceedings from the outside.

"Hey!" Jianzhu said. "You forgot your other daughter!"

"That one ain't mine," the farmer said as he thumped down the steps into the street. "That one ain't anyone's."

An orphan then? Jianzhu hadn't spotted the unchaperoned girl around town in the days before, but maybe he'd glossed over her, thinking she was too old to be a candidate. She was much, much taller than any of the other children who'd been brought in by their parents.

As Jianzhu walked over to examine what he'd missed, the girl quavered, threatening to flee, but her curiosity won over her fright. She remained where she was.

Underfed, Jianzhu thought with a frown as he looked over the girl's hollow cheeks and cracked lips. And definitely an orphan. He'd seen hundreds of children like her in the inner provinces where outlaw *daofei* ran unchecked, their parents slain by whatever bandit group was ascendant in the territory.

She must have wandered far into the relatively peaceable area of Yokoya.

Upon hearing about the Avatar test, the families of the village had dressed their eligible children in their finest garments as if it were a festival day. But this child was wearing a threadbare coat with her elbows poking through the holes in the sleeves. Her oversized feet threatened to burst the straps of her too-small sandals. None of the local farmers were feeding or clothing her.

Kelsang, who despite his fearsome appearance was always better with children, joined them and stooped down. With a smile he transformed from an intimidating orange mountain into a giant-sized version of the stuffed toys behind him.

"Why, hello there," he said, putting an extra layer of friendliness into his booming rumble. "What's your name?"

The girl took a long, guarded moment, sizing them up.

"Kyoshi," she whispered. Her eyebrows knotted as if revealing her name was a painful concession.

Kelsang took in her tattered state and avoided the subject of her parents for now. "Kyoshi, would you like a toy?"

"Are you sure she isn't too old?" Jianzhu said. "She's bigger than some of the teenagers."

"Hush, you," Kelsang said. He made a sweeping gesture at the hall festooned with relics, for Kyoshi's benefit.

The unveiling of so many playthings at once had an entrancing effect on most of the children. But Kyoshi didn't gasp, or smile, or move a muscle. Instead she maintained eye contact with Kelsang until he blinked.

As quick as a whip, she scampered by him, snagged an object off the floor, and ran back to where she was standing on the porch. She gauged Kelsang and Jianzhu for their response as intently as they watched her.

Kelsang glanced at Jianzhu and tilted his head at the clay turtle Kyoshi clutched to her chest. One of the four true relics. Not a single candidate had come anywhere near it today.

They should have been as excited for her as they'd been for evil little Suzu, but Jianzhu's heart was clouded with doubt. It was hard to believe they'd be so lucky after that previous head-fake.

"Good choice," Kelsang said. "But I've got a surprise for you. You can have three more! Four whole toys, to yourself! Wouldn't you like that?"

Jianzhu sensed a shift in the girl's stance, a tremor in her foundation that was obvious through the wooden floorboards.

Yes, she would like three more toys very much. What child wouldn't? But in her mind, the promise of *more* was dangerous. A lie designed to hurt her. If she loosened her grip on the single prize she held right now, she would end up with nothing. Punished for believing in the kindness of this stranger.

Kyoshi shook her head. Her knuckles whitened around the clay turtle.

"It's okay," Kelsang said. "You don't have to put that down. That's the whole point; you can choose different . . . Hey!"

The girl took a step back, and then another, and then, before they could react, she was sprinting down the hill with the one-of-a-kind, centuries-old Avatar relic in her hands. Halfway along the street, she took a sharp turn like an experienced fugitive throwing off a pursuer and disappeared in the space between two houses.

Jianzhu closed his eyelids against the sun. The light came through them in scarlet blots. He could feel his own pulse. His mind was somewhere else right now.

Instead of Yokoya, he stood in the center of an unnamed village deep in the interior of the Earth Kingdom, newly "liberated" by Xu Ping An and the Yellow Necks. In this waking dream, the stench of rotting flesh soaked through his clothes and the cries of survivors haunted the wind. Next to him, an official messenger who'd been carried there by palanquin read from a scroll, spending minute after minute listing the Earth King's honorifics only to end by telling Jianzhu that reinforcements from His Majesty's army would *not* be coming to help.

He tried to shake free of the memory, but the past had set its jagged hooks into him. Now he sat at a negotiating table made of pure ice, and on the other side was Tulok, lord of the Fifth Nation pirates. The elderly corsair laughed his consumptive laugh at the notion he might honor his grandfather's promise to leave the southern coastlines of the continent in peace. His convulsions spattered blood and phlegm over the accords drafted by Avatar Yangchen in her own holy hand, while his daughter-lieutenant watched by his side, her soulless gaze boring into Jianzhu like he was so much prey.

In these times, and in many others, he should have been at the right hand of the Avatar. The ultimate authority who could bend the world to their will. Instead he was alone. Facing down great beasts of land and sea, their jaws closing in, encasing the kingdom in darkness.

Kelsang yanked him back into the present with a bruising slap on the back.

"Come on," he said. "With the way you look, people would think you just lost *your* nation's most important cultural artifact."

The Airbender's good humor and ability to take setbacks in stride was normally a great comfort to Jianzhu, but right now he wanted to punch his friend in his stupid bearded face. He composed his own features.

"We need to go after her," he said.

Kelsang pursed his lips. "Eh, it would feel bad to take the relic away from a child who has so little. She can hang on to it. I'll go back to the temple and face Dorje's wrath alone. There's no need for you to implicate yourself."

Jianzhu didn't know what counted for wrath among Airbenders, but that wasn't the issue here. "You'd ruin the Air Nomad test to make a child happy?" he said incredulously.

"It'll find its way back to where it belongs." Kelsang looked around and paused.

Then his smile faded, as if this little blot of a town were a harsh dose of reality that was only now taking effect.

"Eventually." He sighed. "Maybe."

NINE YEARS LATER

TO KYOSHI, it was very clear—this was a hostage situation.

Silence was the key to making it through to the other side. Waiting with complete and total passivity. Neutral *jing*.

Kyoshi walked calmly down the path through the fallow field, ignoring the covergrass that leaned over and tickled her ankles, the sweat beading on her forehead that stung her eyes. She kept quiet and pretended that the three people who'd fallen in beside her like muggers in an alley weren't a threat.

"So like I was telling the others, my mom and dad think we'll have to dredge the peakside canals earlier this year," Aoma said, drawing out the *mom* and *dad* intentionally, dangling what Kyoshi lacked in front of her. She crooked her hands into the Crowding Bridge position while slamming her feet into the ground with solid *whump*s. "One of the terraces collapsed in the last storm."

Above them, floating high out of reach, was the last, precious jar of pickled spicy kelp that the entire village would see this year. The one that Kyoshi had been charged with delivering to Jianzhu's mansion. The one that Aoma had earthbent out of Kyoshi's hands and was now promising to drop at any second. The large clay vessel bobbed up and down, sloshing the brine against the waxed paper seal.

Kyoshi had to stifle a yelp every time the jar lurched against the limits of Aoma's control. *No noise. Wait it out. Don't give them anything to latch on to. Talking will only make it worse.*

"She doesn't care," Suzu said. "Precious servant girl doesn't give a lick about farming matters. She's got her cushy job in the fancy house. She's too good to get her hands dirty."

"Won't step in a boat, neither," Jae said. In lieu of elaborating further, he spat on the ground, nearly missing Kyoshi's heels.

Aoma never needed a reason to torment Kyoshi, but as for the others, genuine resentment worked just fine. It was true that Kyoshi spent her days under the roof of a powerful sage instead of breaking her nails against fieldstones. She'd certainly never risked the choppy waters of the Strait in pursuit of a catch.

But what Jae and Suzu conveniently neglected was that every plot of arable land near the village and every seaworthy boat down at the docks belonged to a *family*. Mothers and fathers, as Aoma was so fond of saying, passed along their trade to daughters and sons in an unbroken line, which meant there was no room for an outsider to inherit any means to survive. If it hadn't been for Kelsang and Jianzhu, Kyoshi would have starved in the streets, right in front of everyone's noses.

Hypocrites.

Kyoshi pressed her tongue against the roof of her mouth as hard as she could. Today was not going to be the day. Someday, maybe, but not today.

"Lay off her," Aoma said, shifting her stance into Dividing Bridge. "I hear that being a serving girl is hard work. That's why we're helping with the deliveries. Isn't that right Kyoshi?"

For emphasis, she threaded the jar through a narrow gap in the branches of an overhanging tree. A reminder of who was in control here.

Kyoshi shuddered as the vessel dove toward the ground like a hawk before swooping back up to safety. *Just a little farther*, she thought as the path took a sharp turn around the hillside. A few more silent, wordless steps until—

There. They'd arrived at last. The Avatar's estate, in all its glory.

The mansion that Master Jianzhu built to house the savior of the world was designed in the image of a miniature city. A high wall ran in a perfect square around the grounds, with a division in the middle to separate the austere training grounds from the vibrant living quarters. Each section had its own imposing, south-facing gatehouse that was larger than the Yokoya meeting hall. The massive iron-studded doors of the residential gate were flung open, offering a small windowed glimpse of the elaborate topiary inside. A herd of placid goat dogs grazed over the lawn, cropping the grass to an even length.

Foreign elements had been carefully integrated into the design of the complex, which meant that gilded dragons chased carved polar orcas around the edges of the walls. The place-ment of the Earth Kingdom–style roof tiles cleverly matched Air Nomad numerology principles. Authentic dyes and paints had been imported from around the world, ensuring that the colors of all four nations were on full, equitable display.

When Jianzhu had bought the land, he'd explained to the village elders that Yokoya was an ideal spot to settle down and educate the Avatar, a quiet, safe place far away from the outlaw-ravaged lands deeper in the Earth Kingdom and close enough to both the Southern Air Temple and Southern Water Tribe. The villagers had been happy enough to take his gold back then. But after the manor went up, they grumbled that it was an eyesore, an alien creature that had sprouted overnight from the native soil.

To Kyoshi it was the most beautiful sight she could ever imagine. It was a home.

Behind her, Suzu sniffed in disdain. "I don't know what our parents were thinking, selling these fields to a Ganjinese."

Kyoshi's lips went tight. Master Jianzhu was indeed from the Gan Jin tribe up in the north, but it was the *way* Suzu had said it.

"Maybe they knew the land was as worthless and unproduc-tive as their children," Kyoshi muttered under her breath.

The others stopped walking and stared at her.

Whoops. She'd said that a bit too loud, hadn't she?

Jae and Suzu balled their fists. It dawned on them, what they could do while Aoma had Kyoshi helpless. It had been years since any of the village kids could get within arm's reach of her, but today was a special occasion, wasn't it? Maybe a few bruises, in remembrance of old times.

Kyoshi steeled herself for the first blow, rising on her toes in the hope that she could at least keep her face out of the fray, so Auntie Mui wouldn't notice. A few punches and kicks and they'd leave her in peace. Really, it was her own fault for letting her mask slip.

"What do you think you're doing?" a familiar voice snarled.

Kyoshi grimaced and opened her eyes.

Peace was no longer an option. Because now Rangi was here.

Rangi must have seen them from afar and stalked across the entire great lawn unnoticed. Or lain in ambush for them all night. Or dropped out of a tree like a webbed leopard. Kyoshi wouldn't have put any of those feats past the military-trained Firebender.

Jae and Suzu backed away, trying to swallow their hostile intent like children stuffing stolen candy into their mouths. It occurred to Kyoshi that this might have been the first time they'd ever seen a member of the Fire Nation up close, let alone one as intimidating as Rangi. In her formfitting armor the color of onyx and dried blood, she could have been a vengeful spirit come to cleanse a battlefield of the living.

Aoma, rather impressively, held her ground. "The Avatar's bodyguard," she said with a faint smile. "I thought you weren't supposed to leave his side. Aren't you slacking off?"

She glanced to the left and right. "Or is he here somewhere?"

Rangi looked at Aoma like she was a wad of foulness the Firebender had stepped in during the walk over.

"You're not authorized to be on these grounds," she said in her charred rasp. She pointed upward at the jar of kelp. "Nor to lay your hands on the Avatar's property. Or accost his household staff, for that matter."

Kyoshi noticed she personally landed a distant third in that list of considerations.

Aoma tried to play it cool. "This container is enormous," she said, shrugging to emphasize her still-ongoing feat of elemental control. "It would take two grown men to lift it without earthbending. Kyoshi asked us to help her bring it inside the house. Right?"

She gave Kyoshi a radiant smile. One that said *Tell on me and I'll kill you.* Kyoshi had seen that expression before countless times when they were younger, whenever a hapless adult blundered into the two of them "playing" around town, Kyoshi badly scraped up and Aoma with a rock in her hand.

But today she was off her game. Her normally flawless acting had a plaintive, genuine tone to it. Kyoshi suddenly understood what was going on.

Aoma really did want to help her with her delivery. She wanted to be invited inside the mansion and to see the Avatar up close, like Kyoshi got to every day. She was *jealous.*

A feeling akin to pity settled in Kyoshi's throat. It wasn't strong enough to hold Rangi back from doing her thing, though.

The Firebender stepped forward. Her fine jawline hardened, and her dark bronze eyes danced with aggression. The air around her body rippled like a living mirage, making the strands of jet-black hair that escaped her topknot float upward in the heat.

"Put the jar down, walk away, and don't come back," she said. "Unless you want to know what the ashes of your eyebrows smell like."

Aoma's expression crumbled. She'd blundered into a predator with much larger fangs. And unlike the adults of the village,
no amount of charm or misdirection would work on Rangi.

But that didn't mean a parting shot was out of the question.

"Sure," she said. "Thought you'd never ask." With a fling of her
hands, the jar rocketed straight up into the air, past the treetops.

"You'd better find someone who's *authorized* to catch that."
She bolted down the path with Suzu and Jae close behind.

"You little—" Rangi made to go after them, fist reflexively
cocked to serve a helping of flaming pain, but she checked herself. Fiery vengeance would have to wait.

She shook her hand out and peered up at the rapidly shrinking jar. Aoma had thrown it really, *really* hard. No one could
claim the girl wasn't talented.

Rangi elbowed Kyoshi sharply in the side. "Catch it," she
said. "Use earthbending and catch it."

"I—I can't," Kyoshi said, quavering with dismay. Her poor
doomed charge reached the apex of its flight. Auntie Mui was
going to be furious. A disaster of this magnitude might get back
to Master Jianzhu. Her pay would get cut. Or she'd be fired
outright.

Rangi hadn't given up on her. "What do you mean you can't?
The staff ledgers have you listed as an Earthbender! Catch it!"

"It's not that simple!" Yes, Kyoshi was technically a bender,
but Rangi didn't know about her little problem.

"Do the thing with your hands like she did!" Rangi formed
the dual claws of Crowding Bridge as if the only missing com-
ponent were a crude visual reminder by a bender who wielded a
different element entirely.

"*Look out!*" Kyoshi screamed. She threw herself over Rangi, shielding the smaller girl with her body from the plummeting missile. They fell to the ground, entwined.

No impact came. No deadly shards of ceramic, or explosion of pickling liquid.

"Get off of me, you oaf," Rangi muttered. She hammered her fists against Kyoshi's protective embrace, a bird beating its wings against a cage. Kyoshi got to her knees and saw that her face and ears were nearly as red as her armor.

She helped Rangi to her feet. The jar floated next to them, waist-high above the ground. Under Aoma's control it had wavered and trembled, following her natural patterns of breathing and involuntary motions. But now it was completely still in the air, as if it had been placed on a sturdy iron pedestal.

The pebbles in the dusty path trembled. They began to move and bounce in front of Kyoshi's feet, directed by unseen power from below like they'd been scattered across the surface of a beating drum. They marched in seemingly random directions, little drunken soldiers, until they came to rest in a formation that spelled a message.

You're welcome.

Kyoshi's head jerked up and she squinted at the distant mansion. There was only one person she knew who could have managed this feat. The pebbles began their dance again, settling into words much faster this time.

This is Yun, by the way. You know, Avatar Yun.

As if it could have been anyone else. Kyoshi couldn't spot where Yun was watching them, but she could imagine the playful, teasing smirk on his handsome face as he performed yet another astounding act of bending like it was no big deal, charming the rocks into complete submission.

She'd never heard of anyone using earth to communicate legibly at a distance. Yun was lucky he wasn't an Air Nomad, or else the stunt would have gotten him tattooed in celebration for inventing a new technique.

What are my three favorite ladles doing today?

Kyoshi giggled. Okay, so not perfectly legible.

Sounds like fun. Wish I could join you.

"He knows we can't reply, right?" Rangi said.

Dumplings, please. Any kind but leek.

"Enough!" Rangi shouted. "We're distracting him from his training! And you're late for work!" She swept away the pebbles with her foot, less concerned with blazing new trails in the world of earthbending and more with maintaining the daily schedule.

Kyoshi plucked the jar off the invisible platform and followed Rangi back to the mansion, stepping slowly through the grass so as not to outpace her. If household duties were all that mattered to the Firebender, then that would be the end of it, and nothing more would need to be said. Instead she could feel Rangi's silence compacting into a denser form inside her slender frame.

They were halfway to the gate once it became too much to bear.

"It's pathetic!" Rangi said without turning around. The only way she could manage her disgust with Kyoshi was by not looking at her. "The way they step on you. You serve the Avatar! Have some dignity!"

Kyoshi smiled. "I was trying to de-escalate the situation," she murmured.

"You were going to let them hit you! I saw it! And don't you dare try and claim you were doing neutral *jing* or whatever earthbending hooey!"

Right on cue, Rangi had transformed from professional Guardian of the Avatar, ready to scorch the bones of interlopers without flinching, into the teenaged girl no older than Kyoshi who easily lost her temper at her friends and was kind of a raging mother hen to boot.

"And speaking of your earthbending! You were shown up by a peasant! How have you not mastered the basics by now? I've seen children in Yu Dao bend rocks bigger than that jar!"

She and Rangi *were* friends, despite what it looked like. Back when the mansion was under construction—while Kyoshi was learning her duties inside the skeleton of the unfinished house—it had taken her weeks to figure out that the imperious girl who acted like she was still in the junior corps of the Fire Army only yelled at the people she let inside her shell. Everyone else was scum who didn't warrant the effort.

". . . So the most efficient course of action would be to surprise the leader—Aoma, was it?—alone somewhere and then destroy her so messily that it sends a message to the others not to bother you anymore. Are you listening to me?"

Kyoshi had missed the greater part of the battle plan. She'd been distracted by the collar of Rangi's armor, which had been mussed in the fall and needed to be straightened so it covered the delicate skin of her nape once more. But her answer was the same regardless.

"Why resort to violence?" she said. She gently nudged the Firebender in the small of the back with the jar. "I have strong heroes like you to protect me."

Rangi made a noise like she wanted to vomit.

THE BOY
FROM MAKAPU

YUN COULDN'T hear what they were saying, but it was possible to read their body language at this distance. Judging from the way she gestured wildly in the air, Rangi was ticked off at Kyoshi. Again.

He smiled. The two of them were adorable together. He could have watched them all day, but alas. He rolled over onto his back and slid down the roof of the outer wall, using the edge of the gutter to arrest his fall. He let the impact turn his motion into a vault, front-flipped into the air, and landed on the balls of his feet in the marble courtyard.

Eye-to-eye with Hei-Ran.

Shoot.

"Impressive," the former headmistress of the Royal Fire Academy for Girls said, her arms crossed behind her back.

"When the spirits ask for a circus clown to intervene on their behalf, I'll know our time together has paid off."

Yun scrunched his face. His personal firebending tutor had a knack for finding his moments of pride and then crushing them.

"I finished my hot squat sets early," he said. "Five hundred reps. Perfect form, the whole way."

"And yet you chose to spend your spare time lounging on the roof instead of moving on to your next exercise or meditating until I returned. No wonder you can't generate flame yet. You can train your body as much as you wish, but your mind remains weak."

He noticed Hei-Ran never tore into him like this while her daughter was around. It was as if she didn't want to diminish the Avatar's stature in Rangi's worshipful eyes. His image had to be carefully groomed and maintained, like the miniature trees that dotted the garden. The spirits forbid he appear human for a moment.

Yun dropped into the Fire Fist stance. He paused for corrections though it was unnecessary. Not even Hei-Ran could fault his body placement, his spinal posture, his breath control. The only thing missing was the flame.

She frowned at him, interpreting his perfection as an act of defiance, but gave him the signal to begin anyway. As he punched at the air, she walked slowly around him in a circle. Fire Fist sessions were also opportunities for lectures.

"What you do when no one is guiding you determines who you are," Hei-Ran said. The motto was probably engraved over a door somewhere in the Fire Academy. "The results of your training are far less important than your attitude toward training."

Yun didn't think she truly believed that. Not for a second.

She was simply picking on the parts of him that she couldn't examine and adjust for immediate improvement. If he couldn't firebend yet under her care, then his flaw resided deeper than in any of her previous students.

His punches became crisper, to the point where the sleeves of his cotton training uniform snapped like a whip with each motion. He was a pair of images in a scroll, two points in time repeating over and over again. Left fist. Right fist.

"Your situation isn't unique," Hei-Ran went on. "History is full of Avatars like you who tried to coast on their talents. You're not the only one who wanted to take it easy."

Yun slipped. An event rare enough to notice.

His motion took him too far outside his center of gravity, and he stumbled to his knees. Sweat stung his eyes, ran into the corner of his mouth.

Take it easy? *Take it easy?*

Was she ignoring the fact that he spent sleepless nights poring over scholarly analyses of Yangchen's political decisions? That he'd exhaustively memorized the names of every Earth Kingdom noble, Fire Nation commander, and Water Tribe chieftain among the living and going back three generations among the dead? The forgotten texts he'd used to map the ancient sacred sites of the Air Nomads to such a degree that Kelsang was surprised about a few of them?

That's who he was when no one was looking. Someone who dedicated his whole being to his Avatarhood. Yun wanted to make up for the lost time he'd squandered by being discovered so late. He wanted to express gratitude to Jianzhu and the entire world for giving him the greatest gift in existence. Taking it easy was the last thing on his mind.

She knows that, he thought. Hei-Ran was purposely goading him by calling him lazy. But an uncontrollable fury rose in his stomach anyway.

Yun's fingers plowed into the smooth surface of the marble, crushing the stone into his fist as effortlessly as if it were chalk. He would never lash out against a teacher. The only way he could put up resistance against Hei-Ran was to disappoint her. To uphold her accusation that he was a wayward child.

His next punch produced a swirling dragon's belch of "flame" worthy of the Fire Lord, each spout and flicker rendered lovingly, mockingly in white stone dust. He let it rage and dance like a real fire reacting to the eddies of the breeze, and then let the cloud of particles fall to the ground.

To cap it off, make the performance complete, he added the smirk that everyone always said reminded them of Kuruk's. A clown needed his makeup, after all.

Hei-Ran stiffened. She looked like she was about to slap him across the face. The blast went nowhere near her, but it didn't exactly fly away from her either.

"In the old days, masters used to maim their students for insubordination," she said hoarsely.

Yun restrained himself from flinching. "What wonderful modern times we live in."

A single clap pierced the air. They both looked over to see Jianzhu, watching from the sidelines.

Yun gritted his teeth hard enough to make them squeak. Normally he could sense his mentor's footfalls through the ground and get his act together, but today . . . today was all kinds of off-balance.

Jianzhu waved Yun over like he hadn't just caught the Avatar and his firebending master at each other's throats. "Come," he said to his ward. "Let's take a break."

The training grounds had alcoves in the walls for stashing weapons, water jars, and hollow discs made of pressed clay powder that would explode harmlessly on impact. Enough supplies to train an army of benders. Jianzhu and Yun took their tea in the largest of these storage areas, surrounded by straw target-practice dummies.

The floor was thick with dust. While Yun poured, Jianzhu plucked a twig that had snagged on a burlap sack and used it as a stylus, drawing a simplified version of a Pai Sho board on the ground between them.

Yun was confused. The two of them had played the game incessantly while first getting to know each other. But Pai Sho had been forbidden to him for a long time now. It was a distraction from mastering the elements.

Jianzhu contemplated the empty grid, his long face flickering in recollection of past sequences, lines of shining brilliance and outrageous risks unfolding in the tiles. The markers of age radiated outward from his eyes. The troubles that gave him severe crow's feet and white temples had yet to reach the smooth flat line of his mouth.

"I have some news," he said. "Our emissaries tell us that Tagaka has agreed to sign a new version of her great-grandfather's treaty."

Yun perked up. His master had been trying to pursue a diplomatic solution with the queen of the seaborne *daofei* for years. "What changed, Sifu?"

Jianzhu gestured at him. "You. She learned we finally found the Avatar and that he was one of the strongest benders of this generation."

Yun knew that was true. For earth, at least. It might have been arrogant of him to think so, but it was hard to argue with the evidence left across the ground.

"The Fifth Nation fleet will cease raiding the coastlines along the Xishaan Mountains," Jianzhu said. "They've promised not to raise a sail under her colors within sight of the Eastern Air Temple."

"In exchange for what?"

"For official access to the timber on Yesso Island, though they've been unofficially logging there for the better part of a decade. The other sages are calling it a total diplomatic victory. So much gained, for so little."

The leaves of Yun's tea lost their grip on the surface of the liquid. Water was the last element he'd need to master. He'd always suspected he'd have a better time of it than fire.

"Except it's not a victory, is it?" he said, rolling the cup between his fingers. "She's promising to halt her operations in one sector, but a fleet of marauders isn't going to lay down their arms and pick up the plow overnight. They'll cause trouble in the other oceans, maybe go as far north as Chameleon Bay or the Fire Nation home islands. It's just pushing the violence from one corner of the world to the other."

"What would you do then?" Jianzhu said. "Reject Tagaka's offer?"

Yun took a turn staring at the blank gameboard, especially at the sections where players usually laid their boat tiles. He shuddered at the images that came rushing into his head.

Contrary to what many of the locals thought, Jianzhu did not keep him locked up in the estate like a moon flower that would wither in too much sunlight. In between training, they regularly took trips around the world with Kelsang on his flying bison, Pengpeng, to meet important people from around the Four Nations. The goal was to make sure Yun had a cosmopolitan upbringing since the ideal Avatar was also a diplomat, never showing bias to one people or the other. He learned a lot by their side, exploring great cities and talking with their leaders. Sometimes he had fun.

The last outing was not one of those times.

When Jianzhu told him they were obligated to survey the extent of the damage inflicted by the largest coordinated pirate raid on the southeast coast of the Earth Kingdom mainlands in over a century, Yun had steeled himself for blood. Corpses amid smoldering ruins. A scene of total devastation.

But as they flew low over the shores on Pengpeng's back, scanning the seaside villages for survivors, he was surprised to see the driftwood houses and straw huts intact. Nearly pristine. No sign of the inhabitants anywhere.

They had to touch down and investigate a few structures before things fell into place. Inside the homes, they'd found spears left on racks. Tables set with cooked food that hadn't rotted yet. Fishing nets in the midst of being repaired. There had been no massacre.

By complete surprise, the villagers had been taken. Like they were livestock. Animals stolen from a herd.

Nothing else had been touched by Tagaka's corsairs, except for a common thread of items that Yun noticed at the last minute. They'd stolen the bells. The drums and the gongs. The watchtowers of any village lucky enough to have one were picked clean.

Cast bronze was extremely valuable and nigh irreplaceable in that part of the country, Yun realized. So were the right quality hides for drumskins. The pirates had made it so that the village warning systems couldn't be reused when they returned.

Nearly a thousand people were unaccounted for. Conducting a raid on this scale with such precision was not only a crime but a message. Tagaka was more dangerous than her father, her grandfather, and every other crude, bloody-minded pirate that ran the Eastern Sea.

Yun had spent the better part of that night screaming and raging at Jianzhu after his mentor calmly explained that the Earth King was likely not going to do anything to protect his subjects, not ones of so little marginal value. That they were largely on their own to deal with the problem.

The emptiness of the Pai Sho board taunted Yun as loudly as the missing, unrung bells. *Not if they returned, but when.*

He put his tea down and leaned back on his hands. "We should take her offer and pretend we're glad to do it. It's our only chance of rescuing the surviving captives. It'll buy time for the coastal areas to build up defenses. And if Tagaka is bold enough to sail northwest, there's a chance she'll grow overconfident and pick a fight with the Fire Navy. That's an opponent ruthless enough to destroy her completely."

His proposal spilled out of his lips naturally, despite the unease it created in his core. The idea of manipulating the nations he was supposed to keep balance over was frightening, solely because of how easy and effective it would be. He waited for a rebuke.

Instead he caught Jianzhu smiling at him openly. A rare occurrence.

"See?" Jianzhu said, gesturing at the game board out of habit. *"This* is why you are destined to be a great Avatar. You have the insight to think ahead, to see where people are weak and strong. You know which threads of the future to pull. There's not going to be a solution to the Fifth Nation through powerful bending. But there will be a strategy, a line of play that minimizes the suffering they can inflict. And you've spotted it.

"You're everything Kuruk was not," Jianzhu continued. "And I couldn't be prouder."

That was meant to be a genuine compliment. Kuruk had been a genius of the highest caliber when it came to Pai Sho. Bending too. But according to Jianzhu, who'd known him best, the Water Avatar had been unable to translate his personal talents into effective leadership on the world stage. He'd squandered his time, pursuing pleasures around the Four Nations, and died early.

So I guess that means I'll be unhappy and live forever, Yun thought. *Wonderful.*

He looked across the courtyard where Hei-Ran had taken a post, waiting for them to finish. The woman was a statue. Every piece of grief he got from her was made worse by the fact that she resembled her daughter Rangi so closely, with the same porcelain-doll face, pitch-black hair, and eyes tending toward darker bronze than the usual Fire Nation gold. Having a beautiful, adoring bodyguard close to his own age like Rangi was ruined when her spitting image beat the snot out of him on a regular basis.

"Hei-Ran thinks I'm a little too much like Kuruk," Yun said.

"You have to be more understanding with her," Jianzhu said. "She resigned her commission in the Fire Army to teach Kuruk, and then she left the Royal Academy to teach you. She's sacrificed more than any of us for the Avatar."

Hearing that he'd ruined two different promising careers for the same woman didn't make him feel any better. "That's more reason for her to hate my guts."

Jianzhu got up and motioned for Yun to do the same. "No, her problem is that she loves you," he said.

"If that's true then she has a funny way of showing it."

Jianzhu shrugged. "Fire Nation mothers. She loves you almost as much as I do. Too much, perhaps."

Yun followed his mentor toward the center of the training floor. The transition from cool shade back to the outdoor heat was a harsh swipe.

"You must know that you have the love of many people," Jianzhu said. "Kelsang, the visiting sages, nearly everyone who's ever met you. It's my belief that the earth itself loves you. You feel connected to it at all times, like it's speaking to you. Am I right?"

He was, though Yun didn't know where he was going with this. Feeling connected to the earth was the first, most basic requirement for earthbending. Hei-Ran joined them in the court.

"On the other hand, firebending is unique among the four bending styles in that it typically does not draw from a mass of elements separate from one's own body," Jianzhu said. "You don't form a bond with the element in your surroundings; instead you generate it from within. Am I explaining that correctly, Headmistress?"

Hei-Ran nodded, equally confused as to why they were discussing the obvious.

"Take off your shoes," Jianzhu said to Yun.

"Huh?" Like many Earthbenders, Yun never wore shoes if he could help it, but for firebending training they'd forced him into a pair of grippy slippers.

"Tagaka's conditions are that any new treaties must be signed on grounds of her choosing," Jianzhu said. "I know I said that diplomacy was more important than bending for this mission, but it would be much more ideal if you had *some* mastery over fire. In case the pirates need a little show of force. Take off your shoes."

The sun beat down on Yun's head. The buzz of insects grew louder in his ears, like an alarm. He'd never disobeyed Jianzhu before, so he yanked off the slippers, rolled down his socks, and threw them to the side.

"I don't understand," he said. "What's happening here?"

Jianzhu surveyed the featureless training floor. "Like I said, the earth itself loves you, and you love it. That love, that bond, could be what's holding you back, blocking off the different states of mind necessary to master the different elements. We should try severing that link so that you have nothing to rely on but your inner fire. No outside help."

For the first time in his life, Yun saw Hei-Ran hesitate. "Jianzhu," she said, "are you sure that's a good idea?"

"It's *an* idea," Jianzhu said. "Whether it's good or not depends on the result."

An icy knot formed in Yun's stomach as his mind made the connection. "You're going to have her burn my feet?"

Jianzhu shook his head. "Nothing so crude."

He put his hand out to the side, palm down, and then drew it upward. Around them, the marble floor sprouted little inch-high pyramids, each ending in a sharp point. The grounds were uniformly blanketed in them from wall to wall. It was as if someone had hammered nails into each space of a Pai Sho board and then flipped it over, spikes up.

"Now, let's see you run through the first Sun Gathering form," Jianzhu said. The garden of caltrops surrounded them in a tight ring. "Get out there, right in the middle of it, and show us your stuff."

Yun blinked back tears. He looked at Hei-Ran pleadingly. She shook her head and turned away. "You can't be serious," he said.

Jianzhu was as calm as a drifting cloud. "You may begin when ready, Avatar."

HONEST WORK

STEPPING THROUGH the gate of the mansion was like entering a portal to the Spirit World. Or so Kyoshi imagined, from hearing Kelsang's stories. It was a complete transition from one set of rules to another, from a dull, mindless place where the only currencies you could spend were sweat and time, sowing your seeds and baiting your hooks in the hope of staving off hunger for another season, to a mystical universe where rituals and negotiations could make you supreme in a single day.

Their passage was marked by the cool blip of shade underneath the rammed-earth wall. Rangi nodded at the two watchmen, grizzled veterans of the Earth King's army who stiffened their necks and bowed back to her in deference. Lured by better pay into Jianzhu's service, they'd kept their dished, wide-brimmed helmets but painted them over with the sage's personal shades of green. Kyoshi always wondered whether that was against the law or not.

Inside, the vast garden hummed with conversation. Sages and dignitaries from far-off lands constantly flowed in and out of the estate, and many of them enjoyed conducting their business among the flowers and sweet-smelling fruit trees. An overdressed merchant from Omashu haggled with a Fire Nation procurement officer over cabbage futures, ignoring the cherry blossom petals falling into their tea. Two elegant Northern Water Tribe women, arm in arm, meditatively walked a maze pattern raked into a field of pure-white sand. In the corner, a morose young man with carefully disheveled hair bit the end of his brush, struggling with a poem.

Any of them could have been—and probably were—benders of the highest order. It always gave Kyoshi a thrill to see so many masters of the elements gathered in one place. When the estate was full of visitors, like today, the air felt alive with power. Sometimes literally so when Kelsang was around and in a playful mood.

Auntie Mui, head of the kitchen staff, appeared from one of the side hallways and bounced over to them, looking like a plum rolling down a bumpy hill. She used her momentum to deliver a hard swat to the small of Kyoshi's back. Kyoshi yelped and gripped the jar tighter.

"Don't carry food around where the guests can see it!" Auntie Mui hissed. "Use the service entrance!"

She hustled Kyoshi down the steps of a tunnel, oblivious to the hard bump Kyoshi's forehead took against the top support beam. They shuffled down the corridor that still smelled of sawdust and wet loam through the plaster. It was more obvious down here how new and hastily constructed the complex really was.

The roughness of the hallway was another of the many little details that poked holes in the common illusion those under Jianzhu's roof tried to uphold, from his most exalted guest down to his lowliest employee. The Avatar's presence was an uncomfortably recent blessing. Everyone was going through the motions at an accelerated pace.

"You were out in the sun too much, weren't you?" Auntie Mui said. "Your freckles got darker again. Why don't you ever wear that concealer I gave you? It has real crushed nacre in it."

Kyoshi's skull throbbed. "What, and look like a bloodless ghost?"

"Better than looking like someone sprinkled starpoppy seeds over your cheeks!"

About the only things Kyoshi hated more than gunk on her skin were the warped, infuriating values that older folks like Auntie Mui held around complexion. It was yet another contradiction of the village, that you should make an honest living toiling under the sun but never in the slightest look like it. In the game of rural Yokoyan beauty standards, Kyoshi had lost that particular round. Among others.

They climbed another set of stairs, Kyoshi remembering to duck this time, and passed through a hall for drying and splitting the immense amount of firewood needed to fuel the stoves. Auntie Mui tsk'ed at the splitting maul that had been buried in the chopping block by the last person to use it instead of being hung up properly on the wall, but she wasn't strong enough to pull it out, and Kyoshi's hands were full.

They entered the steamy, cavernous kitchen. The clash of metal pans and roaring flames could have been mistaken for a siege operation. Kyoshi set the pickling jar down on the nearest clear table and took a needed stretch, her arms wobbling with unfamiliar freedom. The jar had been attached to her for so long it felt like saying goodbye to a needy child.

"Don't forget, you have gift duties tonight."

She was startled to hear Rangi's voice. She didn't think the Firebender would have followed her this deep into the bowels of the house.

Rangi glanced around. "Don't waste too much time here. You're not a scullery maid."

The nearby kitchen staff, some of whom *were* scullery maids, looked at them and scowled. Kyoshi winced. The villagers thought she was stuck up for living in the mansion; the other servants thought she was stuck up for her closeness to Yun; and Rangi, with her elite attitude, only made it worse.

There was no pleasing anyone, she thought as Rangi departed for the barracks.

Kyoshi spotted an odd figure among the legions of white-clad cooks pounding away at their stations. An Airbender, with his orange robes rolled up to his blocky shoulders. His massive paws were covered in flour, and he'd tucked his forest of a beard into his tunic to keep it from shedding. It was like the kitchen had been invaded by a mountain ogre.

Kelsang should have been aboveground, watching the Avatar. Or at least greeting a visiting sage. Not cutting out dumpling wrappers among the cooks.

He looked up and grinned when he saw Kyoshi. "I've been banished," he said, preempting her question. "Jianzhu thinks my presence is causing Yun to prematurely dream about airbending, so we're trying to keep him focused on one element at a time. I needed to feel useful, so here I am."

Kyoshi sidled her way over to him through the crowded space and gave the monk a kiss on the cheek. "Let me help." She washed her hands in a nearby sink, grabbed a ball of dough to knead, and fell into work beside him.

For the past decade, Kelsang had essentially raised her. He'd used what leeway he had with the Southern Air Temple to reside in Yokoya as much as he could, in order to look after Kyoshi. When he had to leave, he foisted her upon different families, begged alms to keep her fed. After Jianzhu brought the Avatar to Yokoya for safekeeping, Kelsang twisted his old friend's arm to hire Kyoshi on.

He'd done all this, saved the life of a child stranger, for no reason other than that she needed someone. In a part of the Earth Kingdom where love was reserved solely for blood relations, the monk from a foreign land was the dearest person in the world to Kyoshi.

Which was why she knew his good cheer right now was completely fake.

Rumors flew around the house that the once-legendary friendship between Avatar Kuruk's companions had deteriorated. Especially so between Jianzhu and Kelsang. In the years since Kuruk's death, if the gossip was to be believed, Jianzhu had amassed wealth and influence unbecoming of a sage who was supposed to be dedicated solely to guiding Kuruk's reincarnation. Bending masters came to the house to pay obeisance to him, not the Avatar, and decrees that were normally made by the Earth Kings instead bore Jianzhu's seal. Kelsang disapproved of such power-hungry actions and was at risk of being completely shunted to the side.

Kyoshi didn't have context around the politics, but she did worry about the growing rift between the two master benders. It couldn't be good for the Avatar. Yun adored Kelsang almost as much as she did, but ultimately was loyal to the earth sage who'd found him.

Distracted by her thoughts, she didn't notice the little puff of flour fly up from the table and hit her in the forehead. White dust clouded her vision. She squinted at Kelsang, who wasn't trying to hide the second shot that spun around above his palm, chambered in a pocket-sized whirlwind he'd summoned.

"It wasn't me," he said. "It was a different Airbender."

Kyoshi snickered and grabbed the flour bead out of the air. It burst between her fingers. "Quit it before Auntie Mui throws us out of here."

"Then quit looking troubled on my behalf," he said, having read her mind. "It's not so bad if I take a break from Avatar business. I'll get to spend more time with you. We should go on a vacation, the two of us, perhaps to see the Air Nomad sacred sites."

She would have liked that very much. Chances to share Kelsang's company had gotten rarer as the Avatar and his teachers sank deeper into the mesh of world affairs. But as lowly as her own job was in comparison, she still had the same responsibility to show up every day.

"I can't," Kyoshi said. "I have work." There'd be time enough in the future for traveling with Kelsang.

He rolled his eyes. "Bah. I've never seen someone so averse to fun since old Abbot 'No-Fruit Pies' Dorje." He flicked another blob of flour at her, and she failed to flinch out of the way.

"I know how to have fun!" Kyoshi whispered indignantly as she wiped her nose with the back of her wrist.

From the head of the cutting board tables, Auntie Mui gave a tongue-curled whistle, interrupting their debate. "Poetry time!" she said.

Everyone groaned. She was always trying to enforce high culture on her workers, or at least her idea of it. "Lee!" she said, singling out an unfortunate wok handler. "You start us off."

The poor line cook stumbled as he tried to compose on the spot while keeping count of his syllables. "Uh . . . *the-weath-er-is-nice / sun-shin-ing-down-from-the-sky / birds-are-sing-ing . . . good?*"

Auntie Mui made a face like she'd swigged pure lemon juice. "That was awful! Where's your sense of balance? Symmetry? Contrast?"

Lee threw his hands in the air. He was paid to fry things, not perform in the Upper Ring of Ba Sing Se.

"Can't someone give us a decent verse?" Auntie Mui complained. There were no volunteers.

"*I've got cheeks like ripe round fruit,*" Kelsang suddenly pitched forth. "*They shake like boughs in the storm / I blush bright red when I see a bed / and leap at the sound of the horn.*"

The room exploded in laughter. He'd picked a well-known shanty popular with sailors and field hands, where you improvised raunchy words from the perspective of your object of unrequited affection. It was a game for others to guess who you were singing about, and the simple rhythm made manual labor more pleasant.

"Brother Kelsang!" Auntie Mui said, scandalized. "Set an example!"

He had. The entire staff was already chopping, kneading, and scrubbing to the raucous tune. It was okay to misbehave if a monk did it first.

"*I've got a nose like a dove-tailed deer / I run like a leaf on the wind*," Lee sang, evidently better at this than haiku. "*My arms are slight and my waist is tight / and I don't have a thought for my kin.*"

"Mirai!" a dishwasher yelled out. "He's got it bad for the greengrocer's daughter!" The staff whooped over Lee's protests, thinking it a good match. Sometimes it didn't matter to the audience if they guessed right or not.

"Kyoshi next!" someone said. "She's never here, so let's make the most of it!"

Kyoshi was caught off guard. Normally she wasn't included in household antics. She caught Kelsang's eye and saw the challenge twinkling there. *Fun, eh? Prove it.*

Before she could stop herself, the rhythm launched her into song.

"*I've got two knives that are cast in bronze / they pierce all the way to the soul / they draw you in with the promise of sin / like the moth to the flame to the coal.*"

The kitchen howled. Auntie Mui clucked in disapproval. "Keep going, you naughty girl!" Lee shouted, glad that the attention was off him.

She'd even managed to throw off Kelsang, who looked at her curiously, as if he had a spark of recognition for whom she was describing. Kyoshi knew that wasn't possible when she was simply tossing out the first words that came to her head. She thumped a length of dough onto the table in front of her, creating her own percussion.

"I've got hair like the starless night / it sticks to my lips when I smile / I'll wind it with yours and we'll drift off course / in a ship touching hearts all the while."

Somehow the improvisation was easy, though she'd never considered herself a poet. Or a bawdy mind, for that matter. It was as if another person, someone much more at ease with their own desires, was feeding her the right lines to express herself. And to her surprise, she liked how the inelegant lines made her feel. Truthful and silly and raw.

"For the way I walk is a lantern lit / that leads you into the night / I'll hold you close and love you the most / until our end is in sight."

Kyoshi didn't have time to ponder the darker turn her verse took before a sudden pain shot through her wrist.

Kelsang had grabbed her arm and was staring at her, eyes wild and white. His grip squeezed tighter and tighter, crushing her flesh, his nails drawing blood from both her skin and his.

"You're hurting me!" she cried out.

The room was silent. Disbelieving. Kelsang let go, and she caught herself on the edge of the table. A map of purple was stamped on her wrist.

"Kyoshi," Kelsang said, his voice constricted and airless. "Kyoshi, *where did you learn THAT SONG?*"

REVELATIONS

AFTER KELSANG took her aside into an empty study and spent half an hour tearfully apologizing for hurting her, he told her why he'd lost control.

"Oh," Kyoshi said in response to the worst news she'd ever heard in her life.

She ran her fingers through her hair and threw her head back. The library where they were hiding was taller than it was long, a mineshaft cramped with scrolls, yanked off the shelves and put back without care. Beams of sunlight revealed how much dust was floating around the room. She needed to clean this place up.

"You're mistaken," she said to Kelsang. "Yun is the Avatar. Jianzhu identified him nearly two years ago. *Everyone* knows this."

Kelsang didn't look any happier than she did. "You don't

understand. After Kuruk died, the Earthen traditions around locating the Avatar fell apart. Imagine if the seasons suddenly refused to turn. It was chaos. After so many failures, the sages, Earthbenders especially, felt abandoned by the spirits and their ancestors alike."

Kyoshi leaned back against a ladder and gripped the rungs tightly.

"There was talk of Kuruk being the last of the cycle, that the world was destined for an age of strife, to be torn apart by outlaws and warlords. Until Jianzhu labeled Yun as the next Avatar. But the way it happened had no precedent. Tell me this—with the two of you as close as you are, has Yun ever once told you the details?"

She shook her head. It *was* strange, now that Kelsang mentioned it.

"That's because Jianzhu probably forbade him. The full story would cast the shadow of illegitimacy on him." The monk rubbed his eyes; it was abhorrently dusty in here. "We were in Makapu, surveying the volcano. We'd honestly given up on finding the Avatar, like so many others. On the last day of our trip, we noticed a crowd growing in a corner of the town square.

"They were gathered around a child with a Pai Sho board. Yun. He was hustling tourists like us, and he'd made quite a bit of money at it too. To give his opponents confidence, he was running the blind bag gambit. It's when your opponent plays normally, picking their tiles, but you dump yours into a sack and mix them up randomly. Whatever you draw each turn is what you have to play. An insurmountable disadvantage."

Kyoshi could see it too easily. Yun's silver tongue coaxing money out of people's wallets. A stream of banter and flashing smiles. He could probably bankrupt someone and still leave them happy to have met him.

"What most people don't know, and what Yun didn't know, was that the blind bag is supposed to be a scam," Kelsang said. "You're meant to rig the tiles or the bag itself so you have a way to find the exact combinations you need. But Yun wasn't cheating. He was actually drawing randomly and winning."

"We might have passed it off as a kid enjoying a string of luck, but Jianzhu noticed he was drawing and playing Kuruk's favorite strategies, turn by turn, down to the exact placement of the exact tile. Game after game he was doing this. He displayed tricks and traps that Kuruk explicitly kept secret from anyone but us."

"It sounds like Kuruk took Pai Sho pretty seriously," Kyoshi said.

Kelsang snorted and then sneezed, sending a little tornado spiraling toward the skylight. "It was one of the few things he did. And he was unequivocally one of the greatest players in history. Depending on what rules you're using, you have as many as sixty tiles. There are over two hundred spots on the board where you can put them. To randomly draw and then brilliantly execute a precise line of play that only Kuruk was mad enough to win with in the annals of the game—the odds of it are unfathomable."

Kyoshi didn't have a taste for Pai Sho, but she knew that masters often talked about play styles being as individualistic the boasnizable as a signature. An identity contained within

"After what Jianzhu went through with Xu Ping An and the Yellow Necks, it was as if a mountain range had been lifted off his shoulders," Kelsang said. "Any doubts he might have had completely vanished when we saw Yun earthbend. Granted, the kid can move rocks like no one else. If we identified the Avatar solely through a precision-bending contest, he'd be Kuruk's reincarnation hands down."

Kyoshi thought back to this morning and Yun's incredible manipulation of the earth. In her mind only the Avatar could have done that.

"I don't get it," she said. "All of this is *proof*. *Yun* is the Avatar. Why would you tell me that I'm—that I'm—why would you *do* that to me!?"

Her anguish was absorbed, without an echo, by the masses of faded, crumbling paper that surrounded them.

"Can we get out of here?" Kelsang said, his eyes red.

They walked in silence down the corridors of the mansion. Kelsang's presence justified taking the shortest route, where the visiting dignitaries might see them. They passed works of calligraphy mounted on the walls that were more precious than bricks of gold. Vases of translucent delicacy held the day's flowers cut from the garden.

Kyoshi felt like a thief as they passed the casually displayed treasures, no better than an intruder who might slip past the guards and stuff each priceless item into a gunnysack. Even the servants' dormitory, plain and poorly lit, seemed to whisper *ingrate* at her from its dark corners. Not all of the staff were able to live on-site. And she knew that a bed lifted off the floor and a wooden door that shut tight were better than what many other servants around the Earth Kingdom got.

She and Kelsang squeezed inside her room. It was cramped, the two of them being the same height, but as sizable people they had practice at minimizing themselves. Her quarters were small but still technically more space than she needed. Besides a few knickknacks from her street life, her only two possessions upon moving into Jianzhu's house were a heavy locked trunk that she'd stowed in the corner, and on top, the leather-bound journal that explained what was in it. Her inheritance from the days before Yokoya.

"You still have those," Kelsang said. "I know how valuable they are to you. I remember tracking you down to the little nest you made around the trunk underneath the blacksmith's house. You hugged the book so tight to your chest and wouldn't let me read it. You looked ready to defend it to the death."

Her feelings about the items were more complicated than he understood. Kyoshi had never opened the lock, having thrown the key into the ocean one day in a fit of spite. And she'd nearly burned the journal several times over.

Down the hall someone was moving about, making the pine floorboards squeak, so they waited until the footsteps disappeared. Kelsang sat on the bed, bowing the planks in the middle. Kyoshi leaned against her door and braced her feet like an attacking army was trying to beat it down.

"So you think I'm the Avatar because of a stupid song I made up?" she said. Somewhere between the study and her room she'd found enough backbone to say it out loud.

"I think you *might* be the Avatar because you pulled from thin air the exact lines of a poem Kuruk wrote a long time ago," Kelsang said.

A poem. A poem wasn't proof. Not like the cold hard impossibility of what Yun did.

Kelsang could tell she needed a better explanation. "What I'm about to tell you, you should keep to yourself," he said.

"I'm listening."

"It was about twenty years ago. Kuruk's companions were still very close, but without any real challenges, we drifted toward our separate lives. Jianzhu started working on his family's holdings. Hei-Ran started teaching at the Royal Fire Academy and married Rangi's father, Junsik, in the same year. It was the happiest I'd ever seen her. As for me, that was when Abbot Dorje was alive and I was still in his good graces, so I was being groomed to take over the Southern Air Temple."

Assigning a past to the venerable benders was a strange mix of satisfying and unnervingly voyeuristic. She was spying on things she shouldn't be privy to. "What was Kuruk doing?"

"Being Kuruk. Traveling the world. Breaking hearts and taking names. But one day he showed up on my doorstep out of the blue, trembling like a schoolboy. He wanted me to read over a declaration of eternal love he'd composed in a poem."

Kelsang inhaled sharply through his nose. Kyoshi kept her room dust-free and spotless. "This happened two months after Hei-Ran's wedding and three months before Jianzhu's father got sick," he said. "He used a more formal meter than a sailor's ditty, and he didn't sing it, but its contents were exactly what you produced in the spur of the moment."

That only weakened the argument. "You seem to remember this in overly specific detail," Kyoshi said.

The monk furrowed his brow. "That's because he was going to give the poem to Hei-Ran."

Oh no. She'd heard stories of the Water Avatar's lack of propriety, but that was going several levels too far. "What happened next?"

"I . . . meddled," Kelsang said. Kyoshi couldn't tell if he was regretful or proud of his decision. "I berated Kuruk for his stupidity and selfishness, for trying to ruin his friend's happy relationship, and made him destroy the confession while I watched. To this day I don't know if I did the right thing. Hei-Ran always did love Kuruk with some piece of her heart. Maybe everything would have turned out better if they had run off with each other."

Kyoshi quickly did the math in her head—and, yes, if that had happened, Rangi wouldn't have been born. "You did the right thing," she said, with more ferocity than she intended to show.

"I'll never find out. Not long after, Kuruk met Ummi. That tragedy unfolded so fast that my memory of it starts to blur."

She didn't know who Ummi was, and she had no intention of asking. Matters were complicated enough. And Kuruk . . . Kyoshi was no advanced student of Avatar lore, but she was developing a pretty dim view of the man.

"I wish I could be more certain," Kelsang said. "But if there's anything the last two decades have taught me, it's that life does not work out in certain, guaranteed ways. I'm not supposed to talk about this, but Yun is having problems firebending. I fear Jianzhu is becoming . . . more extreme. He's staked so much on creating his ideal replacement for Kuruk that anytime he faces a setback, his response is to dig in and push harder."

Kyoshi was more shaken by the revelation that Yun couldn't firebend than anything else she'd heard so far. The image he projected was of a boy who could do the impossible. Yes, Yun was her friend, but she still had the same faith in the Avatar as anyone else. Mastering fire should have been easy for someone as clever and talented as he was.

Kelsang seemed to pick up on her fear. "Kyoshi, Yun still has the strongest case for being the Avatar. That hasn't changed." He worried the end of his beard. "But if the criteria we've low-ered ourselves to are 'improbable things that Kuruk once did,' then we have to consider you as well."

The monk ruminated for a moment, fitting pieces together in his head. "To be honest though, I don't know if I'm entirely upset by this new complication. You have Avatar-worthy merits that you won't acknowledge."

Kyoshi scoffed. "Such as?"

He thought it over more before deciding on one. "Self-less humility."

"That's not true! I'm not any more—" She caught Kelsang about to laugh at her and scowled.

He got up, and her bed boards groaned with relief. "I'm sorry," he said. "I might have been able to answer this question years ago, had I the chance to meet your parents like I did with the other village children. More information could have made the difference."

Kyoshi scrunched her face and kicked her heel back against the trunk, releasing the sudden burst of anger that ran through her. The wooden side made a drumlike thud. "I'm sure they would have loved having a child as valuable as the Avatar," she snapped. "A once-in-a-generation prize."

Kelsang smiled at her gently. "They would have been proud of their daughter no matter what," he said. "I know I am."

Normally Kyoshi would have felt comforted by the acknowledgment that she'd become as much of a fixture in Kelsang's life as he had in hers. But if he walked out her door and told Jianzhu what happened, it could tear apart the little corner of the world the two of them had marked off for themselves. Didn't Kelsang see that? Wasn't he worried?

"Can we keep this a secret?" Kyoshi said. "Just for a while, until I can get my bearings? I don't want to be rash. Maybe you'll remember Kuruk's poem differently in the morning. Or Yun will firebend." *Anything.*

Kelsang didn't answer. He'd been suddenly transfixed by her tiny shelf.

It held a gold-dyed tassel, a few beads, a coin she'd pilfered from a shrine donation box and felt too guilty to spend and too afraid to return. The clay turtle she couldn't remember exactly how she'd gotten, other than that it was a present from him. He stared at the junk for a long time.

"Please," Kyoshi said.

Kelsang looked back at her and sighed. "For a little while, perhaps," he said. "But eventually we have to tell Jianzhu and the others. Whatever the truth is, we must find it together."

After he left, Kyoshi didn't sit down. She thought best on her feet, motionless. Her wooden cell of a room was good enough for that.

This was a nightmare. While she wasn't an important political dignitary, she wasn't an idiot either. She knew what kind of bedlam lay behind the precarious balance Jianzhu and Yun had set up, the mountain they'd suspended in the air.

From around corners she'd spied on the bouts of ecstatic sobbing, the sense of utter relief that many of the visiting sages went through when they first laid eyes on Yun. After more than a decade of doubt, he was a solid body, a sharp mind, a belatedly fulfilled promise. The inheritor of blessed Yangchen's legacy. Avatar Yun was a beacon of light who gave people confidence the world could be saved.

"Avatar Kyoshi" would simply be dirt kicked over the fire.

Her eyes landed on the journal lying on the trunk. Her pulse quickened again. Would they have left her behind if they knew there was a chance, no matter how slim, that she held some worth?

A knock came from outside. Gifting duty. She'd forgotten.

She shoved the entire conversation with Kelsang to the back of her mind as she opened the door. She knew from experience there was no trouble so great that she couldn't pack it away. Kelsang wasn't certain, therefore she didn't need to worry. What she needed to worry about was Rangi having her hide for—

"Hey," Yun said. "I was looking for you."

PROMISES

"YOU KNOW, this is much harder when you're around," Kyoshi said to the Avatar.

She and Yun sat on the floor in one of the innumerable receiving rooms. The freestanding screen paintings had been folded up and pushed to the walls, and the potted plants had been set outside to make room for the giant piles of gifts that guests had brought for the Avatar.

Yun lay on his back, taking up valuable free space. He lazily waved a custom-forged, filigreed *jian* blade around in the air, stirring an imaginary upside-down pot with it.

"I have no idea how to use this," he said. "I hate swords."

"A boy who doesn't like swords?" Kyoshi said with a mock gasp. "Put it in the armory pile, and we'll get Rangi to teach you at some point."

There were a lot of guesses around the village about what,

exactly, Kyoshi did in the mansion. Given her orphaned, unwanted status, the farmers' children assumed she handled the dirtiest, most impure jobs, dealing with refuse and carcasses and the like. The truth was somewhat different.

What she really did, as her primary role, was pick up after Yun. Tidy his messes. The Avatar was such a slob that he needed a full-time servant following in his wake, or else the chaos would overwhelm the entire complex. Soon after taking her on, the senior staff discovered Kyoshi's strong, compulsive need to put things back in their rightful place, minimize clutter, and maintain order. So they put her on Avatar-containment duty.

This time, the pile they sat hip-deep in was not Yun's fault. Wealthy visitors were constantly showering him with gifts in the hope of currying favor, or simply because they loved him. As big as the house was, there wasn't enough room to give each item a display place of honor. On a regular basis Kyoshi had to sort and pack away the heirlooms and antiques and works of art that only seemed to get more lavish and numerous over time.

"Oh, look," she said, holding up a lacquered circle set in a crisscross pattern with luminous gems. "Another Pai Sho board."

Yun glanced over. "That one's pretty."

"This is, without exaggeration, the forty-fourth board you own now. You're not keeping it."

"Ugh, ruthless."

She ignored him. He might be the Avatar, but when it came to her officially assigned duties, she reigned above him.

And Kyoshi needed this right now. She needed this normalcy to bury what Kelsang had told her. Despite her best efforts, it kept rising from below, the notion that she was betraying Yun and swallowing up what belonged to him.

As he lounged on his elbows, Kyoshi noticed Yun wasn't wearing his embroidered indoor slippers. "Are those new boots?" she said, pointing at his feet. The leather they were crafted from was a beautiful, soft gray tone with fur trim like powdery morning snow. *Probably baby turtle-seal hide,* she thought with revulsion.

Yun tensed up. "I found them in the pile earlier."

"They don't fit you. Give them over."

"I'd rather not." He scooched backward but was hedged in by more boxes.

She crawled over to peer at the boots from a closer angle. "What did you—did you stuff the extra space with bandages? They're ridiculously too big for you! Take them off!" She got to her knees and grabbed his foot with both hands.

"Kyoshi, please!"

She paused and looked up at his face. It was filled with pure dread. And he rarely ever raised his voice at her.

It was the second time today a person important to her had acted strangely. She forced herself to acknowledge the two incidents weren't related. So he'd suddenly developed an intense taste for footwear. She'd make a note of it.

Yun sat up and put his hands on Kyoshi's shoulders, fixing her with his jade-green eyes. She'd long since become inured to his flirty smiles whenever he wanted a rise out of her, his puppy-dog pout when he wanted a favor, but his expression of earnest desire was a weapon he didn't pull out often. The way his troubled thoughts softened the sharp edges of his face was heart piercing.

"Spill it," she said. "What's bothering you?"

"I want you to come on a journey with me," he said quietly. "I need you by my side."

Kyoshi nearly choked on her surprise. He was offering a taste of the world that only an exalted few got to sample. To be a companion of the Avatar, even for a moment, was an honor beyond reckoning.

Flying into the sunset, huddled close to Yun, the wind in their hair—if Aoma and the other villagers were jealous of her before, they'd go foaming-mad with envy now. "What kind of trip is this?" she said, unconsciously lowering herself to his volume. "Where is this taking place?"

"The Eastern Sea, near the South Pole," he said. "I'm signing a new treaty with Tagaka."

Well, so much for fantasy. Kyoshi knocked Yun's hands off her shoulders and sat back on her knees properly. The motion felt like it helped drain the heat out of her face.

"The Fifth Nation?" she said. "You're going to sit at a table with the Fifth Nation? And you want me to come *with* you?" What was she going to do surrounded by a band of bloodthirsty pirates that was bigger than most Earth Kingdom provincial militias? Sweep up their . . . cutlasses?

"I know how much you hate outlaws," Yun said. "I thought you might appreciate seeing a victory over them up close. It's only political, but still."

Kyoshi puffed her cheeks in frustration. "Yun, I am basically your *nanny*," she said. "You need Rangi for this mission. Better yet, you need the Fire Lord's entire personal legion."

"Rangi's coming. But I want you as well. You won't be there to fight if things go wrong." He stared at his own feet. "You'll just stand around and watch me as things go right."

"For the love of—*why?*"

"Perspective," he said. "I need your perspective."

He pulled out a Pai Sho tile he'd nicked from the set she'd put away and squinted at it like a jeweler in the light.

"Is it sad that I want a regular person there?" he said. "Someone who'll be scared and impressed and overwhelmed just like me, and not another professional Avatar monitor? That afterward I want you to tell me I'm as good as Yangchen or Salai, regardless of whether or not that's true?"

He laughed bitterly. "I know it sounds stupid. But I think I need the presence of someone who cares about me first and history second. I want you to be proud of me, Yun, not satisfied with the performance of the Avatar."

Kyoshi didn't know what to do. This idea sounded mind-numbingly dangerous. She wasn't equipped to follow the Avatar into politics or battle, not like the great companions of past generations.

Her stomach wound into a knot as she thought of the secret between her and Kelsang. They wouldn't get the time they needed to figure that matter out. The world demanded an Avatar or else.

"It'll be safer than it sounds," Yun said. "Oddly enough, most *daofei* gangs hold quite a bit of respect for the Avatar. Either they're superstitious about the Avatar's spiritual powers or intimidated by someone who can drop all four elements on their heads at once."

He tried to sound lighthearted, but he looked more and more pained the longer she kept him waiting in silence.

Then again, was it so dire of a choice? Jianzhu would never

risk Yun's life. And she had a hard time believing Yun would risk hers. Really, the situation wasn't as grand or complicated as she made it out to be. Avatar business and the fate of the Earth Kingdom was for other people and other times. Right now, Kyoshi's friend was depending on her. She'd be there for him.

"I'll come," she said. "Someone has to clean up whatever mess you make."

Yun shuddered with relief. He caught her fingers and brought them gently to his cheek, nuzzling into them as if they were ice for a fever. "Thank you," he said.

Kyoshi flushed all the way down to her toes. She reminded herself that his casual tendency to be close to her, to share touches, was just part of his personality. She'd caught glimpses and heard stories from the staff that confirmed it. One time he'd kissed the hand of the princess of Omashu for a second longer than normal and scored an entire new trade agreement as a result.

It had taken her a very, very long time after starting at the house to convince herself she was not in love with Yun. Moments like this threatened to undo all of her hard work. She let herself plunge under the surface and enjoy being washed over by the simple contact.

Yun reluctantly put her hand down. "Three . . ." he said, cocking his ear at the ceramic-tiled floor with a smile. "Two . . . One . . ."

Rangi slid the door open with a sharp click.

"Avatar." She bowed deeply and solemnly to Yun. Then she turned to Kyoshi. "You've barely made any progress! Look at this mess!"

"We were waiting for you," Yun said. "We decided to burn everything. You can start with those hideous silk robes in the corner. As your Avatar, I command you to light 'em up. Right now."

Rangi rolled her eyes. "Yes, and set the entire mansion on fire." She always tried as hard as she could to remain dignified in front of Yun, but she cracked on occasion. And it was usually during the times when the three of them, the youngest people in the complex, were alone together.

"Exactly," Yun said cheerily. "Burn it all to the ground. Reduce it back to nature. We'll achieve pure states of mind."

"You would start whining the moment you had to bathe with cold water," Kyoshi said to him.

"There's a solution for that," Yun said. "Everyone would go to the river, strip down naked, grab the nearest Firebender, and—*pthah!*"

A decorative pillow hit him in the face. Kyoshi's eyes went wide in disbelief.

Rangi looked utterly horrified at what she'd done. She'd attacked the Avatar. She stared at her hands like they were covered in blood. A traitor's eternal punishment awaited her in the afterlife.

Yun burst out into laughter.

Kyoshi followed, her sides shaking until they hurt. Rangi tried not to succumb, clamping her hand over her mouth, but despite her best efforts, little giggles and snorts leaked through her fingers. An older member of the staff walked past, frowning at the trio through the open door. Which set them off further.

Kyoshi looked at Yun and Rangi's beautiful, unguarded

faces, freed from the weight of their duties if only for a moment. Her friends. She thought of how unlikely it was that she'd found them.

This. This is what I need to protect.

Yun defended the world, and Rangi defended him, but as far as Kyoshi was concerned, her own sacred ground was marked by the limits where her friends stood. *This is what I need to keep safe above all else.*

The sudden clarity of her realization caused her mirth to evaporate. She maintained a rictus grin so the others wouldn't notice her change in mood. Her fist tightened around nothing.

And the spirits help anyone who would take this from me.

THE ICEBERG

KYOSHI'S NIGHTMARE smelled like wet bison.

It was raining, and bales of cargo wrapped in burlap splashed in the mud around her as if they'd fallen from great heights, part of the storm. It no longer mattered what was in them.

A flash of lightning revealed hooded figures looming over her. Their faces were obscured by masks of running water.

I hate you, Kyoshi screamed. I'll hate you until I die. I'll never forgive you.

Two hands clasped each other. A transaction was struck, one that would be violated the instant it became an inconvenience to uphold. Something wet and lifeless hit her in the shins, papers sealed in oilcloth.

"Kyoshi!"

She woke up with a start and nearly pitched over the side of Pengpeng's saddle. She caught herself on the rail, the sanded edge pressing into her gut, and stared at the roiling blue beneath them. It was a long way down to the ocean.

It wasn't rain on her face but sweat. She saw a droplet fall off her chin and plummet into nothingness before someone grabbed her by the shoulders and yanked her back. She fell on top of Yun and Rangi both, squashing the wind out of them.

"Don't scare us like that!" Yun shouted in her ear.

"What happened?" Kelsang said, trying to shift around in the driver's seat without disturbing the reins. His legs straddled Pengpeng's gigantic neck, making it difficult for him to see behind himself.

"Nothing, Master Kelsang," Rangi grumbled. "Kyoshi had a bad dream is all."

Kelsang looked skeptical but kept flying straight ahead. "Well okay then, but be careful, and no roughhousing. We don't want anyone getting hurt before we get there. Jianzhu would have my head on a platter."

He gave Kyoshi an extra glance of worry. He'd been caught off guard by Yun's sudden mission, and her agreeing to tag along had amplified the strain. This treaty signing was too important to cast doubt on Yun's Avatarhood now. Until it was over, Kelsang would have to help her shoulder the burden of their secret, their lie by omission.

Below them on the water's surface, trailing only slightly behind, was the ship bearing Yun's earthbending master, as well as Hei-Ran and the small contingent of armed guards. Aided by the occasional boost of wind that Kelsang generated with a whirl of his arms, the grand junk kept pace with Pengpeng, its battened sails billowing and full. Kelsang's bison was dry and well-groomed for the occasion, her white fur as fluffy as a cloud underneath her fancier saddle, but the stiff salt breeze still carried a hint of beastly odor.

That must have been what I smelled in my dream. It had been a very long time since Kelsang had taken her for a ride, and the unfamiliar environment rattled her sleeping mind. The titanic, six-legged animal stretched its jaws wide and yawned as if to agree with her.

And speaking of dressing up, Jianzhu had given Kyoshi an outfit so far beyond her station that she'd almost broken out in hives when she saw it. She'd thought the pale green silk blouse and leggings would have been enough finery, but then the wardrobe attendants brought in two different pleated skirts, a shoulder-length wraparound jacket, and a wide sash with such exquisite stitching that it should have been mounted on a wall rather than tied around her waist.

The other servants had to help her into the clothing. She didn't miss the looks they shared behind her back. That Kyoshi had abused the master's favoritism—again.

But once the pieces were assembled, they melded to her body like she'd been born to wear them. Each layer slid over the next with ease, granting her full mobility. She didn't ask anyone where the clothes that fit her so well came from, not wanting to hear a snippy answer like *Oh, Jianzhu ripped them off the corpse of some fallen giant he defeated.*

And the serious nature of the task ahead made itself clear as she finished dressing. The inside of the jacket was lined with finely woven chainmail. Not thick enough to stop a spearpoint with a person's entire weight behind it, but strong enough to absorb a dart or the slash of a hidden knife. The weight of the metal links on her shoulders said to expect trouble.

"Why are the four of us up here and not down there?" Kyoshi said, pointing at the boat, where more preparations were undoubtedly being made.

"I insisted," Yun said. "Sifu wasn't happy about it, but I told him I needed time by myself."

"To go over the plan?"

Yun looked off into the distance. "Sure."

He'd been acting strange recently. But then again, he was a new Avatar about to enact a decree in one of the most hostile settings imaginable. Yun might have had all the talent and the best teachers in the world, but he was still diving into the abyss headlong.

"Your master has good reason for his reluctance," Kelsang said to him. "At one point it was somewhat of a tradition for the Avatar to travel extensively with his or her friends, without the supervision of elders. But Hei-Ran, Jianzhu, and I . . . the three of us weren't the positive influences on Kuruk that we were supposed to be. Jianzhu views that period of our youth as a great personal failing of his."

"Sounds like a failing of Kuruk's instead," Kyoshi muttered.

"Don't criticize Yun's past life," Rangi said, whacking her shoulder with a mittened hand. "The Avatars tread paths of great destiny. Every action they take is meaningful."

They meaningfully passed another three dull, meaningful hours in southward flight. It got colder, much colder. They pulled on parkas and bundled themselves in quilts as they swooped over otter penguins wriggling atop ever-growing chunks of floating ice. The cry of antarctic birds could be heard on the wind.

"We're here," Kelsang said. He was the only one who hadn't put on extra layers; it was theorized around the mansion that Airbenders were simply immune to the weather. "Hold on for the descent."

Their target was an iceberg almost as big as Yokoya itself. The blue crag rose into the air as high as the hills of their earthbound village. A small flat shelf ringed the formation, presumably giving them a place to set up camp. Most of the far side was obscured by the peak, but as they flew lower Kyoshi caught a glimpse of felt tents dotting the opposite shoreline. The Fifth Nation delegation.

"I don't see their fleet," Rangi said.

"Part of the terms were that the negotiating grounds be even," Yun said. "For her that meant no warships. For us that meant no ground."

The compromise didn't feel even. The vast iceberg was one of many, drifting in an ocean cold enough to kill in minutes. A dusting of fresh snow gave every surface flat enough to stand on a coat of alien whiteness.

Kyoshi knew that though the Southern Water Tribe had long since disowned Tagaka's entire family tree, she still came from a line of Waterbenders. If there was ever a location to challenge an Earth Avatar, it was here.

Kelsang landed Pengpeng on the frozen beach and hopped down first. Then he helped the others off the huge bison, generating a small bubble of air to cushion their fall. The little gesture stirred unease in Kyoshi's heart, the playful bounce like cracking jokes before a funeral.

They watched Jianzhu's ship come in. It was too large and deep-keeled to run aground, and there wasn't a natural harbor formation in the ice, so the crew dropped anchor and lowered themselves into longboats, making the final sliver of the journey in the smaller craft. One of them reached the shore much faster than the others.

Jianzhu stepped out of the lead boat, surveying the landing site while straightening his furs, his eyes narrowed and nostrils flared as if any potential treachery might have a giveaway smell to it. Hei-Ran followed, treating the water carefully, as she was decked out in her full panoply of battle armor. The third person on the longboat was less familiar to Kyoshi.

"Sifu Amak," Yun said, bowing to the man.

Master Amak was a strange, shadowy presence around the compound. Ostensibly, he was a Waterbender from the north who was patiently waiting his turn to teach the Avatar. But questions about his past produced inconsistent answers. There was gossip around the staff that the lanky, grim-faced Water Tribesman had spent the last ten years far from his home, in the employ of a lesser prince in Ba Sing Se who'd suddenly gone from eleventh in the line of succession to the fourth. Amak's silent nature and the web of scars running around his arms and neck seemed like a warning not to inquire further.

And yet the Avatar had regular training sessions with him, though Yun had told Kyoshi outright that he couldn't waterbend yet and wasn't expected to. He would emerge from the practice grounds, bloodied and mussed but with his smile blazing from new knowledge.

"He's my favorite teacher other than Sifu," Yun had said once. "He's the only one who cares more about function than form."

There must have been strategy at work with Amak's attendance. Instead of the blue tunic he wore around the complex, they'd dressed him in a set of wide-sleeved robes, dark green in Earth Kingdom style, and a conical hat that shaded his face. His proud wolftail haircut had been shaved off, and he'd taken out his bone piercings.

Amak took out a small medicine vial with a nozzle built into the top. He tilted his head back and let the liquid contents drip directly into his eyes. "Concentrated spidersnake extract," Yun whispered to Kyoshi. "It's a secret formula and hideously expensive."

Amak caught Kyoshi staring at him and spoke to her for the first time ever.

"Other than Tagaka herself, there are to be no Waterbenders from either side at this negotiation," he said in a voice so high-pitched and musical it nearly startled her out of her boots. "So . . ."

He pressed a gloved finger to his lips and winked at her. The iris of his open eye shifted from pale blue to a halfway green the color of warmer coastal waters.

Kyoshi tried to shake the fuzz out of her head. She didn't belong here, so far from the earth, with dangerous people who wore disguises like spirits and treated life-and-death situations as games to be won. Crossing into the world of the Avatar had been exciting back when she took her first steps inside the mansion. Now the slightest wrong footing could destroy the fates of hundreds, maybe thousands. After Yun told her last night about the mass kidnappings along the coast, she hadn't been able to sleep.

More boats full of armed men landed ashore. They lined up to the left and right, spears at the ready, the tassels of their helmets waving in the frigid breeze. The intent must have been to look strong and organized in front of the pirate queen.

"She approaches," Kelsang said.

Tagaka chose a relatively undramatic entrance, appearing on the edge of the iceberg as a faraway dot flanked by two others. She plodded along a path that ran around the icy slope like a mountain pass. She seemed to be in no hurry.

"I guess everyone dying of old age would count as achieving peace," Yun muttered.

They had enough time to relax and then straighten back up once Tagaka reached them. Kyoshi stilled her face as much as possible and laid the corner of her eyes upon the Bloody Flail of the Eastern Sea.

Contrary to her reputation, the leader of the Fifth Nation was a decidedly unremarkable middle-aged woman. Underneath her plain hide clothing she had a laborer's build, and her hair loops played up her partial Water Tribe ancestry. Kyoshi looked for eyes burning with hatred or a cruel sneer that promised unbound tortures, but Tagaka could have easily passed for one of the disinterested southern traders who occasionally visited Yokoya to unload fur scraps.

Except for her sword. Kyoshi had heard rumors about the green-enameled *jian* strapped to Tagaka's waist in a scabbard plated with burial-quality jade. The sword had once belonged to the admiral of Ba Sing Se, a position that was now unfilled and defunct because of her. After her legendary duel with the last man to hold the job, she'd kept the blade. It was less certain what she'd done with the body.

Tagaka glanced at the twenty soldiers standing behind them and then spent much longer squinting at Kyoshi, up and down. Each pass of her gaze was like a spray of cold water icing over Kyoshi's bodily functions.

"I didn't realize we were supposed to be bringing so much muscle," Tagaka said to Jianzhu. She looked behind her at the pair of bodyguards carrying only bone clubs and then again at Kyoshi. "That girl is a walking crow's nest."

Kyoshi could sense Jianzhu's displeasure at the fact she'd drawn attention. She knew he and Yun had fought over her presence. She wanted to shrink into nothingness, hide from their adversary's gaze, but that would only make it worse. Instead she tried to borrow the face Rangi normally used on the villagers. Cold, inscrutable disdain.

Her attempt at looking tough was met with mixed reactions. One of Tagaka's escorts, a man with a stick-thin mustache in the Earth Kingdom style, frowned at her and shifted his feet. But the pirate queen herself remained unmoved.

"Where are my manners," she said, giving Yun a perfunctory bow. "It's my honor to greet the Avatar in the flesh."

"Tagaka, Marquess of the Eastern Sea," Yun said, using her self-styled title, "congratulations on your victory over the remnants of the Fade-Red Devils."

She raised an eyebrow. "You knew of that business?"

"Yachey Hong and his crew were a bunch of sadistic murderers," Yun said smoothly. "They had neither your wisdom nor your . . . ambition. You did the world a great service by wiping them out."

"Ha!" She clapped once. "This one studies like Yangchen and flatters like Kuruk. I look forward to our battle of wits tomorrow. Shall we head to my camp? You must be hungry and tired."

Tomorrow? Kyoshi thought. They weren't going to wrap this up quickly and leave? They were going to *sleep* here, vulnerable throughout the night?

Apparently, that had been the plan all along. "Your hospitality is much appreciated," Jianzhu said. "Come, everybody."

It was a very, very awkward dinner.

Tagaka had set up a luxurious camp, the centerpiece a yurt as big as a house. The interior was lined with hung rugs and tapestries of mismatching colors that both kept the cold out and served as markers of how many tradeships she'd plundered. Stone lamps filled with melted fat provided an abundance of light.

Low tables and seat cushions were arranged in the manner of a grand feast. Yun held the place of honor, with Tagaka across from him. She didn't mind the rest of their table being filled out by the Avatar's inner circle. Jianzhu's uniformed guardsmen rotated in and out, trading sneers with the pirate queen's motley assortment of corsairs.

The Fifth Nation described themselves as an egalitarian outfit that disregarded the boundaries between the elements. According to the propaganda they sometimes left behind after a raid, no nation was superior, and under the rule of their enlightened captain, any adventurer or bender could join them in harmony, regardless of origin.

In reality, the most successful pirate fleet in the world was going to be nearly all sailors from the Water Tribes. And the food reflected that. To Kyoshi, most of the meal tasted like blood, the mineral saltiness too much for her. She did what she could to be polite, and watched Yun eat in perfect alignment with Water Tribe custom.

As Yun downed another tray of raw blubber with gusto, Tagaka cheering him on, Kyoshi wanted to whisper in Rangi's ear and ask if they should be afraid of poison. Or the prospect of the dinner party stabbing them in the back with their meat skewers. Anything that reflected the hostilities that must have been bubbling under the surface. Why were they being so friendly?

It became too much once they began setting up Pai Sho boards for members of Tagaka's crew who fancied themselves a match for the young Avatar's famous skills. Kyoshi nudged Rangi in the side and tilted her chin at the merriment, widening her eyes for emphasis.

Rangi knew exactly what she was asking. While everyone's attention focused on Yun playing three opponents at once, she pointed with her toe at two men and two women who had silently entered the tent after the party had finished eating, to clean up the plates.

They were Earth Kingdom citizens. Instead of the pirates' mismatched riot of pilfered clothing, they wore plain peasant's garb. And though they weren't chained or restrained, they carried out their duties in a hunched and clumsy fashion. Like people fearing for their lives.

The stolen villagers. Yun and Rangi had undoubtedly spotted them earlier. Kyoshi cursed herself for treating them as invisible when she knew what it was like to move unnoticed among the people she served. The entire time, Yun had been putting on a false smile while Tagaka paraded her true spoils of war in front of him.

Rangi found her trembling hand and gave it a quick squeeze, sending a pulse of reassuring warmth over her skin. *Stay strong.*

They watched Yun demolish his opponents in three different ways, simultaneously. The first he blitzed down, the second he'd forced into a no-win situation, and the third he'd lured into a trap so diabolical that the hapless pirate thought he was winning the whole time until the last five moves.

The audience roared when Yun finished his last victim off. Coins clinked as wagers traded hands, and the challengers received slaps and jeers from their comrades.

Tagaka laughed and threw back another shot of strong wine. "Tell me, Avatar. Are you enjoying yourself?"

"I've been to many places around the world," Yun said. "And your hospitality has been unmatched."

"I'm so glad," she said, reaching for more drink. "I was convinced you were planning to kill me before the night was through."

The atmosphere of the gathering went from full speed to a dead stop. Tagaka's men seemed as surprised as Jianzhu's. The mass stillness that ran through the party nearly created its own sound. The tensing of neck muscles. Hairs raising on end.

Kyoshi tried to glance at Master Amak without making it obvious. The hardened Waterbender was sitting away from the main group, peering soberly at Tagaka over the edge of his unused wine cup. The floor was covered in skins and rugs, but underneath was a whole island of weaponry at his disposal. Instead of freezing up like everyone else, Kyoshi could see his shoulders relaxing, loosening, readying for a sudden surge of violence.

She thought Jianzhu might say something, take over for Yun now that the theatrics were off course, but he did nothing. Jianzhu calmly watched Yun stack the Pai Sho tiles between his fingers, as if the only thing he cared about was making sure his student displayed good manners by cleaning up after a finished game.

"Mistress Tagaka," Yun said. "If this is about the size of my contingent, I assure you I meant no harm or insult. The soldiers who came with me are merely an honor guard. I didn't want to bring them, but they were so excited about the chance to witness you make history with the Avatar."

"I'm not concerned about a bunch of flunkies with spears, boy," Tagaka said. Her voice had turned lower. The time for flattery was over. "I'm talking about those three."

She pointed, her fingers forming a trident. Not at Amak or any of the armored Earth Kingdom soldiers, but at Jianzhu, Hei-Ran, and Kelsang.

"I'm afraid I don't understand," Yun said. "Surely you know of my bending masters. The famed companions of Kuruk."

"Yes, I know of them. And I know what it means when the Gravedigger of Zhulu Pass darkens my tent in person."

Now Yun was confused for real. His easy smile faded, and his head tilted toward his shoulder. Kyoshi had heard of various battles and locations associated with Jianzhu's name, and Zhulu Pass was one of many, not a standout in a long list. He was a great hero of the Earth Kingdom after all, one of its leading sages.

"Are you referring to the story of how my esteemed mentor piously interred the bodies of villagers he found cut down by rebels, giving them their final rest and dignity?" Yun said. The game tiles clacked together in his palm.

Tagaka shook her head. "I'm referring to five thousand Yellow Necks, buried alive, the rest terrorized into submission. The entire uprising crushed by one man. Your 'esteemed mentor.'"

She turned to Jianzhu. "I'm curious. Do their spirits haunt you when you sleep? Or did you plant them deep enough that the earth muffles their screams?"

There was a hollow thunk as one of the game pieces slipped out of Yun's grasp and bounced off the board. He'd never heard of this. Kyoshi had never heard of this.

Now that he was being addressed directly, Jianzhu deemed it proper to speak up. "Respectfully, I fear that rumors from the Earth Kingdom interior tend to grow wilder the closer they get to the South Pole. Many tales of my past exploits are pure exaggerations by now."

"*Respectfully*, I gained my position through knowing facts beyond what you think a typical blue-eyed southern rustic should know," Tagaka snapped. "For example, I know who holds the Royal Academy record for the most 'accidental' kills during Agni Kais, Madam Headmistress."

If Hei-Ran was offended by the accusation, she didn't show it. Instead Rangi looked like she was going to leap on Tagaka and cook the woman's head off her shoulders. Kyoshi instinctively reached out to her and got her hand swatted away for the trouble.

"And Master Kelsang," Tagaka said. "Listen, young Avatar. Have you ever wondered why my fleets stay cooped up in the Eastern Sea, where the pickings are slim, engaged in costly battles for territory with other crews? It's solely because of that man right there."

Of the three masters, only Kelsang looked afraid of what Tagaka might reveal. Afraid and ashamed. Kyoshi already wanted to defend him from whatever charges the pirate might levy. Kelsang was hers more than anyone else's.

"My father used to call him the Living Typhoon," Tagaka said. "We criminal types have a fondness for theatrical nicknames, but in this case, the billing was correct. Grandad once took the family and a splinter fleet westward, around the southern tip of the Earth Kingdom. The threat they presented must have been great indeed, because Master Kelsang, then a young man in the height of his power, rode out on his bison and summoned a storm to turn them back.

"Sounds like a perfect solution to a naval threat without any bloodshed, eh?" she said. "But have any of you pulled a shivered timber the size of a *jian* from your thigh? Or been thrown into the sea and then tried to keep your head above a thirty-foot wave?"

Tagaka drank in the Airbender's discomfort and smiled. "I should thank you, Master Kelsang. I lost several uncles on that expedition. You saved me from a gruesome succession battle. But the fear of a repeat performance kept the Fifth Nation and other crews bottled up in the Eastern Sea, my father's entire generation terrified of a single Air Nomad. They thought Kelsang was watching them from the peaks of the Southern Air Temple. Patrolling the skies above their heads."

Kyoshi looked at Kelsang, who was hunched in agony. *Were you?* she thought. *Is that where you went between stays in Yokoya? You were hunting pirates?*

"A lesson from your airbending master," Tagaka said to Yun. "The most effective threat is only performed once. So you can imagine my distress when I saw you bring this . . . this collection of *butchers* to our peace treaty signing. I thought for certain it meant violence was in our future."

Yun hummed, pretending to be lost in thought. The Pai Sho

tile that he'd fumbled was now flipping over his knuckles, back and forth across his hand. He was in control again.

"Mistress Tagaka," he said. "You have nothing to fear from my masters. And if we're giving credence to gruesome reputations, I believe I would have equal cause for concern."

"Yes," Tagaka said, staring him down, her fingers lying on the hilt of her sword. "You absolutely do."

The mission hinged there, on the eye contact between Yun and the undisputed lord of the Eastern Sea. Tagaka might have been looking at the Avatar, but Kyoshi could only see her friend, young and vulnerable and literally out of his element.

Whatever Tagaka was searching for inside Yun's head, she found it. She backed off and smiled.

"You know, it's bad luck to undertake an important ceremony with blood on your spirit," she said. "I purified myself of my past crimes with sweat and ice before you arrived, but with the stain of so much death still hanging over your side, I suddenly feel the need to do it again before tomorrow morning. You may stay here as long as you'd like."

Tagaka snapped her fingers, and her men filed out of the tent, as unquestioningly as if she'd bent them away. The Earth Kingdom captives went last, ducking through the exit flaps without so much as a glance behind them. The act seemed like a planned insult by Tagaka, designed to say *they're more afraid of me than they're hopeful of you.*

Jianzhu swung his hands together. "You did well for—"

"Is it true?" Yun snapped.

Kyoshi had never heard Yun interrupt his master before, and from the twinge in his brow, neither had Jianzhu. The earth sage sighed in a manner that warned the others not to speak. This matter was between him and his disciple. "Is what true?"

"Five thousand? You buried five thousand people alive?"

"That's an overstatement made by a criminal."

"Then what's the truth?" Yun said. "It was only five hundred? One hundred? What's the number that makes it justified?"

Jianzhu laughed silently, a halting shift of his chest. "The truth? The truth is that the Yellow Necks were scum of the lowest order who thought they could plunder, murder, and destroy with impunity. They saw nothing, no future beyond the points of their swords. They believed they could hurt people with no repercussions."

He slammed his finger down onto the center of the Pai Sho board.

"I visited *consequences* upon them," Jianzhu said. "Because that's what justice is. Nothing but the proper consequences. I made it clear that whatever horrors they inflicted would come back to haunt them, no more, no less. And guess what? It *worked*. The remnants of the *daofei* that escaped me dispersed into the countryside because at last they knew there would be consequences if they continued down their outlaw path."

Jianzhu glanced at the exit, in the direction Tagaka had gone. "Perhaps the reason you've never heard about this from decent citizens of the Earth Kingdom is because they see it the same way I do. A criminal like her watches justice being done and bewails the lack of forgiveness, conveniently forgetting about what they did in the first place to deserve punishment."

Yun looked like he had trouble breathing. Kyoshi wanted to go to his side, but Jianzhu's spell had frozen the air inside the tent, immobilizing her.

"Yun," Kelsang said. "You don't understand the times back then. We did what we had to do, to save lives and maintain balance. We had to act without an Avatar."

Yun steadied himself. "How fortunate for you all," he said, his voice a hollow deadpan. "Now you can shift the burden of ending so many lives onto me. I'll try to follow the examples my teachers have set."

"Enough!" Jianzhu roared. "You've allowed yourself to be rattled by the baseless accusations of a pirate! The rest of you get out. I need to speak to the Avatar, alone."

Rangi stormed out the fastest. Hei-Ran watched her go. Maybe it was because they used the same tight-lipped expression to hide their emotions, but Kyoshi could tell she wanted to chase her daughter. Instead Hei-Ran walked stiffly out the opposite side of the tent.

When Kyoshi looked back, Kelsang had vanished. Only the trailing swish of an orange hem under a curtain betrayed which way he'd gone. She gave a quick bow to Jianzhu and Yun, avoiding eye contact, and ran after the Airbender.

She found Kelsang a dozen paces away, alone, sitting on a stool that had presumably been abandoned by one of Tagaka's guards. The legs had sunk deep into the snow under his weight. He shivered, but not from the cold.

"You know, after Kuruk died, I thought my failure to set him on the right path was my last and greatest mistake," he said quietly to the icy ground in front of his toes. "It turned out I wasn't finished disgracing myself."

Kyoshi knew, in an academic sense, that Air Nomads held all life sacred. They were utmost pacifists who considered no one their enemy, no criminal beyond forgiveness and redemption.

But surely exceptional circumstances allowed for those convictions to be put on hold. Surely Kelsang could be forgiven for saving entire towns along the coasts of the western seas.

The strain in his voice said otherwise.

"I never told you how far I fell within the Southern Air Temple as a result of that day." Kelsang tried to force a smile through his pain, but it slipped out of his control, turning into a fractured, tearful mess. "I violated my beliefs as an Airbender. I let my teachers down. I let my entire people down."

Kyoshi was suddenly furious on his behalf, though she didn't know at whom. At the whole world, perhaps, for allowing its darkness to infect such a good man and make him hate himself. She threw her arms around Kelsang and hugged him as tightly as she could.

"You've never let *me* down," she said in a gruff bark. "Do you hear me? Never."

Kelsang put up with her attempt to crush his shoulder blades through the force of sheer affection and rocked slightly in her embrace, patting at her clasped hands. Kyoshi only let go when the sound of a plate shattering pierced the stillness of the night.

Their gazes snapped toward the crash. It had come from the tent. Yun and Jianzhu were still inside.

Kelsang stood up, his own troubles forgotten. He looked worried. "Best if you head back to camp," he said to Kyoshi. The muffled sound of arguing grew louder through the felt walls.

"Are they all right?"

"I'll check. But please, go. Now." Kelsang hurried to the tent and ducked through the curtain. She could hear the commotion stop as soon as he re-entered, but the silence was more ominous than the noise.

Kyoshi paused there, wondering what to do, before deciding she'd better obey Kelsang. She didn't want to overhear Yun and Jianzhu have it out.

As she fled, the moonlight cast long, flickering shadows, making Kyoshi feel like a puppeteer on a blank white stage. Her hurried exit took her too far in the wrong direction, and she found herself among the outskirts of the pirate camp, near the ice cliff.

She slammed against the frozen wall, trying to flatten herself out of sight. Tagaka's crew was in the midst of retiring for the night, kicking snow over dying campfires and fastening their tents closed from the inside. They had guardsmen posted at regular intervals looking in different directions. Kyoshi had no idea how she'd come so close without being noticed.

She edged as quietly as she could back the way she came, around the corner, and bumped into the missing sentry. He was one of the two pirates who'd accompanied Tagaka to greet them. The man with the mustache. He peered up at her face like he was trying to get the best view of her nostrils.

"Say," he said, a rank cloud of alcohol fumes wafting out of his mouth. "Do I know you?"

She shook her head and made to keep going, but he stuck his arm out, blocking her path as he leaned against the ice.

"It's just that you look very familiar," he said with a leer.

Kyoshi shuddered. There was always a certain kind of man who thought her particular dimensions made her a public good, an oddity they were free to gawk at, prod, or worse. Often they assumed she should be grateful for the attention. That *they* were special and powerful for giving it to her.

"I used to be a landlubber," the man said, launching into a bout of drunken self-absorption. "Did business with a group called the Flying . . . Something Society. The Flying Something or others. The leader was a woman who looked a lot like you. Pretty face, just like yours. Legs . . . nearly as long. She could have been your sister. You ever been to Chameleon Bay, sweet thing? Stay under Madam Qiji's roof?"

The man pulled the cork from a gourd and took a few more swigs of wine. "I had it bad for that girl," he said, wiping his mouth on his sleeve. "She had the most fascinating serpent tattoos going around her arms, but she never let me see how far they went. What about you, honey tree? Got any ink on your body that you want to show meeeaggh!"

Kyoshi picked him up by the neck with one hand and slammed him into the cliffside.

His feet dangled off the ground. She squeezed until she saw his eyes bulge in different directions.

"You are mistaken," she said without raising her voice. "Do you hear me? You are mistaken, and you have never seen me, or anyone else who looks like me before. Tell me so."

She let him have enough air to speak. "You crazy piece of—I'll kill—aaagh!"

Kyoshi pressed him harder into the wall. The ice cracked behind his skull. "That's not what I asked you."

Her fingers stifled his cry, preventing him from alerting the others. "I made a mistake!" he gasped. "I was wrong!"

She dropped him on the ground. The back of his coat snagged

and tore on the ice. He keeled over to his side, trying to force air back into his lungs.

Kyoshi watched him writhe at her feet. After thinking it over, she yanked the gourd full of wine off his neck, snapping the string, and poured the contents out until it was empty. The liquid splashed the man's face, and he flinched.

"I'm holding on to this in case you change your mind yet again," she said, waggling the empty container. "I've heard about Tagaka's disciplinary methods, and I don't think she'd approve of drinking on guard duty."

The man groaned and covered his head with his arms.

Kyoshi collapsed facedown outside her tent. Her forehead lay on the ice. It felt good, cooling. The encounter had sapped her of energy, left her unable to take the last few steps to her bunk. So close, and yet so far.

She didn't know what had come over her. What she'd done was so stupid it boggled the mind. If word got back to Jianzhu somehow . . .

A bright light appeared over her head. She twisted her neck upward to see Rangi holding up a self-generated torch. A small flame danced above her long fingers.

Rangi looked down at her and then at the liquor gourd still in her hand. She sniffed the night air. "Kyoshi, have you been drinking?"

It seemed easier to lie. "Yes?"

With great difficulty, Rangi dragged her inside by the arms.

It was warmer in the tent, the difference between a winter's night and an afternoon in spring. Kyoshi could feel the stiffness leaving her limbs, her head losing the ponderous echo it seemed to have before.

Rangi yanked pieces of the battle outfit off her like she was stripping down a broken wagon. "You can't sleep in that getup. Especially not the armor."

She'd taken her own gear off and was only wearing a thin cotton shift that exposed her arms and legs. Her streamlined figure belied the solidness of her muscles. Kyoshi caught herself gawking, having never seen her friend out of uniform before. It was hard for her to comprehend that the spiky bits weren't a natural part of Rangi's body.

"Shouldn't you be sleeping with Yun?" Kyoshi said.

Rangi's head turned so fast she almost snapped her own neck.

"You know what I mean," Kyoshi said.

The redness faded from Rangi's ears as quickly as it came. "The Avatar and Master Jianzhu are reviewing strategy. Master Amak only ever sleeps in ten-minute intervals throughout the day, so he and the most experienced guardsmen will keep watch. The order is that everyone else should be well-rested for tomorrow."

They settled beneath their furs. Kyoshi already knew that she wouldn't be able to sleep as she'd been told. Her former life on the street in conjunction with her privileged place in the mansion these days meant that, improbably, she'd never had a roommate before. She was acutely aware of Rangi's little movements right next to her, the air rising in and out of the Firebender's chest.

"I don't think they did anything wrong," Kyoshi said as she stared at the underside of their tent.

Rangi didn't respond.

"I heard from Auntie Mui about what Xu and the Yellow Necks did to unarmed men, women, and children. If half of that is true, then Jianzhu went too easy on them. They deserved worse."

The moonlight came through the seams of the tent, making stars out of stitch holes.

She should have stopped there, but Kyoshi's certainty buoyed her along past the point where it was safe to venture. "And accidents are accidents," she said. "I'm sure your mother never meant to harm anyone."

Two strong hands grabbed the lapels of her robe. Rangi yanked her over onto her side so that they were facing each other.

"Kyoshi," she said hoarsely, her eyes flaring with pain. "One of those opponents was her cousin. A rival candidate for headmistress."

Rangi gave her a hard, jostling shake. "Not a pirate, or an outlaw," she said. "*Her cousin*. The school cleared her honor, but the rumors followed me at school for years. People whispering around corners that my mother was—was an *assassin*."

She spit the word out like it was the most vile curse imaginable. Given Rangi's profession as a bodyguard, it likely was. She buried her face into Kyoshi's chest, gripping her tightly, as if to scrub the memory away.

Kyoshi wanted to punch herself for being so careless. She cautiously draped an arm over Rangi's shoulder. The Firebender nestled under it and relaxed, though she still made a series of sharp little inhalations through her nose. Kyoshi didn't know if that was her way of crying or calming herself with a breathing exercise.

Rangi shifted, pressing closer to Kyoshi's body, rubbing the soft bouquet of her hair against Kyoshi's lips. The startling contact felt like a transgression, the mistake of a girl exhausted and drowsy. The more noble Fire Nation families, like the one Rangi descended from, would never let just anyone touch their hair like this.

The faint, flowery scent that filled Kyoshi's lungs made her head swim and her pulse quicken. Kyoshi kept still like it was her life's calling, unwilling to make any motion that might disturb her friend's fitful slumber.

Eventually Rangi fell into a deep sleep, radiating warmth like a little glowing coal in the hearth. Kyoshi realized that comforting her throughout the night was both an honor and a torture she wouldn't have traded for anything in the world.

Kyoshi closed her eyes. She did her best to ignore the pain of her arm losing circulation and her heart falling into a pile of ribbons.

They survived the night. There had been no sneak attack, no sudden chaos outside the tent, as she'd feared.

Kyoshi couldn't have slept more than an hour or two, but she'd never felt more alert and on edge in her life. When they breakfasted in their own camp at the base of the iceberg, she declined the overbrewed tea. Her teeth were already knocking together as it was.

She looked for signs of trouble between Yun and Jianzhu, Rangi and Hei-Ran, but couldn't find any. She never understood how they managed to wound each other and then forgive each other so quickly. Wrongs meant something, even if they were inflicted by your family. *Especially* if it was family.

Kelsang stayed close by her during the preparations. But his presence only created more turbulence in her heart. Any minute now they were going to walk up that hill and watch Yun sign a treaty backed by the power vested in the Avatar.

It's not me, Kyoshi thought to herself. *Kelsang admitted there was hardly a chance. A chance is not the same thing as the truth.*

Jianzhu signaled it was time to go and spoke a few words, but Kyoshi didn't hear them.

He's jumping to conclusions because Jianzhu sidelined him. He wants to be a bigger part of the Avatar's life. Any Avatar's life. And I'm the closest thing to a daughter he has.

She had to admit the line of reasoning was a little self-important of her. But much less so than, say, *being the Avatar*. It made sense. Kelsang was human, prone to mistakes. The thought comforted her all the way to the top of the iceberg.

The peak came to a natural plateau large enough to hold the key members of both delegations. For Yun's side, that meant Jianzhu, Hei-Ran, Kelsang, Rangi, Amak, and—despite the foolishness it implied—Kyoshi. Tagaka again deigned to come with only a pair of escorts. The mustached man was not part of her guard this time, thankfully. But one of the Earth Kingdom hostages, a young woman who had the sunburned mien of a fishwife, accompanied the pirates. She silently carried a baggage pack on her shoulders and stared at the ground like her past and future were written on it.

The two sides faced each other over the flat surface. They were high enough up to overlook the smaller icebergs that drifted near their frozen mountain.

"I figured we'd use the traditional setting for such matters," Tagaka said. "So please bear with me for a moment."

The pirate queen wedged her feet in the snow and took a shouting breath. Her arms moved fluidly in the form of waterbending, but nothing happened.

"Hold on," she said.

She tried again, waving her limbs with more speed and more strain. A circle rose haltingly out of the ice, the size of a table. It was very slow going.

Kyoshi thought she heard a scoff come from Master Amak, but it could have been the creak of two smaller ice lumps sprouting on opposite sides of the table. Tagaka struggled mightily until they were tall enough to sit on.

"You'll have to forgive me," she said, out of breath. "I'm not exactly the bender my father and grandfather were."

The Earth Kingdom woman opened her pack and quickly laid out a cloth over the table and cushions on the seats. With quick, delicate motions, she set up a slab inkstone, two brushes, and a tiny pitcher of water.

Kyoshi's gut roiled as she watched the woman meticulously grind an inkstick against the stone. She was using the Pianhai method, a ceremonial calligraphy setup that took a great deal of formal training and commoners normally never learned. Kyoshi only knew what it was from her proximity to Yun. *Did Tagaka beat the process into her?* she thought. *Or did she steal her away from a literature school in one of the larger cities?*

Once she had made enough ink, the woman stepped back without a word. Tagaka and Yun sat down, each spreading a scroll across the ice table that contained the written terms that had been agreed upon so far. They spent an exhaustive amount of time checking that the copies matched, that phrasing was polite enough. Both Yun and the pirate queen had an eye for small details, and neither of them wanted to lose the first battle.

"I object to your description of yourself as the Waterborne Guardian of the South Pole," Yun said during one of the more heated exchanges.

"Why?" Tagaka said. "It's true. My warships are a buffer. I'm the only force keeping a hostile navy from sailing up to the shores of the Southern Water Tribe."

"The Southern Water Tribe hates you," Yun said, rather bluntly.

"Yes, well, politics are complicated," Tagaka said. "I'll edit that to 'Self-Appointed Guardian of the South Pole.' I haven't abandoned my people, even if they've turned their backs on me."

And on it went. After Tagaka's guards had begun to yawn openly, they leaned back from the scrolls. "Everything seems to be in order," Yun said. "If you don't mind, I'd like to proceed straightaway to the next stage. Verbal amendments."

Tagaka smirked. "Ooh, the real fun stuff."

"On the matter of the hostages from the southern coast of Zeizhou Province as can be reasonably defined through proximity to Tu Zin, taken from their homes sometime between the vernal equinox and the summer solstice . . ." Yun said. He paused.

Kyoshi knew this was going to be hard on him. Rangi had explained the basics of how people were typically ransomed.

At best Yun could free half of the captives by sacrificing the rest, letting Tagaka save face and retain leverage. He had to think of their lives in clinical terms. A higher percentage was better. His only goal. He would be a savior to some and doom the rest.

"I want them back," Yun said. "All of them."

"*Avatar!*" Jianzhu snapped. The Earthbender was furious. This was obviously not what they'd talked about beforehand.

Yun raised his hand, showing the back of it to his master. Kyoshi could have sworn Yun was enjoying himself right now.

"I want every single man, woman, and child back," Yun said. "If you've sold them to other pirate crews, I want your dedicated assistance in finding them. If any have died under your care, I want their remains so their families can give them a proper burial. We can talk about the compensation you'll pay later."

The masters, save for Kelsang, looked displeased. To them, these were the actions of a petulant child who didn't understand how the world worked.

But Kyoshi had never loved her Avatar more. *This* was what Yun had wanted her to see when he'd begged her to come along. Her friend, standing up for what was right. Her heart was ready to burst.

Tagaka leaned back on her ice stool. "Sure."

Yun blinked, his moment of glory and defiance yanked out from under him prematurely. "You agree?"

"I agree," Tagaka said. "You can have all of the captives back. They're free. Every single one."

A sob rang out in the air. It was the Earth Kingdom woman. Her stoic resolve broke, and she collapsed to her hands and knees, weeping loudly and openly. Neither Tagaka nor her men reprimanded her.

Yun didn't look at the woman, out of fear he might ruin her salvation with the wrong move. He waited for Tagaka to make a demand in return. He wasn't going to raise the price on her behalf.

"The captives are useless to me anyway," she said. She stared out to sea at the smaller icebergs surrounding them. Despite her earlier patience, she sounded incredibly bored all of a sudden. "Out of a thousand people or more, not one was a passable carpenter. I should have known better. I needed to go after people who live among tall trees, not driftwood."

Yun frowned. "You want . . . carpenters?" he said cautiously.

She glanced at him, as if she were surprised he was still there. "Boy, let me teach you a little fact about the pirate trade. Our power is measured in ships. We need timber and craftsmen who know how to work it. Building a proper navy is a generational effort. My peaceable cousins in the South Pole have a few heirloom sailing cutters but otherwise have to make do with sealskin canoes. They'll never create a large, long-range war fleet because they simply don't have the trees."

Tagaka turned and loomed over the table. "So, yes," she said, fixing him with her gaze. "I want carpenters *and* trees *and* a port of my own to dock in so I can increase the size of my forces. And I know just where to get those things."

"*Yokoya!*" Yun shouted, a realization and an alert to the others, in a single word.

Tagaka raised her hand and made the slightest chopping motion with her fingers. Kyoshi heard a wet crunch and a gurgle of surprise. She looked around for the source of the strange noise.

It was Master Amak. He was bent backward over a stalagmite of ice, the bloody tip sprouting from his chest like a hideous stalk of grain. He stared at it, astonished, and slumped to the side.

"Come now," Tagaka said. "You think I can't recognize kinfolk under a disguise?"

The moments seemed to slowly stack up on each other like a tower of raw stones, each event in sequence piling higher and higher with no mortar to hold them together. A structure that was unstable, dreadful, headed toward a total and imminent collapse.

The sudden movement of Tagaka's two escorts drew everyone's attention. But the two men only grabbed the Earth Kingdom woman by the arms and jumped back down the slope the way they'd come, dodging the blast of fire that Rangi managed to get off. They were the distraction.

Pairs of hands burst from the surface of the ice, clutching at the ankles of everyone on Yun's side. Waterbenders had been lying in wait below them the whole time. Rangi, Jianzhu, and Hei-Ran were dragged under the ice like they'd fallen through the crust of a frozen lake during the spring melt.

Kyoshi's arms shot out, and she managed to arrest herself chest-high on the surface. Her would-be captor hadn't made her tunnel large enough. Kelsang leaped into the air, avoiding the clutches of his underground assailant with an Airbender's reflexes, and deployed the wings of his glider-staff.

Tagaka drew her *jian* and swung it on the downstroke at Yun's neck. But the Avatar didn't flinch. Almost too fast for Kyoshi to see, he slammed his fist into the only source of earth near them, the stone inkslab. It shattered into fragments and reformed as a glove around his hand. He caught Tagaka's blade as it made contact with his skin.

Kyoshi stamped down hard with her boot and felt a sickening crunch. Her foot stuck there as the bender whose face she'd broken refroze the water, imprisoning her lower half. Above the ice, Kyoshi had the perfect view of the Avatar and the pirate queen locked together in mortal knot.

They both looked happy that the charade was over. A trickle of Yun's blood dripped off the edge of the blade.

"Another thing you should know," Tagaka said as she traded grins with Yun, their muscles trembling with exertion. "I'm really not the Waterbender my father was."

With her free hand she made a series of motions so fluid and complex that Kyoshi thought her fingers had telescoped to twice their length. A series of earsplitting cracks echoed around them.

There was a roar of ice and snow rushing into the sea. The smaller icebergs split and calved, revealing massive hollow spaces inside. As the chunks of ice drifted apart at Tagaka's command, the prows of Fifth Nation warships began to poke out, like the beaks of monstrous birds hatching from their eggshells.

Yun lost his balance at the sight and fell to the ground onto his back. Tagaka quickly blanketed him in ice, taking care to cover his stone-gloved hand. "What is this?" he yelled up at her.

She wiped his blood off her sword with the crook of her elbow and resheathed it. "A backup plan? A head start on our way to

Yokoya? A chance to show off? I've been pretending to be a weak bender for so long, I couldn't resist being a little overdramatic."

Waterbenders aboard the ships were already stilling the waves caused by the ice avalanches and driving their vessels forward. Other crew members scrambled among the masts like insects, unfurling sails. They were pointed westward, toward home, where they would drive into fresh territories of the Earth Kingdom like a knife into an unprotected belly.

"Stop the ships!" Yun screamed into the sky. "Not me! The ships!" That was all he could get out before Tagaka covered his head completely in ice.

Kyoshi didn't know whom he was talking to at first, thought that in his desperation he was pleading with a spirit. But a low rush of air reminded her that someone was still free. Kelsang pulled up on his glider and beelined toward the flagship.

"Not today, monk," Tagaka said. She lashed out with her arms, and a spray of icicles no bigger than sewing needles shot toward Kelsang.

It was a fiendishly brilliant attack. The Airbender could have easily dodged larger missiles, but Tagaka's projectiles were an enveloping storm. The delicate wings of his glider disintegrated, and he plunged toward the sea.

There was no time to panic for Kelsang. Tagaka levitated the chunk of ice Yun was buried in, threw it over the side of the iceberg toward her camp, and leaped down after him.

Kyoshi grit her teeth and pushed on the ice as hard as she could. Her shoulders strained against her robes, both threatening to tear. The ice gripping her legs cracked and gave way, but not before shredding the parts of her skin not covered by her skirts. She lifted herself free and stumbled after Tagaka.

She was lucky Yun's prison had carved out a smooth path. Without it, she would have undoubtedly bashed her skull in, tumbling over the rough protrusions of ice. Kyoshi managed to slide down to the pirate camp, her wounds leaving a bloody trail on the slope behind her.

Tagaka's men were busy loading their camp and themselves into longboats. An elegant cutter, one of the Water Tribe heirlooms she'd mentioned, waited for them off the coast of the iceberg. Only a few of the other pirates noticed Kyoshi. They started to pick up weapons, but Tagaka waved them off. Packing up was more of a priority than dealing with her.

"Give him back," Kyoshi gasped.

Tagaka put a boot on the ice encasing Yun and leaned on her knee. "The colossus speaks," she said, smiling.

"Give him back. *Now*." She meant to sound angry and desperate, but instead she came across as pitiful and hopeless as she felt inside. She wasn't sure if Yun could breathe in there.

"Eh," Tagaka said. "I saw what I needed to see in the boy's eyes. He's worth more as a hostage than an Avatar, trust me." She shoved Yun off to the side with her foot, and the bile surged in Kyoshi's throat at the disrespectful gesture.

"But you, on the other hand," Tagaka said. "You're a puzzle. I know you're not a fighter right now, that much is obvious. But I like your potential. I can't decide whether I should kill you now, to be safe, or take you with me."

She took a step closer. "Kyoshi, was it? How would you like a taste of true freedom? To go where you want and take what you're owed? Trust me, it's a better life than whatever dirt-scratch existence you have on land."

Kyoshi knew her answer. It was the same one she would have given as a starving seven-year-old child.

"I would never become a *daofei*," Kyoshi said, trying as hard as possible to turn the word into a curse. "Pretending to be a leader and an important person when you're nothing but a murderous slaver. You're the lowest form of life I know."

Tagaka frowned and drew her sword. The metal hissed against the scabbard. She wanted Kyoshi to feel cold death sliding between her ribs, instead of being snuffed out quickly by water.

Kyoshi stood her ground. "Give me the Avatar," she repeated. "Or I will put you down like the beast you are."

Tagaka spread her arms wide, telling her to look around them at the field of ice they were standing on. "With what, little girl from the Earth Kingdom?" she asked. "With what?"

It was a good question. One that Kyoshi knew she couldn't have answered herself. But she was suddenly gripped with the overwhelming sensation that right now, in her time of desperate need, her voice wouldn't be alone.

Her hands felt guided. She didn't fully understand, nor was she completely in control. But she trusted.

Kyoshi braced her stomach, filled her lungs, and slammed her feet into the Crowding Bridge stance. Echoes of power rippled from her movement, hundredfold iterations of herself stamping on the ice. She was somehow both leading and being led by an army of benders.

A column of gray-stone seafloor exploded up from the surface of the ocean. It caught the hull of Tagaka's cutter and listed the ship to the side, tearing wooden planks off the frame as easily as paper off a kite.

A wave of displaced water swept over the iceberg, knocking pirates off their feet and smashing crates to splinters. Out of self-preservation, Tagaka reflexively raised a waist-high wall of ice, damming and diverting the surge. But the barrier protected Kyoshi as well, giving her time to attack again. She leaped straight into the air and landed with her fists on the ice.

Farther out, the sea boiled. Screams came from the lead warships as more crags of basalt rose in their path. The bowsprits of the vessels that couldn't turn in time snapped like twigs. The groan of timber shattering against rock filled the air, as hideous as a chorus of wounded animals.

Kyoshi dropped to her knees, panting and heaving. She'd meant to keep going, to bring the earth close enough to defend herself, but the effort had immediately sapped her to the point where she could barely raise her head.

Tagaka turned around. Her face, so controlled over the past two days, spasmed in every direction.

"What in the name of the spirits?" she whispered as she flipped her *jian* over for a downward stab. The speed at which Tagaka moved to kill her made it clear that she'd be fine living without an answer.

"Kyoshi! Stay low!"

Kyoshi instinctively obeyed Rangi's voice and flattened herself out. She heard and felt the scorch of a fire blast travel over her, knocking Tagaka away.

With a mighty roar, Pengpeng strafed the iceberg, Rangi and Hei-Ran blasting flame from the bison's left and right, scattering the pirates as they attempted to regroup. Jianzhu handled

Pengpeng's reins with the skill of an Air Nomad, spinning her around for perfectly aimed tail shots of wind that drove away clouds of arrows and thrown spears. Kyoshi had no idea how they'd escaped the ice, but if any three people had the power and resourcefulness to pull it off, it was them.

The fight wasn't over. Some of Tagaka's fleet had made it past Kyoshi's obstacles. And from the nearby sinking ships, a few Waterbenders declined to panic like their fellows. They dove into the water instead, generating high-speed waves that carried them toward Tagaka. Her elite guard, coming to rescue her.

Rangi and Hei-Ran jumped down and barraged the pirate queen with flame that she was forced to block with sheets of water. Rangi's face was covered in blood and her mother had only one good arm, but they fought in perfect coordination, leaving Tagaka no gaps to mount an offense.

"We'll handle the Waterbenders!" Hei-Ran shouted over her shoulder. "Stop the ships!"

Jianzhu took a look at the stone monoliths that Kyoshi had raised from the seafloor, and then at her. In the heat of battle, he chose to pause. He stared hard at Kyoshi, almost as if he were doing sums in his head.

"Jianzhu!" Hei-Ran screamed.

He snapped out of his haze and took Pengpeng back up. They flew toward the nearest formation of stone. Without warning, Jianzhu let go of the reins and jumped off the bison in midair.

Kyoshi thought he'd gone mad. He proved her wrong.

She'd never seen Jianzhu earthbend before, had only heard Yun and the staff describe his personal style as "different." Unusual. *More like a lion dance at the New Year,* Auntie Mui once said, fanning herself, with a dreamy smile on her face. *Stable below and wild on top.*

He hadn't been able to earthbend on the iceberg, but now Kyoshi had provided him with all of his element that he needed. As Jianzhu fell, flat panes of stone peeled off the crag and flew up to meet him. They arranged themselves into a manic, architectural construction with broad daylight showing through the triangular gaps, a steep ramp that he landed on without losing his momentum.

He sprinted toward the escaping ships, in a direction he had no room to go. But as he ran, his arms coiled and whipped around him like they had minds of their own. He flicked his fists using minute twists of his waist, and countless sheets of rock fastened themselves into a bridge under his feet. Jianzhu never broke stride as he traveled on thin air, suspended by his on-the-fly earthworks.

Fire blasts and waterspouts shot up from the benders manning the ships. Jianzhu nimbly leaped and slid over them. The ones aimed at the stone itself did surprisingly little damage, as the structure was composed of chaotic, redundant braces.

He raced ahead of the lead ship, crossing its path with his bridge. Right as Kyoshi thought he'd extended too far, that he'd run out of stone and thinned his support beyond what it could hold, he leaped to safety, landing on top of a nearby ice floe.

The precarious, unnatural assembly began to crumble without Jianzhu's bending to keep it up. First the individual pieces began to flake off. Chunks of falling rock bombarded the lead ship from high above, sending the crew members diving for cover as the wooden deck punctured like leather before an awl.

But their suffering had only begun. The base of the bridge simply let itself go, bringing the entire line of stone down across the prow. The ship's aft was levered out of the waterline, exposing the rudder and barnacled keel.

The rest of the squadron didn't have time to turn. One follower angled away from the disaster. It managed to avoid crashing its hull, but the change of direction caused the vessel to tilt sharply to the side. The tip of its rigging caught on the wreckage, and then the ship was beheaded of its masts and sails, the wooden pillars snapped off, a child's toy breaking at its weakest points.

The last remaining warship bringing up the rear might have made it out, assuming some dazzling feat of heroic seamanship. Instead it wisely decided to drop anchor and call it quits. If Tagaka's power was in her fleet, then the Avatar's companions had destroyed it. Now they just had to live long enough to claim their victory.

"You did good, kid," said a man with a husky voice and an accent like Master Amak's. "They'll be telling stories about this for a long time."

Kyoshi spun around, afraid a pirate had gotten the drop on her, but there was no one there. The motion made her dizzy. Too dizzy. She sank to her knees, a drawn-out, lengthy process, and slumped onto the ice.

THE FRACTURE

IT WAS warm. So warm that when Kyoshi woke up in the mansion's infirmary, she thought it would be Rangi sitting in the chair by the bed. She hoped it was.

Instead it was Jianzhu.

Kyoshi clutched her blankets tighter and then realized she was being silly. Jianzhu was her boss and her benefactor. He'd given Kelsang the money to take care of her. And while she'd never crossed the courteous distance that lay between them, there was no reason to feel uncomfortable around the earth sage.

That was what she told herself.

Her throat burned with thirst. Jianzhu had a gourd of water at the ready, anticipating her need, and handed it over. She tried to gulp it as decorously as she could but spilled some on her sheets, causing him to chuckle.

"I always had the hunch you were hiding something from me," he said.

She nearly choked.

"I remember the day you and Kelsang told me about your problem with earthbending," Jianzhu said with a smile that stayed firmly on the lower half of his face. "You said that you couldn't manipulate small things. That you could only move good-sized boulders of a regular shape. Like a person whose fingers were too thick and clumsy to pick up a grain of sand."

That was true. Most schools of earthbending didn't know how to deal with a weakness like Kyoshi's. Students started out bending the smallest pebbles, and as their strength and technique grew, they moved to bigger and heavier chunks of earth.

Despite Kelsang's protests, Kyoshi had long since decided that she wouldn't bother formally training in bending. It hadn't seemed like a problem worth solving at the time. Earthbending was mostly useless indoors, especially so without precision.

"You didn't tell me the reverse applied," Jianzhu said. "That you could move mountains. And you were separated from the ocean bed by two hundred paces. Not even I can summon earth from across that distance. Or across water."

The empty gourd trembled as she put it on the bedside table. "I swear I didn't know," Kyoshi said. "I didn't think I could do what I did, but Yun was in danger and I stopped thinking and I—where is Yun? Is he okay? Where's Kelsang?"

"You don't need to worry about them." He slumped forward in his chair with his elbows on his knees, his fingers knotted together. His clothes draped from his joints in a way that made him look thin and weary. He stared at the floor in silence for an uncomfortably long time.

"The Earth Kingdom," Jianzhu said. "It's kind of a mess, don't you think?"

Kyoshi was more surprised by his tone than his random change of subject. He'd never relaxed this much around her before. She didn't imagine he spoke this informally with Yun.

"I mean, look at us," he said. "We have more than one king. Northern and southern dialects are so different they're starting to become separate languages. Villagers in Yokoya wear as much blue as green, and the Si Wong people barely share any customs with the rest of the continent."

Kyoshi had heard Kelsang express admiration for the diversity of the Earth Kingdom on several occasions. But perhaps he was speaking from the perspective of a visitor. Jianzhu made the Earth Kingdom sound like different pieces of flesh stitched together to close a wound.

"Did you know that the word for *daofei* doesn't really exist in the other nations?" he said. "Across the seas, they're just called criminals. They have petty goals, never reaching far beyond personal enrichment.

"But here in the Earth Kingdom, *daofei* find a level of success that goes to their heads and makes them believe they're a society apart, entitled to their own codes and traditions. They can gain control over territory and get a taste of what it's like to rule. Some of them turn into spiritual fanatics, believing that their looting and pillaging is in service of a higher cause."

Jianzhu sighed. "It's all because Ba Sing Se is not a truly effective authority," he said. "The Earth King's power waxes and wanes. It never reaches completely across the land as it should. Do you know what's holding the Earth Kingdom together right now, in its stead?"

She knew the answer but shook her head anyway.

"Me." He didn't sound proud to say it. "I am what's keeping this giant, ramshackle nation of ours from crumbling into dust. Because we've been without an Avatar for so long, the duty has fallen on me. And because I have no claim on leadership from noble blood, I have to do it solely by creating ties of personal loyalty."

He glanced up at her with sadness in his eyes. "Every local governor and magistrate from here to the Northern Air Temple owes me. I give them grain in times of famine; I help them gather the taxes that pay the police salaries. I help them deal with rebels.

"My reach has to extend beyond the Earth Kingdom as well," Jianzhu said. "I know every bender who might accurately call themselves a teacher of the elements in each of the Four Nations, and who their most promising pupils are. I've funded bending schools, organized tournaments, and settled disputes between styles before they ended in blood. Any master in the world would answer my summons."

She didn't doubt it. He wasn't a man given to boasting. More than once around the house she'd heard the expression that Jianzhu's word, his friendship, was worth more than Beifong gold.

Another person might have swelled with happiness while looking back over the power they wielded. Jianzhu simply sounded tired. "You wouldn't know any of this," he said. "Other than the disaster on the iceberg, you've never really been outside the shelter of Yokoya."

Kyoshi swallowed the urge to tell him that wasn't true, that she still remembered the brief glimpses she'd seen of the greater world, long ago. But that would have meant talking about her parents. Opening a different box of vipers altogether. Just the notion of exposing that part of her to Jianzhu caused her pulse to quicken.

He picked up on her distress and narrowed his eyes. "So you see, Kyoshi," he said. "Without personal loyalty, it all falls apart!"

He made a sudden bending motion toward the ceiling as if to bring it crashing down onto their heads. Kyoshi flinched before remembering the room was made of wood. A trickle of dust leaked through the roof beams and lay suspended in the air, a cloud above them.

"Given what I've told you," he said. "Is there anything you want to tell me? About what you did on the ice?"

Was there anything she wanted to tell the man who had taken her in off the street? That there was a chance he'd made a blunder that could destroy everything he'd worked for, and that her very existence might spell untold chaos for their nation?

No. She and Kelsang had to wait it out. Find evidence that she wasn't the Avatar, give Yun the time he needed to prove himself conclusively.

"I'm sorry," she said. "I truly wasn't aware of my own limits. I just panicked and lashed out as hard as I could. Rangi told me she often firebends stronger when she's angry; maybe it was like that."

Jianzhu smiled again, the expression calcifying on his face. He clapped his hands to his knees and pushed himself up to standing.

"You know," he said. "I've fought *daofei* like Tagaka across the length and breadth of this continent for so long that the one thing I've learned is that they're not the true problem. They're a symptom of what happens when people think they can defy the Avatar's authority. When they think the Avatar lacks legitimacy."

He peered down at Kyoshi. "I'm glad there's at least one more powerful Earthbender who can fight on my side. Despite what I said earlier, I'm only a stopgap measure. A substitute. The responsibility of keeping the Earth Kingdom stable and in balance with the other nations rightfully belongs to the Avatar."

The unrelenting pressure of his statements became so great that Kyoshi instinctively tried to shift the weight onto someone else. "It should have been Kuruk dealing with the *daofei*," she blurted out. "Shouldn't it?"

Jianzhu nodded in agreement. "If Kuruk were alive today, he'd be at the peak of his powers. I blame myself for his demise. His poor choices were my fault."

"How could that be?"

"Because the person who has the greatest responsibility to the world, after the Avatar, is the person who influences the way the Avatar thinks. I taught Kuruk earthbending, but I didn't teach him wisdom. I believe the world is still paying for my mistake in that regard."

Jianzhu paused by the door as he left. "Yun is down the hall. Kelsang across from him. You should rest more though. I would hate to see you not well."

Kyoshi waited until he was gone, enough time for him to exit the infirmary completely. Then she burst out of bed. She pounded down the hallway, rattling the planked floor, and after a frantic moment of hesitation, entered the Avatar's room first.

Yun sat in a chair next to a copper bathtub with his right sleeve rolled up to his shoulder. His arm rested in the steaming water. Rangi stood behind him, leaning on the windowsill, staring at the far corner.

"I keep telling the healers I don't have frostbite," Yun said. "This must have scared them." He raised his dripping hand. It was still stained with black ink, giving it a pallid, necrotic look. Yun picked up a teapot of hot water from the floor and poured it carefully into the bath to maintain the temperature. He dunked his hand back under the surface and swirled it around.

Kyoshi's first instinct was to run over to them and embrace them joyfully, to thank the spirits that they were alive. To see a bit of that happiness reflected back in their eyes. The three of them had made it home, safe, together.

But Yun and Rangi looked like their minds were still floating somewhere in the Southern Ocean. Vacant and distracted.

"What happened?" Kyoshi asked. "Is everyone okay? Is Kelsang hurt badly?"

Yun waved at her with his dry hand to be quiet. "Master Kelsang is sleeping, so we should keep it down."

As if she were the biggest detriment to Kelsang's health right now. "Fine," she hissed. "Now will you tell me what happened?"

"We lost a lot of the guardsmen," Yun said, his face shifting with pain. "Tagaka's hidden Waterbenders dropped an avalanche on them. Rangi and Hei-Ran managed to save those they could by burning through the side of the iceberg after it thinned."

Rangi didn't budge at the mention of her name. She refused to lift her head, let alone speak.

"They freed me, and between us, we managed to knock Tagaka out," Yun went on. "Losing their ships and seeing their leader defeated was too much for the rest of the Fifth Nation forces, and they fled. You should have seen it. Pirates clinging to wreckage while Waterbenders propelled them away. The loss of dignity probably hurt more than the falling rocks."

"What happened to Tagaka?" Kyoshi asked.

"She's in the brig of an Earth Kingdom caravan heading for the capital, where she'll be taken to the prisons at Lake Laogai," he said. "I don't know what they're going to do about the lake part of it if she can waterbend like that, but I have to assume at least someone in the Earth King's administration has a plan. In the meantime, the Fifth Nation is no more."

At her look of confusion, Yun gave her the exact same wan, forced smile that his master did a few minutes ago. "Their ships have been damaged beyond repair," he explained. "Tagaka said it herself—her power lies in her fleet. After what you did, it'll be nearly impossible for her successors to rebuild. They won't pose a threat to the Earth Kingdom anymore."

Kyoshi supposed that was true. And that she should be happy to hear it. But the victory rang hollow. "What about the captives?"

"Jianzhu caught one of her lieutenants and interrogated their location out of him," Yun said. "Hei-Ran pulled a few strings—well, maybe more like the whole rope—and now the Fire Navy is mounting a rescue operation in an act of goodwill.

It'll be the first time they've been allowed to fly military colors in the Eastern Sea since the reign of the twenty-second Earth King."

He was giving her answers but nothing else. No emotion she could hook her fingers around. Hadn't he wanted her there as a confidant? Someone who would be awed by his successes?

"Yun, you did it," she said, hoping to remind him. "You saved them."

In her desperation she borrowed a line from the imaginary voice that had spoken to her on the ice. "People will talk about this for ages to come!" she said. "Avatar Yun, who saved whole villages! Avatar Yun, who went toe to toe with the Pirate Queen of the Southern Ocean! Avatar Yun—"

"Kyoshi, stop it!" Rangi cried out. "Just stop!"

"Stop *what*?" Kyoshi yelled, feeling nearly sick with frustration.

"Stop pretending like everything's the same as it was!" Rangi said. "We know what you and Kelsang were hiding from us!"

The floor spiraled away from Kyoshi's feet. Her foundations turned to liquid. She was grateful when Rangi marched up to her and planted an accusing finger in her chest. It gave her a point to stabilize on.

"How could you keep that from us?" the Firebender shouted in her face. "Was it funny to you? Making us look like fools? Knowing there's a chance that all of our lives are a gigantic lie?"

Kyoshi couldn't think. She was enfeebled. "I didn't . . . It wasn't . . ."

Rangi's finger began to heat up and smoke. "What was your angle, huh? Were you trying to discredit Yun? Jianzhu, maybe? Do you have some kind of twisted secret desire to see the world fall apart at the seams?"

The burn reached her skin. She didn't pull away. Maybe she deserved to be punched straight through, a red-hot hole in her chest.

"Answer me!" Rangi screamed. "Answer me, you—you—"

Kyoshi closed her eyes, squeezing out tears, and readied herself for the blow.

It never came. Rangi stepped back, aghast, hands covering her mouth, realizing what she was doing, and then barreled past Kyoshi out the door.

The room swayed back and forth, threatening to force Kyoshi down on all fours. Yun stood up, navigating the thrashing floor with ease. He came closer, his lips parting slightly. She thought he was going to whisper something reassuring in her ear.

And then he sidestepped her. Slid right by, with a layer of empty space between them as impenetrable as steel.

She had one more stop to make.

Kelsang was waiting for her, propped up to a sitting position in his bed. There was a half-eaten bowl of seaweed soup on his bedside table, a remedy for blood loss. His skin was paler than the bandages swaddling his torso. Even the blue of his arrows seemed faded.

"We woke you up." Kyoshi was surprised at how hard her voice was. She should have been relieved to pieces that he wasn't dead, and instead she was on the verge of snarling at him. "You need to be resting."

"I'm sorry," he said. "I had to tell them."

"Did you?"

"What I said about Yun having the greater chance of being the Avatar isn't true anymore. Not after what you accomplished on the iceberg." Kelsang ran his hand over his shaved head, feeling for the ghost of his hair. "You were asleep for *three days,* Kyoshi. I thought your spirit had left your body. There was no more pretending."

Something delicate inside her snapped at hearing "pretend." The people closest to her were suddenly calling the years they'd spent together fake, imaginary. A made-up prelude to a different, more important reality.

"You mean *you* couldn't wait any longer to make your move," she said, unable to control her bile. "You wanted to teach an Avatar who depended on you more than Jianzhu, and you lost your chance with Yun. That's what I am to you. A do-over."

Kelsang looked away. He leaned back against his pillow.

"The time when any of us could have what we wanted passed years ago," he said.

DESPERATE MEASURES

IF SHE needed evidence things were different now, the food was enough.

On days when Kyoshi had time to eat breakfast, she usually helped herself to a bowl of *jook* from the communal pot bubbling away in the kitchen, garnished with whatever dried-out scraps from the upstairs tables Auntie Mui deemed fit to save from the previous night. Today, another servant surprised her outside her door and led her to one of the dining halls reserved for guests.

The room she sat in by herself was so big and empty that drinking her tea made an echo. The grand zitan table held such an array of boiled, salted, and fried delicacies that she thought the place setting for one had to be a mistake.

It was not. Without knowing which of the children under his roof was the Avatar, Jianzhu seemed to have decreed that Kyoshi was to be fed like a noble until he figured it out. She tried to accommodate his generosity, but a small bite of each artfully arranged dish was all she could manage with her rice. Including, she noted with chagrin, the spicy pickled kelp she'd carried to the house herself, now nestled in a lacquered saucer.

Her waiter checked back in. "Is Mistress finished?" she asked with a bowed head.

"Rin, I went to your birthday party," Kyoshi said. "I chipped in for that comb you're wearing."

The girl shrugged. "You're not to show up for work anymore. Master Jianzhu wants you by the training grounds in an hour."

"But what am I supposed to do until then?"

"Whatever Mistress wishes."

Kyoshi staggered out of the dining room like she'd taken a blow to the head. *Leisure?* What kind of animal was that?

She didn't want anyone to see her up and about the house. *Oh, there's Kyoshi, taking in the flowers. There she goes now, pondering the new calligraphy from the Air Temple.* The prospect of being on display horrified her. In lieu of a better option, she ran to the small library where she'd spoken to Kelsang and latched the door behind her. She hid there, alone with her dread, until the appointed time came.

Kyoshi was as unfamiliar with the flat stone expanse of the training ground as she would have been with the caldera of a Fire Nation volcano. Her duties never brought her here. Jianzhu waited in the middle of the courtyard for her, a scarecrow monitoring a field.

"Don't bother with that anymore," he said when she bowed deeply like a servant. "Come with me."

He led her into one of the side rooms, a supply closet that had been hastily emptied of its contents. Straw dummies and earth-bending discs had been tossed without care outside, irking her sense of organization. Inside, Hei-Ran waited for them.

"Kyoshi," she said with a warm smile. "Thank you for humoring us. I know it's been a trying past couple of days for you."

Kyoshi felt like there would be no end to the awkwardness. Despite her friendship with Rangi, she and the headmistress were more distant than she and Jianzhu. Hei-Ran was acting much friendlier than she'd expected. But Kyoshi looked down and noticed that the woman had been pacing trails in the dusty floor. Rangi often did that when she was upset.

"I'll help in any way I can," Kyoshi said, her throat feeling suddenly parched. Her tonsils stuck to the back of her tongue, causing her words to catch in her mouth.

"Sorry, that's my doing," Hei-Ran said with a gentle laugh. "I dried the air out in this room for an exercise. Please, sit."

There were two silk cushions borrowed from the meditation chamber on the floor. Kyoshi was horrified at the finery thrown on the dirty ground, but she took a position across from Hei-Ran anyway. She was keenly aware of Jianzhu standing behind her, watching like a bird of prey.

"We perform this test on newborns in the Fire Nation to see if they're capable of firebending," Hei-Ran said. "We have to know about our children quick, as you can imagine, or else they risk burning the neighborhood down."

It was a joke, but it made Kyoshi more nervous. "What do I have to do?"

"Very little." Hei-Ran reached into a pouch and pulled out

what appeared to be a ball of tinder. "This is shredded birch bark and cotton mixed with some special oils." She fluffed the material with her fingers until it was wispy and cloudlike. "You just need to breathe and feel your inner heat. If the tinder lights, you're a Firebender."

And therefore the Avatar. "You're certain this will work?"

Hei-Ran raised an eyebrow. "Newborns, Kyoshi. It's essentially impossible for a true Firebender not to make some indication with this method. Now hush. I need to get a little closer to you."

She held the tinder puff under Kyoshi's nose as if she was trying to revive her with smelling salts. "Relax and breathe, Kyoshi. Don't put effort into it. Your natural fire, your source of life, is enough. Breathe."

Kyoshi tried to do as she was told. She could feel strands of cotton tickling her lips. She took in deep lungfuls of air, over and over.

"I'll help you along," Hei-Ran said after two minutes without results. The air around them grew hotter, much hotter. Trickles of sweat ran down Kyoshi's face, drying out before they reached her chin. She was desperately thirsty again.

"Just a tiny spark." Hei-Ran sounded like she was pleading now. "I've done most of the work. Let loose. The slightest push. That's all I'm asking for. Your thumb on the scale."

Kyoshi tried for ten more minutes straight before she collapsed forward, coughing and hacking. Hei-Ran crumpled the tinder in her fist. A puff of smoke drifted from between her fingers.

"It takes children, babies, a few seconds at most under these conditions," she said to Jianzhu. Her voice was unreadable.

Kyoshi looked up at the two masters. "I don't understand," she said. "Didn't Yun already pass this test?"

Jianzhu didn't answer. He turned around and stormed out of the room, slamming his fist into the frame as he left. The earth-bending discs stacked by the door exploded into dust.

Someone had seen Kyoshi coming and going from her new hiding place in the secondary library and ratted her out. There was no other way Yun would have found her, curled up beside a medicine chest that had over a hundred little drawers, each carved with the name of a different herb or tincture.

Yun sat down on the floor across from her, leaning his back against the wall. He scanned over the labels next to her head. "It feels like way too many of these are cures for baldness," he said.

Despite herself, Kyoshi snorted.

Yun tugged on a strand of his own brown hair, perhaps thinking ahead to the day he'd have to join the Air Nomads for airbending training at the Northern or Southern Temple. They wouldn't force him to shave it off, but Kyoshi knew he liked to honor other people's traditions. And he'd still be good-looking anyway.

But then, maybe he would never get the chance, Kyoshi thought miserably. Maybe it would be stolen from him by a petty thief who'd burrowed into his house under the guise of being his friend.

He seemed to pick up on her swell of self-hatred. "Kyoshi, I'm sorry," he said. "I know you never meant for this to happen."

"Rangi doesn't." Saying it out loud made her feel ungrateful for his forgiveness. She could count on Yun's easygoing nature and inability to hold a grudge. But if Rangi truly believed Kyoshi had wronged them, then there was no hope.

It was clear. Kyoshi needed both of them in order to feel whole. She wanted her paired set of friends put back into its original place, before the earthquake had knocked everything off the shelf. This state of not-knowing they were trapped in was a plane of spiritual punishment, separating them from their old lives like a sheet of ice over a lake.

"Rangi'll come around," Yun said. "She's a person of faith, you know? A true believer. It's hard for someone like her to deal with uncertainty. You have to be a little patient with her." He caught himself and twisted his lips.

"What is it?" Kyoshi said.

"Nothing, I was just acting like Sifu for a second there." The smile faded from his face. Yun plunked the back of his head against the wall at the thought of Jianzhu. "It's him I'm really worried about."

That seemed backward. The student anxious about the well-being of the teacher.

"I didn't realize it when I first met Sifu, but determining who should train the Avatar and how is a cutthroat business," Yun said. "You'd think the masters of the world are these benevolent, selfless old men and women. But it turns out that some of them simply want to use the Avatar's power and reputation to profit themselves."

Jianzhu had told her something similar in the infirmary, that whoever taught the Avatar held immense influence over the world. Kyoshi regretted what she'd said to Kelsang the day before. He might have had reasons for wanting her to be the Avatar, but material gain was certainly not one of them.

"It's especially bad in the Earth Kingdom," Yun went on. "We call the prominent elders 'sages,' but they're not true spiritual leaders like in the Fire Nation. They're more like powerful officials, with all the politicking they do."

He held up his hands, comparing his clean one to the one stained with ink during the battle with Tagaka. The color still hadn't faded from his skin.

"But that's partly why Sifu and I have been working so hard," he said. "The more good we do for the Four Nations, the less chance that another sage tries to take me away from him. I don't think I could handle having a different master. They would never be as wise or as dedicated as Sifu."

Kyoshi looked at his darkened hand and wondered if she couldn't hold him down and scrub the ink off his skin. "What would happen to the work you've done if—if—" She couldn't finish the thought out loud. *If it wasn't you? If it was me?*

Yun took a deep, agonized breath. "I think nearly every treaty and peace agreement Sifu and I brokered would become null and void. I've made so many unwritten judgments too. If people found out that it wasn't the Avatar who'd presided over their dispute, and only some street urchin from Makapu, they would never abide by the outcome."

Superb, Kyoshi thought. She could be responsible for the breakdown of law and order around the world *and* the separation of Yun from his teacher.

That was the worst prospect of all. For as long as she'd known him, Yun had staunchly refused to talk about his blood relations. But the reverent way he looked at Jianzhu, despite any arguments or bouts of harsh discipline, made it very clear: He had no one else. Jianzhu was both his mentor and his family.

Kyoshi knew what it was like to founder alone in the dark, grasping for edges that were too far away, without a mother or father to extend a hand and pull you to safety. The pain of having no value to anyone, nothing to trade for food or warmth or a loving embrace. Maybe that was why she and Yun got along so well.

Where they differed, though, was how long they wallowed in sadness. Yun sniffed the air and his gaze wandered until it landed on a porcelain bowl resting on top of the chest. It was filled with dried flower petals and cedar shavings.

"Are those . . . *fire lilies*?" he said, a wide, knowing grin spreading across his face.

Kyoshi flushed beet red. "Stop it," she said.

"That's right," Yun said. "The Ember Island tourism minister brought a bunch when he visited two weeks ago. I can't believe you simply shred the flowers once they dry out. I guess nothing goes to waste in this house."

"Knock it off," Kyoshi snapped. But it was too hard keeping the corners of her lips from curling upward.

"Knock what off?" he said, enjoying her reaction. "I'm just commenting on a fragrance I've come to particularly enjoy."

It was an inside reference that only the two of them shared. Rangi didn't know. She hadn't been there in the gifting room eight months ago while Kyoshi arranged a vast quantity of fire lilies sent by an admiral in the Fire Navy, one of Hei-Ran's friends.

Yun had spent the afternoon watching Kyoshi work. Against every scrap of her better judgment, she'd allowed him to lie down on the floor and rest his head in her lap while she plucked deformed leaves and trimmed stems to the right length. Had anyone caught the two of them like that, there would have been a scandal that not even the Avatar could have recovered from.

That day, entranced by Yun's upside-down features dappled with the flower petals she'd teasingly sprinkled over his face, she'd almost leaned down and kissed him. And he knew it. Because he'd almost reached up and kissed her.

They never spoke of it afterward, the shared impulse that had nearly crashed both of their carriages. It was too . . . well, *they each had their duties* was a good way to put it. That moment did not fit anywhere among their responsibilities.

But since then, whenever the two of them were in the presence of fire lilies, Yun's eyes would dart toward the flowers repeatedly until he was sure Kyoshi noticed. She would try unsuccessfully to keep a straight face, the heat coloring her neck, and he'd sigh as if to mourn what could have been.

Today was no different. With a wistful blush on his own cheeks, Yun stared her down until her defenses broke and she let out a giggle through her nose.

"There's that beautiful smile," he said. He pressed his heels into the floor, sliding up against the wall, and straightened his rumpled shirt. "Kyoshi, trust me when I say this: If it turns out not to be me, I'll be glad it's you."

He might have been the one person in the world who thought so. Kyoshi had to marvel at his forbearance. Her fears were unfounded—Yun could still look at her and see a friend instead of a usurper. She should have believed in him more.

"We're late," Yun said. "I was supposed to find you and bring you to Sifu. He said he has something fun planned for us this afternoon."

"I can't," she said, out of ingrained habit. "I have work—"

He raised his brows at her. "No offense, Kyoshi, but I think you've pretty much been fired. Now get up off that maybe-Avatar rear of yours. We're going on a trip."

THE SPIRIT

"MASTER KELSANG needs more time to heal," Jianzhu said over his shoulder. "In the meanwhile, we can perform a spiritual exercise that might shed light on our situation. Think of it as a little 'Earthbenders-only' outing." He adjusted Pengpeng's course, the breeze blowing her tufts of fur in a new direction.

The group was the unusual combination of Jianzhu, Yun, and Kyoshi. They'd borrowed Kelsang's bison, leaving Rangi and Hei-Ran behind. There should have been nothing wrong with the concept of three Earth Kingdom natives bonding over their shared nationality, but Kyoshi found it unnerving. Without Rangi or her mother present, it felt like they were sneaking away to do something illicit.

She glanced at the terrain below. By her best reckoning, they were somewhere near the Xishaan Mountains that ran along the southeastern edge of the continent, the same ones that the Earth

King incorrectly considered a sufficient barrier to waterborne threats like the pirates of the Eastern Sea.

Kyoshi still wasn't fully comfortable addressing Jianzhu in a casual manner, so it fell on Yun to ask what the point of this trip was. "Sifu," he said cautiously, an idea forming in his head. "Is the reason we're going to a remote area because we're trying to invoke the Avatar State?"

His master scoffed. "Don't be ridiculous."

"What's the Avatar State?" Kyoshi whispered to Yun.

Jianzhu's sharp ears intercepted her question. "It's a tool," he said. "And a defense mechanism. A higher state of being designed to empower the current Avatar with the skills and knowledge of all the past ones. It allows for the summoning of vast cosmic energies and nearly impossible feats of bending."

That sounded definitive enough. Why wouldn't they try it, after the failures they'd suffered?

"But if the Avatar can't maintain conscious control over so much power, then their bending can go berserk, causing elemental destruction on a grand scale," Jianzhu continued. "They'd turn into a human natural disaster. The first time Kuruk practiced entering the Avatar State, we went to a small, uninhabited atoll so we wouldn't hurt anyone."

"What happened?" Yun said.

"Well, after his eyes stopped glowing and he came down from floating twenty feet in the air inside a sphere of water, the island wasn't there anymore," Jianzhu said. "The rest of us survived by the skin of our teeth. So, no, we're not triggering the Avatar State. I shudder to think what would happen if an Earth Avatar started hurling landmasses left and right with abandon."

He took them lower. The westward side of the mountainous ridge was dotted with empty mining settlements. Scapes of brown dust spread from the operating sites like an infection, eating into the treeline and displacing the natural vegetation. Kyoshi looked for signs that the land was growing back, but the scars were permanent. The wild grasses kept a strict cordon around the areas touched by the miners.

Jianzhu set Pengpeng down for a landing in the center of a mud-walled hamlet. Whoever originally earthbent the structures into shape had been so sloppy that it seemed intentional, as if to remind the occupants that they weren't going to stay long. Kyoshi was surprised they didn't cause any further collapses by jumping down from the bison.

"This is an important locus of Earthen spiritual energy," Jianzhu said.

Yun dug his toe into the dust as he surveyed their surroundings. "It looks more like a wasteland."

"It's both. We're here to commune with a particular spirit roused from its slumber by the devastation. I'm hoping one of you can help ease its suffering."

"But talking with spirits is no guarantee," Yun said. "I've read of past Avatars who've had trouble with it. And then there's people like Master Kelsang who have been able to communicate with the spirits effortlessly at times."

"I didn't say the method was perfect," Jianzhu snapped. "If it was, I'd have used it on you long ago."

Yun frowned and bit back more questions. Kyoshi was glad that he shared her apprehension at the very least. The desolate town was eerie, the bones of a once-living thing.

But on the other hand, she was slightly comforted by the

knowledge that it would all be over soon. She knew nothing about spirits. In her opinion, being spiritual simply meant acknowledging the power of forces you couldn't see and coming to terms with the fact that you didn't have control over every aspect of your life. The rituals of food and incense placed at sacred shrines were gestures to that worldview. Nothing more, nothing less.

The stories about strange translucent animals and talking plants might have been true, but they weren't for her. The Avatar was the bridge between the human world and the Spirit World, and whatever test Jianzhu had in mind would settle the matter. Yun would glow with energy or some other final proof, and she would lie there inert, listening for sounds she couldn't hear.

After leaving Pengpeng with some dried oats to chew, they walked up the slope of the mountain on a tiny path that ran alongside a gouged-out sluice canal. It was steep going, and Yun remembered there was a faster way to climb. "You know, I could make a lift and—"

"Don't," Jianzhu said.

Eventually, the incline revealed a large terrace carved into the mountain. It was bigger than the entire settlement below, and it had been constructed with more care. It was perfectly level, and empty postholes indicated it had once held some very heavy equipment.

"Go sit in the middle," Jianzhu told them.

Kyoshi felt the same prickle on the back of her neck as she did when stepping onto the iceberg with Tagaka. It made little sense, seeing as how she was surrounded by her native element.

"Come on," Yun said to her. "Let's get this over with." He

seemed to have a better understanding of how this might escalate. She followed him to the center of the terrace.

"It's not the solstice, but it is almost twilight," Jianzhu said. "The time of day when spiritual activity is at its highest. I will guide you two in meditation. Yun, help her if she needs it."

Kyoshi had never meditated before. She didn't know which leg you folded over the other or how your hands were supposed to touch. Fists pressed together or thumb and forefinger?

"You've . . . basically got it," Yun said after they sat down. "Tuck your tailbone in a bit more and don't hunch your shoulders." He stayed facing her, taking up his own pose not too far off. She could have reached out and poked him.

Jianzhu produced a small brazier and a stick of incense, which he placed between them. "Someone help me light this with firebending?" he said.

They stared blankly at him.

"It was worth a shot," Jianzhu said. He lit the incense with a precious sulfur match and backed away until he reached the edge of the terrace, positioned like the high mark of a sundial.

The air took on a sweet, medicinal note. "Both of you, close your eyes and don't open them," Jianzhu said. "Let go of your energy. Let it spill from you. We want to let the spirit get a taste of it, so to speak, so it knows it can come forth."

Kyoshi didn't know how to control her energy. But if Jianzhu was telling her to throw away the idea of containing herself, to stop minimizing the space she took up, to let herself grow and rise to her full dimensions . . .

It felt *wonderful*.

The next exhalation she made seemed to go on forever,

drawing from a reservoir inside her that had no end. Her sense of balance ran wild, the pull of the earth coming from each and every direction in turn. She swayed within the stillness of her own body. Her eyelids were a theater of the blank.

A rasping noise came from the mountain. The sound of millstones with no grain between them.

"Don't open your eyes," Jianzhu said softly. "Hear sounds, smell smells; take note of them naturally and let them pass. Without opening your eyes."

The breeze picked up for a moment, dispersing the incense smoke. In the time it took to settle back down, Kyoshi thought she detected a whiff of something damp. Almost fungal. It wasn't so atrocious as it was . . . familiar.

Familiar to whom? she thought, giggling silently as the incense took over again.

"You know what would be funny?" she said. "If it was . . . you know . . . neither of us."

"Kyoshi," Yun said. His voice sounded slurred. "I need to tell you. Something important. Me and you."

She tried to speak again but her tongue was too big for it. Jianzhu hadn't told them to shut up yet. That was weird. Jianzhu was Master Shut Up. Was he okay? She had to check if he was okay. It was her duty as a member of his household. She disobeyed and peeked.

Yun was meditating peacefully. Had he spoken at all, or had she imagined it? She tried to turn her head toward Jianzhu but went the wrong way, looking at the mountain instead.

A hole had been opened in the rock, a tunnel of pitch-darkness. In its depths, a great glowing eyeball stared back at her.

Her shriek caught in her throat. She tried to scramble away, but her muscles failed her as if her joints had been sliced by a butcher. Nothing connected to anything.

The eye floating in the mountain was the size of a wagon wheel. It had a sickly, luminescent tinge of green. A web of pulsing veins gripped it tightly from behind, giving the sphere an angry appearance, as if it would burst under its own pressure at any moment.

It swiveled over to look at her, her futile struggle catching its attention.

Yun! her mind screamed. He wasn't moving. His breathing was slow and labored.

Jianzhu was unfazed by the horrific spirit before them. "Father Glowworm," he called out in greeting.

A cordial, mellifluent voice rumbled from deep within the mountain, the echo concentrated by the walls of the tunnel. "Architect! It's been *so* long." The eye darted between the three of them. "What have you brought me?"

"A question."

The spirit sighed, a low, nauseating hum that Kyoshi felt in her bones. "That chatty little upstart Koh. Now every human thinks they can march up to the oldest and wisest of us and demand answers. I thought you had more respect, Architect."

Jianzhu stiffened. "This is an important question. One of these children is the Avatar. I need you to tell me which one."

The spirit laughed, and it felt like the earth bounced. "Oh my. The physical world is in poor shape indeed. You do know I'll need their blood?"

Kyoshi thrashed back and forth. But whatever Jianzhu had drugged them with rendered her flailing into mere twitches of movement, her cries into halting breaths. Yun's eyes opened, but only by the smallest degree.

"I know," Jianzhu said. "I've read Kuruk's private journals. But you've tangled with many of the Avatar's past lives. I must have the unerring judgment of a great and ancient spirit such as yourself."

A carpet of slime spilled from the hole in the mountain, flowing over the terrace. It was the same moldy, rotting green as the eye, and it reached toward Yun and Kyoshi in tendrils, the shadows of fingers against a curtain. There was a scraping noise against the stone floor. It came from pointed flecks of debris floating in the wetness, bone-yellow roots and crowns.

The slime was full of human teeth.

Kyoshi was so scared that she wanted to die. Her heart, her lungs, her stomach had been turned into instruments of torture, clawing and biting against each other like frenzied animals. She wanted to reach the void. Pass into oblivion. Anything to end this terror.

As the ooze reached for her knee, Yun opened his eyes. Summoning his strength, he lunged at Kyoshi, shoving her away, throwing his body between her and the spirit. He choked in surprise as the rasping slime shot underneath his clothing. A damp crimson spot bloomed on the back of his shirt.

Kyoshi's foot lay next to the brazier of incense. A meager contribution after what Yun did, but she screamed with her whole body this time, instead of her vocal cords, and kicked at the little bronze vessel. The burning ash landed on the slime and fizzled out. The plasm nearest them shrank from the heat and the spirit hissed angrily.

Yun struggled to his knees beside her.

"I'm surprised you can move," Jianzhu said to him, more impressed than anything else.

"Poison training," Yun spat through clenched jaws. "With Sifu Amak, remember? Or did you forget every darker exercise you put me through?"

They were distracted from the slime regrouping, wrapping around Kyoshi's ankle, until it latched on tight and ground away, sanding her skin off with the rows of teeth. Her blood formed clouds inside the living mucus.

Yun saw her writhe in pain. He grabbed her hand and tried to pull her away from the spirit, their palms clasped hard enough that Kyoshi felt their bones roll over each other. But the tendril held her fast, tasting her, lapping at her wound.

"It's this one," the spirit said. "The girl. She's the Avatar."

Kyoshi and Yun were looking each other in the eye when it happened. When she saw Yun's spirit break inside him.

He had been lying to her with his body and his smile and his words this whole time. He'd thought it was him. Truly and utterly. He'd never once entertained the notion that it might not be him. Any kindness and warmth he'd shown to Kyoshi since the iceberg hadn't been signs of his acceptance—they'd been layers of armor that he'd furiously assembled to protect himself.

And that armor had failed. Piece by piece, Kyoshi saw the only Yun she'd ever known, the boy who was the Avatar, slough and flake into nothingness. His mantle had been stripped from his shoulders, and the shape underneath was merely wind.

He let go of her.

Jianzhu was on top of them in a flash. He sliced at the branch of slime with a sharp, precise little wall, and using the care of his own two hands, dragged Kyoshi away to safety.

Just Kyoshi.

He laid her on the ground and turned around. But it was too late. The spirit's slime reared into the air between them and Yun, a snake guarding its prey. The eyeball in the tunnel swelled with fury.

"You call me forth, ask for my boon, and then assault me?" Its roar nearly shattered the bones in Kyoshi's ears.

Yun, she tried to shout. *Run. Fight. Save yourself. The Avatar—it never meant anything.*

Jianzhu took an earthbending stance, cautiously settling his feet the way a swordsman might slowly go for his blade. "I couldn't risk you taking your revenge on Kuruk's reincarnation. You had your blood, Father Glowworm. Your price has been paid."

"I'm raising it!"

Instead of attacking the two of them, the tendril wrapped around Yun from neck to hip. His face was as pale as clay. He wouldn't move his limbs. Every fear Kyoshi had of taking from him what he treasured most had come to pass in a thundering instant. There was only one more thing left for him to lose.

No, Kyoshi sobbed. *Please, no.*

The spirit pulled, and Yun flew backward into the tunnel, disappearing into the darkness. As Jianzhu punched his fist upward to seal the passage shut once more with solid mountain, Kyoshi found her voice again.

She screamed pure fire.

The flame shot out of her mouth like the rage of a dragon, in a single explosive burst. It doused the terrace and rendered swathes of lingering ooze into blackened, flaking char. But the tunnel was closed. Her fire washed impotently against the mountainside, until it petered out entirely.

Kyoshi stumbled to her feet, barely able to see past her sticky eyelids. The inside of her mouth was blistered. She could sense Jianzhu's presence in front of her, looming.

"I'm sorry," he said. "This could have been avoided if you had—"

She surged forward and tackled him off the edge of the terrace.

The trip down this time was worse than the iceberg. Kyoshi lost her grip on Jianzhu the instant her shoulder smashed into a withered, hardened tree root. She tumbled wildly, tail over teakettle, and came to a stop at the bottom of the slope.

Ignoring the pain, she looked around for Jianzhu. He wasn't to be found in the thin scrub surrounding the base of the mountain. She snapped her head upward at the sound of stone moving.

The earthbending master descended casually, stepping down a flight of stairs that he created himself. Where a more orthodox bender would simply raise a solid platform from the ground, Jianzhu gathered planks of stone and assembled them at will beneath his feet, using the same technique he'd reached Tagaka's ships with. It looked like the earth itself was bowing to him, prostrating under his immense power.

Kyoshi spotted a boulder behind him large enough for her to lift and rooted her feet to the ground. She pulled it toward them, not caring that she was also in its path.

Jianzhu didn't bother turning his head. He reached behind him with one arm and the room-sized rock split along its grain, letting him pass through the gap. The two half spheres kept going and narrowly missed clipping Kyoshi as well. She forced down a yelp as they collided with the ground behind her.

Jianzhu looked at her with the same thoughtful expression he once reserved for Yun. "I'll have to teach you to do more than simply go big," he said.

Kyoshi tried the only other basic tactic she knew of, breaking the opponent's foundation. She aimed her intent at the base of his stairs. She'd take them out along with a huge chunk of the slope.

But after rooting herself again and throwing the mother of all arrow punches at the mountainside, the only movement she got was a geyser of dust. The stairs barely trembled. She tried again. And again.

Jianzhu was taking deeper stances now, spiraling his arms in time with hers, and suddenly she knew why. He was reading her. Smothering each movement of earth she attempted. Nulling her out. She was a child pulling on a door an adult was holding closed.

Jianzhu stopped right in front of her, his platform raising him up so that he was eye level with her. Aside from the dust on his clothes, he could have been leaving a meeting in his house. She'd been unable to touch him in the slightest.

"Kyoshi," he said with a warmth that made her sick to her stomach. "You are the Avatar. Don't you know what that means? The responsibility that you now have?"

He ran a hand through his hair and bared his teeth like he regretted what kind of bushes he'd planted in his garden. "Kyoshi, I'm not a fool, and neither are you. We're not going to pretend you'll ever truly forgive me for what happened here. What I'm asking you to do is weigh our loss against the future of the world. Don't let Yun's sacrifice be in vain. Embrace your duty and let me teach you."

Yun's sacrifice?

Our loss?

Her teeth crushed fresh wounds into her lips. She'd thought she'd known hate before. Hate had been a hollowness inside her, the dull ache that she'd been forced to cradle as she stumbled through the alleys of Yokoya, dizzy with hunger and sickness. Hate had been reserved for her own flesh and blood.

But now she understood. True hatred was knife-edged and certain. A scale that begged for perfect balance. Yun lay on one side of the fulcrum. Her only *responsibility* in this life, as far as she was concerned, was to even the weight.

She swore to herself. One way or another, she was going to know what Jianzhu looked like when he *did* lose everything he held dear.

Kyoshi hurled a Fire Fist, a move she knew nothing about. But whatever firebending she had in her had been used up. It came out as a normal punch, stopping short of his face.

Seeing her so desperate to harm him cracked his mask of serenity. He frowned an ugly frown and clenched his fingers. Two small discs of stone slammed into Kyoshi's wrists from the left and right.

It happened so fast she didn't have time to flinch. The stones shaped themselves around her hands and joined each other in front of her body, forming a set of thick shackles. They were as snug as a bone-doctor's splint and as unbreakable as iron.

The bands of rock rose into the air, taking her with them. Her shoulders clicked painfully under her own weight, and she writhed like an insect caught on sticky paper, madly kicking her feet without purchase.

Jianzhu held her like that, a carcass for inspection, before slamming her back down. The stone shackles merged with the ground, and she struggled on all fours. He'd forced her into a full *kowtow*, a student's posture of submission to their master.

"Had you the essentials of earthbending, you could free yourself," Jianzhu said. "You've gone neglected long enough, Kyoshi. You're weak."

Her palms sunk deeper into the ground the more she tried to resist. There was no denying that he was right. She was weak, too weak to fight him the way she needed to. The distance between them was simply too great.

"So much wasted time," Jianzhu said. "I could have taught you sooner, if only I hadn't been distracted by that little swindler."

That he wasn't done being cruel to Yun was a final kick to her gut. It was incomprehensible. She couldn't keep the tears from flowing down her face. "How could you say that?" she screamed. "He worshipped you, and you used him!"

"You think I *used* him?" Jianzhu's voice grew dangerously quiet. "You think I profited from him somehow? Let me give you your first lesson. The same one I gave Yun."

He stamped his foot, and a thick layer of soil clamped itself over Kyoshi's mouth, a muzzle with no holes for her to breathe. She began to choke on her own element, her lungs clogging with grit.

Jianzhu swept his arm behind him in a wide, encompassing arc. "Out there is an entire nation crammed full of corrupt, incompetent people who will try to use the Avatar for their own purposes. Buffoons who call themselves 'sages' when all it takes in the Earth Kingdom is having the right connections and paying enough gold to plaster such a title on your brow."

The map of Kyoshi's vision curled in on itself. Her toes gouged furrows in the dirt, trying to push her body toward air. The pounding in her head threatened to burst her skull.

"Without my influence, you'd turn into nothing more than a traveling peddler of favors, flopping here and there with your decisions, squandering your authority on petty boons and handouts," Jianzhu said, unconcerned that she was losing consciousness before his eyes. "You'd end up a living party trick, a bender who can shoot water and breathe fire and spit useless advice, a girl who paints the walls a pretty color while the house rots at its foundations."

She barely made out Jianzhu crouching down beside her, bringing his lips close to her ear. "I have dedicated my life to making sure the next Avatar won't be used in such a manner," he whispered. "And despite your every attempt to fight me, I will dedicate my life to *you*, Kyoshi."

He suddenly ripped away the earthen gag. The rush of air into her lungs felt like knives. She collapsed onto her chest, her hands freed but useless.

For several minutes she lay there, despising each pathetic gulp she took, each time she tried to stand but could not. Finally, she heaved herself to her feet, only to see Jianzhu backing away from her, glancing over her head. A gale of wind washed them in dust and desiccated leaves.

Kelsang landed his glider on the slope and slid down on his feet the rest of the way. Relieved as she was to see him, Kyoshi knew right away that he shouldn't have come. His wounds had reopened, staining his bandages red. He'd traveled too far on his own without his bison. The journey by glider would have been arduous for an Airbender at full health.

"How did you find us?" Jianzhu said.

Kelsang closed the wings on his staff. They'd been repaired so hastily that they wouldn't fold completely into the wood, lumps of glue sticking out of the seams. He leaned heavily on it for support, staring hard at Jianzhu the whole time. "You left a map out on your desk."

"I thought I locked my study."

"You did."

Jianzhu's composure broke fully for the first time today. "Really, Kel?" he shouted. "You think so little of me these days that you panicked when I took the Avatar on a trip by myself and broke into my room? I can't trust the people closest to me anymore!?"

Kyoshi wanted to run to Kelsang, hide behind his robes, and sob like a child. But fear had closed her throat and glued her feet.

She felt like the slightest word from her could prove to be a spark thrown on the oil.

She didn't have to say anything though. Kelsang took one look at her trembling form and grimaced. He stepped carefully between her and Jianzhu, leveling his staff at his old friend.

It looked much more like a weapon than a crutch now. "No one in the house could tell me where you went, Rangi and Hei-Ran included," he said to Jianzhu. "You're saying I had no reason to be suspicious? Where's Yun?"

"Kelsang," Jianzhu said, thrusting his hands toward Kyoshi, trying to get his friend to see the bigger picture. "That girl is the *Avatar*. I saw her firebend with my own eyes! Your hunch was correct! After so many years, we've found the Avatar!"

Kelsang hitched, his body processing the revelation. But if Jianzhu thought he could distract the monk to his advantage, he was mistaken. "Where is Yun?" he repeated.

"Dead," Jianzhu said, giving up the ruse. "We tried to commune with a spirit, but it went berserk. It took him. I'm sorry."

"No!" Kyoshi shrieked. She couldn't let that go. She couldn't let him twist what had happened. "You—you *fed* us to it! You threw Yun to that spirit like meat to a wolf! You murdered him!"

"You're right to be upset, Kyoshi," Jianzhu said softly. "I got so carried away with finding the Avatar that I lost my pupil. Yun's death is my fault. I'll never forgive myself for this accident."

He wasn't wailing with sorrow. That would have been too obvious an act. He kept the face that most people knew, the stoic, plain-speaking teacher.

This was a game to him. With Kelsang as the piece in the center. Kyoshi was gripped by a fresh bout of despair. If the monk believed his friend—the adult, the man of good repute—over her, Jianzhu's crime would be buried along with Yun.

She needn't have worried. "Kyoshi," Kelsang said, never taking his staff off Jianzhu. "Stay behind me."

Jianzhu rolled his eyes, his ploy having failed.

"I don't know what's going on here," Kelsang said. "But I'm taking Kyoshi and we're leaving."

He staggered, still weak from his injuries. She caught him by the shoulders and tried to keep him upright. The only way they could keep stable was by holding on to each other.

"Look at the two of you," Jianzhu said. "What you're doing is you're coming home with me. Neither of you are in any shape to argue."

Kelsang felt Kyoshi tremble through her hand on his back. Felt her fear. He ignored his own pain and drew up to his full height.

"You will have nothing to do with Kyoshi for the remainder of your life!" he said. "You are no longer fit to serve the Avatar!"

The cut landed deep on Jianzhu. "*Where will you go?*" he roared, frenzied and frothing. "*Where?* The Air Temples? The abbots will hand her back to me before you can finish telling your story! Have you forgotten how far you've fallen in disgrace with them? Didn't Tagaka jog your memory?"

Kelsang tensed into a solid carving of himself. The grain of his staff squeaked from how tightly he held it.

"I know everyone in the Four Nations who could possibly help you!" Jianzhu said. "I put out the message, and every lawman, every sage, every official will be tripping over their own feet to hunt you down on my behalf! *Being the Avatar will not protect her from me!*"

"Kyoshi, run!" Kelsang shouted. He pushed her away and leaped at Jianzhu, bringing his staff down to create a gale of wind. Jianzhu brought earth up to meet him.

But they weren't fighting the same fight. Kelsang meant to blast his friend away, to knock the madness out of him, to overwhelm him with the least amount of harm done, in the way of all Air Nomads.

Jianzhu shaved off a razor of flint no longer than an inch, sharp and thin enough to pass through the wind without resistance and slice at where his victim was exposed and vulnerable.

A spurt of blood came from the side of Kelsang's neck, from a finger-length cut so clean and precise it was almost elegant.

Jianzhu's expression flickered with a sadness that was deeper and truer than what he'd given to Yun, as he watched his friend fall.

Kelsang collapsed to the ground, his head bouncing lifelessly off the hard-packed earth.

Those were the last things Kyoshi saw before the white glow behind her eyes took over her entire being.

THE INHERITANCE

ONE TIME, when she was ten or thereabouts, a traveling fireworks vendor came to Yokoya. The village elders, in an unusual fit of decadence, paid him to put on a show celebrating the end of the first harvest. Families packed the square, gazing up at the booming, crackling explosions racing across the night sky.

Kyoshi did not see the display. She lay on the floor of someone's toolshed, twisted by fever.

The morning after, the heat in her skull forced her awake at dawn. She staggered around the outskirts of town, seeking cool air, and found the field where the vendor set his explosives the night before. The ground was scorched and pitted, utterly ravaged by a fiend born of no natural element. It was covered in a layer of ash and upturned rocks. Water creeping in slow, black rivulets. The wind smelling like rotten eggs and urine.

She remembered now being suddenly terrified that she'd catch blame for the destruction. She'd run away, but not before scuffing her footprints off the path she'd taken.

When Kyoshi regained her vision, she thought for a moment she'd been thrown back in time to that unreal, violated land-scape. The trees were gone behind her, snapped at their trunks and torn by their roots to expose damp clumps of soil. Before her, it was as if some great hand had tried to sweep away the mountainside in a convulsion of fear and shame. Deep rips crisscrossed the stone like claws. The hilltops had been pushed over, the traces of landslides pouring down from their crests.

Kyoshi had the vague notion that she was too high up. And she couldn't see Kelsang anywhere. She'd wiped away his existence.

There was an animal howl floating on the wind, the scream of rosin on warped strings. It came from her.

Kyoshi dropped to the ground and lay there, her face wet with tears. She pressed her forehead to the earth, and her use-less cries echoed back in her face. Her fingers closed around the dust, sifting for what she'd lost.

It was her fault. It was all her fault. She'd pushed Kelsang away instead of listening to him, allowed cowardice to rule her thoughts and actions. And now the source of light in her life was gone.

She had nothing left. Not even the air in her lungs. The heaving sobs coursing through her body wouldn't allow her to breathe. She felt like she was going to drown above water, a fate she would have accepted gladly. A just punishment for an unwanted girl who'd squandered her second chance: Kelsang, a miraculous, loving father conjured from thin air. And she'd cursed him with death and ruin.

There was a tremor in the distance. The rubble around a certain spot was sinking, parting. Someone had escaped the havoc she'd wreaked in the Avatar State by burrowing deep down in the earth. Now he was tunneling back to the surface, ready to claim his property.

Kyoshi scrambled to her feet in a blind, wild panic. She tried to run in the direction they'd come, stumbling past landmarks she prayed she remembered correctly. The baked ruins of the mining villages were so similar in their crumbling appearance that, for a second, she thought she was caught in a loop. But then, right as her legs were about to give out, she found Pengpeng waiting where they'd left her.

The bison took a whiff of Kyoshi and bellowed mournfully, rearing on her back four legs before crashing down hard enough to shake the dirt. Kyoshi understood. Maybe Pengpeng had felt her spiritual connection with Kelsang dissipate, or maybe Kyoshi simply smelled of his blood.

"He's gone!" she cried. "He's gone and he's not coming back! We have to leave, now!"

Pengpeng stopped thrashing, though she looked no less upset. She allowed Kyoshi to climb on her back, using fistfuls of fur as a ladder, and soared into the air in the direction of home, without being told.

Yokoya, Kyoshi corrected herself. *Not home. Never again home. Yokoya.*

She stayed back in the passengers' saddle. She was unwilling to straddle Pengpeng's withers in Kelsang's place, and the bison didn't need guidance for the return journey. From high up in the sky, she could see dark, rain-filled clouds approaching over the ocean in the opposite direction. If they flew fast enough, they could reach Yokoya before meeting the storm.

"Hurry, please!" she shouted, hoping Pengpeng could understand her desperation. They'd managed to strand Jianzhu in the mountains, but the man's presence felt so close behind. As if all he needed to do was reach his arm out for her to feel his hand clamping down on her shoulder.

That same year she'd caught sick and suffered through the fireworks, Kelsang had returned to the village. He looked askance at the farmer who swore that Kyoshi had been well taken care of with the money he'd left behind. The weight she'd lost and her pallid skin told a different story. Afterward, Kelsang promised Kyoshi that he'd never leave her for so long again.

But Kyoshi had long forgotten about any nights she'd spent ill without medicine. She'd been more concerned with the new kite-flying craze that had taken hold of the village children. For weeks, brightly colored paper diamonds and dragons and gull-wings had hypnotized her from the sky, dancing on the wind. Not surprisingly, she hadn't the supplies or guidance to make one of her own.

Kelsang noticed her staring longingly at the kites dotting the sky while they shared a meal outside. He whispered an idea in her ear.

Together, they scavenged and spliced enough rope for him to tie one end around his waist. That afternoon, he took off soaring on his glider while Kyoshi held the other end from below. They laughed so loud they could hear each other across the great heights. For her, he was the biggest, fastest, best kite in the whole world.

She'd misjudged the weather. The first drops of rain pattered on her cheek, waking her from her slumber of exhaustion. She and Pengpeng still had some ways to go when it quickly became a torrent that blotted out the sun. They narrowly managed to get down to Yokoya in time to avoid the lightning spreading its fingers across the sky.

They arrived at the mansion. Kyoshi jumped off Pengpeng near the stables and landed ankle-deep in mud. She waded through the blinding rain to the house. The staff and the guests had been driven inside to their quarters.

The ride had given her time to think. And she'd concluded that every decision from here on out was easy. An inevitability she would follow into the darkness.

The only person who could have made her falter was waiting inside the servants' entrance for her, under the archway of the wall. Rangi looked like she had confined herself to this area the entire day. She'd worn out a groove in the floor with her pacing back and forth.

"Kyoshi, where were you?" Rangi said, a scowl on her face from having been left in the dark for so long. "What happened? Where are the others?"

Kyoshi told her everything. About the powerful and terrible spirit that had identified Kyoshi as the Avatar. About the way Jianzhu had offered Yun up as a sacrifice and murdered Kelsang when he came to rescue them. She even included how she'd entered the Avatar State.

Rangi stumbled backward until she knocked her head against a support beam. "What?" she whispered. "That's not—*What!?*"

"That's what happened," Kyoshi said. She dripped rainwater on the floor, each *plip* another precious second lost. "I have to go. I can't stay here."

Rangi started pacing again, running her fingers through the ends of her hair, which had fallen loose. "There's got to be a misunderstanding. An explanation. You said there was a spirit? It must have played tricks on your mind—that's been known to happen. Or maybe you simply got confused. Master Jianzhu can't have . . . He wouldn't . . ."

She watched Rangi attempt to will a different reality into existence. It was the same trap Kyoshi had fallen into the day Kelsang told her she might be the Avatar.

"We've got to get to the bottom of this," Rangi said. "When Jianzhu gets home, we'll make him explain himself. We'll find out what really happened to Yun and Master Kelsang."

"RANGI! THEY'RE DEAD! I HAVE TO GO!"

Throughout the journey back, Kyoshi had been thinking only about the shards of her life buried on that mountain. She'd forgotten there was still one more piece, and Rangi's stunned silence let her know she'd lost that too. Kyoshi pushed past her without saying goodbye and headed to her room.

It was easy to fill a sack with her clothes. She barely had any. She was going to leave everything on her shelf behind, but the thought of Kelsang made her grab the clay turtle and throw that in. The item that gave her pause was the beautiful green battle outfit that she'd worn on the iceberg and was now hanging on her wall.

For some reason Jianzhu had let her keep it in her room. The thought of taking, of using, a gift from him made her insides clench. But she would need armor like that where she was going. A protective shell.

She took it down, hastily rolled it up, and stuffed it in the sack. The leather journal went on top. She was truly grateful she'd never given in to her urge to destroy the book. In the past it may have been incriminating evidence, but now it was a war plan.

Tucking the bundle under one arm, she stooped down, grabbed the handle of her trunk with the other, and dragged it out into the hallway.

The corners of the trunk screeched as they gouged out a trail in the polished wooden floors. She supposed the reason that no one stopped her was that they were scared. She saw the hems of robes disappearing around corners, frightened whispers behind closed doors as she passed.

The guardsmen, she remembered, had been decimated on the iceberg. And there had always been an undercurrent of suspicion in the way the other servants looked at her. Now her aberrant behavior must have pushed it over the edge into fear. She looked like a swamp ghost dripping with the water she'd drowned in. She could only imagine what terrors her face held.

Each fork in the hallway brought another flash of raw, sawbladed pain to her heart as if she were one of the target dummies in the courtyard, collecting jagged arrows with her body. The routes she'd taken in her daily life unfolded down the corridors of the mansion, leading inevitably, over and over again, to the dead.

The way to Yun's room, the one area he never let her clean, flustering over his privacy. The path to the little nook where Kelsang would meditate when the weather was too harsh. The grass where the three of them had spat watermelon seeds, only to run away when Auntie Mui yelled at them for making a mess.

She would never tread these lines again. She would never arrive to see Yun and Kelsang's smiling faces at the end of her steps.

By design, Kyoshi took the long way past the wood-chopping station. The splitting maul was there, the wedge buried in the block. Kyoshi placed her bag between her teeth and picked up the maul with her free hand. The entire block came with it, stuck to the blade, so she smashed the whole agglomeration against the wall until the heavy tool was freed from the wood.

She kept walking.

Outside, the rain had doubled. The interval between lightning and thunder was nonexistent. She dropped her bag and flung the heavy wooden trunk in front of her. It slid in the mud before coming to a stop.

The chest had been a focal point for her anger in the past, collecting the flows of her hatred like the water barrels positioned under the gutters of the house. It had been left behind in Yokoya, like her, by the people who'd relegated her to a life of a starving, desperate, unloved creature for so many years before Kelsang came into her life.

Her parents would have to take a lower place on the shelf for now. She had someone new to focus on.

Another lightning flash illuminated which side the iron lock was on. Raising the maul high above her head with both hands, she swung it down, aiming for the weakest point.

The wedge of the maul bounced off the metal. The trunk sank deeper into the mud. She struck it again. And again and again.

The thunder and rain drowned out her senses, leaving her with nothing but the painful vibrations rebounding up the haft of the maul into her hands. She struck again and felt a crunch.

Rather than the lock breaking, the trunk had splintered where the metal was fastened to the wood. But it was open. Kyoshi tossed the maul aside and raised the creaking lid.

Inside were two ornate metal war fans the color of gold alloyed with bronze. The weapons were packed in a softer wood frame that held them open while protecting them from rough treatment like the sort she'd just doled out.

A headdress made out of the same material rested in between them. It complemented the fans by mounting smaller versions of them on a band, forming a semicircular crest at the forehead.

Lastly, there was a plain leather pouch with a case that she knew contained makeup. A lot of makeup.

She snatched each item from its moorings. The headdress and fans were much sturdier than they appeared—they were meant to be worn and wielded in combat, after all. They and the pouch went inside her bag. The trunk served no further purpose and would be left in the mud.

With that, Kyoshi was finished. She was taken aback at how completely and utterly finished she was. How little she had put on display how much she'd lost, like the black night sky around the burst of a firework. She'd held on too hard to a treasure that might have been shaped like a home and a family, only to discover that her touch had dissolved it entirely. She wiped her eyes with her forearm and ran around the edge of the mansion, slipping and falling in the rain at least twice, and reached the stables.

There was a shock waiting for her.

Rangi was busy securing bedrolls, tents, and other bales of supplies to Pengpeng's saddle. She looked up at Kyoshi from under the hood of her raincloak.

"Let me guess," she shouted over the downpour, pointing at several waterproof baskets and sacks of grain. "You didn't pack any food, did you?"

She reached down, grasped Kyoshi's hand, and pulled her onto Pengpeng's back. Then she hopped into the driver's seat and took up the reins. "We'll have to fly low and head southwest, out of the storm."

Kyoshi's throat was a solid lump. "Why are you doing this?"

"I have no idea what's going on right now," Rangi said over her shoulder. She flicked rain off her brow. Her face underneath looked like she was heading into combat. "But I'm not going to let you ride off on your own and die in this storm. You won't last an hour without help."

Kyoshi nodded, stricken dumb with gratitude to Rangi. *For Rangi.* She pleaded with the spirits that it wasn't a final cruel trick, the form of her friend sitting before her. She maintained a safe distance so as not to dispel the precious vision.

The Firebender snapped Pengpeng's reins with authority. "Up, girl!" Rangi shouted. "Yip yip!"

THE DECISION

THE SUNRISE after the storm had no idea what Kyoshi had been through. It shined its warm hues of orange through the clouds like a loud boor of a friend insisting that everything would work out. The waves below flowed neatly under the steady breeze, making it appear that they were flying over the scaled skin of a giant fish.

Fighting the weather throughout the night had blasted them, body and mind. Pengpeng's flight path was starting to ramble. But they were no longer in danger from wind and lightning. It was as good a time as any to address the *other* life-shattering piece of news.

Rangi rubbed at the dark shadows under her eyes. "You're the Avatar," she said. She spread her fingers and stared at the back of her hands, checking whether she was intoxicated. Or dreaming. "After all of this, it's you. You really had no idea until now?"

Kyoshi shook her head. "I don't know what went wrong with the search when we were younger, but from what Kelsang told me, it sounded like a complete mess. No one knew. Not even . . ." It was difficult to spit out his name. "Not even Jianzhu."

"I've never heard of this happening before," Rangi said. She closed and opened her fists to make sure they were still working. "At least not in Fire Nation history. When the Fire Sages reveal the Avatar, it's a done deal."

Kyoshi fought the urge to roll her eyes. Of course, in the Fire Nation the caravans arrived on time, and the identity of the most important person in the world was never in doubt.

"And then there's a festival," Rangi said, lost in thought. "According to tradition, there's a celebration bigger than Twin Sun Day. We eat special foods like spiral-shaped noodles. School is canceled. Do you know how rare it is for school to be canceled in the Fire Nation?"

"Rangi, what does that have to do with anything?"

The Firebender stretched her elbows behind her back, her mind made up. "My point is that there are set ways this is supposed to pan out," she said. "If you're the Avatar, you need the trappings of the Avatar. We need to find masters who know what they're doing to recognize your legitimacy and give you the right guidance."

Rangi vaulted over the saddle edge onto Pengpeng's neck and took up the reins. The bison dipped lower over the shimmering water. Up ahead, a small crag jutted from the surface, a finger of rock poking through the ocean sheet. It was too steep for ships to use it as a dock, but there were a few level surfaces near the top, covered in soft green moss.

"I'm going to drop you off here, where you can camp safely," Rangi said. "There's a protocol in the event the compound came under attack and I had to flee with the Avatar. Those bags were prepacked; there's everything you need for a week in them. Once I return to the village and figure the situation out, I'll bring someone who can help."

"*No!*"

She couldn't go to another master, especially not a well-known one. Any earthbender in a position to aid her was more likely than not to be part of Jianzhu's web. Looking back on her time at the house, she'd seen the evidence of his reach every day. The gifts, the ceremonious visits, and the dictated letters were simply tokens that marked the flow of power and control in the Earth Kingdom. And for as long as she'd known, it all filtered up to Jianzhu.

Kyoshi scrambled over to Rangi and yanked the reins out of her hands. Pengpeng swerved to the side and roared in complaint.

"Stop that!" Rangi shouted.

"Rangi, please! You'd only be sending me right back into his hands!" Kyoshi nearly bit through her tongue as she remembered the horror Jianzhu unleashed from deep within the mountain and his complete callousness while he did so. Rangi couldn't have known the extent of her fear. Kyoshi was certain the man hadn't shown that side of himself to anyone but her and Yun.

Rangi fought with her for the reins. "Let go! You're being ridiculous!"

"*Rangi, as your Avatar, I command you!*"

The Firebender recoiled like she'd been struck by a whip. The order wasn't one of Yun's jokes. It was an exploitation of Rangi's oath to protect and obey the Avatar. An attack on her honor.

Rangi blew a long strand of black hair out of her face. It didn't go very far, the end of it sticking to her mouth. "I suppose I have to get used to you saying that."

There was an agonizing distance in her voice, and Kyoshi despised it. She didn't want a professional bodyguard obeying her orders. She wanted *her* Rangi, who scolded her without hesitation and never backed down.

They spent a long time in silence, listening to the breeze pick up.

"Yun is gone," Rangi said. "He's really gone." Her voice seemed thin, drawn out by the passing wind, like the notes of a flute. She sounded hollow inside.

Kyoshi had no comfort to give her. Both of their lives had centered around duty. Kyoshi's for the sake of survival, Rangi's for pride and glory. But Yun had managed to pierce both their shells. Their friend had been stolen, and as far as Kyoshi was concerned, there was a single path laid out before her that she could take in response, lit by the clean, bright fires of hatred.

"I'm not ready to confront Jianzhu," Kyoshi said. "I'm not nearly strong enough yet. I have to find bending masters who can teach me to fight and who aren't in his pocket."

In fact, it was more than that. She'd need teachers who were completely unknown to Jianzhu. If he suspected she was after training, he'd look for her in schools around the Four Nations.

And she'd have to conceal she was the Avatar. That news would spread so fast it would act as a beacon for Jianzhu, allowing him to close in on her before she was prepared. She didn't have a good idea how she'd obtain instruction in all four elements without giving the game up, but she'd make it work somehow.

The idea sounded ludicrous in her head. It *was* ludicrous. And yet Kyoshi knew she would walk off this cliff without hesitation. She would stick both hands into a dragon's mouth if it meant the slightest chance she could pay back Jianzhu what she owed him.

Rangi dragged her hand down her face. "Fine. Bending masters. Where do you want to look first? You're talking like you have a plan, so let's hear it."

"You're not coming with me," Kyoshi said. "I have to do this alone."

The Firebender gave her a look of such utter contempt for that notion that it could have been grounds for an Agni Kai. Kyoshi was afraid this might happen. Rangi's powerful faith, her need to fulfill her duty, would spiral around with no spot to land on but her.

She had to stand strong. She'd lost so much already, and she wasn't going to risk her one remaining connection to this world on a fool's quest. "You're not coming with me," Kyoshi repeated. "As your Avatar I command you to stay behind. Rangi, I'm serious."

She wanted to sound angry, but the effect was ruined by the overwhelming tide of relief she felt at Rangi's rejection of her demand. A strictly professional servant of the Avatar couldn't disobey her, but a companion might.

"I have no idea how long this journey will take," Kyoshi said. "And there are secrets about me that I haven't told you."

"*Oh no, Kyoshi's keeping a secret from me*," Rangi moaned an octave lower than normal. "I think I'll be okay with whatever your little revelation is, given the last thing you sprung on me was only the most important piece of information ON THE PLANET."

The crag passed them by, a silent onlooker that wanted no part of the conversation. The last marker of reason in an ocean of uncertainty. From this point onward there was nothing but trouble ahead.

But at least Kyoshi had her friend back.

"We need rest, or we'll lose effectiveness," Rangi declared, nestling herself under the corner of a tarp that had come loose. "If you've got a destination in mind then I'm taking the first sleep shift. You owe me that much."

"Rangi." Kyoshi tried one last time to growl in threat. Instead the name came out like a dedication of thanks to the spirits for this fiery blessing of a girl. It was futile trying to mask how Kyoshi felt toward her.

"Where you go, I go." The Firebender rolled to her side and yawned. "Besides, there's only one bison, rocks-for-brains. We can't split up now."

Despite how tired they were, Rangi only dozed fitfully, shivering though it was no longer cold. Watching her from a distance, Kyoshi had an answer regarding the little snips of breath she'd listened to for so long in their shared tent on the iceberg. It was how Rangi cried in her sleep. Every so often, she would burrow her face into her shoulders to wipe her tears.

With their eyes on each other, it was easy to be brave. *Maybe that's the only way we get through this*, Kyoshi thought. *Just never look away.*

She stared at the water until the sun's reflection became too much, and then reached for her single bag of belongings. Digging around, she found the clay turtle. It was made of earth. It was tiny. She could use it for practice.

Small, she thought as she cradled it with both hands. *Precise. Silent. Small.*

She curled her lips in concentration. It was like crooking the tip of her pinky while wiggling her opposite ear. She needed a whole-body effort to keep her focus sufficiently narrow.

There was another reason why she didn't want to seek instruction from a famous bending master with a sterling reputation and wisdom to spare. Such a teacher would never let her kill Jianzhu in cold blood. Her hunger to learn all four elements had nothing to do with becoming a fully realized Avatar. Fire, Air, and Water were simply more weapons she could bring to bear on a single target.

And she had to bring her earthbending up to speed too.

Small. Precise.

The turtle floated upward, trembling in the air.

It wasn't steady the way bent earth should be, more of a wobbling top on its last few spins. But she was bending it. The smallest piece of earth she'd ever managed to control.

A minor victory. This was only the beginning of her path. She would need much more practice to see Jianzhu broken in pieces before her feet, to steal his world away from him the way he had stolen hers, to make him suffer as much as possible before she ended his miserable worthless life—

There was a sharp crack.

The turtle fractured along innumerable fault lines. The smallest parts, the blunt little tail and squat legs, crumbled first. The head fell off and bounced over the edge of the saddle. She tried to close her grip around the rest of it and caught only dust. The powdered clay slipped between her fingers and was taken by the breeze.

Her only keepsake of Kelsang flew away on the wind.

ADAPTATION

JIANZHU PUSHED open the doors of his house to find it in static, silent chaos.

The servants lined up in rows to the left and right, bowing as the master entered, forming a human aisle of deference for him to walk through. It was overly formal, a practice he'd dismissed long ago.

He hadn't bothered to clean himself before entering, so he left a trail of dust and rubble in his wake. There was an ache in his chest as he passed the bashed-in door to his study, a testament to his Airbender friend's great strength and personal conviction.

He had no time to grieve for what had happened to Kelsang. He went straight to the Avatar's room in the staff quarters, followed the path of damage outside to the empty bison pen and then back to his cowering servants in a loop.

"Can someone tell me what happened here?" he said in what he thought was an admirably neutral, collected tone given the circumstances.

Instead of answering they shrank further into their shoulders, quaking. Whoever spoke up first was sure to take the blame.

They're afraid of me, he thought. *To the point they can't do their jobs properly.* He cursed the fact that the girl had no official supervisor watching her, and pointed at his head cook, Mui. He'd seen the Avatar doing favors for the woman in the kitchen.

"Where is Kyoshi?" he said, snapping his fingers.

Mui went crimson. "I don't know. I'm so sorry, Master. None of us had ever seen her act that way before. She—she had a weapon. By the time we could find a guardsman, she was gone."

"Did any of the guests see her leave?"

Mui shook her head. "Most of them left early to try and beat the storm, and the others were in their rooms in the far wing."

He supposed it wasn't the middle-aged cook's fault that she was unable to stop a rampaging, axe-wielding teenager who could break a mountain whenever she remembered she had the ability. Jianzhu dismissed the staff without another word. Better to have them uncertain, fearing his next command.

He drifted through the halls of the house until he found himself in an aisle of the gallery, staring at some of his artwork but not seeing it. That was where Hei-Ran found him after she returned from an offshore meeting with the delegation from the Fire Navy.

She frowned at his appearance, ever the disciplinarian. "You look like you were spat out by a badgermole," she said.

Better to tear off this bandage quickly. He told her the version of events she needed to hear. Kyoshi being the true Avatar. The disappearance of both Yun and Kelsang, caused by a treacherous spirit. The Avatar holding a grudge against him for it.

She slapped him across the face. Which was about as good a result as he could get.

"How can you stand there like that?" she hissed, her bronze eyes darkening with fury. "How can you just stand there!?"

Jianzhu worked his jaw, making sure it wasn't broken. "Would you rather I sit?"

A less-controlled person than Hei-Ran would have been tempted to scream her disbelief to the skies, letting the secret out. *You had the wrong Avatar? You introduced a boy to the world as its savior and then got him killed? You let the real Avatar run off to who knows where? Our oldest and closest friend is dead because of you?*

He was grateful for Hei-Ran's iron character. She thought those things at him instead of saying them, fuming strategically. "How are you not going to lose face over this?" she whispered. "All of your credibility? What are you going to do?"

"I don't know." He leaned against the gallery wall, as surprised at his own response as she was. Out of Kuruk's companions, he had been the planner. Normally Jianzhu had every contingency, every fork in the road mapped out to its logical end. He found the change of pace rather liberating.

Hei-Ran couldn't believe he was drifting like this. She pulled her lips back over her teeth.

"We can minimize the damage if we get her back quickly," she said. "She can't have gone far on her own—she's a maid, for crying out loud. I'll send Rangi to hunt her down. The two of them are friends; she'll know where Kyoshi would run to."

Hei-Ran found the nearest summoning rope and gave it a yank. The soft yellow cables ran throughout the house, held by eyelets across certain walls. The bells at the other ends let the staff know where help was needed.

Given that his employees were busy avoiding him like the plague, it was a minute or two before someone answered. Rin or Lin or whatever. The girl was out of breath, and she limped slightly, like she'd stubbed her toe in her hurry to arrive.

"Rin, please fetch my daughter," Hei-Ran said kindly. "Tell her it's very important."

"I'm so sorry!" Rin shrieked. She was trying so hard not to mince her words in fright that she erred on the side of ear-splitting volume. "Miss Rangi's disappeared! One of the stable-hands said he saw her leave with Kyoshi last night!"

"Rin, please leave my sight immediately," Hei-Ran said with warmth of a different kind this time.

The girl bowed and backed away, eyes lowered, her socked feet thumping a pattern down the hallway that was almost as fast and loud as her heartbeat. Jianzhu waited until she vanished around the corner.

"Before you hit me again," he said to Hei-Ran. "I believe whatever Rangi does is your fault, not mine."

Her face contorted like she was living a thousand lifetimes right then and there, in most of which she melted his eyeballs using his skull as a cauldron.

"This is a positive," Jianzhu said. "Your daughter will keep her safe until we find them."

"Until we find them?" Hei-Ran screamed in whisper. "*My daughter* is an elite warrior trained in escape and evasion! We can already forget about an easy chase!"

She thrashed in place, the waves of bad news buffeting her around, challenging her equilibrium. When she came to a stop, her face was lined with deep sorrow.

"Jianzhu, Kelsang is dead," she said. "Our friend is dead. And instead of mourning him, we're standing here, plotting how to maintain our grip on the Avatar. What has happened to us? What have we become?"

"We've grown old and become responsible, is what," Jianzhu said. "Kelsang made the same promise to Kuruk that we did. We can honor his memory, both of their memories, by continuing on our path."

He found his usual energy coming back, his dalliance with helplessness finished. There had been too many futures to consider before. The individual degrees of catastrophe were overwhelming. But really he only needed to focus on one solution. The piece that was critical to every scenario.

"We'll get the Avatar back," he said. "Finding her ourselves would be ideal, obviously, but it'll be fine if she turns up on the doorstep of another sage to seek refuge. I'll find out and respond quick enough to smother the news from traveling further."

He wasn't worried about the Avatar hiding in the other nations either. His personal networks extended further than the Earth King's diplomacy. If anything, his foreign contacts would inform him faster and with more discretion, hoping to avoid an international incident.

"And what if she falls in with one of Hui's allies?" Hei-Ran asked.

Jianzhu grimaced at the mention of the chamberlain's name. "I suppose that's always a risk. But I'm fairly certain she wouldn't know who he is or which masters he's got his hooks into. *I* don't even know who's sided with him yet."

Jianzhu got off the wall. "My reputation will certainly take an unavoidable hit once we have to reveal her identity to the world, but that won't matter in the end," he said. "As long as the girl is back here when we do it, under my roof, following my orders, it will all work out. I have capital to burn within the Earth Kingdom. Time to put it to good use."

Hei-Ran grudgingly appreciated her friend's return to his usual self. "It doesn't sound like the girl wants to be here."

"We'll worry about that later. Besides, she's still a child. She'll learn what's in her best interests."

He dusted himself off, the first attempt he'd made to get rid of the filth of the mining town so far. The plan molded itself together in his head, like clay under the guidance of an invisible tool. "I need you to write a letter for me."

Hei-Ran looked at him sideways.

"I know, I know," he said. "You're not my secretary. But there has to be a Fire Nation stamp on this message."

"Fine. Who's it to?"

"Professor Shaw, Head of Zoology at Ba Sing Se University. Tell him you're interested in borrowing some specimens he brought back from his latest expedition. You want to display them in the Fire Nation, because they're so very adorable and cuddly, as part of a goodwill tour between our countries."

Jianzhu eyed the piece of art behind him, a painting of the Northern Lights on vellum by a master Water Tribe artist. He grabbed its wide frame with his outstretched hands and ripped it off its moorings. "Send him this as well, to butter him up. It's worth more than what he makes in a year."

Hei-Ran seemed slightly disgusted by his reliance on brib-ery, but that was an Earth Kingdom cultural quirk that people from the other three nations often had trouble getting used to. "Which adorable and cuddly animals are we talking about?" she said.

Jianzhu twisted his lips and sniffed. "The shirshus."

THE INTRODUCTION

KYOSHI STRUGGLED to open the small metal box. She'd opened the visible latch, yes, but no matter how hard she gripped and twisted the container, the false bottom that concealed the true contents wouldn't budge.

"You can't force it," a gentle voice said. "Use too much strength, and it's liable to break. The goods would spill everywhere. You don't want to leave a trail behind, do you?"

Kyoshi looked up from the floor to see a tall, beautiful woman with freckles splashed across the tops of her cheeks and serpent tattoos running down her arms. Next to her was a man, stocky and strong, his face bedecked in red-and-white makeup. The streaks of crimson met each other to form a wild, animalistic pattern, but his expression underneath was warm and mirthful.

The metal box suddenly grew hot, singeing Kyoshi's flesh, and she dropped it. She tried to shout and found her teeth loose and swimming in her mouth. The painted man wiped his face, and in the streaks between the colors, his features had turned into Jianzhu's.

Kyoshi surged forward with rage but couldn't close the distance. The woman found her helplessness amusing and winked at her with a green glowing eye. Her eyeball swelled and swelled, growing so large that it burst out of its socket and kept expanding until it consumed her other eye and then the entirety of her face and then the four corners of the world. Kyoshi flailed in terror inside the cavernous darkness of its pupil, trying to reach solid ground.

We'll never leave you, Jianzhu whispered. *You will always have us, in the distance, behind you, right next to you, watching you. The two of us will always be there for you.*

At the height of her panic a hand gripped Kyoshi by the shoulder. The warmth and solidity of it told her not to flinch, not to worry. She sat up slowly and blinked in the fading daylight.

"Wake up," Rangi said. "We're here."

Rangi insisted on making a single pass over Chameleon Bay before landing. She leaned off Pengpeng's side, drawing in the layout of the ramshackle port town with the single-mindedness of a buzzard wasp, as if every trash-strewn alley and patchy roof were vitally important. Kyoshi let Rangi take her time. She needed a moment to make sure she'd fully climbed out of the depths of her nightmare.

After she collected her thoughts, she joined in on looking. To Kyoshi the mass of buildings was indistinguishable, a curving scab around the bay that should have been picked off long ago. There was only one location that she was interested in, the one that matched the description in her journal.

"There," she said, pointing at one of the few structures that rose above a single story. The yellow roof stood out among its green neighbors like a diseased leaf. "That should be Madam Qiji's teahouse."

They pulled up, retracing their route through the sky. There was no place to land Pengpeng within the town limits, and a sky bison with no Airbender on it was surely one of the first signs Jianzhu would order his network to search for. The reconnaissance sweep itself had risks.

The small copse they found on the outskirts felt like a dose of luck. Perhaps their reserves of good fortune would be drained by the simple act of hiding Pengpeng in the trees.

"We'll be back, girl," Kyoshi said to her, stroking the beast's nose. Pengpeng gently bumped her with her skull, telling her they'd better.

Kyoshi and Rangi set out on foot, the pressure of firm ground against their soles a welcome sensation after so much flying. As they followed a dirt path into Port Chameleon Bay, they were treated to a ground-level view of the town in all its glory.

It was a miserable sight.

For the past nine years, Kyoshi had never laid eyes on open flatland going to waste without some attempt to grow food on it. But the dusty, hard-packed fields they passed through made it clear it wasn't worth trying. The ground here was rawhide, impenetrable.

The port sustained life, in the barest sense. They encountered a surrounding band of slums, wooden lean-tos and moth-eaten tents. The inhabitants stared at them with glassed eyes, not bothering to adjust their bodies from where they sprawled. The few who stood up, in wariness that they might be hostile, were hunched by malnutrition and sickness.

"People shouldn't live like this," Rangi said.

Kyoshi felt her sinews tying into knots. "They can and they do," she said as casually as she could.

"That's not what I mean." Rangi rubbed her own elbow, considering the pros and cons of what she was about to say. "I know about the time you spent in Yokoya on your own, before Jian—before Master Kelsang took you in. Even though you tried to hide it from me."

Kyoshi's stride faltered, but she gathered herself and kept going. They couldn't stop here simply because her friend wanted to have a heart-to-heart about one of the oldest, deepest scars running through her soul.

"Auntie Mui told me," Rangi said. "Kyoshi, you should never have been put through that experience. The thought of the other villagers ignoring you when you needed them, it makes me sick. That's why I was always pushing you to fight back."

Kyoshi laughed bitterly. She'd long laid the blame for those years on a different party than the Yokoyans. "What was I supposed to do, drop the mountain on them? Smack around a bunch of children half my size? Anything I did would have been completely disproportionate."

She shook her head, wanting to change the subject. "Anyway, is the Fire Nation so perfect that prosperity gets shared with every citizen?"

"No," Rangi said. Her lips scrunched to the side. "But maybe one day it could be."

They entered the town proper, the edges marked by a change to brick and clay shanties, some of them earthbent into being and others laid by hand. The streets twisted and angled like they'd been set over animal paths instead of following human needs. If it hadn't been for the landmark of the teahouse jutting above the roofline, Kyoshi would have been lost after a few steps.

The merchants who'd closed up shop for the night had done so with vigor, coating their storefronts in so many locks and iron bars that she wondered how some of them afforded the expense. A number of deer dogs, hidden behind walls and fences, set off barking as they passed.

No one bothered them. Thankfully. Reaching the teahouse felt like making it through a field of trip wires. Madam Qiji's was an island in the haphazard layout of the town, ringed by the broadest avenue of open space they'd seen so far. It was as if someone had aggressively claimed the public square and plunked down the wooden building in the center.

Light flickered through the paper windows. They stepped onto the large, creaking porch, approaching cautiously. There was an old man sprawled across the doorway, wrapped in canvas blankets, blocking their entry. His loud snores caused his wispy white beard to flutter like cobwebs in the breeze.

Kyoshi was debating whether to prod him gently or try leaping over him when he woke up with a start, grumbling at the impact his shoulder made with the doorframe. He blinked at her and frowned.

"Who're you?" he mumbled.

She noticed his hands shaking as they poked out from his cocoon. From hunger, no doubt. She hadn't given enough thought to money as she made her getaway from the mansion, but there were a few coppers in the pockets she'd sewn into her dress long ago. She fished the coins out and placed them on the porch in front of him. If the instructions in her journal were correct, she and Rangi wouldn't have any need for money once they were inside.

"Get yourself something to eat, Grandfather," she said.

The old man smiled at her, his wrinkles clawing over his face. But his happy expression turned to outright shock when Rangi added a silver piece to the pile.

Kyoshi glanced back at her.

"What?" Rangi said. "Weren't we just talking about this kind of thing?"

The inside of Madam Qiji's was only halfway finished.

The ground level was dedicated to serving food and drink. Tables for visitors were arranged over a layer of straw and sand. But where there should have been a second floor with rooms for overnight guests and weary travelers, there was no floor. Doors floated in the walls twelve feet off the ground with no way to reach them. No mezzanine, no stairs.

The handful of hooded figures sitting in the corners didn't seem to think that was unusual. Nor did they look up as Kyoshi and Rangi came in. If anything, they leaned farther into their cups of tea, trying to remain inconspicuous.

Kyoshi and Rangi took seats in the middle. Near them was an exquisite, heavily constructed Pai Sho table, by far the nicest object in the room. It sat on four sturdy legs, surrounded by ratty floor cushions, a jewel nestled in the petals of a wilted flower.

They were in the right place. And they were in the right chairs. It was supposed to be only a matter of time before someone came over and said the phrase she was waiting for.

For Kyoshi it was an eternity. The Pai Sho table was an agonizing reminder of Yun. And she didn't need a visual aid to feel the raw wound of losing Kelsang. That pain was a bleeding trail leading back to Yokoya. It would never wash away.

Rangi kicked her chair. A man made his way over to them. A young man, really. A boy. Each step he took into the better-lit center of the room regressed how old he looked. His sleeves were bound with thin strands of leather, and he wore headwraps in the style of the Si Wong tribes. They hung loose around his face and neck, framing his barely contained fury. Kyoshi could sense Rangi getting ready for the worst, gathering and storing up violence to unleash if things went wrong.

"What would you like to drink?" the boy said through his teeth.

Here it was. The moment of truth. If the instructions in the journal were wrong, then her vaunted single path forward would be cut off at the first step.

"Jasmine picked in fall, scented at noon, and steeped at a boil," Kyoshi said. Such a combination didn't exist. Or if it did, it would have tasted like liquid disaster.

The reply came out of his mouth like it needed to be dragged by komodo rhinos, but it was the reply she was looking for. "We have every color blossom known to man and spirit," he said.

"Red and white will suffice," she replied.

He clearly had been hoping for any response but that one. "Lao Ge!" the boy suddenly shouted toward the door. "You were supposed to keep watch, you useless piece of dung!"

The old man who'd been lying across the porch leaned half-way inside. He was suddenly much less infirm than when they'd first met.

"I *was* standing guard, but then those two lovely young women gave me enough money to buy a drink or ten," he said with a big, toothy grin. "They must have slipped by me while I stepped out to the wineshop. Quite the tricksters, those two." He tilted a liquor bottle to his lips and drank deeply, his ragged sleeve falling down his arm to reveal sheaves of corded muscle under papery skin.

The boy ground the heel of his hand into one of his eyes. He stormed away to the kitchen, muttering expletives at the old man the whole way. Kyoshi could sympathize.

Rangi leaned on the table. Though her pose was relaxed, her eyes fluttered around the room, sizing the occupants up, including and especially Lao Ge, who was busy finding the bottom of his second bottle of drink.

"You know," she whispered to Kyoshi. "You told me we were going to a *daofei* hideout; you told me you were going to get access to help through *daofei* code; here we are, I heard you speak it, and yet I still can't believe this is happening."

"It's still not too late for you to get out of here and save your honor," Kyoshi said.

"It's not *my* honor I'm worried about," Rangi hissed.

Before they could get further into the matter, the boy returned with a tray of steaming cups. He placed one in front of Kyoshi, Rangi, and then himself, taking a seat across from them. He was much calmer now. It may have had less to do with the tea than with the backup that slowly filed in behind him.

A huge man in his thirties, as tall as Kelsang and half again as thick, blotted out the lamplight coming from the kitchen. He had a smooth, clean-shaven face over a body that threatened to burst from expensive robes, his clothes having been chosen for flash over fit. Kyoshi saw Rangi's eyes dart to the man's feet instead of his scarred knuckles or protruding gut, and realized why. As big as he was, he hadn't made the floorboards creak.

One of the doors suspended in the wall above the ground flew open. A young woman stepped out of the room, not caring about the drop that awaited her.

She was dressed in an Earth Kingdom tunic, but with a fur skirt over her trousers. Kyoshi had seen pelts like that worn by visitors from the poles. The stronger indication of the woman's Water Tribe heritage was her piercing, sapphire-blue eyes that no amount of spidersnake formula could possibly hide.

She landed on the ground with her toes pointed like a dancer's. Kyoshi could have sworn she'd fallen slower than normal, a feather's descent. It was the only way to explain how she made the journey from the second story to the table without breaking stride or the bones in her foot. She stood behind the other shoulder of the boy, her wolflike features unreadable as she assessed Kyoshi and Rangi.

I'm not afraid, Kyoshi told herself, finding to her surprise that it was true. She'd tussled with the Lord of the Eastern Sea. A single street-level *daofei* crew wasn't going to intimidate her.

The boy in the desert hat tented his fingers. "You come in here, total strangers, unannounced," he said.

"I have the right," Kyoshi said. "I gave the passwords. You are obligated to provide me and my partner succor, by the oaths of blood you have taken. Lest you suffer the punishments of many knives."

"You see, that's just it." The boy slouched back in his chair. "You're using these big, old-timey words like you've got these grand ideas of how this is supposed to work. You rattle off a senior code that we haven't heard in years like you're pulling rank on us. You did it like you were reading from an instruction manual."

Kyoshi swallowed involuntarily. The boy noticed and smiled.

He tilted his head at Rangi. "Coupled with the fact that Gorgeous over here practically screams 'army brat,' it makes me think the two of you are lawmen."

"We're not," Kyoshi said, swearing silently inside her head at how badly this was going. "We're not abiders."

There were three men scattered around the teahouse who were not part of their little confrontation. They all hastily plunked down coins and beat it out the door, eyes wide with fright.

The boy placed a small, hard object on the table with a click. Kyoshi thought it was a Pai Sho tile at first, but he withdrew his hand to reveal an oblong stone, polished smooth by a river or a grinder.

"I'm pretty good at spotting an undercover," the boy said. "And I think this is your story. Your daddy bought you an officer's commission from a crooked governor, and the first thing you decided to do with it is play detective and come knocking on our door." He thumbed at Rangi. "She was assigned to watch your back, but she didn't do a very good job, because you're here now, and you're going to die. The cause will be recorded as acute terminal stupidity."

Kyoshi could almost hear Rangi's thought process, counting the limbs of the three people across from them, calculating out the sequence of damage she'd inflict. "I'm telling you, we're not lawmen."

The boy angrily kneed the underside of the table hard, knocking over the teacups and spilling the liquid across the surface.

Kyoshi acted before she thought. But in retrospect, it was more about stopping Rangi than anything else. She kicked upward as well. The entire foundation of the teahouse, the patch of earth it was built on, jumped by half an inch.

The boy nearly fell out of his chair. His two bodyguards wobbled. The shocked looks on their faces said that didn't happen very often, not with the large man's stability and the Water Tribe girl's impeccable balance.

Kyoshi spoke over the groans of resettling wood and the dust drifting in clouds around them. "You're right," she said. "I don't belong here."

They didn't bum-rush her immediately, deciding that she needed to be attacked with caution. That bought her time to speak.

"The truth is that I despise *daofei*," Kyoshi said. "I hate your kind. It makes me sick to be in your presence. You're worse than animals."

"Uh, Kyoshi?" Rangi said as the big guy and the woman sidled into better flanking positions. "Not sure where you're going with this."

The boy remained where he was. Kyoshi could tell he wanted to put up a brave front. So did she. "But that doesn't matter right now," Kyoshi said, staring through the hardening layer of rage in his eyes. "You are going to give me everything I demand, because you are bound by your outlaw code. You will do as I say because of your idiotic, clownish, make-believe traditions."

Her blood sang in her ears. Her hand went to her belt. The man and woman would certainly interpret that as the signal to attack. She was aware of Rangi leaving her seat.

Only by moving faster did Kyoshi prevent complete disaster. She slammed one of the war fans on the table, its ribs spread wide to reveal the golden leaf. The Waterbender and the big guy stopped in their tracks. The boy looked like someone had reached into his chest and seized his heart.

"Spirits above!" Lao Ge said. "That's Jesa's fan!"

The sudden appearance of the old man at the table startled both sides equally. He'd managed to squeeze in between Rangi and Kyoshi without them noticing, and he leaned inward, giddily examining the details of the weapon.

The boy leaped out of his seat. "Where did you get that?" he shouted.

"I *inherited* it," Kyoshi said, her pulse racing. "From my parents."

The Water Tribe girl looked at her with wonder. "You're Jesa's daughter?" she said. "Jesa and Hark were your mother and father?"

Kyoshi didn't know why she was getting more worked up over simple facts than the prospect of a brawl earlier. "That's right," she said. It felt like her mouth had become her stomach, unwieldy and sour. "My parents founded this group. They're your bosses."

"Our baby has come home!" Lao Ge crowed. "This calls for a drink." He stepped back so he could have room to pour a third bottle into his gullet.

The boy was still angry, but in a different flavor now. "We need to confer for a minute." He snatched up his rock from the table and pointed accusingly at Kyoshi. "In the meantime, I suggest you get your story straight, because you have a lot of explaining to do."

"Yes," Rangi said. "She does."

Lao Ge perched on a table off to the side with his containers of booze, like a strange bird arranging shiny objects in its nest. The rest of the gang filed back to the kitchen without him. Given that they seemed to treat him like background furniture, Kyoshi could only do the same. She turned to Rangi and found the Firebender giving her a critical stare.

"What?" Kyoshi said. "This happened exactly the way I said it would. We're in. This is the first step to gain access to this world."

Rangi remained unmoved.

"I told you everything before we landed," Kyoshi said. "The truth about my parents being *daofei* smugglers who abandoned me in Yokoya. Rangi, you came in here with me knowing this."

The words poured out of her in a churning waterfall. Her knee was jogging rapidly up and down. The motion did not escape Rangi's notice.

"As bizarre as it is for me to say this, your secret family history is not the issue," Rangi said. "Don't you think you played that situation a little . . . aggressively?"

That was news to Kyoshi, coming from her "burn it first and ask questions later" friend. "It's the kind of behavior these people respect," she said. "Tagaka knew we were calm and rational, and look what she tried to do to us."

Rangi's teeth clicked. "You didn't see yourself back there. It was like you were begging them to attack you. There's being brave, and then there's having a death wish."

She reached out and clamped her hand on Kyoshi's leg to still the shaking. "We're not in our element," Rangi said. "You might have the keys to certain doors, but this is not our house. You have to be more careful."

And if I back down from a few daofei, *I have no chance of standing up to Jianzhu.* "I'm sorry, all right?" Kyoshi said. This argument wasn't going to resolve anytime soon, and the gang was coming back. The last thing they needed was to show a fractured front to the criminals they were trying to coerce.

Rangi let it go, seeing the same value in unity. The Si Wong boy, Water Tribe woman, and bulky man arranged themselves in front of Kyoshi with great formality. She had often stood that way to greet important guests, always in the back of the group due to her height.

The man made a gesture with one open palm down, and the other hand clenched into a fist on top. It was unlike any other greeting Kyoshi had witnessed and made it seem like his right side was smashing the left for trying to steal food off a table.

"Flitting Sparrowkeet Wong," he said, bowing slightly. If he seemed embarrassed by having such a delicate-sounding nick-name, he didn't show it.

The lithe Waterbender stepped forward and made the same pose, though in a slouchy way to let everyone know she thought the concept of professional names silly. "Kirima," she said. "Just Kirima."

"Bullet Lek," the boy snapped with great pride. He had rearranged his headwraps behind his ears to a more dignified, indoor style. "Though some call me Skullcrusher Lek, or Lek of the Whistling Death."

Kyoshi made sure not to mirror the faces that Wong and Kirima made behind Lek's back, or the boy would have certainly been insulted. "Kyoshi," she said. "This is my associate, Rangi."

Rangi made a little snort of disapproval that Kyoshi took to mean: *Oh, so we're giving them our real names now?*

"How did you come to us tonight?" Kirima asked. "Start as far back as you can."

That far, huh? "I don't remember much from when I was little," Kyoshi said. Though her legs had settled down, the front of her neck now ached with tension. "Only that my parents and I never stayed in one place very long, and they never told me where. You could say I grew up in 'the Earth Kingdom.'"

"That would have been before any of you joined," Lao Ge said to the others. "Jesa and Hark slowed down considerably for several years and barely ran any jobs. They never told me why they stopped gathering the old crew for so long. I thought maybe they'd quit the game."

The old man's memory helped Kyoshi fit pieces together into a completed puzzle. The result was uglier than she'd imagined.

"Well, they must have wanted back in very badly, because they abandoned me in a farming village when I was five or six," she said. "I can't be sure exactly when. I never saw them after that." *Or forgave them.*

"That can't be," Lek said. "Jesa and Hark would never do that to family. They were the most loyal bosses anyone could ask for. You must be mistaken."

Kyoshi wondered what it would be like to pick him up, like she did to that pirate, and shake him until he saw spots. Kirima intervened before she could explore the idea.

"Are you telling their own daughter what happened to her?" the Waterbender snapped at Lek. "Shut up and let her finish."

"There's not much more to tell," Kyoshi said. "I nearly died of neglect in that village before I was taken in by the household of a rich and powerful man. A sage. The only possessions I had to my name were my mother's gear and her journal, which had information about my parents' *daofei* customs, obligations I could call on. It was an instruction manual. Like you said."

She glanced at Rangi. "I kept my parents' past a secret from the village the whole time. Given how I was treated as an outsider, I don't think I would have fared well if the townsfolk knew I was also the spawn of criminals."

Rangi clenched her jaw. Kyoshi could tell she was thinking about the what-ifs, how their relationship might have been different had she known Kyoshi was a tainted child from the start. Would she have looked past that and befriended Kyoshi all the same? Or would she have condemned her to the rubbish heap like she'd done to Aoma and Jae and the others?

"And one day you just decided to leave and come here?" Lek said. He was still incredulous, like a sequence of events that started with Kyoshi's parents being anything but perfect was not possible.

"I did not just decide," Kyoshi snarled, turning her attention back on him. "The man whose house I lived in decided, when he murdered two people dear to me. I swore by the spirits that turn this world on its axis that I would make him pay for it.

"That's why I'm here," she said, pounding her fist on the table for emphasis. "He's too powerful and influential to be brought down by the law. So I need the opposite side of the coin. I need my parents' resources. If they can give me one gift at all in this life, then let it be revenge for those I've lost."

Her face was red. Kyoshi felt ready to explode. She didn't know what she'd do if another door in the wall opened and her mother and father stepped out. It would have been as volatile and uncharted as her encounter with the cave spirit.

Lek solemnly took his headwraps off and wrung them between his hands. His hair was sandy and cropped underneath. "You came all this way to find Jesa and Hark," he said in a mournful mutter. "Kyoshi, I'm so sorry. I don't know how to break this to you, but . . . but . . ."

Relief came like a monsoon. She did not have to meet them. She didn't have to discover what kind of person she was when the past unearthed itself and took solid form.

"What, are they dead or something?" Kyoshi said, waving her hand at him flippantly. "I don't care."

A lie. Had they appeared in front of her, she might have had to run screaming from this room.

Lek's grief was replaced by outrage, a funeral guest who caught her stealing the altar offerings. "We're talking about your mother and father! They were taken by a fever three years ago!"

She found it so easy to be cruel now that she knew for certain they couldn't defend themselves. "Wow," Kyoshi said. "I guess there're some things you can't outrun, huh?"

His eyes goggled out of his head. "How can you be so vile? No one in the Four Nations disrespects their own kin like that!"

"They left me behind because I took up too much cargo space," Kyoshi said. "So I would say it's a family tradition."

She snapped the war fan closed, intending to punctuate her sentence in an intimidating way. Instead the arms fell out of alignment and the leaf folded the wrong way, ruining the effect. She would need to learn how to use it properly at some point.

"I'm not here to confront my parents, or their ghosts," Kyoshi said. The raw nervous energy coursing through her bones had slowed. "I'm here to seek what's owed me by blood ties."

She counted off on her fingers. "I want access to safehouses in the bigger cities where I can stay hidden at length. I want introductions with the rest of the network, starting with the strongest benders. And, most of all, I want training. Training until I'm strong enough to take down my enemy personally."

A silence fell over the group.

Kirima made an awkward little choke. Kyoshi thought maybe she'd gotten some saliva down the wrong pipe, but then the Waterbender burst out laughing.

"Other cities!" she guffawed. "Let me guess. Your journal mentioned secret bases in Ba Sing Se, Omashu? Gaoling maybe? Filled with a brotherhood of bandits who honor the old ways?"

"I'll blow my trumpet," Wong said. "I'm sure they'll come running."

Kyoshi frowned. "What's so funny?"

Kirima spread her arm. "This is our one and only base of operations. *This* is the network. Us. Whatever assistance you thought you could personally demand outside the law ends here, within these walls."

Kyoshi remembered the most tired she'd ever been in her life. It was not long after she'd been dropped in Yokoya, when she still saw the journal and chest as her birthright treasures and not as incriminating evidence her parents wanted to ditch alongside her.

She'd been chased away from every door, forced to drag the heavy trunk with her. It was a lot for a child to carry back then, even one as outsized as her. As the day wore on, the exhaustion had seeped into her fingernails and teeth. Her thoughts had turned gray. There had been no room in her body for hunger and thirst. It was all given over to fatigue.

Kyoshi felt the same fragments of weariness threatening to undo her now. They drove into her joints like nails, beckoning her to give up. Looking at the *daofei* before her, she saw it clearly now. They weren't the vanguard of some shadow army she could use to march upon Jianzhu. They were haggard, hunted people. Like her.

"We've fallen on hard times," Wong said. She gathered he didn't speak much, so when he did, it was likely true and to the point. "Crackdowns on smuggling across the Earth Kingdom have been pretty severe in recent years. We've been cut off from gangs in other cities without much news or any jobs to speak of."

"Your journal must be at least a decade old, with entries that go back further," Lek said. "In those days, groups like ours had real influence." He stared at his hands like a deposed king longing for the grip of his scepter. "We had territory. The governors asked *us* for permission to do business."

"Lek, you would have been three years old during our heyday," Kirima said. "We hadn't even picked you up yet."

He wheeled on her furiously. "That means the rest of you should be more upset than me!"

"We understand," Rangi interrupted. "It's painful to know what should have been."

Kyoshi detected a streak of satisfaction in her voice at the way things had turned out. The hole went no deeper than a dilapidated teahouse and a few cutpurses. As far as Rangi was concerned, they could still extricate themselves.

"Kyoshi, we tried," she said. "You did what you could. But this isn't what we came for." She glanced at the room doors and their unusual placement. "We could stay here overnight, perhaps, but it'd be no safer than camping. We should get back to Pengpeng and fly to the nearest—"

Lek slammed his hands on the table. *"Fly?"* His voice broke with excitement. "You *flew* here?"

The rest of the group perked up. "Are you telling me you have a sky bison?" Kirima said. There was an interested gleam in her eye.

Rangi cursed at her slipup. "Why?" Kyoshi said. "What difference would it make?"

"Because now you have something we want," Kirima said while Lek bounced off the walls. "Being Jesa and Hark's kid means we're obliged to keep you safe from harm. It doesn't mean we'll follow your orders or help you on some personal quest for vengeance. You want that level of commitment, then you make us an offer."

"No," Rangi snapped. "Forget it. We're not giving you our bison. We're not giving you anything of the sort."

"Simmer down, Topknot," Kirima said. "I'm merely suggesting a partnership. We need to get out of this dried-up town to where the prospects are better. Kyoshi wants training. We should travel together for a while. It's her best shot at finding earthbending teachers of ill repute."

Hearing her, Kyoshi suddenly realized she'd made a critical mistake. She'd shown her earthbending. While she greatly needed improvement in her native element, there wasn't a straightforward way to get training in the others without revealing she was the Avatar.

Rangi was still opposed to the idea. "We didn't come here to revive a two-bit smuggling operation," she said to Kyoshi. "We'd just be taking on more risk than we need."

"First of all, *our* operation was top-notch!" Lek said, full of umbrage. "And second, you two are the baggage here. You wouldn't last a day moving in our circles without a guide. For crying out loud, *we* almost killed you."

Rangi narrowed her eyes. "Is that your impression of what happened?" She sounded perfectly willing to test his theory.

Kyoshi buried her face in her hands while they argued. Ideas that had been so clear in her mind before were becoming trampled and muddy. Her singular path turned out to be full of brambles and false turns.

Lao Ge interrupted her wallowing by slamming an empty bottle on the table. He'd been forgotten until now, and his smile folded in on itself like he was bursting with the world's best secret.

"I know it's a tough decision, my dear girl," he said, cocking his ear toward the door. "But don't take too long. The police are coming."

ESCAPE

THE SOUND of marching boots hitting the road filled the air. "You stupid old man!" Lek shouted. "I'm never putting you on watch again!"

"Finally," Lao Ge said. He winked at Kyoshi.

Officers wearing constabulary green hustled into the teahouse. They fanned out along the sides to accommodate their numbers, reaching to the corners. Twenty or so, wearing quilted armor with single *dao* broadswords on their backs.

At the head of their formation, still in plainclothes but now wearing the same headband adorned with the prefectural badge of the law as the others, were the same three men who'd been in the teahouse earlier.

"Remind me again who's good at spotting undercovers, Lek?" Kirima snarled.

In a moment of panic Kyoshi thought the officers had come

for her on behalf of Jianzhu, but that couldn't have been the case. If he'd sent out messengers immediately, they still wouldn't have beaten a bison.

No, she thought with a grimace. They were here for the girl who'd walked into an outlaw hideout and started making demands with outlaw codes. She'd incriminated herself in public, like a fool.

"In the name of Governor Deng, you are under arrest!" the captain said. Instead of a sword, he pointed a ceremonial truncheon topped with the Earth King's seal at them, but it looked heavy enough to break bones regardless. "Put down your weapons!"

Deng. The name brought more terror to Kyoshi's heart than a charging saber-tooth moose lion. Stout, red-nosed Governor Deng was a frequent visitor to Jianzhu's house and one of his closest allies. Kyoshi glanced at Rangi. The Firebender's worried headshake confirmed her fear. If they got caught here, tonight, the whole operation was over. They'd be back in Jianzhu's grasp before his breakfast got cold.

The captain did not like the eye contact between her and Rangi. *"I said put down your weapons!"* he shouted, bristling for a fight.

The *daofei* looked at their empty hands in confusion. Kyoshi realized that unless the man felt particularly threatened by Lao Ge's bottles, the only armed one was she. The glinting war fan was still in her hand, its mate stuck in her belt. She stood up so that she could have room to yank the other fan out.

The captain took a step back in astonishment. He'd interpreted her unfurling to her full height as a hostile act. He wasn't the first. "Take them!" he shouted to his men.

There were so many of them. Crammed in the dark confines of the teahouse, the police force seemed larger in number than Tagaka's marauders. Five of the officers made a beeline for Kyoshi, the obvious target.

They were knocked down by a blast of fire. Kyoshi glanced back at Rangi again. She had her fist extended, her skin smoking. Her face was upset but unrepentant. If they were in, they were in full-measure. Rangi didn't do things by halves.

Inspired by her decisiveness, Wong picked up Lao Ge and threw the drunkard bodily at the captain like a rag doll. Lao Ge's warlike screech as he flew through the air was the only sign that he'd agreed to the act. The two of them must have done it before. The element of surprise worked strongly in their favor as Lao Ge's wiry arms wrapped around the captain's neck and his legs scissored around the waist of his subordinate, becoming a human net.

Another blast from Rangi sizzled past Kyoshi's ear. She no longer knew what was going on. Men closed in on her with swords drawn. She picked up the nearest, heaviest object, the Pai Sho board, by one of its legs and swung it in an arc.

The policemen were bowled over like wheatstalks by the dense wooden bludgeon. The ones who tried to block her wild strikes with their *dao* had their swords bent and crushed against their torsos for their trouble.

Fresh officers ran in through the door only to slip on a sheet of ice that Kirima laid down using nothing but the remaining wine from Lao Ge's stash. Kyoshi jolted in surprise at the reserved, minimalist twirl of her wrists and fingers. For a moment it looked like Tagaka of the Fifth Nation was fighting on her side.

"Girl!" Lao Ge said, clamping swords inside their scabbards wherever his bony fingers and toes could reach. "Bump the table!"

She didn't have the same previous working relationship with him as Wong, but Kyoshi caught his drift. She raised her foot high and stomped the floor.

The teahouse jumped into the air again, this time tilted higher from the back. Lao Ge and several of the policemen fell through the door. The others were knocked prone, scrambling on the straw and frozen wine.

Kyoshi's new compatriots managed to stay upright, having seen the trick before. "Out the other side!" Lek yelled.

"What about Lao Ge?" She hadn't meant to dump him into the thick of the enemy.

"He can handle himself! Move!"

She flung the Pai Sho board at the nearest officers and followed the others through the kitchen. It was empty, just a little room with a clay stove that smoldered from the one attempt Lek had made at tea. Another door gave way, and they were in the town square behind the building.

The passage had been disguised, painted over without a frame, and there were no windows, so it was the side of the house that was least well-guarded by the police. Only two men held positions there. Kyoshi heard a *zzip-zzip* noise, and they crumpled to the ground before they could wave their swords.

Lek tucked something back into his pocket. "Where's your ride?"

Rangi answered, which was good because Kyoshi had lost her bearings and had no idea. "Southwest corner of town," she said. "If everyone follows me, I can get us there."

There was a harsh scrape of clay from above. A whole section of roof tiles sloughed off and came crashing down at their heels as they ran. Reaching Pengpeng meant running along the edge of the square, seeking one outlet from the many cramped alleyways branching and forking in different directions like the veins of a leaf.

Kyoshi caught sight of the reason why they hadn't been swarmed by more lawmen. Lao Ge was tangling with a whole platoon of them by the main entrance. They slashed wildly at the air he occupied only to come up empty every time. He folded and rolled his body like the wine still fogged his mind, dodging and flipping, his movements seemingly designed to taunt and frustrate them. Kyoshi saw him leaning over at impossible angles nearly parallel to the ground and realized he was subtly earthbending supports underneath his torso, changing his center of gravity to confound his opponents.

"We can't leave him!" she shouted to the others.

Apparently they could, because no one else gave Lao Ge a second thought. "This one!" Rangi said, darting down a passage into the darkness. But before anyone had a chance to follow, a thick stone wall shot up from the ground, reaching the height of the neighboring roofs, closing the exit off. The police force had brought Earthbenders of their own.

Lek kept running after her as if he were oblivious to the obstacle in his path. Kyoshi though he was going to dash his brains out against the wall. And then he did one of the most amazing things she had ever seen.

He stepped up into the thin air.

Lek ran higher and higher on invisible stairs. It was only after he'd gone above eye-level that she saw how. The thinnest columns of earth she'd seen anyone earthbend shot up from the ground with each of his steps, anticipating where his foot would land next. They provided a moment's support and then crumbled into dust immediately once his weight shifted off them. His rising path left no trace behind him.

Kyoshi had watched children around the village play by bending the ground they stood on into the air. It was sometimes a test of courage, who could make their pillar the highest, or a game of coordination, taking turns with a partner to seesaw back and forth. But it was always highly destructive to the ground, leaving jagged markers of what had happened. And the players had to remain still, or they'd fall off their platforms.

Lek had none of those concerns. He floated, weightless, free of the earth's pull. He stepped over the top of the wall and onto a rooftop before disappearing.

The feat wasn't limited to Earthbenders. Kirima uncorked a small pouch at her waist and wisps of water spilled forth, gathering under her feet. She stepped higher into nothingness much as Lek had, only her stairs were powerful, thin little jets that provided the same resistance as earth. If the timing was more difficult for her, or the water less stable, she compensated with supreme grace.

Wong glanced at Kyoshi as if to check what she was thinking. *You can't possibly*, was what.

He shrugged at her skepticism and followed his teammates skyward, using earth and dust as Lek had, like it was no big deal. The sight of the gigantic man defying all notions of gravity made her jaw drop. It looked less like bending and more like spiritual chicanery, an invisible hawk lifting Wong's bulk over the roofline. Kyoshi watched him and Kirima run over eaves and windowsills and the blank spaces of alley gaps with equal ease.

The whole show had happened in less than seconds. It was a mind-blowing stunt. And highly unfortunate.

Because no one had taken into consideration that Kyoshi could not do that. She expressly, with utmost certainty, could not do that.

"Cut her off!" a policeman shouted behind her. A second slab of rock shot up to her right.

Left, then. She sprinted for the nearest remaining avenue and made it out of the square before it was blocked shut. Immediately she knew it was a mistake. The alley veered sharply away from the direction the others had gone. The forks in the narrowing street had no markers, and each subsequent guess she made only got her more lost. The houses squeezed in on her as she ran, promising to throttle her by the gills like a fish in a net.

A blast of flame shot into the darkening sky. And then another, the source slightly to the right. Rangi was signaling to her where to go. Kyoshi felt her heart skip a beat for her friend. It was either that or a conniption from running at full speed for so long.

She followed the upcoming bend in the direction of the fire, but so did the lawmen. In fact, they used their knowledge of the town layout to steal a march on her, suddenly popping into view closer behind her. She couldn't double back. And up ahead, a dead end loomed. The alley had been walled up with bricks.

"No way out, girl!" an officer with admirable lung capacity bellowed.

Step, she thought to herself. Do the thing like they did. Her self-berating voice sounded a lot like Rangi in her head.

It should be easier with more speed, right? She hurled herself toward the wall, praying that she could Avatar herself into picking up a technique she'd only seen once. Her on-the-run attempt to bend the necessary struts without destroying the whole town resulted in only pitiful bumps of earth appearing before her. They collapsed under her weight, tripping her up. She fell forward uncontrollably, face-first. She wasn't able to cross her arms in front of her before she made impact.

Kyoshi shut her eyes as she slammed into the wall. There was a terrible crash, an explosion of snapping bricks and tearing mortar. When she opened them again, she was on the other side, still running.

She'd plowed straight through without feeling a thing. She must have bent reflexively, flinched and wrapped herself in her own power like a cloak. A quick glance back showed a Kyoshi-sized hole in the wall and surprised guards trying to decide whether to leap through or go over the top.

In her distraction she collided with the corner of a house. Fear of broken bones caused her to force her way through the clay structure the instant she felt the pain of impact on her shoulder. The building stayed standing, a neat chunk of it ripped off like a sampled loaf of bread.

Ahead of her the spaces between closed-up merchant shops were so narrow that a person smaller than her would have had to stop and wedge through sideways. Rangi sent up another beacon. The only way to get there was as the bird flew. Kyoshi sent an apology into the cosmos for the damage she was about to cause and barreled straight into the cluster of buildings. If she couldn't be a creature of grace, then she'd be a battering ram.

She smashed through the first wall like it was rice paper. Inside, she crossed the floor in a few steps and burst into the neighboring section, boring a passageway through the cluster of storerooms. Each section she stampeded through offered a momentary glimpse of different merchandise. Dry goods, wet goods, weapons, ivory that was certainly illegal, fancy hats. She was glad that she was only ruining inventory and not harming living occupants with flying debris.

Her face felt tight and she wondered if she'd injured herself, ripped her skin open. But no, she determined. She was grinning with a locked, maddened expression, mindlessly exulting in her own power and destruction. Once she realized it, she quickly worked her jaw back into a grim frown and splashed through the next wall.

An unfamiliar sensation caused her to flail after hitting the last barrier. It was freedom. She was in a broad street, going the right way for once. Up above her on the rooftops, the whole crew sprang deftly from surface to surface, bolstering themselves with their element when necessary.

"I see you made your own shortcut," Kirima shouted. The water lifting her up sparkled prettily in the moonlight, making her look like a lunar fairy.

Kyoshi checked behind her to see if anyone had followed the trail of utter devastation she'd left through the town. "Where's Rangi?"

"Still in the lead. That's quite a companion you've got."

There was another blaze of light that resembled a rocket climbing into the night. Rangi had joined the *daofei* on their level. She ran as nimbly as they did on the roof tiles, and when there was a leap too great to make naturally, she stepped on jets of fire that blasted out of her feet, bounding in propulsive arcs across the sky.

The sight made Kyoshi's breath come to a standstill at the very time she needed it flowing. Rangi was so beautiful, illuminated by moon and fire, that it hurt. She was strength and skill and determination wrapped around an unshakable heart.

Kyoshi had always admired Rangi. But right now, it felt as if she were gazing at her friend through a pane of glass freshly cleaned. Some mighty and loving spirit had reached down from the heavens and outlined the Firebender in new strokes of color and vibrance.

There was a struggle in Kyoshi's chest that had nothing to do with how hard she was running, notes of longing and fear played in one chord. She tamped the feeling down, not wanting to confront what it meant right now. In any case, it was a poor time to be distracted.

Soon they exhausted their supply of houses to leap over. They reached the shanties in the outskirts, causing more confusion for the residents who'd seen Kyoshi and Rangi head inward for the night but now flee for their lives in the opposite direction with three other people in tow.

Lek raced for the copse of trees without being told, perhaps understanding that there were only a few places you could hide a ten-ton bison. Kyoshi reached the copse in time to catch the boy as Pengpeng roared and blasted him backward with wind.

"Easy, girl!" She coughed, her lungs burning from the run and inhaled building dust. "They're with us."

Walking across the sky must have been a highly efficient technique, because no one else seemed as tired as she. Rangi leaped onto Pengpeng's neck and unwound the reins from the saddle horn. The *daofei* climbed onto the bison's back, gripping her fur with strange familiarity. Once they were settled, Rangi took Pengpeng up above the treeline.

Lek was ecstatic. "A bison!" he screamed, drumming on the saddle floor. "A real bison!"

"Calm down!" Rangi said. "It's not like you can't see them near any Air Temple."

"He's just excited because we used to have one of our own," Wong said. "Cute little fella named Longyan."

Despite their need to move quickly, Rangi paused, leaving Pengpeng swooping around in a gentle, idling circle. "Wait, how?" she said. "Only Air Nomads can tame bison. The animals won't listen to strangers if they're stolen."

"We didn't steal Longyan," Kirima said. "He was Jesa's bison."

Rangi squinted in confusion and turned to Kyoshi. "But wasn't Jesa . . . *your* mother?"

Kyoshi winced. She spotted a reprieve from the awkward conversation, albeit only a temporary one. On the ground below them, waving his hands, was Lao Ge. He'd managed to escape the dozens of men who had him surrounded and made it to the hiding spot in better time than anyone else.

The *daofei* didn't look one bit surprised to see him. Rangi took Pengpeng low and Wong leaned over, clasping hands with Lao Ge and swinging him onto the saddle, again with the smooth ease of practice. "I thought we might finally be rid of your stinking hide," Lek yelled.

"Not quite so easy," Lao Ge said. "Is anyone else thirsty? I could use—"

"Shut up," Rangi snapped. She fixed Kyoshi with her gaze again. "Does that mean what I think it means? About your mother?"

She looked hurt at another secret being kept from her. But Kyoshi had honestly, sincerely forgotten to bring it up. It hadn't been relevant until now.

"Yes," Kyoshi said sheepishly. "My mother was an Airbender. I'm half Air Nomad."

She felt terribly guilty. She'd forced Rangi to absorb a lot in the past day. Finding out that Kyoshi wasn't the fully Earth Kingdom girl that Rangi had assumed this whole time was yet another small weight added to the pile.

But hearing that a despicable criminal and gang boss was an Air Nomad would have been enough to shock and confuse anyone. People around the world looked up to Airbenders as enlightened paragons who were free of worldly concerns. They belonged to a benign, peaceful, monastic culture that was so spiritually pure that every single member had bending ability.

Rangi resembled a child who'd just been told that the sweets tucked underneath her pillow had been left by her parents instead of the Great Harvest Spirit. Kirima and Wong detected the awkwardness between them and remained silent. Lek wasn't so observant.

"What's everyone looking sour for?" he said, slapping Rangi and Kyoshi on their backs. "We finally have a bison again! Our best days are ahead of us!" He thrust his fists into the air and let out a whoop. "The Flying Opera Company is back in business!"

They camped along the bank of a dried-up creek, hiding themselves by virtue of being way out in the middle of nowhere. If the officers in Chameleon Bay knew what direction they'd gone in, it still would have taken at least a day by ostrich horse to catch up. They didn't bother hiding the fire Rangi blasted into the ground for them. It burned larger than they needed, sputtering and crackling from unseasoned fuel. They ate the last of the dried food.

Kirima and Wong fell asleep first, without asking about shifts. Lek waded in the waterless creek, picking up a few polished stones that caught his fancy before he settled in for the night.

Rangi was holding a grudge over how badly the day's events had gone—almost getting arrested by the local police, the *daofei* insinuating themselves into their camp, the revelations about Kyoshi's heritage—so the two of them engaged in a silent, petty contest of wills to see who would fall asleep next. Kyoshi had the advantage, knowing that there was probably a nightmare waiting for her. She made sure Rangi was truly out cold before laying the good blanket they'd kept hidden from the others over the Firebender's shoulders.

Kyoshi walked along the river, wobbling over pavestone-sized rocks that had once been underwater, until she found Lao Ge sitting under a gnarled tree. Half its roots had been washed clean in some long-ago flash flood, while the rest clung tightly to the bank. The tree's efforts were in vain. It was dying.

Lao Ge's eyes were closed in meditation. "You're very loud," he said.

She frowned. She'd practiced stepping lightly for years as a servant, to move like a whisper so as not to distract guests.

"I mean your spirit is loud," the old man said. "It rings in the air. Sometimes it screams. Like right now—your body may be all the way over there, but your spirit is grabbing me by the shoulders and howling in my face. If you went to the Spirit World in your current condition, you'd cause a typhoon the size of Ba Sing Se."

"I know who you are," Kyoshi said. "It took me a while to figure it out, but after seeing you fight so many men at once, it was clear."

He opened one eye a crack. Kyoshi had a theory that people who liked meditating practiced that gesture to look good-humored and wise.

"You're Tieguai the Immortal," Kyoshi said.

"Oh?" Lao Ge said, fully interested now. "I suppose there was a description of me in Jesa's journal? Long white hair, great dancer, devastatingly handsome?"

"It didn't have that much detail. It said you were an underworld legend rumored to be two hundred years old, but that's obviously a tall tale."

"Of course. I'm a man, not a spirit, after all."

"I know it's you because of a different description," Kyoshi said. "*Tieguai fights with a crutch.* I was looking for someone with a wooden crutch or a bad leg. Then I saw you leaning on your earthbending while you fought the lawmen in the square."

Lao Ge sighed, as if he pitied her for putting two and two together. He put his hands on his knees and raised himself to his feet. Then he tiptoed down the web of roots until he was in Kyoshi's face.

"Why would one such as yourself seek out Immortal Tieguai?" he said, no longer an old man but a human-headed monster asking a riddle in exchange for safe passage. "After all, your mother never did. She only called me Lao Ge."

The root he perched on shouldn't have been able to support a bird let alone a human being. Kyoshi swallowed hard. She had a sense of tumbling downhill, her inner ears roiling like choppy seas. An inability to go back to the harbor.

"Because she was afraid of you," Kyoshi said. "She didn't know when you first joined the group, but her suspicions grew over time that you were Tieguai the Assassin. Tieguai who killed the fortieth Earth King. She figured out that you were using her smuggling gang as cover, to travel from place to place as you eliminated targets for your own purposes. She was too scared to confront you."

The entries in her mother's hand had been completely fearless while describing dangerous smuggling jobs, burglaries, and skirmishes with local militias. They were the musings of someone who'd thrilled to the life of a *daofei*. But the journal also had patches that were rife with criminal superstition, none more so than the scattered stories about a shadow who moved across the Earth Kingdom, snuffing out lives both exalted and lowly according to some unknowable design.

Jesa the smuggler had pieced together the pattern. Whenever the silly old man in her gang slipped away by himself, a death would happen nearby. Sometimes it would be a prominent noble who should have been safe behind thick walls and numerous guards.

Lao Ge—the name had stuck hard—lowered his head and mouthed a quick prayer for the dead. "That woman always was very observant. I'm surprised I didn't catch her catching me. So what is it that her daughter wants? To bring me to justice?"

"No," Kyoshi said. "I want you to teach me how to kill someone."

If Lao Ge was surprised by her answer, he didn't show it. "Hit them in the head really hard with a rock."

"No," Kyoshi repeated. "Bending and killing are not the same thing." The image raced through her mind, the way Jianzhu had so casually done the unspeakable, first to Yun and then to Kelsang. As easy as breathing.

It needed to be that easy for her. She could afford no mental block, no hesitation when it came to taking his life. She had to be ready in all regards when she next saw Jianzhu.

A breeze in the night air puckered her skin. "You should go to sleep, girl," Lao Ge said. "Because you've already learned lesson one."

"So does that mean we'll continue later"—she decided to test the waters—"Sifu?"

"If and when I believe the time is right."

She bowed and left him to his meditations, backing away out of distrust as much as respect. Her footing was unsteady and threatened to roll her ankles. Right before she was about to turn, Lao Ge spoke up again.

"I'd appreciate it if you didn't tell the others about my independent ventures," he said. "I don't wish to complicate matters with our little merry band."

The relationship between Lao Ge and the other *daofei* was not her problem. But if that was the only leverage she had in order to get him to teach her, she'd use it. "I wouldn't dream of it, Sifu."

Lao Ge smiled benignly. It reminded her of Jianzhu's, only more genuine. It reached his eyes. He had no need to hide what he was from her.

"And in return, I'll keep *your* secret," he said. "Kyoshi."

THE AGREEMENT

KYOSHI SLEPT poorly, fretting during the night over what the old man had said. *Her secret.* First Tagaka and now Lao Ge. If every old person could look into her eyes and deduce she had unusual power, or was the Avatar, then she'd be in trouble. The only benders she'd be able to learn from would be infants like Lek.

A toe in her ribs woke her. She clawed at the hard surface under her, dirt filling her fingers instead of her sheets. She found herself blearily missing her bed.

"Get up," Rangi said. The sun hadn't risen yet, and the fire still had a few red embers glowing in it. Lao Ge was nowhere to be seen, and the others were engrossed in a three-way snoring contest. Gray predawn light made the dusty riverbank appear like it had been treated with lye, leached of color and vitality.

Kyoshi staggered to her feet. Having moved in the night, the good blanket fell off her onto the ground. "Wha-what?"

Rangi shoved her along the bank, in the opposite direction she'd taken last night. "You wanted training? Well, you're getting training. Starting today. Now."

They walked, Kyoshi feeling like a prisoner as Rangi prodded her sharply every so often for not moving fast enough. They put some distance between themselves and the camp, but much less than Kyoshi thought they would by the time Rangi ordered her to stop.

A series of grassy mounds shielded them from view of the others, but the small hills weren't very high. "Let's see your Horse stance," Rangi said. "You don't get a pass on the basics that earthbending has in common with firebending."

"We're firebending? Here?" Anyone who came searching for them would certainly check this place. They'd left Pengpeng alone with criminals who coveted her.

"We're reviewing basics, not making flame," Rangi said. "I doubt you need a lot of nuanced, high-level instruction at this point. Can you even hold a deep bending stance for ten minutes?"

"*Ten* minutes!?" Kyoshi had heard five was an admirable goal, one that she'd never reach.

There was a hint of a smirk on Rangi's lips. "Horse stance. Now. I don't say things to my students twice."

Three minutes in, and Kyoshi knew what this was. Punishment. The burning in her thighs and back, the ache in her knees, was retribution for not telling Rangi everything.

"Look, I'm sorry," she said.

Rangi rested her elbow in her other hand and examined her nails. "You're allowed to talk once your hips get to parallel."

Kyoshi swore and readjusted her bones. This had to be an exercise meant for short people. "I should have told you my mother was an Airbender. I didn't think it was relevant."

Rangi seemed satisfied with the apology. Or the amount of pain she was inflicting on Kyoshi. "It *is* relevant!" she said. "Air Nomads aren't outlaws! This is like finding out you had a second head hidden under your robes the whole while."

Maybe satisfying Rangi's curiosity would get her out of Horse stance early. "My mother was a nun born in the Eastern Air Temple," Kyoshi said. "I don't know much about her early life other than she became a master at a young age and was highly regarded."

Talking provided a useful distraction from the acid eating her muscles. "Then, on a journey through the Earth Kingdom, she met my father in a small town somewhere. *He* was the *daofei*. An Earthbender and small-time thief."

"Ugh, I can already see where this is going," Rangi said.

"Yes. He dragged her into a scheme, and she fell in love with both him and the life of an outlaw. She must have been born into the wrong existence as an Air Nomad, because she tattooed over her arrows with serpents and dove into the underworld with her whole being, seeking out more 'adventure.'"

Rangi shook her head, still not able to get over an Airbender going rogue. "That's just . . . so bizarre."

"You heard the others talk about her. She became a relatively big figure among *daofei*, more so than my father. But her airbending suffered from a spiritual taint. Or so her journal says. Letting herself be absorbed by worldly concerns, and greedy ones at that, caused her power to dwindle. So she compensated."

"With a set of fans," Rangi said, snapping her fingers at a mystery solved. "For the life of me I couldn't figure out why you had fans as an Earthbender. I didn't ask because I thought it might have been a touchy subject."

"It *is*." The searing pain in her legs had been replaced by a duller, more manageable agony. "Why do you think I never told Kelsang? *'Oh, by the way, I'm the product of one of the worst disgraces to your culture in recent memory?'* By the time I was old enough to consider bringing it up, there was no point. I had my job. I'd met you."

"Five minutes," Rangi said. "Not bad."

Kyoshi pushed the hurt to the back of her mind. "I think I can keep going."

Rangi took a lap around her, checking her posture from all angles. "It's galling. A master Airbender abandoning her spirituality for a lowlife. No offense."

"None taken. It doesn't sit well with me either."

Rangi poked her in the small of the back. "Promise me you'll never throw your life away over a *boy*," she said, her voice coated thickly with disdain.

Kyoshi laughed. "I won't. Besides, who could possibly be worth—"

The full weight of what she was saying slammed down on her midsentence like a heavy gate. Her insides boiled with disgust at her own weakness.

She'd let herself laugh. She'd spoken Kelsang's name out loud without cursing Jianzhu's in the same breath. And worst of all, she'd forgotten Yun. It didn't matter how long the lapse was. To release her grip on him, even for a second, was unforgivable.

Rangi knew it too. Her face crumpled, and she turned away. Kyoshi remembered what Lao Ge had said about her spirit making too much noise. Seeing Rangi stilled with grief in front of her drove the lesson home. The two of them held storms inside.

Kyoshi had to be stronger, in body and mind. Moments of happiness were like useful proofing, liquid testing the cracks in a jar. The less they occurred, the greater the chance she was on the right track for vengeance.

She was still in a low stance. She remembered the ineffectual Fire Fist she'd thrown in Jianzhu's face. Perhaps if she'd embraced her firebending ability earlier, she could have ended him right then and there.

"Let me try producing flame," Kyoshi said.

Rangi looked up and frowned.

Kyoshi's rededication to her cause felt hot and bitter inside her, like steam in a plugged tea kettle. She was sure that if she let it out, she could firebend. "Fire Fists," she said. "I think I can do them with real flame now. I feel like it'll work."

"No," Rangi said.

"No?" Kyoshi was taken aback by her certainty. Firebending felt so real, so close. "What do you mean, no?"

"I mean no. You're as tense as a rolled-up armadillo lion right now. You're going to produce the wrong kind of flame and develop bad habits. Watch."

Rangi stepped to the side. Without warning, she dropped into her stance and punched the air, snapping her sleeves with the force of her motion. Kyoshi could see her knuckles smolder like the tip of an incense stick.

"You need to work on relaxation and mental coordination first," Rangi said. "Early lessons in firebending are all about suppressing flame and keeping it controlled. For a beginner, making visible fire means failure."

Kyoshi scoffed to herself. Not producing flame had been the cause of her problems from the start. "Then let me try what you did." She planted her feet in mimicry of Rangi and chambered her fists.

"Kyoshi, *don't*."

She imagined Jianzhu's face, inhaled, and struck.

Her one experience at flamespitting had jiggled something loose, made it easy for her breath to spiral outward from her lungs and combust. Too easy. Energy raced down her arm and crashed into her fingers. It caused her nerves to light up with signals, as if she'd gripped a red-hot coal straight from the stove.

Instead of the crisp glow that Rangi produced, the heat that came out of Kyoshi's fist was erratic, toggling, the popping of water added to hot oil. It went on for far too long and caused far too much pain. Kyoshi fell on her back and tried to get herself pointed away from any target. She managed to aim her hand at the sky in time. A tiny, contorted spout of black smoke belched upward from her fingers.

Kyoshi sat up. Rangi watched the pathetic yarnball of vapor climb into the air. Then she gave Kyoshi a stare that was hard enough to flatten iron.

They were saved from a difficult conversation by Lek. He crested the hill next to them and traced the path of the smoke with his finger.

"What kind of broke-down firebending was that?" he said

with a snicker. He directed the question at Rangi, not having seen the source.

Rangi crossed her arms. "I had a momentary collapse of discipline," she said, still glaring at Kyoshi. "It won't happen again. Not if I ever want to firebend properly."

Lek shrugged. "Lighten up; I was just asking. If the two of you are done collapsing, breakfast is ready."

Breakfast was some manner of rodent, hunted, gutted, skinned, and burnt to the point of unrecognizability. Kyoshi and Rangi ate with big, angry bites as they sat with the *daofei* around the rebuilt fire, each trying to show the other how upset they were through aggressive gnawing.

Lek forgot his portion as he watched them, amazed. "I didn't think an army princess and a servant girl from a fancy mansion would take to elephant rat."

"Survival training at the academy," Rangi said, breaking a bone with her fingers to get at the marrow. "We learned to accept whatever food we could find in the wild."

"I used to eat garbage," Kyoshi said.

That drew stares from the group.

"I thought Jesa and Hark left you in a farming village," Kirima said.

"That doesn't mean the farmers shared food with me." Kyoshi worked her tongue around a stringy fiber of meat caught in her teeth. "They might not have known I was the child of outlaws, but I was still an outcast there. They treated me like I was unclean. And then I had to do things like this to survive, so you know. Self-fulfilling prophecy."

"Reasons like that are why I can't stand law-abiding, salt-of-the-earth folk," Wong said. "It's the holier-than-thou attitude. The hypocrisy." He wiped his hands on a leaf. "If anything, they *deserve* to be knocked out and robbed on a regular basis."

He noticed Kyoshi staring at him. "What?" he said. "I practice what I preach."

"You must have hated their guts," Kirima said.

"The villagers? Not really." Kyoshi found she meant it. "Not as much as the people who left me with them."

Lek threw the remnants of his meal into the fire and walked off, fuming silently. He disappeared behind the other side of Pengpeng, the only member of the party who seemed to make him happy.

"All right, what's his problem?" Kyoshi snapped. "Every time I state a fact or an opinion about my parents he has a fit."

"That's because he idolized them," Kirima said. "We picked him up in a town outside the Misty Palms Oasis. He'd just lost his brother, his last remaining family. Hark and Jesa took him in for a few days, and he proved useful on a job, so they taught him more and more of the trade until he grew into a stricter follower of the outlaw code than the rest of us. He worshiped the ground they walked on."

Perhaps Kirima had meant to soothe the beast inside Kyoshi, but instead she'd smeared its nose with fresh blood.

"Oh, I'm sorry," Kyoshi said, a lifetime's worth of unused irony pouring forth. "I'll remember to be nicer to the boy my mother and father decided to raise instead of me."

Kirima made a gesture with her thumbs to indicate how little she cared about the issue. "What about you?" she said to Rangi. "What's a sparky young noble like you doing with an Earth peasant?"

The mere reminder of her duty caused Rangi to sit up straighter. "I'm honor bound to follow and protect Kyoshi—"

"Nope!" Kirima said, regretting she'd asked. "Gonna cut you off right there. The last time I listened to a Firebender talk about 'honor' my ears nearly rotted off my skull. Had to kick him out of my bed with both feet."

She and Wong got up. The two older *daofei* didn't feel the need to reciprocate with their life stories. Wong pointed two fingers at the campfire and sunk it a few feet into the ground before covering it up. His size belied the dexterity of his earthbending. In fact, she'd confirmed last night that every member of her parents' gang had finesse to spare. The exact quality she was lacking.

"We need to talk," Kyoshi said, getting up as well. "Last night we were interrupted before I agreed to anything."

"Oh, come on, really?" Kirima said. "After what we've been through, you want to take your bison and ditch us in the middle of nowhere?"

"We shared a meal," Wong said, looking genuinely hurt. "We beat up lawmen together."

"My demands haven't changed," Kyoshi said. "I want bending training, and the only benders around are you lot. *You'll* teach me. Personally."

"What are you lumping me in for, Earth girl?" Kirima said. "You want to learn waterbending forms to relax and improve your circulation?"

Kyoshi had prepared an answer overnight for this purpose. "'Wisdom can be gleaned from every nation,'" she said, using a quote of Kelsang's. "If learning about the other elements can make me stronger, then I'll do it."

"That desperate for revenge, huh?" Kirima said. "Who is this powerful man who's wronged you? You never told us his name."

"That's because you don't need to know." Kyoshi didn't want to talk about Jianzhu. He was too renowned throughout the Earth Kingdom. The same went for her identity as the Avatar. Information about their link could spread, giving him a trail to hunt her down before she was ready to fight him.

Every edge would count in this battle. Kyoshi recalled the way her parents' gang had flown over the rooftops last night, unimpeded. They'd practically reached the same heights Jianzhu had with his stone bridges.

"I want to learn how to run across the sky," she said. "Like you did in town."

"Dust-stepping?" Wong said. His usually impassive face took on an edge of seriousness.

"It's our group's signature technique," Kirima said. "Though for me it's 'mist-stepping.' And it's not something you get for free."

The atmosphere had changed. Previously the *daofei* had treated Kyoshi's demands as amusing, the barking of a puppy trying to look fierce. This was the first time they'd gotten truly cautious and guarded, as if they might be swindled in the trade.

Rangi noticed their reservations. "You're acting pretty serious about a technique I cribbed after seeing it once," she said.

Kirima fixed her with a stare. "Other groups probably would have killed you for that," she said without a hint of jest. "You don't last long in our world by letting everyone see your advantages. Secrets are how we survive."

She turned back to Kyoshi. "We teach you, that means you're in. For real, and for life. You'd have to swear our oaths and follow our codes. In the eyes of those who abide by the law, you'd be a *daofei*."

I'd be like Tagaka, Kyoshi thought. *I'd be like my parents.* She stilled the revulsion inside her and nodded. "I understand."

"Kyoshi, think about what you're doing!" Rangi yelled.

"Topknot's right, for once," Wong said. "You don't take these vows lightly. It means accepting us as your brothers and sisters." He raised his brows, showing the whites of his eyes. "Since we've met you've been looking down your nose at us. Can your honor take the hit, associating with such *unclean* folk?"

The big man was more incisive than he looked. Kyoshi knew what it was like, being on the receiving end of disdain.

Her answer was yes. As far as she was concerned, her personal honor and reputation had no value. Trading them for more power was an easy choice. She would do it. For Kelsang and Yun.

She could practically feel Rangi's disappointment vibrating through the ground. "What are these oaths?" Kyoshi asked.

According to Kirima, the swearing-in ceremony was supposed to take place in a grand hall, with the initiate standing under an arch of swords and spears. They'd have to improvise. Kyoshi took a spot by the riverbank while Wong stood behind her and held a pocketknife over her head.

Kirima had Kyoshi make the same odd salute the gang had

used the night before in the teahouse. The flattened left hand represented the square folk, the law-abiding community, while the right fist hammering it down represented followers of the outlaw code. Just in case Kyoshi forgot she was joining the forces of darkness.

Rangi stalked some ways off to the side, making sure to stay within their field of vision so everyone could see how angry and disapproving she was the whole time. Kirima ignored her while conducting the ceremony. According to the Waterbender, there were normally fifty-four oaths that had to be taken, recited from memory by the new member of the gang. She had decided to let Kyoshi off easy with just the most important three.

"O spirits," Kirima exclaimed, "a lost one comes to us, seeking the embrace of family. But how will we know her heart is true? How will we know that she follows the Code?"

"I shall swear these oaths," Kyoshi said in response. "I swear to defend my brothers and sisters, and obey the commands of my elders. Their kin will be my kin, their blood my blood. Should I fail to uphold this vow, may I be hacked to death by many knives."

The words were easy to say. They caused no tugs of conflict on her spirit. Yun and Kelsang had been her lifeblood. She should have defended them with every scrap of her being. They might have lived, had she embraced her power more fully.

"Next," Kyoshi said, "I swear to follow no ruler and be beholden to no law. Should I become the lackey of any crown or country, may I be ripped apart by thunderbolts."

As a good citizen of the Earth Kingdom, this line made her a little more nervous. Yun had always said the Avatar had to act independently of the Four Nations. But to disregard law and order entirely felt like an extreme for the sake of extremes. Did her parents walk down the street trying to flaunt every statute and custom they could think of?

"Stop drifting," Kirima hissed.

Kyoshi coughed and straightened up. "Last, I swear never to make an honest living from those who abide the law. I will take no legitimate wage, and work for no legitimate man. Should I ever accept coin for my labors, may I be sliced to bits by a variety of knives."

She didn't see the difference between the first and third punishments. And the last oath was perhaps the one most inimical to her being. Back in Yokoya, a steady job had been the only barrier between her and death.

I'm not that person anymore, Kyoshi reminded herself. *That girl is gone and will never come back.*

With her third vow, she was done. "I see no stranger before me, but a sister," Kirima said. "The spirits have borne witness. Let our family prosper in the days to come." She saluted Kyoshi and stepped back.

A heavy weight slammed down on Kyoshi's collarbones, and she momentarily panicked, fearing an attack from behind. The sensation was too similar to the rock that Jianzhu had locked around her wrists. But it was just Wong giving her a congratulatory pat on the shoulders.

"Welcome to the other side," he said, unsmiling. He brushed past her like they'd finished rearranging furniture and joined Kirima in trudging back to the campsite.

Kyoshi blinked. "That's it? What happens now?"

"What happens is we leave this place on your bison," Kirima said without looking back at her. "As soon as we can."

They left her alone with Rangi. Instead of scolding Kyoshi, the Firebender simply gave her a shrug that said, *You get what you pay for.*

Kirima and Wong were already cleaning up the remnants of camp once they caught up. The big man took special care to cover their footprints, sweeping dust over the signs of their presence with little pivots of earthbending.

"The deal was for lessons," Kyoshi said.

"And you'll get them, once we pick up a score," Kirima said. She checked the level of her water pouch and made a face. "Even little baby vengeance seekers need food and money to survive. In case you haven't noticed, we're out of both. I'm not eating elephant rat for two days in a row."

Kyoshi pulled her lips over her teeth in frustration. They'd touted the seriousness of the oaths so much that she'd thought they'd start treating her like an equal after she took them. Instead they were treating her like Lek.

She had to establish a better position in the hierarchy or else this would go on forever. As Wong reached down to pick up a blanket, she stepped on it, pinning it to the ground.

He stood up and gave her a stare that had probably heralded countless brawls in the past. Kyoshi crossed her arms and met his gaze. He wasn't more dangerous than Tagaka or Jianzhu.

After trying to deal death through the power of his mind alone, Wong broke the silence. "Keep being a brat, and I'll never teach you how to use your fans," he said.

Kyoshi was going to retort out of instinct, but the implication made her pause and step back. She pulled out one of her fans. "You . . . know how to use these?"

They'd been a puzzle so far. Rangi had taken a look at the

weapons earlier, tested their balance, and concluded she couldn't teach Kyoshi much about them, other than using them as short, heavy clubs in their folded state. "They're not part of the Fire Academy curriculum," she'd said with a shrug. "Maybe you can sneak them into places you couldn't take a sword."

Wong plucked the fan out of Kyoshi's hand and snapped it open. He tossed it into the air and it spun perfectly around its pivot pin, the leaf tracing circles as it flew. He twirled around himself and caught the fan behind his back before lifting it coquettishly to his face.

"The peony sheds its beauty before the moon," he sang in a deep, beautiful, vibrant voice, using the surface of the fan to reflect and amplify the sound. *"Shamed by the light of a spirit so pure / I leap to catch its petals / and mourn for what I have left unsaid."*

He thrust the fan all around him in a series of flitting gestures, the leaf opening and closing rapidly like the beating of insect wings. It was an expertly performed dance. But Kyoshi knew it could also have been a sequence of attacks, defensive weaving, evasion and retaliation against multiple opponents.

With a flourish, Wong ended the performance in a traditional heroic pose, a deep stance with his arms spread wide, his head intentionally wobbling side to side with the leftover energy from his motions. It was a showcase of classic poetry, older than old school. Auntie Mui would have fainted with delight.

Kyoshi applauded, the only appropriate response to a display of skill that great. "Where did that come from?" she asked.

"Hark. We have a lineage through your father's side that traces back to one of the Royal Theater schools in Ba Sing Se," Kirima said. "And we stay sharp enough at performing to have plausible cover in the cities we visit. We're the Flying *Opera* Company, after all."

She raised a leg behind her, over her head, and kept it going until she completed a forward-facing, no-handed cartwheel, a move that elite dancers saved for the climax of their performances. Kirima looked like she could have done her market shopping, traveling that way.

Kyoshi was astonished. That would explain how they were so light on their feet. Royal Theater performers were known to be some of the most physically capable people in the Earth Kingdom, able to mimic dozens of martial styles on the stage and act out dangerous stunts without getting hurt. It made her feel better about the agreement they'd struck. She could get some extra value out of the bargain.

Wong folded the fan and handed it back to her. "I'll teach you to use this," he said. "For a fifth of your shares on any future jobs we do."

"Deal," Kyoshi said quickly. She didn't know what shares were, but she would have paid nearly any price to better understand her weapons.

Rangi and Kirima both smacked their hands against their foreheads, but for different reasons. "You could have gotten at least half," Kirima said to Wong.

Lek popped his head around the side of Pengpeng. "Do you want to get going, or do you want to sit here rubbing each other's backs all day?" he said.

"Hey, Lek, guess who the newest member of the gang is," Kirima said. "Official and everything."

Lek's eyebrows squeezed together in frustration. "You cannot be serious!" he yelled. He waved his arm at Kyoshi like she was a fake vase they'd brought home. "She doesn't care about the Code! She's abider chaff! She's squarer than the hole in an Earth Kingdom coin!"

"And she has a bison," Kyoshi snapped. "So unless you like walking, I suggest you deal with me being part of your stupid outlaw family." If Kirima or Wong took offense to her regression in attitude toward *daofei*, they didn't show it.

"I am *never* calling you kin," Lek spat. He went back to making final adjustments on Pengpeng's reins. He'd saddled the giant bison by himself—in impressive time too. Neither Kyoshi nor Rangi could find any fault with the work he'd done as they mounted Pengpeng.

Lek took offense at their examination. "I know what I'm doing," he said. "I probably have more practice than you two."

"If we're being perfectly honest, our whole reputation was built on Jesa's bison," Kirima said. "We might talk a good game, but Longyan did all the work. Smuggling's a cinch when you can just fly over checkpoints."

She and Wong finished loading and climbed onto Pengpeng's back. Rangi marked her territory in the driver's seat, daring Lek to challenge her for it. He compensated for his downgrade in the pecking order by pulling a crude map out of his pocket. *Real* leaders navigated and scheduled.

"We're going to a meeting post in the mountains outside Ba Sing Se," he said, denting the paper with his finger. "We'll get the latest news from other groups and find a few easy jobs to get our feet back into the water."

Rangi lifted off. The late-morning sun had yet to turn oppressive. And with the prep work having been done by extra hands, Pengpeng's unhurried climb into the cool air almost felt relaxing.

"How did the two of you get a bison?"

Lek's sudden question was tinged with suspicion and jealousy. "Neither of you were raised Air Nomad," he said. "And this girl would never let you fly her unless she'd already known you for a long time. Did you steal her from an Airbender friend?"

In her head, Kyoshi silently thanked Lek for reminding her of her duty. This was where she needed to stay. Down in the muck, painted in hatred for herself and her enemy, not flying in the wind with Kelsang. "Yes," Kyoshi said. "I did."

Rangi gave her a worried glance, not understanding why she'd lie. Lek shook his head in disgust. "Separating a monk from their bison?" he said. "That's cold. Though I should have expected such low behavior from someone who doesn't respect their mother and father."

Kyoshi said nothing and stared into the distance, where the horizon broke into jagged formations against the sky. The empty feeling was good. It absolved her of choice, allowed her to think of herself as merely a vessel, an agent of balance.

But her tranquility was broken when she noticed something missing. "Wait," she said, turning around in the saddle. "Where's Lao Ge?"

OBLIGATIONS

"I ALWAYS had a feeling I would be undone by a fancy party," Jianzhu muttered.

He and Hei-Ran were in the main library, surrounded by the map collection. The best and comically worst representations of the known world were posted on the walls behind panes of flawless crystal. Ragged, heavily used pages from nautical chartbooks hung next to cloth maps stained the color of smoked tea. Jianzhu liked this room. It portrayed the advancement of human understanding.

Hei-Ran had insisted they meet twice a day since the incident, regardless of whether there had been any updates. This afternoon, there had been an update.

She finished reading the invitation stamped with the insignia of the flying boar and tossed it on the desk. "*'The Beifong family wishes to hold a celebration for the Avatar, commemorating his victory over the pirates of the Eastern Sea in front of the gathered sages of the Earth Kingdom.'* Jianzhu, this is a bigger disaster than that 'victory.' I thought Lu Beifong agreed to be hands-off when it came to the Avatar."

"He did. It's Hui who's behind this." Jianzhu rolled the letter opener between his fingers, longing for a sharper implement and something to stick it in. "He's been at this game for the past year or so, whispering in Lu's ear that training the Avatar shouldn't be left to a man of such humble origins."

He put the blunt metal knife down. "Hui may have a point. Look how Kuruk turned out."

"We were kids back then, and so was Kuruk," Hei-Ran said. "It wasn't our responsibility to raise him."

"Hui still presents it as a strike against us," Jianzhu said. "Did Shaw respond about the shirshus?"

"No. And even if he did, there wouldn't be enough time before this *party*." One thing Hei-Ran shared with Jianzhu was a disdain for frivolities. She cracked her knuckles. "We could say the Avatar is sick."

"We could, but then I look like a bad guardian who can't keep the most important child in the world healthy. Hui will send doctors, herbalists, and spiritual healers, all insisting they see the Avatar in person for treatment. Every time we turn his agents away, it'll sow more suspicion amongst the other sages.

"No, the truth will get out," Jianzhu said, leaning back in his chair. "It's simply a matter of how long we can delay it."

Hei-Ran's military mind was already adapting. "Then we need to consolidate your allies. Find out which sages will stick by you after this debacle comes to light. It's going to end up with your faction against his, and right now we don't have a count of those numbers."

Jianzhu smiled as a possibility dangled in his head, waiting to be tugged. He could always count on his friend to seed him with ideas. These forced meetings had paid off.

"We need to do something like that," he said. He drummed the tips of his fingers together. "What's your wardrobe looking like these days?"

Hei-Ran gave him a stare that said he should be glad she didn't have the letter opener in her hands.

"I just wanted to make sure you have a nice gown ready," he said innocently. "We have a fancy party to attend."

Without Pengpeng, they made the trip to Gaoling the old-fashioned way. Slowly. In a big caravan. With lots of gifts in tow.

By the time they arrived at the estate, Jianzhu had come up with a new policy he would have to enact. Earthbenders, the most elite in the kingdom, needed to flatten out every single inch of the roads. No cost would be too great if it meant never having to suffer another skull-bouncing, teeth-clacking journey over bumpy paths.

He stepped out of his moving prison cell and squinted into the shining glory of Beifong manor. If there was anything he'd learned when he was building his own estate in Yokoya, it was that rich people's houses were all essentially the same. Walls to keep the townsfolk out. A garden as big as possible to display humility before nature. A residential quarter where that humility was tossed on its ear, preferably with as much gold and silver inlay as possible.

Chamberlain Hui greeted them at the head of a column of footmen. The short, stocky bureaucrat shielded himself from the sun with a parasol.

"Master Jianzhu," he said, raising the shade to reveal a grizzled, brick-like face. It always surprised Jianzhu how the man looked as if he spent his days breaking rocks with a pickaxe when the heaviest object he lifted was his master's ivory seal. "How was your journey?"

Unnecessary and grating, like you. "Most pleasant, Chamberlain Hui, most pleasant indeed. It's always the utmost delight to survey our magnificent nation up close."

The next carriage in the train pulled up, ostrich horses stamping their feet until the weight behind them came to a halt. Hui opened the door himself, probably so that he could be the first to take the hand of the occupant.

"Headmistress," he said, providing Hei-Ran unnecessary help out. "You look radiant. I'd swear you've stepped out of the pages of Yuan Zhen's finest love poetry."

He angled his parasol as if the sun would be deadly on her skin. It wasn't like heat and light from the sky were the source of her incredible powers, no.

Hei-Ran barely disguised her shudder at Hui being her first sight out of the carriage. "Former headmistress," she corrected.

"Ah, but educators deserve the utmost respect, for life." Hui said, his words and smile coated in oil. "Or so I've always believed."

Jianzhu felt terrible for his friend in these situations. Being a rich, beautiful, well-connected widow drew a certain breed of suitor out of the woodwork. Men like Hui could interpret the most hostile snubs as part of an ongoing courtship dance, refusing to consider the possibility that Hei-Ran wanted nothing to do with them.

"And when will Master Kelsang be joining us?" Hui said, his fingers lingering on Hei-Ran's until she yanked them away. "I noticed Avatar Yun is not with you. I assume they'll be arriving together shortly?"

The chamberlain's eyes darted around their faces, checking the corners of their lips, the dilation of their irises for involuntary twitches. Jianzhu knew that Hui played a game of details. Induction. He turned slight hints into broad generalizations that he poured into the ears of Lu Beifong and the other sages. Right now, the Avatar choosing to travel with Kelsang was obviously the sign of a slight crack, a burgeoning rift between Yun and Jianzhu. Wasn't it?

Jianzhu thought back to how he'd threatened the true Avatar, on that day everything had gone to pieces. The net cast by his power and influence over the Earth Kingdom was real, but it required constant, exhausting effort to maintain. The challengers he'd stamped out since Kuruk's death were too many to count. And now here was the latest generation of parasite, catching him at his most vulnerable.

"They are together, yes," Jianzhu said. He noticed the way Hei-Ran flinched beside him. Hui saw it too. With a smile, the chamberlain led them to the receiving hall.

The interior of the Beifong estate suffered from the rare sickness of wealth-induced monotony. It was covered from floor to ceiling in the same queasy brownish-green paint that had at one point been the most expensive shade in the Earth Kingdom. It was meant to show off just how rich the family was, but these days the main effect it had was making Jianzhu feel like he was being slowly digested in the acidic maw of a scavenger.

At the gullet of the columned hall was a double-seated dais where, over many generations, the leader of the Beifong clan and their spouse had held court. These days only one side of it remained occupied. Lu Beifong, Jianzhu's old master, sat on the oversized throne, his dust-colored robes making a tent around his wizened head at the peak.

He may have looked like a mummy held together by silk threads and spite, but his mind was aggressive as ever. "Headmistress, wonderful to see you, as always," he squawked, acknowledging Hei-Ran as fast as he could before turning to Jianzhu. "What's this about a loan for the Southern Water Tribe?"

He didn't ask about the Avatar. Nothing like a business transaction to get the old lizard crow tunneled in. Jianzhu had almost forgotten about the request he'd made to Beifong after the battle with the pirates. Work hadn't stopped simply because the Avatar's identity had been in doubt. He bowed deeply before answering.

"Sifu, I made that request because the encounter with Tagaka brought up an issue of balance between the Four Nations," he said. "The Southern Water Tribe could use assistance in developing a legitimate navy. Tagaka's presence was stifling any movement in that direction. With more far-ranging deepwater ships, they could prosper from trade and protect themselves from their neighbors, much like their Northern cousins. The loan would be for the construction of such vessels."

"*We* are their neighbors, Master Jianzhu," Hui said, materializing by Lu's side. "Why would we want to give them any position of strength relative to the Earth Kingdom? Why, they might try to claim the contested Chuje Islands with such a fleet!"

A familiar rage raised the hairs on the back of Jianzhu's neck. Hui had no real stake in this matter, not even personal greed. There was no reason for him to want the Southern Water Tribe to remain poor and undeveloped and vulnerable.

It was simply opposition for opposition's sake. Somewhere down the line, Hui had decided to make his name by using Jianzhu as a ladder, and a straw man, and whatever other analogy applied. It was easier for Hui to gain political power and fame by tearing down Jianzhu's work than doing his own.

No matter how logical and beneficial Jianzhu's actions were, Hui would undercut them. He pushed to end treaties that had taken years to develop, brushing them off as unnecessary when in truth he didn't understand how they worked and didn't care. He stoked petty rivalries he didn't have to, toying with peace that Jianzhu had earned. Had Hui been around during the height of the Yellow Neck atrocities, he would have insisted on treating that madman Xu Ping An like a folk hero.

It was times like these when Jianzhu found himself sorely missing the influence of Lu's wife, Lady Wumei. She had been an intelligent and vivacious woman, beloved across the kingdom, and a source of wisdom in Lu's ear. After her death, the old man had become more obstinate, and Hui's bold destructiveness had accelerated.

"I've spoken to the southern chieftains and they're excited

about the prospect," Jianzhu said. "They've proposed a compact of mutual defense."

"It's a good idea, Master Beifong," Hei-Ran said, adding an outsider's perspective. "Right now, the group most capable of projecting force over the Eastern Sea is ironically the Fire Navy. I'm sure the Earth Kingdom and Southern Water Tribe would prefer to command their own waters."

Lu didn't look convinced. Jianzhu didn't want this opportunity to slip away. "If it's about the Chuje Islands, they're worthless," he said. "They serve no strategic purpose other than puffing up national pride—"

He realized his mistake as soon as he said it. It wasn't like him to blunder so.

"Master Jianzhu!" Hui said with fake horror. "Surely there is no matter more important than the pride and love we have for our country! The Earth King has been vexed over those islands since his coronation. Surely you are not questioning His Majesty's judgment!"

Jianzhu would have liked nothing better than to maroon both the Earth King and Hui on one of those desolate atolls and see which idiot ate the other first. Before he could respond, Lu waved his hand.

"Enough." He heaved himself to a standing position. It was barely noticeable, given his hunch. "I side with the chamberlain. There will be no loan and no Southern Water Tribe navy unless I hear a convincing argument from the Avatar himself. I notice the boy is late. He can find me in the banquet hall with the other guests when he arrives."

Lu shuffled out of the receiving hall, the only noise the rasping of his slippers against the floor. Jianzhu couldn't believe it.

Just like that, the future had changed for the worse. The Southern Water Tribe would remain impoverished and outpaced by the rest of the world all because Hui wanted to win a debate at a party. The stupid, smug whims of one unworthy man had left fingerprints on history that weren't likely to be erased.

The Avatar could have made the difference, Jianzhu reminded himself. The thought stuck through him like a javelin.

"Master Jianzhu, I apologize for making a counterargument," Hui said. "But as you know, it's my duty to Master Beifong to make sure both sides are considered in any important decision."

"Both sides" was a rhetorical weapon used by hypocrites and the ignorant. As far as Jianzhu was concerned, Hui was no better than a *daofei*, wantonly burning fields of grain because he enjoyed watching the smoke rise over the horizon.

I would show you what I do to daofei.

"Chamberlain, it's quite all right," Jianzhu said. "I always appreciate your voice in such matters." He hesitated, adding a hitch of uncertainty to his body language, the trembling of a man who was hiding the strain of a great burden. "In fact, I need your wisdom more than ever right now. Can you join me and the headmistress to talk in private?"

The upside to the sudden confession was watching Hui nearly collapse in surprise. The man grabbed the desk in his office for support and knocked over a bottle of ink. The black liquid dripped down the chamberlain's sleeve like blood from a wound.

"YOU LOST THE AVATAR!?" he shrieked.

Jianzhu wasn't worried about being overheard. He knew from

a glance at the walls that Hui had built his plain, unadorned personal study for soundproofing. It was a safe room of secrets for a man who trafficked in them.

The more dangerous element here was Hei-Ran. Jianzhu hadn't told her he was going to tell Hui, because she would never have agreed to it. He risked driving her away, in this very moment.

"It's as I explained," he said. "Yun and I had an argument about his bending progress. More than an argument, really. I said things to him I never should have said. It got out of hand and he ran away with Kelsang's help. On a bison, the two of them could have gone anywhere in the world."

Hei-Ran's face was remarkably still, but the slight temperature increase in the room betrayed her emotions. It added to the effect of Jianzhu's ploy.

Hui was still shocked, but the wheels in his mind were already beginning to turn, his chest heaving for dramatic effect more than a need for air. "I thought the monk was the equivalent of a decorative hermit living on your estate," he said, not a good enough actor to keep out the sneer of disdain.

He was a companion of Kuruk and my friend, you little toad. "He was, or so I thought. I didn't realize he'd been plotting, waiting to seize the right moment. Our relationship had suffered over the years, but I could never have expected to this extent."

Jianzhu punched at the air, letting his real frustrations shine through. "It's Yun I should have understood better. I don't know if the damage can ever be repaired."

"It can't be that bad," Hui said, hoping with his entire heart it was truly that bad. "Children are volatile at that age."

"He—he swore upon his own Avatarhood that he would

never accept me as his master again." Jianzhu ran his thumb and forefinger over his eyes. "Chamberlain Hui, I am begging you for assistance here. The stability of our nation is paramount. If word gets out that Yun has gone rogue, then there'll be chaos."

The crack that Hui had been hoping for turned out to be a gulf the size of the Great Divide. He hadn't been prepared to strike this much gold. "Master Jianzhu, there are several prominent Earth Kingdom sages, including our benefactor, waiting for the Avatar in the grand hall," he said, thrusting his hands at the walls.

Jianzhu put on a mask he'd never worn before. Helplessness. He let his silence answer for him.

Hui composed himself, wanting to reflect the new state of affairs. He was the man in charge now. He straightened his collar and clicked his heels together. Unfortunately for him, he also forgot about the ink on his sleeve, ruining the effect of tidiness.

"Master Jianzhu, there's no need to worry," he said. "I'll handle this."

In the end, Hui told Lu Beifong and the assembled sages the exact line that Jianzhu had used on his own household. Yun felt he'd been neglecting his spiritual studies. After much pleading, Jianzhu had given him leave to travel alone with Kelsang on a nomadic journey of self-discovery, avoiding such obvious destinations as the Air Temples or the Northern Oasis. Yun had been to those places. He needed to grow along his own path, untrammeled by expectations.

It meant no contact from the Avatar for a while. The world would have to get along without one until further notice.

Jianzhu could have said as much himself, but coming from Hui, the story was so much more effective. It was an open secret among the party guests that the chamberlain was waging political war against him. The only thing they would ever align on were basic, incontrovertible facts. Like the Avatar going on a vacation.

The rest of the visit was spent on trivialities. Jianzhu weathered the severe annoyance and biting remarks of Lu Beifong, wondering how many more years he'd have to put up with groveling before his former *sifu*. The old man seemed like he would never kick the bucket while debtors owed him money, and nearly the entire Earth Kingdom banked with the House of the Flying Boar.

Hei-Ran stood dull-eyed in the corner as men prodded for her thoughts on remarriage, in language they thought was subtle and flattering. Some of them, upon hearing her rebuff, immediately pivoted to inquiring about her daughter. Jianzhu never understood how she resisted the temptation to bend scorched holes into the ceiling when her element was always available.

They left when the party became too much to bear, getting into a single carriage for the journey back. Hei-Ran's admirers could have interpreted that a certain way. But the two of them simply needed to talk.

"I know you're angry at me," Jianzhu said. He slumped back against his seat.

"About what?" Hei-Ran snapped. "The fact that you revealed your biggest setback to your worst enemy? That you're piling lies upon lies for no reason I can see? Why didn't you tell Hui the excuse he gave to the crowd?"

"Because vulnerability equals truth. The only statement of mine Hui would take at face value was one that left me exposed. Now my story's set with the vast majority of the Earth Kingdom. I only have a single opponent to worry about."

She didn't look very confident in his tactic. Firebenders thought in terms of positive *jing*, always staying on the offensive. "It's getting a little difficult to keep track of the wind spewing out of your mouth at this point."

Imagine how hard it is for me. "All warfare is based on deception," he said. "Isn't that a Fire Nation quote?"

Hei-Ran suddenly pulled her hairpin out of her tightly bundled style and hurled it against the wall of the coach. It clattered to the floor, the arms bent.

For the first time today, Jianzhu was truly alarmed. For a Fire Nation native to treat her hair, her topknot, this way meant she felt she was losing her honor. He waited patiently for her to speak.

"Jianzhu, I pushed that boy to the breaking point," she said, her voice hoarse. "He might not have been a Firebender, and he might not have been the Avatar, but Yun was still my student. I had an obligation to him, and I failed."

Hearing his name all night must have been eating at her. The absent Avatar was still the toast of the party, his conquest of the pirates turning into legend through word of mouth.

"We can still make this right," Jianzhu said. "We simply need to find Kyoshi. Everything will be fine after that."

"If that's the case, and I don't think it is, you set ablaze the time we had left and scattered the ashes. As soon as that party is over, Hui is going to march straight to the other sages and tell them what you told him. He might not wait. It'll be the conversation topic over dessert."

"It'll be longer than that," Jianzhu said. "He's not going to waste an opportunity of this magnitude by hurrying. In fact, if he plays the information too quickly and carelessly, it'll bite him in the end. He's a man of self-preservation."

Hei-Ran tucked herself into the corner of the carriage, her bunched-up gown turning her into a shapeless mass. "I wish I could say the same about you these days."

To get the last word in, she aggressively went to sleep. Jianzhu noticed that people who were former military could doze off anywhere, anytime at the drop of a hat. After an hour of silence, he began to drift in and out of consciousness himself, shaken awake by the occasional road bump, his thoughts forming loose connections and ideas that he made no attempt to preserve.

It wouldn't do to plot too far out. Sometimes the best option was to sit quietly until the next step arrived in turn, like an Earthbender should. Neutral *jing*.

When they arrived home in Yokoya, there was a very validating delivery waiting for them. Jianzhu didn't bother waking up Hei-Ran and hopped out of the coach, invigorated by the sight.

In the distance, by the stables, were two extremely large wooden boxes, each the size of a small hut, peppered with little holes. The sides of the crates had *Danger!* and *Give Wide Berth* painted on them in a slapdash manner. Surrounding them was a crew of underpaid university students warily brandishing long forked prods. They pointed their weapons inward at the boxes. Theft of the contents was not the primary concern.

At the head of the group was a portly older gentleman in fine robes, wearing a helmet made of cork. He was geared for adventure in the habit of academics who had no idea how dirty and bloody true adventure could get.

"Professor Shaw!" Jianzhu called out.

The man waved back. Behind him, the boxes suddenly started rattling and jumping, scaring the handlers. A long, whiplike strand shot out of a hole punched in the side and lashed two of the nearest students across the face and neck before they could react. They screamed and collapsed to the ground in a heap like rag dolls.

Professor Shaw looked at his downed interns and then gave Jianzhu a big grin and a thumbs-up.

That must have meant the shirshus were in good health after their journey. Excellent. Jianzhu needed them in peak condition. The beasts' impeccable sense of smell would let them track a target across a continent. Oceans, if the rumors were to be believed.

He'd sent word out to his subordinates across the kingdom, the magistrates and prefects he'd spent years buying off, telling them to be on the lookout for two girls who'd escaped his estate. But it never hurt to have a backup plan that didn't rely on the shifting loyalty and ballooning greed of men.

One way or another, he was going to fulfill his promise to the Avatar. There would be no hiding for Kyoshi. Not in this world.

THE TOWN

THE TAIHUA Mountains south of Ba Sing Se were treacherous beyond measure. They were said to have swallowed armies in the days of the city's founding. Howling blizzards could freeze a traveler's feet to the ground, snapping them off at the ankles. Once every decade or so, the winds would shift, carrying red dust from Si Wong to the peaks of Taihua, polluting the snow a fearsome bloody color, turning the mountains into daggers plunged through the heart of the world.

Pengpeng sailed over the dangerous terrain, unbothered. From their vantage point Kyoshi and the others could see any weather sneaking up on them, and right now it was clear in every direction.

"This is the life," Lek said. He rolled over onto his side, reaching over the saddle, and patted her fur. "That's a good girl. Who's a good girl?"

He'd been trying to get the bison to like him more than Kyoshi and Rangi at every available opportunity. Kyoshi didn't mind so much. It meant Lek took care of foraging and watering for Pengpeng. Like she had her own stablehand.

"Oof, I'm glad you remembered to come back for me," Lao Ge said. "There's no way I could have made it here on my own." The old man yawned and stretched, catching as much of the breeze between his arms as he could. "I have to remember not to wander off by myself for too long."

His comment made Kyoshi's stomach constrict. The journal said that Lao Ge came back from his jaunts with blood on his hands. She wondered if her mother had sat this close to him as they traveled, afraid that she might be one of his victims in the future.

"We're way past the last charted outposts," Rangi said from the driver's seat. "Beyond that, the mountains haven't been mapped."

"Yeah, an outlaw town isn't going to be on a map," Kirima said. "This is the exact flight path we used to take with Jesa. Keep going."

As they flew toward a line of jutting gray peaks, the mountains separated, gaining depth. The formation was less a ridge and more of a ring that obscured a crater from all sides. The depression held a small, shallow lake that Kyoshi thought was brown and polluted at first. But as they flew closer, she saw the water was as clear and pure as could be. She'd been looking straight through the lake to the dirt bottom.

Next to the lake, built into the slope like a rice terrace, was an encampment slightly more handsome than the slums of Chameleon Bay. Longhouses had been constructed out of mountain lumber hauled from the forests down below. Several of them sat on makeshift piles, fighting a losing battle against erosion. Glinting with openly carried weapons, people filed in between the gaps and along the streets.

"Welcome to Hujiang," Kirima said. "One of the few remaining places in the world where Followers of the Code gather freely."

"Is everyone down there a *daofei*?" Kyoshi said.

"Yes," Wong said. He frowned at the crowds below. "Though it seems more busy than usual."

They'd approached with the sun behind them out of caution. Lek pointed Rangi toward a cave farther away where Kyoshi's mother used to hide Longyan. They landed Pengpeng there, camouflaged her with fallen branches and shrubs, and suffered the lengthy hike to town.

The longtime members of the Flying Opera Company were prepared for the fine silt that rose from the winding, narrow path, stirred by their footsteps. They pulled close-woven neckerchiefs over their noses and mouths and smirked underneath when Kyoshi and Rangi looked askance at them with reddened eyes. The group was still figuring out what courtesies to share. Apparently spare dust masks fell by the wayside.

Rounding the mountain, they entered Hujiang from above, carefully picking their way down crudely carved steps that were oversized to cut down on the number needed. Kyoshi wondered why they weren't earthbent into shape.

They came to one of the large streets and lowered their scarves. "You should probably keep your head down this time," Rangi said to Kyoshi. "Instead of barging in like you own the place." The debacle in Chameleon Bay still weighed on her mind.

"No!" Kirima hissed. "You act meek in this town, and everyone will think you're weak! Follow our lead."

As they joined the flow of traffic, the Waterbender seemed to grow in stature, expanding her presence. Kirima normally retained a certain amount of elegance to her movements, but now she stepped through the crowd with exaggerated purpose and delicacy. She gazed through lidded eyes down the length of her chin as she walked, a picture of sophistication, a swordswoman moving through a form with a live blade. Interrupting her flow would mean getting cut to shreds.

"Gotta look like you're ready to take someone's head off at any moment, for any reason," Wong said. "Or else you'll get challenged." He followed Kirima with angry stomps, abandoning the agility Kyoshi knew he possessed. His feet sent seismic thuds through the ground.

"Topknot's got it," Lek said, pointing at Rangi. "Look at her, boiling away with Firebender rage. See if you can pull that off."

"I'm not doing anything," Rangi protested. "This is my normal face."

"You could also try to be like me!" Lao Ge said. He hunched inside his threadbare clothes, hiding his muscles, and flashed his manic, gap-toothed smile. He looked like the group's shameful grandfather who'd escaped from the attic.

"Picking a fight with you would be a disgrace," Lek said.

"Exactly!"

They made their way toward the bazaar in the center of town. It was slow going, trying to look tough. And not just for them. The other outlaws swaggered along the avenues, chests thrust out, elbows wide. A few favored Kirima's approach of razor-edged refinement, carrying narrow *jian*s instead of broadswords to complete the image.

Practically everyone was armed to the teeth. Most with swords and spears, but more exotic weapons like three-section staves, deer-horn blades, and meteor hammers were surprisingly common as well. Kyoshi spotted a few people wielding arms that should have been flat-out impossible to fight with. One man had a basket with knives lining the edge and a tether trailing off it.

"Is that guy carrying a muck rake?" Rangi whispered, tilting her head at a pug-nosed man waddling by.

"That's Moon-Seizing Zhu, and don't stare at the rake," Lek said. "I've seen him puncture the skulls of two men at once with it."

The Flying Opera Company had by far the least amount of metal on their persons. "Most of these people don't seem like benders," Kyoshi said.

"What, are you looking to trade us in for better teachers?" Kirima said. "Because you're right—they're not benders. Most outlaws live and die by the weapons in their hands. Our crew is a rarity."

"Honestly, I think you should appreciate us more," Wong said.

Kyoshi was distracted by a clatter of metal to the side. Two men, both carrying swords, had bumped into each other as they rounded a corner in opposite directions. The street slowed around them. Kyoshi's stomach churned as she anticipated a surge of violence, gore running through the gutters.

It never came. Blades stayed in their scabbards while the men apologized profusely to each other, acting as friendly as two merchants who were planning a marriage between their children. There were promises to buy cups of tea and wine for each other before they parted ways. The happy smiles stayed on their faces long after the encounter.

"They'll meet on the challenge platform tonight," Lek said. "Probably during the weapons portion of the evening." He made a bloody, strangled noise that made it obvious what the outcome would be.

"What?" Kyoshi said. "That wasn't a big deal!"

"You don't understand," he said. "In this world, the only currency you have is your name and your willingness to defend it. If either of those men showed fear or poor self-control, they'd never get taken on by an outfit again. They had no other options."

"They could stop being *daofei*," Rangi muttered.

"Like it's so easy to do whatever you want!" Lek's face was full of bitterness. "You think honest work rains down from the sky? This is why the two of you are the worst! No one takes up this life on purpose!"

"Lek," Kirima warned.

His shouting had drawn attention. Eyes watched them from the windows and porches of houses, anticipating a second act to tonight's performance.

Lek calmed down. "Keep walking," he said to Rangi and Kyoshi. "Show them we're together, and it'll be fine."

Kyoshi had no objection to following his lead this time. She controlled her posture with renewed seriousness. They resumed picking their way through the town.

"There's an expression in these parts," Wong said, his low grumble giving the argument a close. "When the Law gives you nothing to eat, you turn to the Code. Then at least you can feast on your pride."

The Hujiang bazaar was . . . a bazaar. Not much different from the one in Qinchao Village, which neighbored Yokoya. Vendors sat cross-legged next to piles of their wares on tarps laid over the ground, scowling at passersby who kicked up too much dust or lingered without buying. The sounds of haggling rang out in the air. Here, it was safe to let loose with aggression. There seemed to be a distinction between the warriors and the black marketeers who supplied them.

Kyoshi noticed that most of the peddlers specialized in traveling food: dried and smoked meats, beans and lentils. Rice was expensive: produce more so. The "fresh" vegetables were brown and wilted, and the rare pieces of shriveled fruit looked more like decorative antiques.

"How did this stuff travel up here?" she asked. "For that matter, how did the people?"

"There're unmarked passageways through the mountains," Kirima said. "More trade secrets. The royal surveyors in Ba Sing Se don't have a clue."

That must have been a big part of why *daofei* were so hard to stamp out for good. Kyoshi reflected on what Jianzhu had told her, about the Earth Kingdom being too big to police. If underground networks like this one could thrive so near the capital, then the rot must be worse throughout the far reaches of the continent. A whole other community existed below the surface of the Earth Kingdom.

The moniker of the Fifth Nation pirate fleet suddenly took on a defiant meaning. *We're here,* Kyoshi imagined their formidable leader saying with an ice-blue stare. *We've always been here. Ignore us at your peril.*

Wong's foot caught on a brass oil lamp. The vendor it belonged to cursed before looking upward and silencing himself willingly. With his size, the Flitting Sparrowkeet didn't need name recognition. First glances were enough.

"It's crowded," Wong repeated. He'd been fixated on that since they'd arrived.

Kirima and Lek took his complaint seriously. They lifted their heads higher, scanning the bazaar. Kyoshi tried to help, but she had no idea what to look for.

"East by northeast," Rangi said. "They're listening to someone speak."

Sure enough, the people gathered in that corner of the bazaar had their backs turned, showing *dao* broadswords or other weapons strapped to their torsos. They nodded intently, absorbing whatever message was being preached to them. Someone found the leader a stool or a crate, because he stepped upward to reveal an ugly face bisected by a leather strap.

Lek and Kirima both swore loudly. "We've got to get out of here," Lek said. "Now."

"What's the problem?" Rangi said.

"The problem is we shouldn't have come here," Kirima said. "We've got to leave town. As fast as possible."

"Don't make eye contact!" Lek said as Kyoshi tried to get one last glance at the man. The strap looked like it was holding his nose in place. His speech had reached a fever pitch, his jaws working up and down like he had a chunk of meat between them. Strangely, he had a moon peach blossom tucked into his collar.

She didn't have time to see any more details. They hustled back the way they came. Only to run into someone in the exact same spot as the earlier encounter they'd witnessed. That blind spot was a death trap.

Lek's face fell in despair. He backed up a few steps and bowed sharply using the same fist-over-hand salute from when he'd greeted Kyoshi for the first time. So did Kirima and Wong.

"Uncle Mok," they said in chorus, keeping their heads lowered.

The man they waited on for a response was dressed in plain merchant's robes. His spotlessness stood out in the dusty filth of the town. He was strikingly handsome, with narrow eyes resting over fine cheekbones. And there was a moon peach blossom tucked into his lapel.

He couldn't have been older than Kirima. Kyoshi didn't understand why they were calling him "Uncle."

"Bullet Lek," Uncle Mok said. "And friends. You made the long journey from Chameleon Bay."

"It had been too long since we felt the embrace of our brethren," Lek said, trembling. In the short time she'd known him, Kyoshi had never heard the boy speak with such deference. Or fear.

"And you brought extra bodies?" Mok eyed the two new members of the group.

Rangi had already matched the bows of the others, calculating that sometimes it was better to keep quiet and play along. Kyoshi tried to do the same, but not without Mok catching her using the wrong hands at first.

"Fresh fish," Kirima explained, raising her head only slightly. "We're still beating respect and tradition into them. Kyoshi, Rangi, this is our elder, Mok the Accountant."

There was no mention of an "elder" Mok in the journal. As far as Kyoshi knew, her parents were the elders of the group.

"See that you do," Mok said with what he deemed a warm smile. "Without our codes, we are nothing but animals, begging for fences. It's fortuitous that you're here, for I have business to discuss with you."

"How lucky we are," Wong said. If it rankled him, bowing to a younger man, he kept it to himself. Kyoshi noticed that Lao Ge had managed to disappear yet again. She wondered if it was solely so he didn't have to call Mok "Uncle."

"Let's discuss it tonight," Mok said. "Why don't you join me as my guests at the challenge platform? When there's this many people in town, blood runs high. Should be fun!"

"It would be our distinguished honor, Uncle," Rangi said, beating the others to the punch. "Our gratitude for the invitation."

Mok beamed. "Fire Nation. It's wonderful how respect comes so naturally to them." He reached out and knocked Lek's headwrap to the ground so he could tousle the boy's hair.

"I remember when I first met this one," he said as he fixed Kyoshi with his slitted gaze. His fingers gripped Lek's scalp, yanking and twisting his head around, making sure it hurt. "He was such a mouthy little brat. But he learned how to act."

Lek put up with the manhandling without a noise. Mok cast him to the side like an apple core. "I hope you're an equally quick study," he said to Kyoshi, making a clicking noise with his teeth.

After Mok left, no one spoke. They waited for Lek to pick up his hat off the ground and smooth his hair. His eyes were red from more than dust.

Kyoshi had questions, but she was afraid of saying them out loud in the street. She knew exactly what kind of man the Accountant was.

Jianzhu had once implemented a policy that any member of the staff, no matter how lowly, could talk to him personally about any household concern. Kyoshi saw the gesture of kindness devolve into some of the servants ratting each other out over minor grievances, hoping to curry favor. She knew now that had been his intent all along.

The longhouse-lined streets of Hujiang felt like the walls of the mansion during the worst of the paranoia. She had no doubt that a careless word risked making it to Mok's ears. She followed her group to a termite-eaten inn that hadn't been painted since Yangchen was alive. Many of the outlaws they passed along the way had moon peach blossoms in various states of freshness placed somewhere on their person. She couldn't believe how dumb she was not to have noticed before.

They paid for a single room and tromped up the stairs, a funeral procession. Inside their lodgings, the bare planks of the floor had been oiled by the touch of human skin. There weren't enough beds if they were planning to sleep here tonight.

"This is one of the tighter-built houses," Kirima said after she shut the door and slumped against a wall. "It'll be safe to talk as long as you don't shout."

Wong stuck his head out the window and did a full sweep of the street below, craning his head upward to check the roof. He pulled himself back in and latched the shutters closed. "I suppose you want an explanation," he said.

"Those hard times we mentioned back in Chameleon Bay," Kirima said. "They were pretty hard. After your parents died, Jesa's bison escaped, and we never saw him again."

Kyoshi understood that much. The link between Air Nomads and their flying companions was so strong that the animals would normally run away and rejoin wild herds if they lost their Airbender. It was a complete miracle that Pengpeng had stuck around to help her.

"We were trapped in the wrong city with too many debts to the wrong people," Kirima continued, ignoring the irony that by most standards *they* were *the wrong people*. "We were desperate. So we accepted the Autumn Bloom Society as our elders in exchange for some favors and cash."

"The peach flower guys," Wong said.

Moon peaches normally bloomed in spring, but then again these were *daofei*, not farmers. "I take it this group is now beholden to the Autumn Bloom?" Rangi said.

"It seemed like a safe move at the time," Kirima said. "After the Yellow Necks scattered, there were so many smaller societies grubbing for the scraps. Mok and the Autumn Bloom started off as nothing special. But then they began to squeeze the other outfits."

"And by squeeze we mean crush them to a pulp and suck on the bloodstains," Wong said.

"They were barely concerned with turning a profit," Kirima said, shaking her head at the greatest outrage of all. "The law hasn't caught wind of them yet because they've yet to make any big plays aboveground."

"Well, I can guarantee you that's about to change," Rangi said. "What we saw in the bazaar was a campaign muster. A recruitment drive. Mok has big plans ahead."

"And we're signed up now," Kirima said. "If we disobey a summons by our sworn elders, our name will be worth less than mud. We'll be worse off than before we met the Autumn Bloom."

"Plus he'll, you know, kill us," Wong said.

Lek thumped the back of his head against the wall. "Mok owns us now," he said. He sounded like he was speaking through an empty gourd. "Our independence was Jesa and Hark's pride. And we threw it away. Because of me."

"Lek," Kirima said sharply. "You were injured and would have died without treatment. We've been over this."

"Stung by a buzzard wasp," Lek said to Kyoshi and Rangi. He laughed with a bitterness that had to have been developed over many nights of reflection. "Can you believe it? Like I was fated to be this group's downfall."

"Jesa and Hark would have made the same decision in a heartbeat," Kirima said.

Kyoshi's breath rushed in and out through her nose. Slowly at first, and then faster and faster, until her lungs felt like they'd escape through the holes in her skull.

She remembered scraping her head against the frozen ground when she was little, trying to seek relief for the fever blazing within her body. She remembered trying to walk again after untreated sickness sapped her muscles, not being certain if the shaking would ever go away.

Was it possible to enter the Avatar State through sheer contempt? She stared at the *daofei*, lost in their own histories. What did they know, huh? *What did they know?* They'd had each other. Family willing to make sacrifices. She had no doubt that Jesa and Hark would have done anything for their gang. Just not their daughter. Sworn ties trumped blood ties. Wasn't that the lesson that needed to be etched into her bones?

"Oh, *boo-hoo*," Kyoshi snapped. "How pathetic of you."

They turned their heads toward her. She refused to look at any one of them, instead staring at a blank spot on the wall where a knot had fallen out of the wood, leaving a dent in the plank.

"So your choices had consequences," Kyoshi said. "That's not the definition of a raw deal. That's life. You made your bed with Mok's, and I made mine with yours. *I* should be the one complaining."

She wished she had a spitting habit so she could add the appropriate color to what she was saying. "If he wants us to show up tonight, then we show up tonight. We do whatever he wants us to do. And then we all can *get what we came here for*."

She ended her statement a hair's breadth from shouting. A long silence followed.

"Kyoshi's got a point," Kirima said. The wall creaked as she took her shoulder off it. "We have no choice but to take things one step at a time."

"She didn't have to be so mean," Wong muttered.

After Kyoshi's outburst, Rangi asked the others for a moment alone with her. They filed out like sullen children. The room transformed from too small to too big.

"Don't yell at me," Kyoshi said preemptively. "None of this Autumn Bloom nonsense was in the journal."

"And yet here we are anyway," Rangi said. She seemed at a loss for what to say. She pointed in different directions to emphasize rants she hadn't made yet.

Eventually she settled for a question. "Do you know what it's like, watching you sink deeper into this muck?"

"I'm doing what's necessary," Kyoshi said. "If you want me to make faster progress, then let's go find an isolated spot and practice more firebending."

"Kyoshi, you're not listening to me." Rangi instinctively lowered her voice to protect their secret. "You're the Avatar."

"I remember, Rangi."

"*Do* you?" she said. "Do you really? Because the last time I checked, the Avatar is supposed to be shaping the world for the good of humans and spirits, not risking their neck to help a bunch of second-story thieves pay off their debts!"

She held back from punching the nearest wall. "Did you know that the Avatar is supposed to be able to commune with their past lives, gaining access to the wisdom of centuries?"

she said. "With the right lessons, you could have been asking Yangchen herself for guidance right now. But no! You don't have that option, because my guess is that spiritual teachers are a little hard to come by in our current social circle!"

Rangi waved her hand around at the room, at Hujiang, at the Taihua Mountains themselves. "To see you here? It kills me. The fact that you're stuck here, where no one knows who you truly are, makes me die a little inside with each passing moment. You're meant to have the best of everything and instead you have *this*."

She rubbed at the creases in her forehead with her fingers. "A *daofei* town! A normal Avatar would have been responsible for wiping this encampment off the face of the earth!"

So she was upset about Kyoshi neglecting her duties. And nothing more. Rangi wanted a normal Avatar. Not whatever Kyoshi was.

She's a true believer. Yun's words came back like he was standing beside her, whispering in her ear. Rangi couldn't handle any more disgrace to the office. Kyoshi was poor raw material for an Avatar to begin with, and her selfish choices had only defiled the position further.

"Rangi." Kyoshi's heart felt harder than it ever had, dull metal weighing her chest down. "The world waited years for an Avatar. It can wait a little longer. And so can you."

She thought she heard a little puff of breath come from behind Rangi's hands. But when the Firebender lowered her arms, she was as calm and stony as the mountain.

"You're right," Rangi said. "After all, I'm just your bodyguard. I have to do what you say."

Nightfall did Hujiang a favor in appearance. Unlike honest folk who went to bed soon after the sun went down, the *daofei* settlement lit up with torchlight to continue business. The slope of the mountain spread out below the inn looked like it had attracted a cloud of fireflies.

A meal of rice gruel and dried sweet potato did little to help them relax. Before they left the inn, Lek tightened the thongs covering his sleeves with such ferocity that Kyoshi was afraid his hands would go purple.

"Are you okay?" she asked.

"I'm worried about Pengpeng, is all," he said defiantly. "Don't let it slip that we have her. Mok would probably kill us and try to tame her himself."

It made more and more sense, the degree to which outlaws coveted a sky bison. Flight was normally a feat restricted to the pure of heart. As an Airbender willing to sully herself with dirty work, Kyoshi's mother must have been in high demand.

The streets were emptier than during the day. The *daofei* had gathered inside drinkhouses, and drinkhouses seemed to comprise half the town. Kyoshi could hear laughter and arguments and poorly composed poetry spilling from the windows they passed. She imagined Lao Ge was in one of the taverns, swindling for booze. Or indulging in his other hobby.

They came to a house bigger than the others. A broad, high barn that shook with noise. The shouting inside rose and fell in waves, punctuated with cries of delight or disappointment. Another man wearing a peach flower in his hat greeted them at the door.

"Uncle Mok is waiting for you on the balcony," he said as he bowed.

Going inside, they were immediately absorbed by a throng of spectators. The center of the floor held a large wooden platform covered with a tightly drawn layer of canvas held down with ropes, giving the structure the appearance of a great drum. Two men circled each other warily on top, stepping through stances, refusing to blink as sweat gathered on their faces.

"*Lei tai*," Kirima said to Kyoshi. "Ever seen one before?"

She hadn't. She knew of earthbending tournaments with a similar concept—knock the opponent off the platform and you win. But this stage was made of unbendable material, and the two men were fighting bare-knuckled and empty-handed. Throwing the opponent off would require closing the distance and getting to grips in ways benders normally disregarded.

Lek had mentioned a weapons portion of the evening. Now must have been the unarmed combat rounds, serving as a warm-up. The two men charged each other. Fists cracked against skulls. One of them got the better of the exchange and followed up with a devastating kick to the side of his opponent.

"Liver shot," Kyoshi heard Rangi mutter. "It's over."

She'd seen the outcome before the loser did. He tried to resume his fighting stance but couldn't raise his arms. In a slow, teetering arc that reminded Kyoshi of a cut tree, he fell to the surface of the platform, clutching his torso.

Kyoshi expected the standing man to peacock in victory, spend some time basking in the adulation of the crowd. Instead he pounced on his downed opponent, who was clearly unable to continue, and began punching him viciously in the head.

"Here's a lesson for you square folk," Wong said. "It's over when the winner says it's over."

Kyoshi had to turn away. She heard dull, wet thuds inter-spersed with the cheers of the crowd and nearly threw up on her feet. She was listening to a man get beaten to death.

There was a round of boos, and she looked up. The man left standing had decided to stop the assault, though Kyoshi could tell the decision was less about mercy and more about saving energy. He went back to one corner of the platform where attendees had placed a stool for him to sit. He held out his hand, and a cup of tea appeared in it. Being the champion came with some perks.

Two volunteers carried off his vanquished opponent by the arms and legs. Only a cough of blood spray gave any indication the man was still alive.

Kyoshi wanted to get this over with as fast as possible. "Where's Mok?" she said.

"There." Kirima pointed to the second level. Kyoshi's suspi-cions were correct; this place *was* a barn. The "balcony" was a converted hayloft. Mok sat on a giant, thronelike chair that had to have been lifted into place with pulleys. Beside him stood the strap-nosed man from the bazaar, the one who'd been recruiting outlaws with spiritual zeal.

The Flying Opera Company went up the old-fashioned way, and they had to do it one at a time. The three more experienced members went first. Kyoshi felt eyes on her as she climbed the long ladder, vulnerable with each bounce and sway of the wooden struts.

Mok had no guards with him, other than the street preacher. And the others had told her neither of them were benders. Either *daofei* were stingy when it came to personal protection, or they preferred to display strength this way. "This is my lieutenant,

Brother Wai," Mok said, gesturing to the wild-eyed man. "You will pay him the same respect that you do me."

Kyoshi bowed along with the others, but Wai was silent. He stared at the group with seething contempt, like he detected the taint of evil buried deep in their bones. She became conscious of her flayed leg that had scabbed over, of the waking nightmare she'd pushed to the back of her mind. But Wai paid her no special attention. He despised them all equally.

Mok, on the other hand, singled Kyoshi out. "New girl," he said. "You seemed a little blood-shy just now. Not a trait I like in my subordinates."

Wong and Kirima tensed up. They'd warned her about the need to keep a certain mask on, and she hadn't taken them seriously enough. Kyoshi tried to think of something to say that would placate Mok.

"She's tough when it counts, Uncle," Lek interjected. "I personally saw Kyoshi wipe the floor with a whole squad of lawmen back in Chameleon Bay."

Mok made a signal with his finger. In a motion so smooth that it looked rehearsed, Wai pulled out a knife, grabbed Lek by the hand, and slashed him across the palm. Lek stared disbelievingly at the fresh red wound for a moment.

"Funny," Mok said. "I don't think I was talking to you."

A spatter of blood landed on the floor. Lek doubled over, clutching his hand to his stomach, and stifled a scream. Wong and Kirima's faces were white with anger, but they maintained their positions, shoulders hunched in deference.

Kyoshi forced herself to look this time, to watch Lek suffer. Mok was testing her, she realized. Her weakness had gotten her companion hurt, and this was the price.

Her limbs went cold as a vision of the future swept her in its embrace. She was going to sort this Mok one day. Neatly on the shelf, right below Jianzhu. Him and Wai both. They'd have a place of honor in her heart.

But for now, the face she gave them was made of stone. She saw Lek straighten up and tug his sleeve over the wound, clenching his jaw and fist tight. He stared at the space between his shoes. Other than the bloodstain blooming at the end of his shirt, she would have been hard-pressed to tell that he was injured.

"Better this time," Mok said to Kyoshi. "Unless for some reason you don't like the boy."

She made a noncommittal little shrug. "There's not many people I hate, Uncle." The truth made it easier to remain calm.

"A fast learner indeed!" Mok caught a glimpse of something interesting happening below. The crowd roared, half of them booing and the other half expressing wild approval for whatever it was. He grinned and turned his full attention back to the center of the barn. "Not as fast, though, as your Firebender friend."

Kyoshi followed his gaze. It took all of her newfound willpower not to shriek in horror.

Rangi was standing on the fighting platform.

"The beautiful thing about *lei tai* is that anyone can issue a challenge," Mok said. "Simply by doing what she's doing."

Kyoshi had to look at the empty ladder again to make sure she wasn't dreaming, that Rangi hadn't followed right behind her as usual. To confirm that she could have gone so long without noticing her friend's presence.

The champion, still sitting in the opposite corner, cocked his head in interest. Rangi met his gaze as she stripped off her bracers and shoulder pieces, throwing her heirloom armor to the ground like a fruit peel. Ignoring howls and whistles from the crowd, she disrobed until she was in the sleeveless white tunic she wore beneath her outer layers.

Rangi was above the average height for a girl. The muscles in her arms and back were well-formed and strong from years of training. But her opponent was taller and outweighed her by a third, if not more. She looked so tiny and vulnerable on the canvas, a small flower in the corner of a painting.

Kyoshi nearly jumped down from the hayloft to throw herself between the combatants. But Kirima and Wong gave her the same glance and imperceptible headshake from when Lek was cut. *Don't. You'll make it worse.*

The champion ran a hand down his braided queue and squinted at Rangi with beady eyes. He dabbed himself with a towel and flung it behind him. As he rose, his attendant plucked the stool off the platform. He'd rested enough. The man raised his chin and said a few words that Kyoshi couldn't hear, but she guessed their meaning well enough.

No firebending.

Rangi nodded in agreement.

A lance went through Kyoshi's heart as the two of them approached each other. The champion didn't take a stance immediately. If he took the challenge of a young girl too seriously, he'd lose face.

Rangi let him know how wise that decision was by whirling a kick at the knee he was about to put his weight on. Only pure reflex saved him. He snatched his leg back before it snapped in half, and stumbled awkwardly around the platform, a drunk that had lost his footing. The crowd jeered.

"*This* girl," Mok said with a tone of appreciation that sent fresh loathing down Kyoshi's throat.

The champion righted himself and took up a deep stance. The disciplined movement in his lower body was at odds with the wrath coursing through his face.

As if to taunt him further, Rangi slid forward fearlessly until she was within his striking distance. Her expression was cool, impassive. It didn't change when the man launched a flurry of blows. She read his limbs like the lines of a book, letting his momentum pass right by her as she made pivots so small and sharp that her feet squeaked against the canvas.

After he missed a straight punch that hung over her neck like a yoke, she bumped him in the armpit with her shoulder, timing it with his retraction. He went flying back, worse than before, his feet making a clownish attempt to support him. Kyoshi's hope rose, forcing her to her tiptoes as he neared the edge. If he fell off the platform then this bad dream would end.

He managed to catch himself. Kyoshi heard a swear come from someone other than her. Rangi followed her opponent to the boundary but seemed unconcerned about pushing him over. She could have ended it with a nudge.

The man saw this and lost his composure. He lashed out with a wild punch devoid of technique. It was so telegraphed that Kyoshi could have ducked under it.

But in that instant, Rangi looked upward and locked eyes with Kyoshi. The blow struck her squarely in the face. She let it happen.

She tumbled across the platform and landed in the center, a lifeless heap. The weight difference had done its work. Kyoshi's cry was drowned out by roar of the crowd.

The champion wiped his mouth as he sauntered over to Rangi's body. The girl had humiliated him. He was going to take his time destroying her.

Kyoshi screamed to the rafters, invisible and unheard in the frenzy. Nothing mattered anymore but Rangi. She couldn't lose the center of her being like this. She would have obliterated the world to undo what was happening.

Only Wong's hands clamping down on Kyoshi's shoulders held her in place as the man raised his foot high above Rangi's skull. There was a blur of motion and the sound of muffled snapping.

Kyoshi's mind caught up with her eyes. Her comprehension played out like a series of pictures, changed between blinks.

Rangi had spun out from under the man's foot, rotating on her shoulders like a top, and wrapped her body around his standing leg. She'd made a subtle twist, and his limb shattered along every plane it could. The champion lay out on the canvas, writhing in pain, his leg reduced to an understuffed stocking attached to his body. Rangi stood over him, bleeding from the mouth. Other than the single punch she'd taken, she was fine. She hadn't broken a sweat.

The spectators were silent. Her footsteps bounced off the canvas like drumbeats. She hopped lightly off the platform and gathered up her armor.

A single person clapping broke the pall. It was Mok, applauding furiously. It gave the crowd permission to react. They whooped and hollered for their new champion, surging toward her. A single glare made them hold off on slapping her back or lifting her onto their shoulders, but they got as close as they could, forming a little ring of appreciation around her.

Rangi made her way over to the ladder and climbed up with one hand, her gear bundled under the other arm. Her head peeked up over the edge of the hayloft, and then the rest of her body. She tossed the armor into the corner and bowed.

No one responded. They all waited on her next move, Mok and Wai included.

Rangi shrugged at the unasked question. "It seemed like fun," she said calmly.

Kyoshi knew that was complete and utter bull pig. There was no reason for her to have such a lapse in judgment, to commit such a mind-bogglingly stupid act. Kyoshi wanted to punch Rangi so hard that she'd land on her rear end back in Yokoya. She was going to throttle the Firebender until flame came out of her ears.

Mok slapped his thighs and burst into laughter.

"A future boss in the making!" he said. "Dine with me tonight. I'll tell you the plans I have in store."

"How could we refuse, Uncle?" Rangi said with the biggest, sweetest, falsest smile Kyoshi had ever seen.

Attendants carried chairs for everyone up the ladder with great difficulty, followed by a table, and then food and drink. Unlike the large manors of legitimate society, there was no servant class here. Junior toughs and swordsmen did the task, their weapons clanking in their scabbards as they juggled trays like rookie maids.

No one let on that they'd already eaten. The meal was an attempt to mimic a wealthy sage's table, with more than one course. Shaped flour paste substituted for ingredients that would have been impossible to get in the mountains, and yellowing vegetables made up the rest. There was plenty of wine though.

Mok sat with his back facing the edge of the balcony. The fights no longer interested him. Judging by the clash of metal coming from below, the challenges had moved from unarmed combat into the weapons section. The occasional scream and gurgle made it difficult to concentrate.

"Have any of you heard of Te Sihung?" he asked, dropping the endless displays of puffery and dominance. As foolhardy as Rangi's fight had been, there was no denying she'd changed the energy of the meeting.

Te Sihung. Governor Te. Kyoshi had never seen him in person at the mansion, but the last gifts she remembered him sending to Yun were an original, unabridged copy of *Poems of Laghima,* and a single precious white dragon seed.

"Governor in the Eastern Provinces," she said. "Likes to read and drink tea. Certainly isn't hurting for money."

"Very good," Mok said, impressed, even though she could have been describing half of the rich old men in the Earth Kingdom. "Te's a little unique among prefectural leaders. He's not so quick with the axe when it comes to sentencing crimes." He made a hacking motion to the back of his own neck. How lighthearted they were being.

Mok took a sip of wine and smiled when Kyoshi refilled his cup without being told. "He keeps prisoners instead," he went on. "His family inherited an old mansion dating back to the Thirty-Somethingth Earth King, complete with a court-house and a jail where criminals could serve out their sentences instead of facing swift modern justice. I believe the romantic notion of mercy went to his head."

"Sounds nice of him," Rangi said, a bit insouciantly. Her face had begun to swell, her words slurring as her lip grew puffy. The other members of their company had willingly retreated into the background, letting her and Kyoshi do the talking. They were playing the tiles they'd been dealt.

"Don't go putting up statues just yet," Mok said. "He's had one of our own locked up for eight years."

Behind him, Wai positively vibrated, his body thrumming with rage. "We need to get our man out of Te's cells," Mok said. "That's what this job is about. A jailbreak on a fortified position is going to take a lot of bodies, more than the Autumn Bloom has sworn members. So we're calling in our associates. Every favor will be repaid in one night."

"This prisoner—is he important?" Rangi asked. "Does he have information you don't want leaking?"

For the first time tonight Mok looked displeased with her. "This mission is about *brotherhood*," he said. "First and fore-most. My sworn brother has been rotting in the hands of the law for almost a decade. It's taken that long for the Autumn Bloom to grow strong enough to attempt a rescue mission, but Wai and I have never forgotten him."

His passion was real, carved into his spirit with deep grooves. He resembled Lek when the boy talked about Kyoshi's parents.

Propped up by an iron framework larger than himself. Kyoshi wondered if she'd appear the same if she ever spoke about Kelsang at length to anyone. She hoped so.

"Apologies, Uncle," Rangi said. "I thought knowing the facts would be helpful to our cause."

"The only facts I need you concentrating on concern how your group is going to help spring my man out of Governor Te's prison," Mok said.

"Our group?" Kyoshi preemptively tilted in apology for not understanding. "It sounded like we were to band together with the Autumn Bloom in this mission."

"Originally, yes. But after giving it some thought, that would be a waste of an elite team of benders such as yourselves. A two-pronged assault should double our chances. I have numbers at my disposal but not stealth or bending prowess. While my men beat down the doors in a frontal assault, I want the Flying Opera Company to take the quiet route. Whoever succeeds first, it doesn't matter to me."

Rangi was still in professional, intelligence-gathering mode. "Are there plans to Te's palace? Layouts? Staff schedules? Any inside people we can count on?"

Mok's face darkened. He kicked the table away, sending dishes clattering to the floor. "What do you think this is, a robbery?" he snapped. "Figure out your approach on your own!"

Kyoshi realized why he was so angry. Rangi's questions had exposed him as not much of a tactician. He knew nothing of leadership besides making demands and doling out cruelties when they weren't met.

Control by tantrum, Kyoshi thought. She had a label for the way Mok wielded power.

He stood up and dusted himself off. "I plan on being at Governor Te's palace thirty days from now with my forces. I know how swift the Flying Opera Company tends to be, so if you arrive early, you should have all the time you need to prepare yourselves. But! I don't want you acting on your own before we arrive. Do you hear me?"

I hear many things about you. "Of course, Uncle," Kyoshi said. The clash of steel and a scream filled the air as she bowed.

The five of them stood outside their inn, not knowing what to say to each other. Fresh distance had come between them. Self-consciousness reigned supreme.

Kyoshi broke the silence. "Can we agree to leave this forsaken town first thing in the morning?"

"Yes," Wong said. "I'm going to drink myself stupid until then. If I run into any of you, I'm going to pretend I don't know you. Even if you challenge me." He frowned. "*Especially* if you challenge me." Wong stomped off into the darkness, disappearing beyond the glow of the nearest lantern.

Lek hadn't spoken a word on the way back. His sleeve was plastered to his palm with dried blood, a good sign as far as his wound was concerned. But he was possessed by a rigid coldness that had Kyoshi worried.

"Lek," she said before he vanished too, inside his own head. "Thank you. For standing up for me."

He blinked and looked at her, as if they'd only met a minute ago. "Why wouldn't I?" he said, caught waking up from a dream.

"I have to take care of his hand," Kirima said. She looked at Rangi. "I'm not the best healer, so it'll be awhile before I can get to your face."

"I don't need it," Rangi said. She turned and walked away in the opposite direction of Wong, down the slope the town was built on.

"Rangi!" Kyoshi snapped. The Firebender didn't listen to her. She was Kyoshi's bodyguard. She was *obligated* to listen to her. "Get back here! Rangi!"

"After tonight's display, she's the safest person in Hujiang," Kirima said. There was a sly edge to her smile. "But I still think you should go after her."

Having grown up in Yokoya, Kyoshi had walked enough hills for two lifetimes. Going down fast threatened to buckle her ankles, strained at her knees. She found Rangi sitting at the edge of the shallow lake, less by light and more by heat. The Firebender was a dark silhouette curled up against the lapping water. Kyoshi entertained the notion of shoving her straight in.

"You want to tell me what that was about?" she yelled.

Rangi sneered at the question. "Mok was treating us like dung, and now, slightly less so. I impressed a *daofei*. Hasn't that been our goal?"

"My mother's gang belonged to my *mother*! Mok is a rabid animal whom we have no leverage with! It was a stupid risk!"

Rangi got to her feet. She'd been letting her toes dangle in the water, and now she stood ankle-deep in it.

"Of course it was!" she said. She nearly rammed her finger into Kyoshi's chest out of instinct but caught herself. She wrung her hands out and forced them to remain at her side. "I did exactly what you've been doing this whole time!

"Let me tell you something," Rangi said. "I blacked out when I got hit. If I hadn't woken up quickly, that man would have killed me."

Kyoshi's mind went white with fury. After the fight ended, she'd assumed that Rangi had been faking unconsciousness to lure her opponent in. She wanted to march back to the barn and break the rest of his limbs.

"You know what you felt, watching me lie on the canvas?" Rangi said. "That helplessness? That sensation of your anchor being cut loose? That's what I've been feeling, watching you, every single minute since we left Yokoya! I got on that platform so you could see it from *my* perspective! I had no idea what else would get through to you!"

She kicked at the surface of the lake, slicing a wave between them. For an instant she looked like a Waterbender. "I watch you throw yourself headlong into danger, over and over again, and for what? Some misguided attempt to bring Jianzhu 'to justice'? Do you know what that even means anymore?"

"It means he's gone for good," Kyoshi snapped. "No longer walking this earth. That's what it has to mean."

"Why?" Rangi said, her eyes begging and combative at once. "Why do you need to do this so badly?"

"Because then I don't have to be afraid of him, anymore!" Kyoshi screamed. *"I'm scared, all right? I'm scared of him, and I don't know what else will make it go away!"*

Her words carried over the surface of the lake to any man and spirit who might be listening. Kyoshi's obsession wasn't the mark of a great hunter on a relentless stalk of her quarry. That was the lie that had sustained her. The truth was that she was a frightened child, running in different directions and hoping it would all work out for the best. She couldn't feel safe with Jianzhu loose.

She heard it again. Those soft, sharp little breaths. Rangi was crying.

Kyoshi fought back her own tears. They wouldn't have been as graceful. "Talk to me," she said. "Please."

"It wasn't supposed to be like this," Rangi said. She tried to smother herself with the palm of her hand. "It shouldn't have gone this way."

Kyoshi understood her friend's disappointment. The shining new era the world was supposed to get after so many years of strife, the champion whom Rangi had trained to protect, had been stolen from them and replaced with . . . with Kyoshi.

"I know," she said, her heart aching. "Yun would have been a much better—"

"No! Forget Yun, for once! Forget being the Avatar!" Rangi lost the battle to restrain herself and smacked Kyoshi hard across her collar. "It's not supposed to be this way for *you!*"

Kyoshi went silent. Mostly because Rangi had hit her too hard, but also from surprise.

"You think you don't deserve peace and happiness and good things, but you do!" Rangi yelled. "You, Kyoshi! Not the Avatar, but you!"

She closed the distance and wrapped her arms around Kyoshi's waist. The embrace was a clever way to hide her face.

"Do you have any idea how painful it's been for me to follow you on this journey where you're so determined to punish yourself?" she said. "Watching you treat yourself like an empty vessel for revenge, when I've known you since you were a servant girl who couldn't bend a pebble? The Avatar can be reborn. But you can't, Kyoshi. I don't want to give you up to the next generation. I couldn't bear to lose you."

Kyoshi realized she'd had it all wrong. Rangi *was* a true believer. But her greatest faith had been for her friends, not her assignment. She pulled Rangi in closer. She thought she heard a slight, contented sigh come from the other girl.

"I wish I could give you your due," Rangi muttered after some time had passed. "The wisest teachers. Armies to defend you. A palace to live in."

Kyoshi raised an eyebrow. "The Avatar gets a palace?"

"No, but you deserve one."

"I don't need it," Kyoshi said. She smiled into Rangi's hair, the soft strands caressing her lips. "And I don't need an army. I have you."

"*Psh*," Rangi scoffed. "A lot of good I've been so far. If I were better at my job you would never feel scared. Only loved. Adored by all."

Kyoshi gently nudged Rangi's chin upward. She could no more prevent herself from doing this than she could keep from breathing, living, fearing.

"I *do* feel loved," she declared.

Rangi's beautiful face shone in reflection. Kyoshi leaned in and kissed her.

A warm glow mapped Kyoshi's veins. Eternity distilled in a single brush of skin. She thought she would never be more alive than now.

And then—

The shock of hands pushing her away. Kyoshi snapped out of her trance, aghast.

Rangi had flinched at the contact. Repelled her. Viscerally, reflexively.

Oh no. *Oh no.*

This couldn't—not after everything they'd been through— this couldn't be how it—

Kyoshi shut her eyes until they hurt. She wanted to shrink until she vanished within the cracks of the earth. She wanted to become dust and blow away in the wind.

But the sound of laughter pulled her back. Rangi was coughing, drowning herself with her own tears and mirth. She caught her breath and retook Kyoshi by the hips, turning to the side, offering up the smooth, unblemished skin of her throat.

"That side of my face is busted up, stupid," she whispered in the darkness. "Kiss me where I'm not hurt."

THE BEAST

THE MORNING sunrise had never been so warm. Kyoshi had slept better on the hard-packed shore of the lake, without a bedroll, than she had any of the nights spent camping between Chameleon Bay and Hujiang. Perhaps that was because she had her own fire now. She didn't have to share it with anyone else.

Rangi murmured into the base of her neck, a soft thrumming sensation. A shadow loomed over them both. Kyoshi blinked until she saw a pair of leather boots next to her head. Kirima squatted down closer to their level, her hands on her knees and her chin in her hands.

"Have a nice night?" the Waterbender said, batting her eyelashes. She grinned wider than the open sky.

Kyoshi rose to her elbows. Rangi slid off her chest and thumped her head on the ground, startling awake. The leg she'd thrown across Kyoshi's body reluctantly unwound itself.

"Must have been nice," Kirima said, barely able to contain her laughter. "Sleeping under the stars. Just two friends. Having a close, private moment of friendship."

Kyoshi rubbed the drowsiness out of her face. She could leap to her feet and deny everything. She had no idea what would happen if she and Rangi kept pulling on this thread together. Few people in the Earth Kingdom would react anywhere near as well as Kirima.

But ever since that day in Yokoya, when she'd learned her fate while her hands were still dusted in white flour, her life had been an endless refusal, full of secrets unhappily kept to their destructive ends. She was sick of denying herself.

Not this time. This time would be different. A steady thought. The drumbeat in her head and heart let her know the truth. She would never back down from how she felt about Rangi.

Rangi caught her gaze and smiled, making a slight, barely there nod. A *ready if you are* signal.

She was. And they were.

"It's exactly what it looks like," Kyoshi said. "You have a problem?"

Kirima shrugged and waved her fingers, dipping into a moment of quiet seriousness. "I'm not the type to give you grief over whom you love," she said. Her mirth returned immediately. "I am, however, going to give you *tremendous* amounts of grief about romancing within your own brotherhood. That's like doing laundry in the outhouse. It never ends clean."

Kyoshi got up. "First off, we knew each other before we met you. Second, my parents founded this stupid gang, and they were obviously a pair!"

"Good to see you carrying on the family tradition," Kirima said. "Jesa and Hark were mad about each other."

Nothing could douse the moment for Kyoshi like a reminder of her parents. She wondered if they still kissed, made eyes, whispered jokes after they'd dropped her in Yokoya. Perhaps unburdening themselves had made their relationship all the sweeter. She didn't want to ask.

The darkness of her abandonment must have boiled to her surface as the three of them trudged uphill back toward town, because Rangi ran the back of her nails down Kyoshi's hand, a playful and teasing distraction that held more meaning now than a hundred volumes of history. Kyoshi nearly tripped and fell on her face.

If this was what being true to herself felt like, she could never go back. Her heart was nestled somewhere above her in the nearest cloud. She wanted to scoop up Rangi in her arms and run, stepping higher and higher using that technique she still had to learn, until they found it.

Kyoshi was so happy that Hujiang itself looked prettier in the new light of day. Splotches of color caught her eye that weren't visible in the torchlight of the previous evening, blues and reds from beyond the Earth Kingdom. The longhouses, she could see now, had individual touches like carved shrine alcoves and Fire Nation rugs hung over doors. It reminded her of the way ships would get personalities imprinted on them by their sailors. Dust had yet to be kicked up by the day's business, and the air was cleaner, easier to breathe without the dingy haze.

They strolled through town—when was the last time Kyoshi had a *stroll*? Had she ever?—and sidestepped the strewn bodies of men who slept off hangovers, or beatings, or both. Kirima led them to one of the larger establishments, where she ducked through a door with one of its posts destroyed, like someone had been thrown out but not very accurately. She returned moments later, bending a large blob of water that she had to have found inside. It rolled down the steps like a slug.

Wong floated inside the reverse bubble, his head poking out the top. He snored comfortably.

"Wake up!" Kirima shouted. With a flick of her arms, the water froze. The big man jolted awake from the cold. He resembled a small iceberg with his face poking out of the summit.

"Ugh, leave me in this for a while," he said, bleary-eyed.

Kirima liquified the water again, dropping him to his feet, and bent it away from his body, leaving him dry as a bone. She hurled the water back inside the building, where it landed with a giant splash. Someone inside screamed and sputtered.

"We've had enough of this town," she said. Then she grinned at Kyoshi and Rangi, without any attempt to hide the meaning in her stare. "Or at least I have."

Wong didn't get the chance to interpret her stage gestures. A loud crashing noise from somewhere near the bazaar punctured the silence of the morning. It sounded like a house might have collapsed. Birds rose into the sky, fluttering in distress.

Rangi frowned and leaned her ear toward the disturbance. "Was that a landslide?"

"I don't know," Kirima said cautiously. "But the birds have the right idea."

Now the clamor of men shouting in horror could be heard over the rooflines. "Never wait to find out what the trouble is,"

Wong said, already jogging away from the source. "By then, you're already too close."

If that wasn't ancient wisdom, it should have been. They followed him briskly back toward the inn. Hopefully Lek and Lao Ge were both there, ready to fly. Judging by how fast the ruckus was catching up, they wouldn't have time to search the town on Pengpeng.

A horrendous snorting, choking sound rolled through the streets. Back in her mansion days, Kyoshi had once seen an ambassador bring a pet poodle monkey that was so inbred in the name of "cuteness" that it had trouble breathing through its miniaturized snout. That was what she heard now, on a scale a thousand times larger. The exhortations of a creature that would never get its fill of air.

Two men ran screaming out of a longhouse, right on their heels. An instant later, the building front exploded, planks and beams torn to shreds by a dark, wiry mass that writhed with fury. A rope or a whip flung out with the speed of a cable under tension and lashed the men across the back. They fell to the ground, skidding on their faces, momentum making their legs scorpion over their heads.

"Tui's gills!" Kirima shouted. "What is that thing!?"

Behind them was a beast that Kyoshi had never seen the likes of before, a black-and-brown four-legged monstrosity that stood higher at the shoulder than some of the huts. It managed to be hulking with muscle and yet lissome as a serpent at the same time. Claws as long and sharp as sickle blades reaped at the ground, opening damp wounds under the dusty surface.

But the most hideous part of the creature was its dark void of a face. The furry, elongated skull had no eyes, only a flowering pink snout that wriggled with its own fleshy protuberances. It was as if a parasite from another world had attached itself to the nose of an earthly beast and taken control over the entire animal. Two large dark holes, nostrils, sucked air in all directions until they pointed straight at Kyoshi.

She backed away slowly, ineffectually, surprised she could manage that. The nausea of terror chained her, robbed her of survival instinct. Her skin felt wet and cold.

Again, was the only thought running through her mind. Again, Jianzhu had loosed a nightmare on her, an inhuman specter that would drag her away into the darkness, screaming. It had to be him. There was no one else who could have scraped the depths of her fear like this. Somehow, she knew in her bones it was he who taunted her with this living aberration.

A wall of earth shot up between her and the animal. She hadn't bent it.

"What are you doing?" Wong roared as he followed through on his attack. "Either fight or run! Don't stand there where we can't help you!"

The monster clambered over the wall he made with ease, its claws letting it climb as fast as it ran. Kirima pulled more water from a nearby trough and smashed at the beast's shoulders, trying to knock it off-balance. Rangi kicked low sheets of flame at the places it tried to land its forepaws, reasoning that it was as effective to break an animal's root as it was a normal opponent.

That's right, Kyoshi thought. *I'm not alone this time.*

The street was wide enough to accommodate her earthbending weakness. She knifed at the air in front of her, and the entire surface of the road began to grind and shift. A fissure opened, and one of the animal's paws fell in. If she could close the gap fast enough, she could pin it by the—

The monster, rather than avoid the jaws of her trap, dove headfirst into the rift. Its entire body disappeared belowground, leaving a pile of castings behind.

"This thing can *burrow*!?" Kirima sounded more aggrieved than afraid, like an experienced gambler discovering the table they'd joined was blatantly rigged against them.

Kyoshi felt vibrations beneath her. It was impossible not to, with a creature that size, but they were indistinct and directionless. Not a help in this situation.

"Spread out," Rangi said, eying the ground.

"Shouldn't we stay close?" Kyoshi said.

"No," Rangi said. "Then it'll get more than one of us in a single bite."

Kyoshi may have been feeling warm with newfound camaraderie for her gang, but no one had told Wong and Kirima. After hearing Rangi, they immediately leaped onto the roof of the nearest house, elements trailing below the soles of their feet, leaving her and Kyoshi down below.

The soil loosened around them, a perfect circle caving in. Rangi tackled Kyoshi out of the center of the formation, boosting herself sideways with flame jets from her feet. They landed hard on their sides, shoulders bruising. The creature burst through the surface, rearing toward the sky, the ground giving birth to a shape of death that blacked out the sun above.

There was a zipping sound, and then a thud. The animal screamed, and its claws came down short of Kyoshi and Rangi's bodies. It shook its head furiously.

Another impact, and this time Kyoshi saw it. A smooth,

fist-sized stone had struck the beast hard on the tip of its sensitive nose, sending it reeling. She looked up and made out Lek's silhouette on the roof of their inn, the sun behind him shrouding his face.

"Move, maybe?" he shouted.

A hail of perfectly aimed stones gave them cover, each missile landing uncannily on the one spot that the animal seemed to feel pain, no matter how much it thrashed about. It backed away, trying to hide its nose. As Kyoshi and Rangi fled toward Lek, several arrows struck it in the hindquarters. It turned to face the new threat.

The *daofei* had gotten over their surprise and were now mobbing the beast, thrusting spears at it and pricking its fur with shortbows. They sought the glory of bringing it down. The animal lashed out with its tongue, sending a row of men falling to the ground, but more swordsmen-turned-hunters stepped over their limp bodies to replace them.

Kyoshi didn't care to understand the bizarre scene playing out before her. She and the rest of the group ran for the hills.

They arrived at Pengpeng's cave in the mountainside winded, their legs and lungs burning, to find Lao Ge feeding the bison a pile of cabbages. He tossed them one at a time high in the air for Pengpeng to catch between her broad, flat teeth. There was probably no use asking him how he'd acquired the produce.

"A lot of help you were!" Lek shouted. He was assuming, like Kyoshi was at this point, that Lao Ge was completely aware of what had transpired.

The old man gave him a pitying look. "Fighting a shirshu? That's just a bad investment of effort. I left as soon as I felt it coming."

"You knew what that abomination was?" Kirima said.

"It's a legendary subterranean beast that hunts by scent," he explained dismissively, like they would have known this if they'd paid better attention to his ramblings. "Supposedly it can track its quarry across stone, water, dirt, thin air. In the old days, Earth Kings would use them to execute their political enemies. *For the traitor, let them be hounded by shirshu until they drop where they stand, far from their homes and the bones of their ancestors.*"

Lao Ge fed Pengpeng another cabbage. "Or at least that's how the saying went. Shirshu haven't been seen in the wild for at least a generation, so I assume this one was being used to hunt a fugitive too. Same as in the days of yore."

Kyoshi felt Lek's gaze boring into her. "It was going for you," he said. "I could see it from the roof of the inn. It was sniffing out your scent. *You* brought it here."

She hesitated. Had she been as smooth as Yun, she could have come up with a convincing denial on the spot.

Before she could say anything, she was preempted by the metallic clanking of blades rattling in their scabbards. They leaned over the cave ledge to see a party of swordsmen down below. At the back of the group, exhorting them onward, was Brother Wai. Mok's inquisitor looked like he wished to speak with whomever he was searching for, very much.

"I can explain," Kyoshi said quickly. "But maybe once we're in the air?"

There was silent and unanimous agreement as they scrambled onto Pengpeng. The truth took a back seat to survival.

THE AVATAR'S MASTERS

PENGPENG GRACED the skies over the plains of Ba Sing Se. The Impenetrable City watched them pass like a silent sentry, the monolithic brown walls a blank face devoid of features.

Kyoshi watched the capital sail by. Somewhere in the center of those titanic fortifications was the Earth King, nominally the most powerful person on the continent, with armies to command and the wealth of the world at his disposal. Though she'd never dug deep into history lessons, she knew that the records were full of instances where Avatars and Earth Kings came to each other's aid.

And yet she couldn't go ask him for help. There were no means for a peasant to approach the Earth King that wouldn't result in immediate refusal, or capture, or death. Moreover, courts and cities were Jianzhu's realm. He'd spent decades cultivating influence among the bureaucrats of Ba Sing Se. Barging in there would be no better than surrendering to Governor Deng back in Chameleon Bay.

She looked at her parents' gang. These were the only people she could trust, as sad as that was. Out there was a city that essentially belonged to her enemy. Her allies could fit on the back of a single bison.

And they weren't happy with her right now.

"All right, spill it," Kirima snapped. "Who is this man you're feuding with? You said he was a rich and powerful sage. Which one, exactly? Tell us the truth!"

Kyoshi stared at the saddle floor. Before, she'd felt within her rights, keeping his name a secret. But the decision seemed completely foolish in retrospect.

". . . Jianzhu," Kyoshi said weakly. "Jianzhu, the companion of Kuruk."

"The Architect?" Lao Ge said, rubbing his chin. "You aim high, my dear. I'm impressed."

The rest of them were not as amused. Their jaws dropped in chorus. "Jianzhu the Gravedigger!?" Lek yelled. "You picked a fight with the *Gravedigger*!?"

"I didn't pick the fight!" Kyoshi protested. "I wasn't lying when I said he killed two people I loved!"

"Oh no, we believe that!" Kirima shouted. "We can believe that plenty! That man has a higher body count than septapox!"

"And you ticked him off so badly that he sent a beast out of myth to track you all the way into the Taihua Mountains," Wong said with a sigh. "We might as well jump off Pengpeng right now and save ourselves the trouble."

"Thanks a lot, you numbskull!" Lek said. "We had a chance

of surviving Mok, but if the Butcher of Zhulu Pass wants you feeding the worms, then it's only a matter of time before he puts you *and* us belowground!"

So Kyoshi wasn't the only one terrified of him. It was a small comfort, but a comfort nonetheless, that made her feel like she was standing on firmer footing. Outlaws were perhaps the one group who would understand how brutal and dangerous Jianzhu really was.

She closed her eyes. She hadn't known these people for very long. But to her own surprise more than anyone's, she would have felt intolerably guilty if Jianzhu's efforts to capture her caused them any grievous harm. They deserved . . . not to be swindled, was the way she'd put it. They were owed the full story.

"He's not trying to kill me," Kyoshi said. "He doesn't want me dead."

"Well, that would be new for him!" Kirima said. "How are *you* so privy to his inner thoughts and goals?"

"Because." She took a deep breath to steady herself. "I'm the Avatar."

It was the first time she'd ever knowingly said the truth out loud. Somehow she'd managed to avoid speaking those three specific words in that specific order to Rangi the night they fled Yokoya in the drenching rain. Rangi had already known the Avatar was either her or Yun, so context had sufficed.

Kyoshi's confession hung in the air, as visible as smoke. She waited for the rest of them to recover from the blow that had staggered Rangi, Kelsang, and everyone else who belonged to the small circle of knowledge at one point in time or another. They might have needed a moment to recalibrate their view of the world . . .

"Ha!" Lek said. *"Ha!"*

. . . Or maybe they'd just laugh in her face?

Lek rolled back on the floor of the saddle, finding her moment of ultimate honesty a good joke, a relief from his jangled nerves. "You, the Avatar? Man, I have heard some whoppers, but that might be the best yet!"

"I know I let you gloss over a bunch of the oaths," Kirima said to her. "But at least five of them are about never lying to your sworn family."

"She *is* the Avatar!" Rangi said. "Why do you think she has a Fire Nation bodyguard?"

"Dunno," Wong said with a shrug. He pointed his thumb at Kirima. "Why do you think we've got her?"

The Waterbender gave him a dirty look before continuing. "Look, you can believe in your weird little two-person cult all you want," she said to Kyoshi. "Just tell us what you stole from the Gravedigger. You wouldn't be the first servant who bungled a theft and had to flee from their angry boss."

Kyoshi couldn't believe it. She'd had it all wrong. She'd thought that her Avatarhood was the final secret, a gilded treasure that needed to be kept in a series of locked chests until the exact right moment. It turned out that without proof, the information was worth less than the paper it was written on. She squeezed one of the fans in her belt out of frustration.

"Do you even bend all four elements?" Wong said. "Do you?"

"I firebent once," she said, realizing how stupid she sounded as she said it. "Under duress. It, uh, came out of my mouth. Like dragon's breath." She thought about trying to do a Fire Fist, but it felt like a bad idea, given the lack of space and how badly her last one went.

"Yeah, I once got food poisoning from dodgy fire flakes too," Lek said. "Doesn't mean I'm the reincarnation of Yangchen."

"Well, *I* believe her," Lao Ge said with a proud, upturned chin. Judging by the others' expressions, his endorsement had the opposite effect.

"Okay, okay," Kirima said. "Everyone calm down. Take a breather. Let's consider this rationally for a minute. Assuming she is the—*KYOSHI, THINK FAST!*"

She'd uncorked her water skin with a sleight of hand. A pellet of liquid flew at Kyoshi's face.

Kyoshi made an undignified squeal that should have disqualified her from holding any office whatsoever. She still couldn't bend any piece of earth smaller than a house, and the water aimed at her eyes made her flinch like a prickle snake had wandered into her sleeping bag. She threw her arms over her face.

"Spirits above," Lek whispered.

Her cheeks burned in shame. Sure, she looked bad, but *that* bad?

"Kyoshi," Rangi said, breathless and thrilled. "Kyoshi!"

The fan she'd been holding had come out of her belt as she clenched up in surprise. She was gripping it the wrong way, like a dagger. The tip of the weapon pointed to the little blob of water hovering in midair.

"Is that you?" Rangi said to Kirima. The stunned Waterbender shook her head.

Rangi dove at Kyoshi. The water fell on her back, splashing

them both. She squeezed Kyoshi in a ferocious embrace. "You did it!" she yelled. "You bent another element!"

As Kyoshi struggled to breathe with an ecstatic Firebender wrapped around her neck, she stared at the fan in her hand. Her mother's weapon had made the difference somehow, in both the element and the amount. She was sure of it.

She looked up at the faces of the *daofei*. Lao Ge had a cool, knowing expression, but the rest were shocked into submission. They'd been smuggling valuable cargo the whole time.

They settled down in one of the innumerable abandoned quarries that supplied the middle and upper rings of Ba Sing Se. The marker of wealth for most Earth Kingdom citizens was whether your house was built with stone from the ground below it. The farther the rock had to travel, the fancier it was.

This quarry followed a seam of marble. The small canyon had been mined out in perfectly square blocks, leaving the edges protruding with right angles. They landed on a flat surface of swirled gray and white, resembling tiny figures on a giant fountain basin. The regularity of the stone fractures laid on top of the natural rock formations made Kyoshi's vision blur.

The first sign that something was off was Wong. He dismounted first and then reached up to help Kyoshi down. She frowned, assuming he was more likely to pick her pocket than act as a footman. She jumped off the other side of the saddle.

Once they were all on solid ground, the original members of the Flying Opera Company backed away from her. "We need a moment to confer," Kirima said.

Kyoshi and Rangi shared uncertain glances with each other while the *daofei* huddled on the far side of the marble cube, murmuring and whispering. Occasionally one of them would poke their head up like a singing groundhog and give Kyoshi a hard, assessing stare before returning to their debate.

"If they turn on us," Rangi whispered sideways through a forced smile, "I want you to take Pengpeng and run. I'll buy you time to escape."

Kyoshi found that scenario too distressing to think about. The sudden end of the gang's discussion forced her backbone straighter. They filed back over to Kyoshi and Rangi, as grim and wary and determined as the first night they'd met. Kyoshi sucked in her breath through her teeth as Lek stepped forward, a mirror of that night they'd almost come to blows.

"It's been our honor to have traveled with the Avatar," he said. "We regret that we have to part ways." They bowed in unison. Not using the *daofei* salute, but with their hands formally at their sides.

Kyoshi blinked. "Huh?"

"It doesn't have to be right now, if that's not to your wishes," Kirima said. "I suppose you might want the night to plan your next move and leave us in the morning."

It was the politeness more than anything that threw her off. *"Huh?"*

They seemed as confused as she was. "You're the Avatar," Wong said. "You can't stay with people like us. It'd be an offense to the spirits or something."

"Not to mention too dangerous," Lek said. He ran his fingers over his palm where a blotchy red line remained, the artifact of Kirima's imperfect healing. "We're still obligated to join the attack on Governor Te's. If we bail, Mok would find us eventually. When he does, well . . . being killed by a shirshu would be kinder."

"You'll be safer the farther away you are from us," Kirima said.

Kyoshi's mind reeled. Were they *protecting* her? She'd been so certain that the first people who discovered her identity would take her hostage or rat her out to Jianzhu. The Avatar was a tool. The Avatar was leverage. The master of all four elements lay somewhere between a bargaining chip to get what you wanted and a blunt-force hammer to be swung at the many imperfections riddling the world.

No. You just thought that way because of how Jianzhu treated Yun.

"Kyoshi, they have a point," Rangi said. "If you fall deeper into Mok's clutches, it will taint you forever."

That was true. If she cared at all about *being* the Avatar, about someday holding the office and performing its duties as Yun had already begun to do, then she had to part ways with the Flying Opera Company and their debts. Otherwise the association with criminals would mark her indelibly.

She'd be unclean.

The history of the Avatars contained rebels, enemies of tyrants, those who stood alone against the armies of the Four Nations when necessary. But as far as Kyoshi knew, none had been self-serving outlaws. Time had always proven her predecessors in the right and shown them as champions of justice.

Yun had told her that most *daofei* respected the Avatar. She looked at her parents' gang and saw their swagger gone, their cloak of daring and confidence torn wide open. They'd laid themselves bare in the presence of the living bridge between mankind and spirits.

She couldn't explain what was so familiar about this situation, nor why she felt so compelled. The Flying Opera Company was not a bunch of innocent victims like the hostages kidnapped by Tagaka, needing a higher power to reach down and change their futures. They should have been capable enough without her, just like—

Yun. They reminded her of Yun, when he needed Kyoshi beside him on the iceberg. They were her friends, and they were in a bind.

Kyoshi didn't turn her back on her friends. She swallowed her own misgivings and made up her mind.

"I'm not going anywhere," she said. "I'm staying. And if I can help with the Autumn Bloom, I will. I haven't gotten my end of the bargain yet."

The gang perked up. Logically, her promise should have made no difference to them. She'd been deadweight since the beginning, only useful because of Pengpeng. But they glanced at her with wonder in their shifting eyes, the same nervousness she knew she felt when Kelsang had tracked her down for the first time and lifted her out of the dirt. *You'd sully yourself with me?*

"Kyoshi," Rangi said. "Think about this to its end. The Avatar can't be seen attacking the residence of an Earth Kingdom official."

"As far as the abiders are concerned, I'm not the Avatar yet,"

Kyoshi said. "I took the oaths of this group. I won't abandon my sworn brothers and sisters."

Her choice of words was not lost on them. Or Rangi. The Firebender was torn between being critical of Kyoshi's judgment and being proud that she'd brought personal honor into the issue.

"You are not ready for anything resembling a real fight," Rangi said. "Currently, *you* are this group's biggest weakness. You're too valuable to lose, and you don't have the skills to defend yourself."

"That's a little harsh," Lek said. Of all people.

"Hairpin's right," Kirima said to Kyoshi. "*Currently*. We have until the next full moon to link up with Mok's forces for the assault. We can finally give you the training you were hoping for. That's what we promised you, wasn't it?"

"It takes years for the Avatar to master all four elements!" Rangi snapped. "And that's with world-class teachers! I don't get the impression that any of you have a bending lineage to speak of."

Kirima grinned. "No, but I've always wanted to start one. I'm not going to pass up the chance to go down in history as the Avatar's waterbending master."

Kyoshi could practically hear Rangi's blood boil. Through her mother's side, her family belonged to an unbroken line of bending teachers who were considered some of the finest in the Fire Nation. They'd tutored members of the royal family. This plan required her to accept the shame they'd put off for so long. The most important bender in the world would have to bow to rabble.

The *daofei* watched the agony play out on Rangi's face. They were highly amused. "Lighten up," Lek said. "We'd be teaching

Kyoshi to survive, not turning her into Yangchen. Consider the raid on Te's a practical exam."

Whatever worshipfulness Kyoshi detected earlier had completely vanished from their attitude. Kyoshi supposed she only had herself to blame, telling them to think of her as their sister instead of the Avatar.

"Speaking of Yangchen, we're out of luck for airbending anyway," Kirima added. "Either the two of you accept a few improvisations, or Kyoshi remains the way she is. Weak. Defenseless. A helpless, pitiable babe in the woods who can't—"

Kyoshi aimed beyond Kirima's shoulder and pulled a massive cube of stone out of the far side of the canyon. It went crashing down the cliff face, its corners shearing off, a die cast by a spirit the size of a city. The boulder hit the canyon floor and fractured into an army of slabs and shards that teetered on their ends before falling over flat.

Despite the noise, Kirima didn't give the landslide a single glance. She stared at Kyoshi, impassive, unimpressed. "This is exactly what I'm talking about," she said. "You need more than one trick in your bag."

Kyoshi felt the evening wash by her like the wind passing through the branches of a tree. The gang was content to leave her be, for now. They chattered excitedly to themselves around the fire. The Avatar had volunteered to stay by their side. Their every move forward carried a tinge of spiritual righteousness.

Kyoshi gave it a day before the shine wore off.

Rangi was in a mood all her own. After camp chores were

finished, she hopped to a different stone cutout entirely, to meditate. By herself, it was made pretty clear. They'd talked about the anguish of watching each other take risks, but neither of them had made any promises to stop.

They couldn't. Not now.

Kyoshi watched the stars fade in and out of the sky, screened and unveiled in turn by the clouds that were as invisible in the darkness as black-clad stagehands moving the settings of a play. She was waiting for the others to fall asleep. She waited for a particular hour that belonged neither to this day nor the next, when time felt jellied and thick.

Kyoshi got up and moved to the next cubical platform of the quarry, and then the next. Without dust-stepping, it was slow going. She had to clamber up and down the height changes. She didn't want to wake the others with noisy, orthodox earthbending.

The old man stood at the mouth of the marble seam with his back turned to her. Sometimes she wondered if Lao Ge wasn't a shared hallucination. Or an imaginary friend exclusive to her. The others could have been humoring her, nodding and smiling every time she talked to a patch of empty space.

"I thought you would come to me in Hujiang," he said. "I suppose you had other priorities on your mind."

Kyoshi bowed, knowing he could tell if she did. "Apologies, Sifu." But in her thoughts, the unease ballooned. If he had a problem with Rangi, then . . .

Lao Ge turned around. There was a smile in his eyes. "You don't have to forsake love," he said. "Killing's not some holy art form that requires worldly abstinence. If anything, that's lesson two."

She swallowed around the block in her throat. She'd been

full of bluster the first night she went to him in secret. But she'd been so used to false starts and stymied progress that continuing their conversation felt like foreign territory. More doubt seeped into her cracks.

"Lesson two should scare you to the bone," Lao Ge said. "You can take a life before the sun comes up, eat breakfast, and go about your day. How many people might you pass on the street who are capable of such callousness? Many more than you think."

Jianzhu certainly was. He'd pulled her alone to safety, leaving Yun behind in the clutches of that unholy spirit. That was the moment he'd marked his once-prized pupil as having no further use, the way a dockworker might paint an X on a crate of cargo fouled by seawater. Total loss, not worth the recovery effort.

And then there was what he'd done to Kelsang.

"Fancy yourself different?" Lao Ge said, noticing her stillness.

She could still feel Jianzhu's hands gripping her. "I won't know until I try," she said.

The old man laughed, a single bark that pierced the night. "I suppose you'll get the chance soon. In the heat of battle, you can excuse the act away well enough. Fling an arrow here, hack away with a sword there. You and your victim are just two of many, acting in self-preservation. Is that how you want to deal with your man? With chaos as your shroud? Do you want to shut your eyes, hurl an overwhelming amount of death in his direction, and hope he's disposed of when you open them?"

"No," she said. Remembering what she'd been robbed of, what she'd never get back because of Jianzhu, brought a surge of conviction. "I want to look him in the eye as I end him."

Lao Ge reacted as if she'd made a saucy quip, pursing his lips in amusement. "Well, then!" he said. "In that case, during the raid, you and I are going to split off from the others. We'll head farther into the palace than anyone else. And we're going to assassinate Governor Te."

"Wait, what?" The certainty she had regarding Jianzhu caused her to mentally stumble at the mention of another target. It was as if she were the *lei tai* fighter throwing an all-or-nothing punch at Rangi, who'd deftly turned her momentum against her. "Why would we do that?"

"For you, it's practice," Lao Ge said. "For me, it's because he's my man. Listen. Governor Te is *brutally* incompetent and corrupt. His people go hungry, he skims from the Earth King's taxes to enrich his own coffers, and in case you haven't noticed, he doesn't have a good policy for handling *daofei*."

"Those aren't excuses to murder him!"

"You're right. They're not excuses—they're ample justifications. I guarantee you that many citizens have suffered immeasurably from his greed and negligence, and many more will die if he is allowed to keep breathing."

Lao Ge spread his hands wide as if to embrace the world. "Te and his ilk are parasites leeching strength and vitality from the kingdom. Imagine yourself as the predator that keeps the land healthy by eliminating the sources of its weakness. It was said of Kuruk that he was the greatest hunter that ever walked the Four Nations, but from what I know, he never made man his quarry. I'm hoping you can be different."

The idea of becoming a beast free of thought and culpability was supposed to help, but it made her shudder instead. "What gives you the right to decide?" she asked. "Are you part of another brotherhood? Are there more people like you? Is someone paying you?"

He shook his head, dodging her questions. "Doesn't everyone have the right to decide?" he said. "Isn't the Avatar a person like me? Someone who shapes the world with their choices?"

She was going to protest that no, the Avatar had the recognition of the spirits and Four Nations, but she found her tongue tied in the wake of his argument.

He gripped his forearms behind his back and gazed across the canyon. "I would declare the lowliest peasant is like the Avatar in this regard. All of our actions have an impact. Each decision we make ripples into the future. And we alter our landscapes according to our needs. To keep her crops alive, a farmer uproots the weeds that nature has placed in her fields, does she not?"

"People aren't weeds," Kyoshi said. It was the best she could manage.

He turned to face her. "I think it's a bit late to claim the moral high ground, given what your aims are."

She flushed hot in her cheeks. "Jianzhu murdered two of my friends with his own hands," she spat. "He doesn't deserve to get away with it. If you took him out for me, instead of targeting some random governor, I could reveal myself as the Avatar." *I would be safe.*

Her resolve was wavering left and right. Not a minute ago she was yowling about doing the deed herself, feigning a hard soul, and now she was begging Grandfather to make the bad man go away.

Lao Ge smirked. "No one in this world is random. I don't care to kill Jianzhu. He's competent, and he surrounds himself with competent people. I wish the Earth Kingdom had a hundred Jianzhus. We'd enter a new golden age."

"And yet you're not trying to stop me from ending him."

"For this case, I won't intervene one way or the other. Besides, what kind of teacher would I be if I took my student's examination for her?"

"A rich one," Kyoshi muttered. Tutors swapping identities with the children of wealthy families so they could pass the government tests needed for prestigious administrative jobs was a common practice across the Earth Kingdom. Pulling off the con paid very well.

Lao Ge burst out laughing. "Oh, I do like our little chats. Here's an assignment for you in the meantime."

He jumped up to a higher level without the aid of bending and without much effort at all. The leap was higher than Kyoshi's head.

"Many of Governor Te's personal guard will die in Mok's raid," he said, disappearing past the edge of the stone, his voice already beginning to fade. "Soldiers who are simply doing their jobs. His servants will be caught in the violence as well. What will you do then, Avatar?"

Kyoshi hopped in place, her eye poking above the surface of the cube he'd landed on, trying to catch one last glimpse. It was empty. Lao Ge was already gone.

She slumped against the marble wall. The concept of collateral damage had lingered in the back of her mind, but Lao Ge had circled it in ink, made it ache, the same way Rangi pointed out flaws in her Horse stance. She had no idea how she was going to take part in this action, fulfill her promise to her newfound brotherhood, without getting her hands dirty.

The promise had been so easy to make at the time. She stared miserably at the opposite side of the mined-out gulf, sleep coming to her before a solution could.

She woke up, sprawled flat on the hard marble surface. She must have shifted during the night.

Four figures loomed over her, making an arc of their upside-down faces. "Oh, look," Kirima said. "Our precious little student is trying to get away and shirk her training."

Wong stomped the ground. The marble under Kyoshi tilted like a frying pan, dumping her to her feet. He proffered her fans, handles toward her. "I get you first," he rumbled. "A warm-up before you start bending."

"Topknot told us all about your little weakness," Lek said, backing away with a look of superiority on his face. "That you can't bend small pieces of earth."

"I believe my words were 'completely and utterly lacks precision,'" Rangi said, sniffing in contempt. She ignored Kyoshi's glare.

"Don't worry," Lek said. "By the time we're done with you, you'll be able to bend the crud out of your own eye. Catch!"

He whipped the stone that appeared in his hand at Kyoshi's face. Only the fact that Wong had her fans held out, right there, let her snatch one in time to protect herself. As the arms snapped open and she earthbent through the weapon, the stone stopped in midair. It reversed course at full speed and struck Lek in the forehead.

He doubled over. "Ow!" he screamed. "I was aiming above you!"

"Wait, so you *can* bend small things?" Kirima said, upset by the revelation. "Were you lying to us again? I have to tell you, I'm getting really fed up with the secrets."

"I'm bleeding here! This is worse than Hujiang!"

"That's not how you open the fan!" Wong roared indignantly. "You could have damaged the leaf!"

Amid the shouting, Rangi buried her face in her hands. She seemed to have a headache that rivaled Lek's.

Kyoshi agreed with her. The official training of the Avatar was off to a great start.

PREPARATIONS

THE JOURNEY to Te's palace was a painful blur. Each moment spent on solid ground was devoted to training. The *daofei* adopted their new roles as her teachers with relish. Criminals liked their hierarchies, and the Flying Opera Company had just established a brand-new one, with Kyoshi at the bottom.

"No!" Wong shouted. "It's fan open, fan closed, high block, dainty steps backward, big lunge forward, leg sweep! The fan is not a weapon! It's an extension of your arm!"

The man had never been much for words before, but when it came to fighting with the fan, he transformed into a tyrannical stage director, with the ego and perfectionism to match. "I could remember the moves better if you didn't make me sing the full works of Yuan Zhen while we do this!" Kyoshi said, huffing and puffing in the open field they'd landed in. The rest of the group sat in the shade of a persimmon tree overlooking an empty field, munching on the astringent fruit and enjoying the breeze while Kyoshi toiled under the sun.

Wong was highly offended. "The singing is breath control practice! Power and voice both come from the center! Again! With emotional content this time!"

No matter how difficult fan practice got, she toughed it out. The rewards were bounding leaps in progress with her earth-bending. With her fans in hand, she could narrow her focus to kick rocks at targets and raise walls of stone like a normal Earthbender, albeit one with a sloppy, informal technique. Still, after all those years of fearing she'd destroy the countryside with the smallest act of bending, using her mother's weapons was liberating. It was so effective, it felt like cheating.

"It *is* cheating," Lek said as they volleyed pebbles back and forth at each other in the mouth of a cave while the others set up camp. "Sure, some Earthbenders amplify their power with weapons like hammers and maces, but what are you going to do if you don't have your fans? Ask for a rules change?"

"How is someone going to steal my fans?" Kyoshi said. The flight of the pebbles picked up speed, their arcs growing sharper. "I always have them with me."

"It might not be theft," Lek said. "You might voluntarily leave them behind. The first rule of smuggling is *Don't get caught with the goods.* Your parents knew that. That's probably why they stashed the fans with you in that hick abider town."

Kyoshi's temper flared. One, she found herself longing for Yokoya these days, much to her surprise. Not the people, but the harsh, wild landscape where the wooded mountains met the sea and salt air. The interior Earth Kingdom often felt like a brown monotone, a flat expanse that changed little from one landing site to the next. She decided she didn't appreciate people looking down on the unique little part of it where she'd met Kelsang.

And two, she'd never gotten over the resentment she felt toward Lek, each moment her parents had spent with him instead of her. It didn't matter if he was simply a gang member to them. They'd found him useful, decided he had a purpose. Her? Not so much.

She could have explained her feelings to him. Instead, she sliced at the flying pebbles with her fans, cracking them cleanly into hemispheres, and sent twice as many projectiles back at Lek. *Can you do* that, *with or without a weapon?*

He yelped and threw himself to the floor. The shot blast of stone zinged into the cave wall above him, showering him in dust. Playtime had gotten far too rough.

"I'm sorry!" Kyoshi cried out, covering her mouth in horror with the spread fan. She could have put out his eye, or worse.

He got up with a scowl on his face. But then he remembered something. His glower turned into a grin so smug it could have illuminated the rest of the cave.

"It's fine," he said, patting the dirt off his pants. "Though I'll have to tell Rangi about your lapse in control."

Whatever remorse Kyoshi felt vanished. "You snot-nosed little—"

He raised a finger patiently like an enlightened guru. "*Bup-bup.* That's *Sifu* Snotnose to you."

Kyoshi could firebend without her fans.

That one bad attempt after their escape from Chameleon Bay was a distant memory. Since then, some kind of blockage had cleared. The flame felt straightforward, a power that merely needed to be set free instead of prodded or manipulated like earth.

It made no sense to her how she had a critical weakness with her native element but could produce fire decently for a beginner. The reason could have been that Rangi was a great teacher, as might be expected from the scion of great teachers.

"No," Rangi said. "It's your emotional state."

The little training area they'd built stood at the end of an isolated shepherd's path leading away from a small town in a valley below. Rangi faced her on a long, narrow beam of earth that she'd ordered Kyoshi to raise from the ground. Balancing on it was hard enough, but then they'd started to run through firebending forms and light sparring. The linear exercise meant she'd need to concentrate on resisting and overcoming with positive *jing* instead of staying still or evading.

"Of all bending disciplines, fire is the most affected by inner turmoil," Rangi said, punching a flame downward at Kyoshi's front foot, forcing her to pull it back. "The fact that its coming easier to you now means you're feeling more relaxed and natural."

Kyoshi snap-kicked her new leading leg. A crescent of fire sliced upward, and Rangi had to reconsider how much pressure she wanted to apply. "Isn't that a good thing?" Kyoshi asked.

"No! Why would it be? You feel loose and breezy when you're surrounded by *daofei*, about to risk your life for them in what's essentially an act of treason against the Earth Kingdom!?" Rangi spun on the balls of her feet, perfectly centered, with more dance-like beauty than Kyoshi could ever have mustered. A horizontal skirt of flame billowed out from her waist, exactly at a height too awkward for Kyoshi to jump over or duck easily.

Rangi hadn't accounted for her opponent's complete lack of shame. Kyoshi dropped to her belly like a worm, hugging the sides of the beam for stability, and let the wave of fire pass over her. She popped back up to see Rangi looking at her with disapproval in her eyes. And it was about more than her lowly escape.

"You're firebending now," Rangi said. "Dare I say, you might even be good at it. There's no reason to continue on this path. We could go to the sages and prove you're the Avatar."

Kyoshi thought this matter had been settled, but apparently not. "Which ones, exactly?" she said. "Because the only sages I know are the names from Jianzhu's guest lists! Should we try Lu Beifong? The man who thinks of Jianzhu like his own son? Or maybe someone at the court of Omashu! Omashu is practically his summer home!"

"We could go to my mother," Rangi said, her voice barely audible.

Kyoshi dropped her fighting stance. If she caught a fireball to the face, she deserved it. She'd essentially separated Rangi from her only family. It was a nagging guilt that Kyoshi had been able to ignore, solely because of her friend's strength. This was the first time Rangi had cracked along that plane.

"Do you really think she'd take our side over his?" Kyoshi asked. She didn't mean for the question to be defiant. The friendship between the Avatar's companions in eras past was the stuff of legend. It was said that two of Yangchen's close friends and bending teachers had died protecting her from her enemies. The prospect of Hei-Ran choosing Jianzhu over her own daughter had to be considered.

Rangi's face wilted further. "I don't know," she said after a while. Her shoulders were heavy with dejection. "I couldn't be certain. I guess if we can't trust my own mother, then we can't trust anyone."

It did not feel good to win this argument. Kyoshi stepped along the beam carefully until she could put her arms around Rangi. "I'm sorry," she said. "I've taken so much from you. I don't know how to make it right."

Rangi wiped her nose and pushed Kyoshi away. "You can start by promising me you'll be a great Avatar. A leader who's virtuous and just."

The comment knocked Kyoshi off-balance better than a kick to her knee. She couldn't reconcile her friend's righteous desires with the dark conclusions of Lao Ge. Entertaining the wisdom of an assassin was already a betrayal of Rangi's trust. What would happen if Kyoshi took the old man's test and passed?

Rangi lined up a big attack to knock her off the beam, purposely exaggerating her own motions and openings to let her student counter-hit her. But Kyoshi couldn't capitalize on them.

She backed away until she ran out of space, forlornly waving her hands in a mockery of firebending, heat sputtering from her fingers.

Luck intervened before she humiliated herself further. "You two have been here all morning," Kirima called out as she approached along the trail. "It's my turn with Kyoshi."

"Buzz off!" Rangi yelled. She took the fire she'd been winding between her hands and redirected it high above Kirima's head.

Since the night they spent in the marble quarry, Rangi's personal attitude toward Kirima had gone steeply downhill. Kyoshi had no idea why. They were both talented benders who married intelligence with precision. She'd trust either of their judgments in a pinch.

Kirima didn't flinch from the fire blast. The waves of heat fluttered her hair and illuminated her sharp face in golden hues, an effect that was rather pretty. "You're not setting a very good example for the baby Avatar, Topknot. Too much rage will stunt her growth."

"Stop calling me that!" Rangi fumed.

Maybe that was it, the constant teasing. Kyoshi wondered how Rangi put up with the nickname for so long. In the Fire Nation, hair was heavily linked with honor. She'd heard that sometimes the losers of an important Agni Kai would shave parts of their head bald, laying patches of their scalp bare to symbolize an extra level of humility from their defeat, but the topknot was always sacred. It was never touched except in circumstances akin to death.

Kirima bowed in mockery. "As you wish, my good Hotwoman. I'm coming back in five minutes."

After she disappeared, Kyoshi put her hand on Rangi's shoulder. "Did something happen between the two of you?"

Rangi responded with her new favorite way of avoiding the subject. "Stance training," she said.

"We already did stance training!"

"Lek said you went berserk in the cave. We're moving to two a day. Horse. Now."

Kyoshi groaned and pressed her feet together. She shuffled them to the sides, alternating between heels and toes, until they were wider than her shoulders. She kept quiet as she lowered her waist, or else Rangi would make her hold a log or some other heavy object they could find lying around.

Rangi circled her, looking for any weakness where she could strike. "Do not move," she said, right before stepping carefully onto Kyoshi's bent knee.

"I hate you so much!" Kyoshi yelled as Rangi draped her bodyweight over her shoulders.

"The exercise is to maintain composure in the face of distraction! Now maintain!"

Kyoshi put up with the asymmetrical agony until Rangi dropped back down to the ground. "I don't want her teaching you waterbending," Rangi said as she moved threateningly into Kyoshi's blind spot.

"Why?" Kyoshi felt Rangi leap onto her back, clinging to her like a rucksack. *"Agh! Why!"*

"There's a proper order to training the Avatar," Rangi said. "The cycle of the seasons. Earth, fire, air, water. It's not good to deviate from that pattern. You have to master the other elements before water."

"Again, why?" There were only four airbending temples in the world. If she tried to seek out a master there, Jianzhu would find her more easily than anywhere else.

"Because!" Rangi snapped. "They say bad things happen when an Avatar tries to defy the natural order of bending. Ill fortune befalls them."

Kyoshi had never known Rangi to lean on superstition. Tradition, however, was another matter. She could tell that each time they ignored an established practice regarding the Avatar, the knife twisted in Rangi's heart a little bit more.

But Kyoshi owed it to her not to make a promise she couldn't keep. "I'm going to use every weapon I have at my disposal," she said. That was the truth.

Rangi let go of her. "I know. I can't stop you from training with Kirima. It's just that as soon as you start waterbending in earnest, our chance to do things the right way dies. Forever. It can't be brought back."

Hearing it phrased that way made Kyoshi glummer than she'd expected. She stared at the ground in front of her. Rangi's feet came into view.

"Come on," she said. "Cheer up. I didn't mean to send you into a spiral."

"I can't cheer up. I'm in Horse stance."

"I like your focus," Rangi said. "But see if you can withstand this."

She slid between Kyoshi's arms and gave her a head-tilting, knee-buckling kiss, as powerful and deep as the ocean after a storm.

Kyoshi's eyes went wide before they shut forever. She sank into heavenly darkness. Her backbone turned to liquid.

"*Maintain*," Rangi murmured, her lips like a feather on Kyoshi's before she attacked again, with added ferocity this time.

Kyoshi never wanted the torment to end. Rangi pressed into her like metal glowing on an anvil, scorching her where their skin met. Fingers ran through Kyoshi's hair, twisting and pulling to remind her how delightfully at the Firebender's mercy she was.

After a hundred years had passed, Rangi broke contact, gently and deliberately breathing a wisp of steam down Kyoshi's neck, a parting gift of heat that drifted underneath her clothes.

She leaned in for one last seductive whisper. "You still have seven minutes left to go," Rangi said.

Kyoshi kept her complaints to herself. It was a decent trade, all things considered.

"Your water and air chakras are overflowing," Lao Ge said.

He sounded like it was an embarrassment, as if Kyoshi had wandered outside her home without being fully dressed. She'd braved coming to him while the others were still awake, bedded down by the embers of the campfire. Rangi was probably staring at the sky, vigilant to her last moments of consciousness.

Lao Ge lay on his side in the grass, his head propped upon his hand so he could watch a pair of fireflies circle each other, tracing erratic patterns through the air. Kyoshi had long since gathered that the man had very little need to ever look at her.

"I don't know what chakras are," she said.

"What they are is either open or closed. For the sake of predictability, I prefer working with people who have all seven of them open or all seven of them closed. An accomplice with only some of their chakras unblocked can be easily swayed by their strongest, most gnarled-up emotion."

Kyoshi assumed the term had something to do with energy movement within the body. Not much of a stretch, since controlling internal *qi* was the basis of all bending.

"Your feelings of pleasure and love are butting up against a wall of grief," he said. "And guilt. Grief I can work with, but guilt makes for a poor killer. Have you second thoughts about your man?"

"No," she said. "Never." Lao Ge rolled over to his other side. She waited, letting him examine her to see she wasn't bluffing. Jianzhu was part of her blood by now. He was the back of her hands.

But this Te person was not. "I don't know if I can help you kill the governor," she said. "Helping Mok free a prisoner is one thing, but an assassination in cold blood is another." Kyoshi wondered why she didn't reject Lao Ge immediately the other night. Speaking the action out loud made it ludicrous. "There's no reason for me to help you."

The old man blew his nose on his sleeve. "Have you ever heard of Guru Shoken?" he asked. Kyoshi shook her head.

"He was an ancient philosopher, a contemporary of Laghima's. Not as popular though. He had a proverb: *'If you meet the spirit of enlightenment on the road, slay it!'*"

She wrinkled her brow. "I can see why he's not popular."

"Yes, he was considered heretical by some. But wise by others. One interpretation of that particular saying is that you cannot be bound by petty concerns on your personal journey. You must walk with a singular purpose. The judgment of others, no matter how horrific or criminal they label your actions, must hold no meaning to you."

"I can't do that," Kyoshi said. "I care what she thinks of me. I don't know if I could handle disappointing her."

Lao Ge knew whom Kyoshi was talking about. "Your hesitation seems to be less about your own morals than hers. In fact, without your Firebender tethering you to this world, you might feel no compunction at all. Perhaps that's why you feel guilt. You're only one step away from Guru Shoken's ideal, and it disturbs you."

This was the sorry state of Kyoshi's Avatarhood. Heartlessness the new enlightenment. Murder the means to self-discovery. If she ever resurfaced in the legitimate world, she would create a stain as dark as loam in the history books.

"Don't look so compromised," Lao Ge said. "Yangchen was a devoted reader of Shoken."

Kyoshi glanced up at him.

"She studied his opponents as well," he said. "But I don't feel like giving you their philosophical arguments. It doesn't serve my purposes."

She remembered the notes in her mother's journal, about the rumored longevity of Tieguai the Immortal. "Are you him?" she said. "Are you Shoken?" If her wild accusation was right, it would have made the man before her older than the Four Nations themselves.

Lao Ge snorted and rolled on his back, closing his eyes. "Of course not." He settled in to sleep. "I was always much better looking than that fool."

CONCLUSIONS

JIANZHU HAD learned his lesson. No caravans. No roads. As soon as he received the message from the shirshu tracker team, delivered by hawk, he'd gone through the enormous, preposterous expense of buying rare eel hounds. The fastest cross-country mounts besides a flying bison. A whole herd of them.

In the annals of the Earth Kingdom, ancient nomadic barbarians had traveled great distances, surprising footslogging armies with such tactics. A single rider would bring multiple mounts on a journey, switching between them on the fly to keep the animals as fresh and speedy as possible. From the ranks of his newly replenished guardsmen, he'd chosen two on the basis of their riding ability and set out with eight eel hounds between them. They'd been told as little as possible, but from his urgency it was easy to guess that their quest was important.

They reached the mountains of Ba Sing Se in astonishing time, with barely a witness to mark their passing. Early on, one mount had broken its leg in a singing groundhog's hole and needed to be put down. Another died from exhaustion on the far shore of West Lake.

But other than that, the constant, mindless riding, the wind in his hair, had been good for Jianzhu's spirit. As much as he missed Hei-Ran's company, he needed the occasional freedom from her watchful gaze. The party had brought more messenger hawks with their baggage, carefully caged and hooded. Jianzhu had promised to send word to her as soon as possible.

The location where he was set to meet the trackers was a small trailhead leading into the foothills of the southern Taihua range. The gentle slope of grassy green knolls was punctured by rows of red-stone crags jutting upward, uniformly following the same angle and grain. The rocks were as tall and numerous as the trees in a forest.

Jianzhu saw a lone figure in the middle of the stones waving them over and frowned. The message that had brought him here in such a hurry had explained, with overflowing apologies, that the shirshu had followed the scent trail to these mountains. Right before they'd lost control of the animal. It had escaped and run up the peaks in pursuit of its prey. For all he knew, it might have eaten the Avatar.

The handlers must have drawn lots to see which one would face his wrath in person while the rest looked for the shirshu. He spurred his hound toward the unlucky representative. The man's waving was stiff and forced, like the motion of a waterwheel.

"You can stop," Jianzhu called out. "I see you—"

A whistle and then a thump. The lone tracker keeled over, two arrows in his back.

Jianzhu cursed and leaped off his mount, more arrows crossing the air above his saddle. He tented slabs of earth around him and hunkered down in his cover, listening to the thunks of projectiles landing around him.

I am getting much too old for this. He never would have fallen for such an obvious trap in his younger days.

There was a pause in the firing. He chambered his fists and punched outward. The slabs that had protected him now splintered and flew outward in all directions like shrapnel from a bombard. He heard screams from the rocks above.

Taking in his surroundings as quickly as possible, he saw a few archers who'd fallen from their perches lying at the base of the crags. But, better safe than sorry. He lowered his stance, shook his waist, and whirled his arms. From base to top, every stone he could see violently sprouted thin spikes the size of *jian*s, like they'd instantly transformed into the same species of Si Wong cactus.

He heard more screams from the archers who remained hidden in their cover behind the rocks. That should have been it for elevated opponents. Fighters who fancied themselves professionals, but weren't, often made the mistake of taking the high ground without planning a way out.

His eel hound had run off. But two of them were still nearby, tethered by their reins to a heavy weight. The corpse of one of the guardsmen, studded with arrows. The reins had snagged on his wrist.

Good job, whatever your name was, Jianzhu thought.

The other guardsman was busy wiping the blood off his

dao with a hank of grass. Three attackers lay at his feet. They'd charged him with melee weapons, and bizarre ones at that. Jianzhu thought he spotted an abacus made of iron on the ground.

He was still impressed. "What do they call you, son?"

The guardsman snapped to attention and stared above Jianzhu's head with youthful, bright eyes. He had the strong brow of Eastern Peninsula ancestry. "Saiful, sir."

It was likely Saiful didn't understand how close of a call this was. Talent would only let you survive so many encounters. After that, the odds tended to catch up with a vengeance. "Excellent work, Saiful. There's always opportunity for a quick blade on my staff. I'll remember this."

The young guardsman kept his thrill contained as best he could. "Thank you, sir."

Jianzhu nudged a body onto its back. The dead man was clothed in the standard attire of a bandit, in the sense that he wore whatever peasant clothing he'd taken with him from his last legitimate occupation. This one had the trousers of a sailor or a sailmaker, mended repeatedly with fine sewing skill.

But there was an odd detail on his shirt. He'd stuck a flower in his lapel. It was too ruined to see what kind.

Jianzhu checked another body. It had no decoration on its person, but he backtracked along the path the man had charged and found what he was looking for on the ground. A dried moon peach blossom.

A badge, Jianzhu thought with some vehemence.

He straightened up and looked around. The mountains loomed nearby. They were said to be uninhabited. Practically impassable. Yet these men weren't clothed for an expedition.

With a sudden burst of energy he slammed his palm against the ground. Tremors rang through the earth, spreading wide like ripples in a pond.

"Sir, are you . . . searching for something underground?" Saiful asked.

"Maybe," Jianzhu said, his attention skimming over the grass. "Though what I'm doing right now is preserving their footprints."

He continued along the trail left by Saiful's opponents, watching the indentations they made with their heels and toes in the dirt, examining where they left mud on grass. A long time ago, he'd tracked criminals down in such a way, by listening to the earth and reading its marks.

The prints, in reverse, led to a clearing with a conspicuous gray rock the size of a chair. Jianzhu waved it away with a brush of his hand. Underneath was a wooden trap door.

"A hidden passage?" Saiful asked.

Jianzhu nodded grimly. "Hidden passage. Through the mountains."

"Sir . . . is this town supposed to be here?" Saiful said.

"No," Jianzhu said, his teeth grinding together.

Though he couldn't see underground, knowing the tunnel was there allowed Jianzhu to make various educated guesses with earthbending and knowledge of stonework to determine a path. They'd followed the network up the mountain on their eel hounds, forcing aside blocked passages and relying on the agility of their unusual mounts to see them through. Eventually the obstacles parted to reveal a great crater nestled in the heights, and in that bowl, waiting for them, was a village that neither of them had ever heard of before.

An entire settlement not on any map, out of reach of the law. Jianzhu's rage was almost too great for him to swallow. He was a storekeeper who would never be rid of vermin, a servant who would never be able to polish the silver clean.

The town appeared to be abandoned. They rode through empty streets, between longhouses that made a mockery of the Four Nations with adornments either looted or crudely imitated from their places of origin. One particular scrap-quilted banner had been fastened together so that characters from multiple signs clumsily formed the syllables *Hu* and *Jiang*.

Hujiang. So that was the name of this dungheap.

"There's our shirshu, sir," Saiful said. He pointed down the street where a dark, foul-smelling mound blocked the way.

The beast lay in relatively dignified repose. Other than the flies buzzing around its face—or lack thereof—it was still whole. Any trophy hunters would have found very quickly that toxins still coursed through its dead body.

Professor Shaw would be upset though. Jianzhu would need to come up with a cover story and a convincing amount of hush money to keep the man's anger from casting suspicion.

A brief scraping noise came from the house to his right. There was someone inside. Jianzhu dismounted and approached the darkened building.

"Sir?" Saiful whispered. "Going alone is a bad idea."

Jianzhu waved him off. "Patrol the street."

He slipped inside, contouring against the door frame rather than standing fully in the entrance, where he would be outlined by sunlight. Judging from the long tables and low backless stools, the building was some kind of inn or tavern. It made him furious again, that these outlaws had enjoyed enough peace in these mountains to build gathering places and sell each other wine.

Jianzhu walked around the tavern's counter. He found the person who'd made the noise.

It was a man sitting on a pile of pillows. He was muscled and scarred like a fighter, though it would seem he'd fared poorly in his last outing. One of his legs was wrapped in cloth and splinted up to his hip.

The injured man stared at Jianzhu with the empty, wary expression of being caught out. Jianzhu noticed empty bottles within his arms reach, jars of half-eaten food. He pieced it together. The inhabitants of the settlement had evacuated some days ago, probably scared away by the shirshu. The ambush at the base of the mountain had been a rearguard, or a bunch of greedy opportunists who'd lagged behind. This man with the broken leg couldn't make the journey down at all, so his companions had left him here to recover.

Jianzhu's eyes went to a small, out-of-place vase. It had a moon peach blossom in it. "I'm looking for a girl," he said to his recuperating friend. "She was here at some point. A very tall girl, taller than you or me. Pretty face, freckles, doesn't speak much. Have you seen her?"

The man's eyebrows twitched. It could have been an attempt to conceal the truth, or it could have been his memory sparking but failing to light.

"She would have been accompanied by a Firebender. Another girl, black hair, military bearing—"

Jianzhu caught the spear-hand strike aimed at his throat and redirected it into the nearby shelf, smashing the uprights. The man could add a broken wrist to his troubles. Jianzhu watched him seethe with pain.

The injured fighter tucked his bad hand under his good arm. "I am Four Shadows Guan," he snarled with pride. "And I will tell you nothing. I know a man of the law when I see one."

Jianzhu believed him. Once these types told you their professional name, there was no more rational conversation to be had. He would try one more tactic, a play on the *daofei*'s emotions.

He plucked the moon peach blossom from its vase and twirled the stem between his thumb and forefinger. "Times have changed," he said. "In my younger days I remember tracking this small group around the edges of the desert, from watering hole to watering hole. The Band of the Scorpion, they called themselves. There couldn't have been more than a dozen members."

Jianzhu caught what he was looking for, the man snorting in derision at a brotherhood that small. Which meant his group was much larger.

"The funny thing was, when I caught up with them, I found out why they were moving so slowly," he went on. "Two of their members had caught foot rot and couldn't walk. The others fashioned litters and carried them through the desert, the whole time. The group would have escaped me if they had left their sick behind, but they chose to stay together. They chose brotherhood."

He crushed the flower. "That's what Followers of the Code used to be like. When I look at you, abandoned by your sworn brothers, I don't see that tradition. I don't see honor."

Jianzhu let a flying gob of spit hit him in the face. "The brothers of the Autumn Bloom are willing to die for each other," the man said, wiping his lips. "You would never understand. Our cause makes us—"

He paused, realizing that Jianzhu was manipulating him. Four Shadows Guan was smarter than he looked. He clenched his jaw and slammed back against his makeshift bedrest.

Jianzhu grimaced and rolled up his sleeves. So much for doing this the easy way.

He stepped into the sunlight and wiped his hands on a nearby saddle blanket that had been hung up to dry and forgotten.

The Autumn Bloom, he thought to himself. *The Autumn Bloom.*

Who in the name of Oma's bastard children were the Autumn Bloom?

Jianzhu really was getting too old. He'd never heard of this gang before. He, the man who'd once single-handedly kept half the continent from falling into lawlessness, had let a new criminal outfit large enough to populate a good-sized village operate within shouting distance of the capital. The Autumn Bloom, whoever they were and whatever their goals, had a level of organization high enough to evacuate the settlement the moment they suspected an intrusion.

And more importantly, *most* importantly, the *only* thing that was important, was that they now held the Avatar in their clutches. The girl had been here at some point, that was certain. She must have planned to hide in the remote mountains and fallen into an ambush, like he nearly did. She'd been captured and taken to this headquarters. Shirshu followed living scents, and the animal would not have come here if she were dead.

Jianzhu cursed the spirits and mankind alike, cursed the threads of fate that had formed this knot. The Avatar had been kidnapped by *daofei*.

He threw his head back and stared at the sky for answers. Out of the corner of his eye he watched a bird fly away, its long tail plumage trailing behind it like a streamer. Some obscure cultures read the future through the patterns of winged creatures. Jianzhu wondered if that would have worked, if birds could have found the girl at birth and saved them this trouble. He heaved a great sigh.

Saiful rounded the corner and came back into the street, trotting back over to his boss. "Did you find anything inside, sir?"

"Just a corpse." He looked at the young swordsman. Saiful, along with a handful of other men, had answered Jianzhu's call for more fighters after the encounter with Tagaka left the ranks of his guard depleted. Perhaps a little too quickly and conveniently, now that he thought about it.

"Saiful, I didn't tell you to send a message with one of our hawks," Jianzhu said.

The young man looked surprised. "I was, uh, relaying ahead for supplies," he said. His hand drifted toward his weapon. He was a capable warrior, unafraid to kill for pay. A mercenary who swore loyalty as long as the wages were good. When you got right down to it, there was really no difference between him and a *daofei*.

But lying was something he needed more practice at. "You're from the Eastern Peninsula, aren't you?" Jianzhu said. He clasped his hands behind his back. "I have a good friend who does a lot of business in the Eastern Peninsula. His name is Hui. Have you met him before, by chance? Perhaps he was the one you relayed for supplies just now?"

. It had only been a twinge of suspicion on Jianzhu's part, a bluff really, but mentioning Hui's name let loose a flood of tells from Saiful's face and body language.

"Let me guess," Jianzhu said, digging deeper along this productive seam of ore. "Hui sent you to infiltrate my household, didn't he? With orders to find out what happened to the Avatar."

The slight step backward Saiful took let Jianzhu know that he'd struck upon the truth. "And being the smart young man you are, you realized the implication of the shirshu trail ending here. The Avatar—and, let's be clear, we *have* been following the Avatar—has been lost to outlaws. That was the message you sent to Hui just now."

Saiful was astonished that Jianzhu had performed the supernatural feat of reading his mind. Really, all Jianzhu had done was follow lines of information as they unfolded, like any good Pai Sho player.

The swordsman decided to follow a gambit of his own. He'd been found out, but they were in the isolated mountains, and he had his weapon and his youthful reflexes on his side. He warily drew his *dao* again.

Jianzhu rolled his neck, his joints creakier than in years past. The thing about Pai Sho was that most games didn't need to be played to completion. Masters usually recognized when they were beaten and resigned while the action was still technically in progress. If this dance between him and Hui had taken place on the grid, then right here would be where Jianzhu was supposed to bow and pick up his tiles in defeat.

There was no stopping the message from reaching Hui now that the bird was in the air. The chamberlain would realize how big a mess he was hiding and assemble a case against him to the rest of the sages of the Earth Kingdom. If the girl was found alive and her identity proven, she'd be delivered straight into the hands of Hui, who in the end wouldn't care which version of the Avatar he got, so long as he was taking it from Jianzhu.

By all logical reasoning, he was ruined. He'd lost.

But what only his close Pai Sho partners knew about him was that Jianzhu had never surrendered a game early in his life. On the rare occasions when an opponent got the best of him, he forced them to play out the lines to the bitter end. He made them jump hurdles for every piece of his they captured, and ran the late-night candles down to their last inches of wick out of sheer spite.

Jianzhu smiled grimly as he closed in on the young swordsman. Beating him always required a price in blood. He wasn't about to drop the habit now.

QUESTIONS AND MEDITATIONS

KYOSHI KEPT pace behind Lao Ge through the streets of the market. The two of them were alone, a girl and her elderly uncle taking a relaxing stroll. Nothing out of the ordinary.

Except Lao Ge, when not in the presence of the rest of the Flying Opera Company, walked with the bearing of a dragon wrapped in the clothes of a beggar. And Kyoshi was . . . Kyoshi. Vendors in their stalls craned their necks to gawk at her as she passed.

"Aren't we here to buy rice?" she muttered, feeling the pressure of so many gazes. "We passed two different peddlers already."

"Any one of us could have done that alone," Lao Ge said. He winked at a matron sweeping her stoop. She frowned and pushed a pile of dust at him. "You're here to observe."

Zigan Village was the main town that supplied food and man-power to Governor Te's palace. Kyoshi had been impressed by its size as they walked in from the outskirts, but quickly noticed that the solidly built houses and traditional Earth Kingdom trappings were somewhat of a front. They hadn't encountered an actual person until they were well into the heart of the village. Kyoshi found it hard to believe that the outer districts were completely vacant, but she'd seen nothing to the contrary.

Her ears perked toward the sound of an argument. A peddler and the farmer supplying him were nearly at blows.

"You can't fool me!" shouted the peddler. "I know the harvest was good this year! What you're charging me is an outrage!"

The farmer gestured wildly with the straw hat in his hand. "And I'm telling you, most of it gets confiscated for the governor's silos! I have to set the price based on the grain I have leftover!"

"How can you keep raising prices when there's an ocean of rice sitting behind his walls?" The peddler was beside himself. "For Yangchen's sake, I can see the roof of the storehouse from here!"

"Te hasn't opened the silos for over five years! You might as well consider that food eaten by the spirits!"

Lao Ge pushed Kyoshi along. Apparently, they were not here to offer solutions to people who needed them.

She knew what he was trying to prove, that Te's impending death was justified. "Reserving food for an emergency isn't foolish or corrupt," she said.

"No, but secretly selling your reserves for off-the-books profit is. To enrich himself, Te has traded away the grain he's collected every year since he was appointed governor. He's persisted during bad harvests, when his citizens have gone hungry enough to abandon their homes. Most famines are man-made, and he is on the verge of making one."

Lao Ge kicked a pebble at a shuttered window. There was no response to the noise. "Tell me, has Jianzhu ever failed his people in this manner?"

Kyoshi was forced to admit that Yokoya had only grown and prospered since Jianzhu planted his flag there. The townsfolk she'd seen in Zigan had the sinking, harried look of men and women running out of time. They weren't starving yet, but they would be soon. She recognized the weight of hunger on their shoulders, the same one she felt on hers as she went from door to door in Yokoya after being dumped there, rejected in turn by every family, her options dwindling.

She knew intimately what would happen next to the villagers. How their humanity would break down as starvation and helplessness took over. How it felt to watch death encroach a little closer every week. It had taken an intervention by Kelsang to save her from that fate.

Now Lao Ge was claiming to be that mercy for Zigan, for hundreds of people instead of just one girl. She had no reason to call him wrong.

It was a long, serpentine hike up the hillside to their encampment. She noticed the Flying Opera Company preferred elevated positions—maybe her mother's influence seeping through. It made perfect sense in this context. The rocky terrain hid them from view, and from this high up they could see the layout of Te's palace as clearly as a well-drawn map.

The governor is tactically incompetent not to have scouts monitoring these passes, Kyoshi thought, before noticing the strange mix of Rangi and Lao Ge that had rubbed off on her.

Lek looked up from stoking the campfire. "Did you get the rice?"

"We got sweet potato." She tossed the burlap sack to the ground. "Rice is . . . an issue."

"I'm sick of sweet potato," he groused.

Kyoshi ignored him and climbed higher to the flat outcropping where Kirima and Rangi lay on their stomachs, surveying the palace. They'd come to a temporary truce over their mutual appreciation for intelligence gathering. Casing a joint was pretty much the same thing as planning an assault.

She sat down behind them, unnoticed.

"We're looking at a traditional *siheyuan* design dating back to the Hao line of Earth Kings," Rangi said to Kirima, fixated on the complex below. It was ancient compared to the mansion back in Yokoya. There were four courtyards instead of two. And instead of being walled by rooms in continuous, smooth construction, it appeared as if more than a dozen houses of varying sizes and heights had been placed end to end along square patterns drawn in the ground. The ancient owners must have grown in wealth over time, adding more and more extensions haphazardly, a far cry from the singular vision Jianzhu had in constructing his own home.

It was still obscenely extravagant, especially when compared to the declining village of Zigan. One of the courtyards held a gaudy turtle-duck pond that was too large for its surroundings. Kyoshi knew that was a new trend in imitation of the Fire Nation royal palace.

"There's overlapping fields of view for the guards in each of the high points," Rangi said. She pointed at three lumps of roof on the closest edge. "We have to assume they'll be fully manned. So, coming at the best angle, that's three sentries we'll have to deal with on the approach."

"Lek can drop two of them from a distance, but the third would have time to sound the alarm," Kirima said. "How do you know so much about old Earth Kingdom architecture?"

"In the academy we studied how to attack any kind of fortification," Rangi said. "Walled Fire temples, Earth Kingdom stockades . . ."

Kirima looked at her carefully. "Polar ice walls?"

"Yes," Rangi said without hesitation. "Preparedness carries the day. There was even a plan for Ba Sing Se, though I'd pity the troops who carried it out."

The Waterbender set aside the comments made toward the other nations. "Mok will want to attack the south gate directly," Kirima said. "If we time our approach with his, we could assume the sentries posted on the other walls will divert toward him."

Rangi frowned. "That's a killing field." The ground south of the complex was hard-packed dirt strewn with fieldstones the size of a man's head. "A few Earthbenders in Te's guard could cause massive casualties."

"I don't think Mok cares," Kirima said. "I don't know what poison Wai's been pouring in the ears of his men, but they've turned into fanatics. He's going to breach the walls with sheer numbers."

Kyoshi shuddered to think of the slaughter that would follow if the *daofei* succeeded. She'd never heard of a siege where the attackers didn't repay the cost of victory in blood.

"We have one last option," Kirima said. "We still don't know which building the prison cells are in, or under. Capturing the entire palace might be the only way we get enough time to search for the person we're trying to free. So instead of trying to penetrate the compound, we simply take out the watchmen on the south wall, open the gate from the inside, and let Mok stroll right through."

"That's not going to happen," Kyoshi said.

"Gah!" Kirima launched herself to her knees and nearly fell off the outcrop. "How are you so stealthy on those giant hooves of yours?"

"Servants have to be quiet." Kyoshi appraised the pair of benders, who were probably more alike than either cared to admit. She needed some wisdom in a hurry. The conventional sort, not the turned-around mind games of Lao Ge. Right now, these two women were her best sources.

"We have to talk," she said to them.

The last hours of daylight were devoted to more training. The training never ended. The training would invade her dreams. She was certain the next Fire Avatar would be born with her muscle memory imprinted in their little fire-baby limbs.

"Let's go already!" Wong shouted. "You're the one who wanted to learn dust-stepping."

"Are you sure about this?" Kyoshi said, justifiably nervous. "When I saw the rest of you do it, you started on solid ground and worked your way higher. That seems a lot safer."

She perched on a rock column, one of many that studded a

ravine. The distance between each pillar was at least twelve feet. On the far side of the gully, Wong waited for her.

"Practice should be more difficult than the real thing," he said. "The goal is to reach me without slowing down. If you stumble you have to go back to where you started and try again. You're doing it three times."

Kyoshi peered down at the ground below. There was nothing that would break her fall on the hard stone floor. "Can I at least use my fans?"

"I don't know," Wong said. "Can you?"

She pulled her weapons from her belt. The heft in her hands was comforting as she spread them open. She had the thought that maybe if she flapped hard enough, she could take to the air like a bird.

"Either shoot or go hungry," Lek called out.

She should have just went for it without hesitating. Now she'd drawn an audience. The entire group, including Lao Ge, watched from various seats around the camp.

Precision, she thought to herself. *Timing. Precision. Timing.*

She leaped into thin air. In the same instant, pebbles and dust rose from the bottom of the ravine, stacking on each other, solidifying into a rigid structure that only needed to support her weight long enough for her to take her next step. She felt the ball of her foot land gracefully on the miniature, temporary stalagmite, the fragile tower of earth.

Then she crashed right through it. She dropped like . . . well, a stone.

In her panic Kyoshi let go of her fans and reached for the column with her hands, a drowning victim ready to pull the entire lifeboat under the surface with her. She struck the side and bounced off, scrabbling for the top of the column with her fingers but unable to find any purchase. Her back collided with the formation behind her, sending her pinwheeling face-first into the bottom of the ravine.

She lay there, a smear along the ground. Two thuds sounded, her fans landing after her. She had a distinct feeling, mostly because she was still alive, that someone had earthbent the ground under her to be softer, covered the rock with a layer of sand. Her guess was Lao Ge.

"Zero," she heard Wong call out. "Start over."

Every attempt at dust-stepping failed. Painfully. It was so bad that Rangi relented and let Kirima try teaching her to use water as a support instead of earth. That meant Kyoshi still ended up sprawled on the ground, only wetter.

"Maybe you should sit the mission out," Lek said after a particularly brutal fall. For once he was speaking out of genuine concern instead of taunting her.

"I don't think she can," Kirima said. "The only decent plans we came up with require all of us working together."

"I think there's ways we can make use of Kyoshi's raw power," Lao Ge said. He hadn't offered any opinions on the matter until now. "She may be a hammer on a team of scalpels, but sometimes a brute-force approach is necessary. I'll babysit her on the raid."

Kyoshi almost had to admire the way the old man spun events

into the patterns he desired, a weaver looking at raw flax and seeing the cloth it would become. "Maybe that would be for the best," she said. "We can keep each other out of trouble."

Each night, Kyoshi looked at the moon growing fuller, as if it were gorging on her dread. The date of the raid drew nearer and nearer, and the mood around camp turned grim. Roles had been determined, rehearsals walked through using props of nut shells and loose coins laid on diagrams traced in the ground. The gnawing in Kyoshi's stomach had little to do with hunger, and cold sweat kept her awake no matter her distance from the campfire or how close Rangi slept near her.

On the bright side, the two most useless members of the group being paired up gave Kyoshi and Lao Ge plenty of time to talk in private.

"Haven't you wondered why Mok's goal isn't to kill Governor Te?" Lao Ge asked, moments after he ordered her to sit and meditate with him.

The thought had crossed Kyoshi's mind. "He knows you're going to do it?"

Lao Ge laughed. "And I used to believe you didn't have a sense of humor. No, the reason is that he has the same piece of information I do. Palaces built in the Hao period often had an iron saferoom hidden in their depths. In case of an attack, the lord of the manor would flee there and lock himself behind impenetrable metal doors. The vaults had supplies to last a month, which was more than enough time for reinforcements to arrive. Mok knows trying to kill the governor would be a waste of effort."

The more Kyoshi heard about this Te person, the more she despised him. She opened her eyes. "He's going to abandon his household to an army of *daofei*?"

"What did you expect from a wealthy official?" Lao Ge said. "You sound disappointed. Perhaps you assumed Te would stride onto the field of battle at great risk to himself and fight off Mok's forces single-handedly with an incredible display of earthbending, protecting scores of innocent lives? I don't know where you got that image from."

Her hackles rose. It seemed like the old man never let an opportunity to sing Jianzhu's praises go by. She tried to calm herself by returning to her meditation.

Kyoshi had been denied access to this kind of training in Yokoya, but Rangi had found moments to teach her the basics on their journey. With their bloody task looming over her head, she found the practice calming, centering. She was like cool stone deep below the—

"So you're telling me you've never wondered about my age?"

Now he was trying to goad her on purpose. It was astounding how easily he flipped from the hypnotic, terrifying vision she knew he could be into an oafish child with wrinkles and white hair. She was wrong to have thought that calling him *sifu* a few times would have given her consistent, uninterrupted access to a guru of death.

"I can't say that I have," Kyoshi muttered through her teeth.

He sounded slightly wounded by her lack of interest in his secrets. "It's just . . . the people who've openly confronted me in the past with the name 'Tieguai the Immortal' . . . to a man, they all begged me for the secrets of longevity. The only ones who didn't were you and your mother."

First, she didn't believe he was anywhere near as old as he claimed. And second, desperately grasping for more power and control over life was what people like Jianzhu did. Te too, probably.

"Sifu," she drawled. "Oh, please, impart upon me the mysteries of immortality, for I wish to watch eras pass before my eyes like the grains of an hourglass."

"Of course!" Lao Ge said brightly. "Anything for my dear student. You see, it all comes down to maintaining order. Keeping things neat, clean, and tidy."

"Excuse me?" This was genuinely offensive to Kyoshi, as a former housekeeping servant. She'd let go of her standards for cleanliness the first morning outside of Yokoya, after waking up covered in Pengpeng's shed fur. But with his drinking and aversion to changing clothes, Lao Ge toed the line of rancidity. What did he know about tidying up?

"Aging is really just your body falling apart, on the smallest, most invisible levels, and neglecting to put itself back together," he said. "With the right mental focus, you could take an inventory of your own body and place each little piece that's not where it should be back into the correct order."

Kyoshi had to assume he was tailoring his lessons to her background and that the real process was much more complicated. "The way you describe it, you'd have to decide what version of yourself you'd be stuck as, forever."

"Exactly! *Those who grow, live and die. The stagnant pool is immortal, while the clear flowing river dies an uncountable number of deaths.*"

"Is that another proverb of Shoken's? Because it doesn't sound like any spiritual lesson I've heard."

"It's *my* proverb," Lao Ge whined, his feelings hurt again. "All this fretting about spirits. I'm trying to teach you about the *mind*. An infinite world that's been neglected by far too many explorers."

The mind. Kyoshi's mind drifted to another existence, one where she was sitting happily across from Kelsang in a green field as he told her about the wonders of the Spirit World. His warm and gentle voice guiding her consciousness until they crossed the boundary, hand in hand, to a land where human concerns couldn't weigh them down.

She'd lost that. She'd lost him, and the sickness that followed would never fully heal. Kelsang's absence had put her in stasis. If Lao Ge wanted her to be stagnant and forever trapped, she'd already mastered the lesson.

Kyoshi looked at this substitute who sat before her, the strange joke she got instead of her true teacher. It was an exchange poor enough to make her weep. "Spirit creatures are more interesting than mental riddles," she said.

"My dear," Lao Ge said softly. "As you'll discover one day, the mind has specters of its own."

THE FACE OF TRADITION

THE TIME had come. The moon was full to bursting. It spilled its light over the fields surrounding Te's palace, sharpening corners and altering colors in ghostly detail. Mok knew enough to schedule his raid when his men could see what they were doing.

The Flying Opera Company picked its way down the rocky hillside. "Does everyone know the plan?" Rangi said.

She was asking as a formality. Rangi had drilled each step into their skulls. It had been satisfying to see the others get a measure of Fire Nation discipline as revenge for what they'd put Kyoshi through.

Going to see Mok before the assault was part of the operation. If he let them move as they pleased, and did not let his temperament and vanity reign, then with luck on their side they would deliver him exactly what he wanted. One prisoner, unharmed.

Te's foolishness was on full display as they approached Mok's encampment south of the palace. Kyoshi counted at least five hundred *daofei* preparing for battle, sharpening their swords and honing their spear thrusts. Had none of Te's household guard noticed this many armed men converging on his location? Jianzhu would have smothered this miniature uprising before it—

She shook her head. For one night, and one night only, Jianzhu was immaterial.

They tiptoed by a large group of bare-chested men arranged in neat rows, deep in Horse stance, chanting gibberish in unison. Their captain walked among them holding a bundle of lit incense sticks in his hand. He ritualistically swept the smoking ends over their torsos, leaving trails of ash on their skin. Kyoshi looked closer and saw that each man had the characters for "impervious" inked on their forehead.

"Who are they?" she whispered to her companions.

"Those are members of the Kang Shen sect," Kirima said. "They're nonbenders who believe that performing secret purification ceremonies will make them immune to the elements. Mok must have recruited a bunch to serve as his front line."

"That's madness!" Kyoshi said. "If they charge straight into a formation of Earthbenders, they're going to be slaughtered!" The men she saw had no armor, no shields. Many of them seemed to be empty-handed fighters, lacking a weapon entirely.

"It's amazing what the mind can be led to believe," Lao Ge said.

"Especially if you're desperate," Lek muttered. "They say that people turn to the Kang Shen sect after seeing a friend or loved one killed by a bender. Be made to feel powerless that way, and you'll do anything that gives you courage."

They approached the center of camp. Mok was easy to spot. He'd set up a fancy wooden desk in the middle of the outdoors that served no purpose other than to show he could. He sat behind it with his fingers tented, as if he were the governor of these parts and not Te. Wai stood next to him, a nightmarish imitation of a secretary.

"My beloved associates," Mok said after they bowed. "Come closer."

They glanced at each other nervously and shuffled toward the desk.

"Closer still," Mok said. They crowded around him. Kyoshi noticed Lek was on the flank, in the most danger. His head was low and still. She regretted not standing between him and the *daofei* leader.

"I didn't get the chance to bid you farewell in Hujiang," Mok said. "You missed the excitement." He stared pointedly at Rangi and Kyoshi. There was no evidence to link them to the shirshu attack, but a man like him wouldn't need it. They were the pieces that didn't fit, and that was enough.

"A great beast came on the morning you left," he continued. "It killed several of my best men. What do the two of you have to say about that?"

Wai drew his knife before Kyoshi could answer. It was Lek, brave, stupid Lek, who either never learned or was too selfless for his own good, who spoke up for her again. "We don't know anything about that, Uncle. Kyoshi and Rangi aren't to blame."

Wai lunged.

Certainty lent Kyoshi a speed she never knew she had. In one swift motion she caught Wai's knife hand before it reached Lek, pinned it to the desk by his wrist, and drew her fan with her other hand. She kept the heavy weapon closed as she smashed it like a hammer on Wai's fingers, breaking them in a single blow.

The knife clattered to the ground. The eyes of the Flying Opera Company were as big and wide as the moon overhead. Everyone was shocked into silence, including Wai, who seemed numbed by sheer disbelief from the pain coursing up his arm.

"Forgive me, Uncles," Kyoshi said, finding it supremely easy to speak now. "I saw a poisonous insect and thought to save your lives."

Wai clutched his broken hand and bared his teeth at Kyoshi, a vine cobra about to spit.

She was still calm. "But if Uncle Wai believes my actions inappropriate, he can always teach me the meaning of discipline on the *lei tai*, after our mission is over."

Mok leaned back in his chair and crowed with laughter. "So much progress in only a few weeks! This is the influence I have on people. Come, Kyoshi. Since your brothers and sisters have had their tongues stolen by a spirit, tell me what plans you've come up with since we last saw each other."

She carried on as if nothing had happened, ignoring the surprise of her friends and the fury of Wai. She'd heard the strategizing between Rangi and Kirima enough times to be convincing. "We believe the prison where your—*our*—sworn brother is being held is below the northeast courtyard. Assuming it was constructed at the same time as the oldest part of the palace, we should be able to defeat the security."

He noticed her pause. "But?"

"Provided we have enough time. If Te's guards choose to defend the prison, our group alone may never be able to spring our man. There's also a chance that if we show our hand too early, they realize what we're doing and preemptively kill the hostage."

"Then it's as I anticipated," Mok said, stroking his chin like a wise man. "We'll need a direct attack in concert with your clandestine efforts." Kyoshi had to give him some measure of credit. He did foresee this outcome back in Hujiang.

Mok reached inside the desk and pulled out two sticks of timing incense. Kyoshi watched him pluck Wai's knife off the ground and carefully cut them to the same length before handing them to Rangi. "If you would, my lovely."

She lit both tips with one finger and handed one back to Mok.

"Get to your positions," he said. "We attack in one hour."

The Flying Opera Company bowed and got out of there as fast as they could. Step one had been passed. Rangi cradled the timing incense as they left the camp, trying to shield it from breezes that might accelerate the burn and throw them off schedule.

One hour, Kyoshi thought. In the distance a few bright lights from the palace could be seen, the fires lit by servants like her for cooking and warmth, lanterns carried by guards like the watchmen who always greeted her kindly at the gates of Jianzhu's mansion. She looked at the Kang Shen acolytes working themselves into a frenzy, vulnerable and naked but for their faith. One hour until blood was spilled.

"Steady on," Lao Ge whispered to her.

His words, meant to be comfort, only reminded her. One hour until she became the killer she was trying to be.

Lek, Kirima, and Wong hustled them back to camp. "What's the rush?" Rangi said, covering the dwindling stick of incense. "There's no reason to be hasty at this point." She and Kyoshi were already wearing their armor.

"We have to put on our faces," Kirima said. She rummaged around her limited belongings. "It's tradition before a job."

Lek failed to find what he was looking for and grunted. "I forgot we left Chameleon Bay in a hurry," he said. "I'm out. Does anyone else have some makeup they can spare?"

Kyoshi blinked, having difficulty comprehending. "I . . . do? I think there was some in my mother's trunk, along with the fans?"

Wong helped himself to Kyoshi's rucksack until he found the large kit of makeup that had been completely neglected until now. "It would be a disgrace for an opera troupe to perform barefaced. And stupid for thieves not to hide their identities."

Kyoshi remembered. Classical opera was performed by actors wearing certain patterns of makeup that corresponded with stock characters. The tiger-monkey spirit, a popular trickster hero, always had a black cleft of paint running down his orange face. Purple meant sophistication and culture, and often appeared on wise-mentor types. Her mother's journal had mentioned the makeup, but she'd overlooked it in favor of the more practical fans. And the headdress. Didn't she have a headdress too?

Wong brought the kit to her and opened it. "It looks like the good stuff, from Ba Sing Se, so it hasn't dried out," he said. "I'll do yours first. It takes practice to put on your own face correctly."

Kyoshi shuddered at the thought of the oily paste on her skin but decided not to complain. "Wait a second," she said. "There's nothing in here but red and white." The indentations that should have held an assortment of colors had been filled multiple times over with deep crimson and an eggshell-colored pigment. There was a small amount of black kohl as well, but not enough to cover the whole face.

"Those are our colors," Wong said as he dipped his thumb and began to gently apply the paint to her cheeks. "White symbolizes treachery, a sinister nature, suspicion of others, and the willingness to visit evil deeds upon them."

Kyoshi could hear Rangi snort so loudly Te might have heard it in his palace.

"*But*," Wong said, scooping into the other side of the case with his forefinger. "Red symbolizes honor. Loyalty. Heroism. This is the face that we show our sworn brothers and sisters. The red is the trust we have for each other, buried in the field of white but always showing through in our gaze."

Kyoshi closed her eyes and let him put more paint on.

"Done," Wong said. He smoothed the last of the black eyeliner on her brow and stepped back to examine his handiwork. "I can't promise it'll stop a sharp rock or an arrow, but I can guarantee you'll feel braver. It always does that for me."

"Lean down," Kirima said. She'd pilfered the headdress out of Kyoshi's bag while her eyes were closed. "You're wearing your mother's face, so you should wear her crown as well."

Kyoshi lowered her head so that Kirima could place the band around it. She'd never tried on the headdress before. It fit like it had been made for her.

She rose to her full height. "How do I look?" she asked.

Wong held up a tiny mirror that had been nestled in the lid of the makeup kit while Rangi angled the glow of the incense so she could see. The glass wasn't wide enough to display her entire face, just a slash of reflection running down the arc of gold atop her brow, across her flaring eye, and over the corner of her red-dened mouth.

The narrow mirror resembled a tear in the veil of the universe, and from the land that lay beyond the other side, a powerful, imperturbable, eternal being stared back at Kyoshi. A being that could pass as an Avatar someday. "I'm not thrilled you're wearing *daofei* colors," Rangi said, biting her lip as she smiled. "But you look beautiful."

"You look terrifying," Lek added.

A lifetime ago, Kyoshi had never thought she would be either of those things. "Then it's perfect."

THE RAID

THEY CREPT to the staging point, a small promontory a few hundred feet from the walls of the palace. They huddled around Rangi and watched the timing incense die out in her fingers, the last embers lighting their painted faces. Kyoshi glanced at the group, their features muted or exaggerated by strokes of red on white. Even Rangi and Lao Ge had donned the colors. The markings tied them together.

The incense crumbled to where Rangi could no longer hold it. "Go," she whispered.

Lek dust-stepped to the top of the boulder they were hiding behind. He grabbed his sleeve and pulled it up over his shoulder, exposing a long, wiry arm wrapped in more thin leather straps than Kyoshi had previously thought.

He shook his elbow forward, and the bindings released, revealing the pocket of a sling.

Rangi, Kirima, and Wong took off running for the palace.

Without slowing his motion, Lek kicked a stone bullet the size of a fist into the air and snatched it up in the sling pocket. The projectile whined with speed as it whirled around his head, accelerated with bending. As he stood astride the rock, legs bracing against the powerful momentum of the bullet, his face tranquil with concentration, he looked much older to Kyoshi. Less a boy, and more a young man in his element.

He let the stone fly. Kyoshi could barely see the guard on the roof he was aiming at and would have guessed that such a target was too impractical to hit, but Lek's talents—physical, or bending, or both—created a tiny *plink* sound off in the distance. The blurry shape that was the guard dropped out of view.

Lek was already winding up his next shot before the first one landed. Rangi and the others closed the gap. They were within spotting distance of the guards. He loosed the second stone.

But right as he let go of the sling end, a horn blasted through the silence of the night. It came from the south. The *daofei* forces had decided to announce their presence.

The sudden noise fouled Lek's throw. He swore and immediately threw his hands out in a bending stance. Kyoshi watched in disbelief as he applied some kind of invisible pressure to the flying stone. She couldn't see any of the results, but from the way he let out a relieved breath when another *plink* went off, the shot landed. It had happened in an instant. His distance control had to be on par with Yun's. Maybe better.

"Go!" Lek shouted at Kyoshi, not interested in her admiration. "Mok and those idiots have blown our cover! Go!"

Kyoshi and Lao Ge started carrying out their portion of the plan. They sprinted down the hillside toward the southern fields of the palace. Out of the corner of her eye, she saw three figures climbing into the air to vault atop the eastern wall, one of them with twinkling feet as if she were stepping on starlight.

The plain across from the main gate filled with swordsmen charging at the complex. As Rangi had predicted, the front ranks were nothing but fodder for Te's unseen Earthbenders, who lacked Lek's accuracy but didn't need it. The first stones arced through the air from the direction of the palace, pulverizing the unprotected Kang Shen acolytes. The missiles bounced farther, carving swathes through the *daofei* behind them. Screams of pain and anger filled the air.

The outlaws ignored their casualties and picked up speed. Kyoshi and Lao Ge were headed right for the killing ground between them and the palace.

Lao Ge got behind Kyoshi and tapped her twice on the shoulder. "Go!" he shouted.

She took a deep breath, still on the run, and embraced the earth fully.

"We can't let Mok anywhere near the palace," Kyoshi said. "He'll kill everyone inside."

Rangi and Kirima looked up at her from their positions on the overlook. They needed a break from surveying the complex anyway. "There's no way we can prevent him from taking it in the long run," Rangi said. "Do you want to flip to Te's side and try to fight them off?"

Kyoshi shook her head. "I don't think slaughtering Mok's forces is the answer."

"But if Mok doesn't launch his assault, then our team will be sitting turtle ducks," Kirima said. "You're telling us we need to think of a way to attack the palace with an army, save the lives of everyone inside the palace, keep the army from killing itself, *and* rescue a prisoner from inside the walls?"

Lao Ge never said that she wasn't allowed to seek help in answering his riddles. It was the time-honored Earth Kingdom tradition. Cheating on a test with the help of your friends. "That's exactly what I'm telling you."

"We can't make all sorts of fancy plans when we only have a handful of benders," Rangi said.

Kyoshi grimaced. She had to get used to exercising her prerogative, and she might as well start now.

"What kind of plans would you make if you had the Avatar?" she asked.

Kyoshi ran into the ground, descending on a fifty-foot-wide ramp of her own making. The earth yawned to accept her, parting ways to create a titanic furrow that piled the spare dirt to the left and right. Aoma and Suzu could go jump off a pier. Kyoshi had grown up in Yokoya just as much as they had. She *did* know about farming matters. And now she was plowing the ground with more force than the entirety of the village's Earthbenders.

Arrows and stones passed harmlessly overhead. She leveled out once she hit a depth of fifty feet—why not keep things square and tidy?—and kept running across the southern field with Lao Ge keeping pace, creating an impassable trench behind her.

It had become clear during their surveillance that Te's palace had a critical security weakness. It lacked a moat. Kyoshi was providing one for him, free of charge.

"Would you be able to handle going faster?" Lao Ge shouted above the bone-crushing noise.

She nodded. There was no fatigue. No strain. Her bending had changed. To cut loose like this with her full power instead of trying to squeeze it through tiny holes was energizing. It was the difference between eating a bowl of rice one grain at a time versus taking huge, satisfying bites.

Lao Ge bent a section of the ground around them, and suddenly the two of them were surfing on a platform of earth while Kyoshi kept shoving the soil out of their way.

"No sense in traveling by foot when we don't have to," he said.

In this manner it took them no time at all to round the corners of Te's palace and encapsulate it in the trench. She couldn't see aboveground, but she imagined surprise on the faces of the guards and the *daofei*, sheer murder on Mok's and Wai's. She had to hope that phase two of the plan would appease them. The Flying Opera Company still had a promise to fulfill.

"Watch out now," Lao Ge said. "I know you can't dust-step yet."

He raised his hands and the platform rose out of the trench. It soared past ground level and onto the eastern roof of the palace, where it crumbled underneath their feet, leaving them standing on the shingles in the exact spot where Kirima, Wong, and Rangi waited for them, bathed in the moonlight.

"Right on time," Kirima said.

"Are the guards crowded in the southern wall?" Kyoshi

asked. She'd created a standoff between them and the *daofei*, and she needed them staying in place.

"Enough of them," Rangi said. "You have to move quickly though."

This rally point left them temporarily exposed, but it had been chosen for a reason. It lay right above the overlarge, over-deep turtle-duck pond. And they had clear sight of the glowing full moon above.

Kyoshi drank its light, feeling its push and pull as Kirima had taught her, her muscles loosening from the rigidity of earth-bending into the relaxed, flowing state of water. She took a stance and beckoned at the pond.

She knew little of advanced waterbending forms, but that wasn't necessary right now. Nor did she require her fans yet. For this feat, Kyoshi would provide the power, like a draft beast, and Kirima would apply control. As Waterbenders, the two of them would be greatly enhanced by the full moon, like tides rising in a bay.

The sleeping turtle ducks quacked awake in panic and fled as the surface of the water bulged upward. Kyoshi lifted the blob of liquid higher and higher. Where it threatened to protrude too far and spill, Kirima gently nudged it back into place with the skill of a surgeon. The mass of water looked like a jellynemone, pulsating and floating along the current.

Kyoshi felt an impact against her ribs and nearly let the water out of her grip. She looked down to see a tear in the fabric of her jacket and a small metal point broken off in the links of the chainmail underneath. She'd taken a glancing blow from an arrow.

A few guardsmen poured out of the opposite end of the courtyard. "We'll cover you!" Rangi said. "Go!" Everyone who couldn't waterbend leaped off the roof.

"All right, Kyoshi!" Kirima shouted. "Drop the hammer!"

Kyoshi relaxed and lowered her center of gravity with such vigor that it felt like her skeleton outraced her muscles. The heavy formation of water punched through the interior wall of the southern portion of the compound, rushing in through the breach. There was so much that it would flood every corridor from wall to wall, floor to ceiling. Little windows and vents dotting the interior walls gave them the line of sight they needed, though with this amount of water, it was hard not to feel the element's presence intuitively.

The locations of the screams told them it was working. The guardsmen who'd been focusing on the *daofei* assault, concentrated in the southern fortifications, were being violently scrubbed from their posts.

Kyoshi and Kirima swept the tidal wave from left to right, then around the corner to the west for good measure, before releasing the pressure. They wanted to knock the soldiers out, not drown them. With a synchronized pull, they burst a portion of the west wall, letting the water flow into the other courtyard. Piles of groaning, coughing bodies spilled through the gap.

In the brief moment Kyoshi spent checking that the men were alive, a battle cry caught her off guard. She turned to see a lone soldier who'd entered the roof from some sally port they'd overlooked charging her with a spear, his feet clattering over the tiles. Her hands went for her fans, but she fumbled the draw.

Right before she was impaled, she heard a familiar zipping noise. The spearman took a stone bullet to the hip and fell off the roof with a scream. Kyoshi glanced back into the night. Somewhere in the distance, Lek was grinning smugly at her.

"What are you doing?" Kirima snapped. "Get moving!"

On to the last phase, the one Kyoshi was truly dreading.

Kirima and Kyoshi hurried down the steps of the service tunnels. Their objective was underground. They came to a fork where Lao Ge was waiting for them.

"They need you to bounce the cell door lock," he said to Kirima, motioning down the right branch. "Kyoshi and I will check the other side for any lurking guardsmen."

The others had explained to Kyoshi that "bouncing a lock" meant shooting water into the keyhole with enough pressure to force the pins higher, releasing the locking mechanism. It was considered faster and more elegant than trying to freeze the metal to its shattering point. It was also beyond Kyoshi's waterbending skill, fans or no fans.

Kyoshi bit her lip as Kirima went down the right tunnel without hesitation, leaving her alone with Lao Ge. The old man watched the Waterbender depart with casual interest. He'd taken a slouching position against the wall as if he didn't have a care in the world.

"Come," he said to Kyoshi, any sense of urgency gone from his voice.

She followed him down the hall. It was more finished than the tunnels under Jianzhu's mansion, lit with glowing crystal and painted clean white. Though her headdress added to her height, she didn't have to stoop.

The dizziness she sometimes felt in Lao Ge's presence when they were alone came back with a vengeance. Each of her footfalls seemed to carry her miles over the endless stretch of tunnel. She lost her sense of up and down.

She had no idea how far they'd gone when they reached the end of the hall. At first Kyoshi thought that it was strewn with bodies, that the violence had leapfrogged them somehow. But the dozen or so people who lay on the floor or pressed themselves against the walls were alive and trembling. They weren't guards. They wore the decorative patterns of ladies-in-waiting, or the plain, neat robes of butlers. Beyond them was a solid iron door, barred by a thick bolt that had no visible opening mechanism.

Lao Ge took a step forward. The entire assembly cowered and hid their faces.

"Your master saved himself and locked you out," he said with wicked humor. The tight corridors caused his voice to echo at a lower timbre, or perhaps it had always been that deep. "You've been left to your fate."

The maid nearest him sobbed. Lao Ge had painted his face in a twisted, horrific jester's leer. And many people considered Kyoshi a tower of menace on her best days. She remembered the effect she had on the staff in Jianzhu's mansion that rainy day she left them, and they'd known her for years. To Te's servants, who'd heard the throes of battle outside, she and Lao Ge must have looked like walking incarnations of death.

An acrid smell wrinkled her nose. She looked down to see a chamberlain, rocking and mumbling to himself with his eyes rolled back in dread. "Yangchen protect me. The spirits and Yangchen protect me. The spirits . . ."

Lao Ge laughed, and the servants shrieked. "Get out," he said. "Today you live."

The staff members scrambled past them on their hands and knees, taking the turn that would lead them to the surface of the palace. Kyoshi watched the unfortunate men and women leave. She said nothing that would relieve their fear or allow them to sleep better tonight.

"The lock," Lao Ge reminded her.

The greater portion of it was on the other side of the door, as he'd explained earlier. But there was a flaw in the design that left part of the thick iron bar exposed. Defeat that, and they could get in.

She gripped the bolt with both hands. It began to glow beneath her firebending. She yanked back and forth rhythmically as the metal grew hotter and hotter. Between her and Lao Ge, they'd come up with the three parts needed for this to work. Sufficient heat to ruin the temper of the iron. Oscillating motions to create fatigue in the structure, weakening it. And last, sheer brute force. Her specialty.

With each successive tug, the metal gave way a little more. Once, Rangi had warned her that heating an object like this without injury took much, much more skill than preventing your own flames from singeing your skin, which was an act so instinctive to Firebenders it didn't need to be taught. This trick with the iron was prolonged, dangerous contact with a hot surface. Kyoshi felt her hands start to burn.

"You're almost there," Lao Ge said with a hint of admiration. "Honestly, I wasn't completely sure this was possible."

The metal angled farther and farther off its bearings until, right before the pain became too much to bear, it snapped. The severed ends of the bolt jutted out like red-hot pokers. The heavy door groaned on its hinges.

Kyoshi wrung the heat from her fingers and shouldered the vault open. It was brighter inside than in the hallway. She blinked as she took in her surroundings.

The interior of the large room was not what she expected. Lao Ge had described it as an emergency survival measure. She expected water stores, preserved food, weapons.

It had been redecorated. Someone had removed the necessities for lasting out a siege and replaced them with luxurious carpets, silken pillows. One wall was racked with jugs of wine, not water. Any fool who locked himself inside would have died within a few days.

There was a single figure standing against the far wall. A boy in his nightclothes. Kyoshi made the deduction that Te's son had converted this room, made for war, into a clubhouse.

"Where is your father?" she said, the words coming out a harsh growl. "Where is Governor Te?"

The boy stared at her with a round, soft face full of defiance. "I'm Te Sihung," he said. "I'm the Governor."

Kyoshi looked at Lao Ge. He smiled at her knowingly. *This* was the test. Whether she was cold-blooded enough to help him kill a boy who didn't look old enough to shave. She cursed the old man, cursed the stupid youth in front of her, cursed the corruption and incompetence of her nation that allowed such a mistake of authority to occur.

"How old are you?" she asked Te.

"I don't owe *daofei* an answer," he sneered.

She rushed forward, grabbed him by the back of the neck and tossed him out the door of the vault. He bounced on the floor and skidded down the hall. Kyoshi walked around to his head and nudged his jaw with her boot. "How old are you?" she asked again.

"Fifteen, soon," he whimpered. His attitude had changed dramatically midflight, and the painful landing sealed the deal. "Please don't kill me!"

"He's Lek's age," Lao Ge said to Kyoshi. "Old enough to know right and wrong. Old enough to shirk his responsibilities, to mismanage, to steal. You saw the state of Zigan. I can still guarantee that you'll save many lives by taking his." He noticed Te trying to crawl away and placed his foot on the boy's ankle, not hard enough to break it, but enough to make it clear he could.

Te gave up on trying to move. "Please," he said. "My father was governor before me. I just acted in accordance with what he taught me. Please!"

That was all anyone in this world did. What they saw their predecessors and teachers do. The Avatar was not the only being who was part of an unbroken chain.

"*You're* not much older than him," she heard Lao Ge say. "Are you immune to consequence?"

No. She wasn't. She picked up Te by his lapels. He blubbered incoherently, tears streaming down his face. "Sorry," she said. "But this is something I decided on, long before I laid eyes on you."

Kyoshi thrust an arm behind her and blasted Lao Ge down the tunnel with a ball of wind.

"Rangi, I can't airbend. You're not an airbending teacher."

It was the day before Kyoshi was scheduled to begin training with Kirima, to see if they could lift an entire pond's worth of water together. Rangi and Kyoshi were off by themselves in a small clearing under a lonely, gnarled mountain tree that had sprinkled its dried leaves over the ground. The two of them walked around in circles, their arms extended, nearly meeting in the center. There was no way they were doing this right.

"I'm not trying to teach you airbending," Rangi said. "I only want you to create wind, once, before you start waterbending in earnest. It doesn't have to be perfect." She spun around and traded the position of her hands. "I think you're supposed to . . . spiral? Feel your energy spiraling?"

Kyoshi had to pivot awkwardly to go the other way before Rangi collided with her. "How are you okay with amateur, self-taught airbending?"

"I'm not. I just—I just have this irrational fear that if you get too good at waterbending before ever airbending once, you'll damage the elemental cycle. Back when you used your fans to waterbend, I was ecstatic at first, but then I panicked. I started having nightmares that you permanently locked out your firebending and airbending. I was afraid you'd become a broken Avatar."

Rangi plunked down on the ground and put her head in her hands. "I know it doesn't make sense," she said. "Nothing makes sense anymore. We're doing everything wrong. Up is down, left is right."

Kyoshi knelt down and wrapped her arms around Rangi from behind. "But the center doesn't change."

Rangi made a little snort. "You know I miss him too?" she murmured. "Master Kelsang. He was so kind and funny. Sometimes when I find myself missing him, I feel guilty that I'm not thinking about my father instead. I wish they were both here. I wish everyone we've lost could be here with us, one last time."

Kyoshi squeezed her tight. She imagined Rangi's energy twining together in place with her own, forming a stronger thread from two strands.

There was a tickle against her brow. She and Rangi looked up to see a swirling dance of leaves, spinning around in a circle, the two of them caught in its eye. Kelsang used to make her laugh in the garden like this, by swirling the air, letting her touch the currents and feel the wind run between her fingers.

Kyoshi let the breeze play against her skin before giving it a gentle push with her hand. The wind spun faster at her request. She could feel Kelsang smiling warmly at her, a final gift of love.

"They'll always be with us," she said to Rangi. "Always."

Lao Ge landed in the vault, which happened to be full of cushions. Which meant that Kyoshi had less of a head start than she'd counted on. She threw Te over her shoulder and ran down the hall.

"Girl!" she heard Lao Ge shout behind her, echoing through the tunnel. She had the distinct feeling he could catch up at a moment's notice no matter how far she'd gone.

The fear lent her more speed. She took the stairs five at a time until she reached the surface.

Te gasped from her grip around his waist. "What are you—"

"Shut up." They were hemmed in by the walls of the courtyard. The stables were on the opposite end of the complex. An immortal assassin was surely only a few paces behind.

Kyoshi ran at the far wall. And then she ran higher. And higher. The earth flicked at the soles of her feet, propelling her upward. She continued to dust-step until she landed on top of the roof.

She spared a glance back. Lao Ge stood by the stairs, choosing not to follow her into the air, for the moment.

"My!" he called out. "You're just full of deceptions, aren't you? To think you were faking so many failed attempts at dust-stepping."

"They weren't all fake!" Kyoshi shouted as she sped away.

She sprinted across the palace, tiles crunching under her feet. She went north until she found the stables abutting the wall. Dropping down to the ground with Te still in hand, she found a sleepy ostrich horse and roused it awake.

Lao Ge was still toying with her, or perhaps he couldn't dust-step. She'd never seen him do it. Either way, they didn't have much time. She dumped the boy astride the mount she'd stolen.

"Thank you," Te said, wobbling from the lack of a saddle. "I'll give you anything you want. Money, offices—"

Kyoshi backhanded him hard across the mouth.

"You should have died tonight," she hissed. "I'll give you one chance to unsully yourself as governor of these lands. You will open the doors of your storehouses and make sure your people are fed. You will give back what you stole, even if it means selling your family's possessions. If you don't by the time I return, I'll make you wish you'd been captured by those *daofei* out there."

She left an open end on that timeline, having no idea when she'd be free to make good on the threat. But she knew she would, if given the chance. She was letting Te know there would be consequences. *Jianzhu would be proud,* she thought darkly.

Te's bleeding face roiled with confusion. "You—you earthbent and airbent. I saw it. How is that possible? Unless . . . you can't be. You're the Avatar?"

She saw the images warring in his head. He must have known of Yun, maybe met him in person. Revealing her identity had always been a risk on this mission. But Te was a loose end, one that ran in the same circles as Jianzhu.

Kyoshi bit her lip. She'd chosen from the start to save this boy's miserable life instead of keeping the secret that her own safety depended on. No sense in regretting it now.

"All the more reason for you to do as I say." She slapped the ostrich horse's flank, sending it careening toward the ditch. Te screamed as she bent a bridge into place at the last minute. He rode off into the darkness, clinging to the neck of his mount for dear life.

Once he was gone, Kyoshi lowered the bridge again. She didn't want Mok's men infiltrating the compound from the rear while so many helpless people were still inside. She dust-stepped over the gap and took her time walking farther north, to the rendez-vous point where the others would be waiting.

At some point during the hike, Lao Ge fell in beside her.

"You're not a very good apprentice," he said tonelessly.

There were a dozen replies she could have given him. Te was too young to die and still had time to redeem himself. The whole exercise was flawed and had nothing to do with her desire to end Jianzhu.

"I haven't failed to take my man in a long time," Lao Ge went on. "My pride is in shambles."

Kyoshi winced. She'd never seen Lao Ge truly angry, and it was a gamble as to what kind of person would emerge when things didn't go his way.

"Te's your responsibility now," he said. "From this point onward, his crimes will be your crimes. More than anything, I'm upset that you've fettered yourself in such a way. It's like you haven't paid attention to my lessons."

She supposed being treated like a disobedient child who'd adopted a stray animal was the best result she could have hoped for. "I'm sorry, Sifu," Kyoshi said. "I'm willing to accept the results of my actions."

"Easy for you to say that now." Lao Ge's upper lip curled with disdain. "Mercy has a higher price than most people think."

She stayed silent. There was no need to further provoke a man who could likely start the Avatar cycle anew in the Fire Nation right now without breaking stride. Any hope she'd had that spar-ing Te was the true goal all along, or that Lao Ge, through the lens of age, would interpret her betrayal as one grand joke in the greater scheme of life, was stifled by his compressed, tangible annoyance with her. There was no deeper-level understanding to be had.

The standoff between them continued until they reached the others. The Flying Opera Company was flush with success. Wong and Kirima held a bound man between them, clothed in a plain, ragged tunic. He had the sweet-potato sack tied over his head.

"We did it!" Rangi said. She ran forward and embraced Kyoshi. "I can't believe we did it! You bent like an —" She stopped herself from saying "Avatar" in the presence of a stranger. "Like a master of old!"

"Let's go make our delivery," Wong said. He picked up the prisoner and threw him over his shoulders, much as Kyoshi had done with Te. "Sorry for the rough treatment, brother. It won't be too long before you're breathing free air."

"It's no problem at all," the hooded man said politely.

The *daofei* nearly filled them with arrows as they approached the southern camp.

"We have your man!" Kirima shouted. Wong dumped the prisoner to his feet. With the hood on, he couldn't see how his rescuers crowded behind him like a human shield.

Mok strode up to them, apoplectic. "What do you think you were doing!? We discussed no such plan!"

Kirima held her hands up. "We got him out of the prison," she said, reminding him again that the mission had technically been accomplished. "The trench was a necessary last-minute improvisation."

That wasn't true. Figuring out how to keep the *daofei* out of the palace had been the primary challenge Kyoshi had set to Rangi and Kirima. Seeing the Waterbender lie for her made Kyoshi feel worse about hiding the additional side mission with Lao Ge and Te from the others. She'd caused her friends undue risk.

"I should flay your skins and put them under my saddle!" Mok screamed. Wai stood behind him, though Kyoshi noticed he wasn't so ready to draw a blade this time. The man stared at her warily, rubbing his bandaged hand.

"Mok, is that you?" the prisoner said, tilting his ear toward the noise. "If so, stop haranguing my saviors and get this bag off my head."

Wong untied his hood while Kirima sliced the ropes off his wrists with a small blade of water. Rangi had recommended the bindings as a precaution since they didn't want a confused captive resisting his own rescuers. The burlap mask fell off his head to reveal a pale, handsome face under shaggy dark hair.

"Big brother," Mok said. The *daofei* leader's mannerisms suddenly took on a reverential, submissive quality. "I can't believe it's you. After so long!"

"Come here," the prisoner said, opening his arms wide. The two men embraced and pounded each other's backs.

"Eight years," the newly freed man said. "Eight years."

"I know, brother," Mok sobbed.

"Eight years," the man repeated, squeezing harder. "Eight years! *It took you eight stinking years to rescue me?*"

Mok gasped, unable to breathe. "I'm sorry, brother!" he choked out with the air he had left. "We tried our best!"

"Your best!?" his elder brother screamed in his ear. "Your best took nearly a decade! What's your second-best? Waiting for my prison to collapse from rust?"

Judging by Mok's squeals of pain, prison hadn't rendered the man physically weak. He tossed Mok aside and surveyed the *daofei*. Wai hadn't made a single move. The surviving Kang Shen followers took a knee and lowered their heads, while the rank and file stood at attention. Kyoshi's eyes fell on the moon peach blossoms, still placed with care on the men's shirts. While it was now obvious that they'd sprung no ordinary outlaw from Te's custody, there was something worse hanging in the air, a dark warning in her imagination.

"Uncles," Kyoshi spoke up suddenly. "If the debt of the Flying Opera Company is repaid, we should be on our way." Her instincts screamed that they needed to get out of here. Immediately.

"Repaid?" the man they'd rescued said. He beamed at them, not with the fake smiles of Mok, but with genuine warmth in his heart. "My friends, you have done more than repay a debt. You have made a new future possible. Forevermore, you shall have the friendship and sworn brotherhood of Xu Ping An. You must stay and celebrate with us!"

Alarms went off in Kyoshi's head, the creeping hint of recognition just out of her sight. Before she and the others could decline, he turned to address his troops. Mok's men had become his men, and there was no protest.

"Brothers!" he said, his pleasant voice ringing through the camp. "For many years you've kept the faith. You are true Followers of the Code! I would die happily this very instant, knowing that there is still honor and loyalty in this world!"

The assembled *daofei* roared and shook their weapons. The sun began to rise dramatically behind Xu, as if he were favored by the spirits themselves.

"But I think we've suffered enough losses, don't you?" Xu said. "Five thousand. Five thousand of our compatriots snuffed out like vermin. I haven't forgotten them, not over the eight years I spent rotting in an abider prison. I haven't forgotten them! Have you?"

Over the frenzied screams of the *daofei*, Xu raised his arms to greet the morning light. "I say there's a price to be paid! A debt that is owed! And collection starts *today*!"

Kyoshi's head swam. They'd been duped. Distracted by small matters when the real danger that threatened the kingdom loomed within reach. She was so stupid.

"Now!" Xu said with theatrical casualness. "Where are my colors? I feel terribly naked without them."

Mok hurried over and handed him a piece of fabric. In unison, the *daofei* reached into pockets and satchels or lifted their shirts to reveal lengths of cloth tied around their waists. They freed the wrappings from wherever they'd hid them and fastened them around their necks.

The sun rose fully, letting Kyoshi see the hues that adorned the bodies of every outlaw present. The moon peach blossoms had been a ruse, a cover story to avoid detection. The Autumn Bloom was a temporary name for an old organization. A behemoth had risen from the depths of the earth to feed once more.

"Much better," Xu said as he patted the bright yellow scarf knotted around his neck. "I was getting a bit chilly there."

THE CHALLENGE

"**WE HAVE** to do something!" Rangi said. "This is our fault!"

"It might be our fault, but it's definitely not our problem," Kirima muttered as she hastily packed her portion of their camp. "It's not our problem." She repeated it like a mantra that might keep them safe from harm.

"I don't understand," Lek said. "Who is this Xu Ping An guy? Who are the Yellow Necks? I thought we were dealing with the Autumn Bloom."

"The Yellow Necks are business that we don't want any part of," Wong said. He rolled up the sleeping blankets with tight, nervous hand motions. "They're not in this life for money or freedom. They take glee in pillage and destruction. They're wanton killers. And Xu Ping An is their brains, heart, and soul."

"He was a bloodthirsty madman *before* he spent the last eight years locked up and dreaming about revenge," Kirima said. "We heard the stories. He used to call himself the General of Pandimu and claimed its residents were beholden to him for the protection he provided."

Lek scratched his head. "Where's Pandimu?"

"Nowhere!" Kirima said. "It's the name for the world he made up himself! My point is he's unhinged!"

Earlier, as they'd mumbled excuses about needing to leave the company of the Yellow Necks, Xu had seemed easygoing, without Mok's pettiness or Wai's outbursts of violence. He'd assured them that though he wished to throw a feast in their honor, a little show of appreciation, anything really, they were free to go with all debts to the Autumn Bloom and Yellow Necks repaid.

Kyoshi knew that veneer of civility meant nothing. Men like Xu simply waited for the right moment to drop it and reveal the beast behind the curtain.

"I don't know how he's alive," Rangi said. She paced in circles around the remnants of the campfire. "I've read copies of reports sent to the Earth King by Jianzhu himself. Xu was listed among the dead at the Battle of Zhulu Pass. This doesn't make sense!"

Kirima kept her argument directed at Kyoshi. "Look, they're—what?—a couple hundred strong now, at the most? Fewer, since the Kang Shen decided to dine on rocks? They're not an army like they were in the past. We can simply wait until the governors summon a militia force to deal with them. I bet Te is the one who rides out to meet him."

Governor Te was currently riding at the head of a one-man column in nothing but his pajamas. It wasn't clear whether Kirima and the others knew how old he was. But he could be a hundred, and he still wouldn't know how to deal with a man who'd given Jianzhu fits.

"That sounds perfect to me," Lek said. His face was unrecognizably dark. "The more dead lawmen, the better." He left the camp to get Pengpeng ready for departure, satisfied with his contribution to the debate.

"Xu first started out with smaller numbers than he has now," Rangi said. "If more Yellow Necks come out of hiding and rally to his banner, we're back to the dark days after Kuruk died."

"*We're* not back to anything!" Kirima shouted. "Xu is the abiders' problem! As far as *we're* concerned, he's a finished job! You don't go back to a job you've already finished!"

"Years ago, I passed through a town caught in the wake of the Yellow Necks," Lao Ge said, reminiscing calmly like it had been a mediocre vacation he'd once taken. "I saw what happened to the residents. They'd been . . ." He twisted his mouth, trying to decide what word to use before settling on one. "Stacked," he said. He made a layering motion with his hands, alternating one on top of the other.

Kirima still wasn't swayed. "We run away from trouble," she said. "Not toward it. That's our policy. It served us well in Chameleon Bay, it helped us survive in Hujiang, and it'll pay off here."

"What do you think we should do, Kyoshi?" Lao Ge said. "Given your newfound taste for making decisions of life and death?"

His question was dripping with petulance. But the rest of the gang didn't know about the botched assassination. They were still thinking of her command to preserve the lives of Te's household while pulling off the raid. No one had argued against her back then.

It didn't seem like they would now either. The group fell silent as they waited on Kyoshi's response, offering her the chance to tilt the scales conclusively.

Her head swam. A single moon ago, she was the weak link, not the shot caller. The others were putting too much stock in her being the Avatar. Conflating bending versatility with leadership. She'd grown more capable in the days since Hujiang, but not wiser.

Kyoshi fell back on the one philosophy she was well-versed in as an Earthbender. Neutral *jing*. "We wait and see what happens," she said. "But we can wait from a higher elevation. Load up Pengpeng."

Rangi and Kirima, the two opposite voices in her ear, united to share a worried look with each other.

They loitered in the air, a physical stamp of Kyoshi's indecision on the blue-and-white cloth of the sky. Pengpeng floated inside a cloud that Kirima had pulled around them. The Waterbender stood upright in the saddle, swirling her arms to prevent the tufts of vapor from parting and revealing their position.

Lek took them slowly over the Yellow Necks so they could monitor the movements of Xu's force. Kyoshi was keenly aware that they occupied a literal halfway point between fleeing and staying, perhaps ruining their chances for either option. She shook the nagging doubt out of her head and peered down below.

The column of men drifted slowly away from Te's palace like ants on the march. They formed a solid mass, Xu no doubt at the front, with the occasional scout sprinting ahead and returning back to report. A colony sending out feelers.

"I hope they're heading toward a militia outpost," Lek said, still clinging to some ember of hate for the law. "Then we could see a good dustup from here."

"They've stopped by a rice field," Rangi said. "Maybe they're trying to pick it? The second harvest wouldn't be ready though." The farming knowledge of Yokoya had rubbed off on her.

Kyoshi watched as the crops provoked some kind of response in the *daofei*. Years ago, when she was still living without a roof over her head, she would sometimes watch her fellow insects crawl through the dirt in search of food. The motions of the bugs always started slow, indistinguishable from randomness, full of hesitant backpedaling, until within the span of a fingersnap they turned into a focused swarm. The army lingered next to the green, burgeoning grain as if the collective had sniffed a target of interest.

Dark lines began to grow across the field. She puzzled over their meaning until she realized it was Xu's scouts infiltrating through the high stalks of rice, parting and trampling the plants. Her eyes darted to the opposite end of the field where a small house and barn stood. Smoke from the morning's water boil puffed gently out the chimney.

Kyoshi had been so preoccupied with the safety of the household staff of the palace that she'd forgotten about the people outside the moat. Large estates often had tenant farmers managing their private lands. In that little house was a family. A target for eight years of Xu's pent-up wrath.

Trying to split the difference with neutral *jing* had been the wrong choice. "I made a mistake," Kyoshi said. "We have to get down there. Now."

Kirima made a choking, indignant noise. "What, exactly, are we going to do?"

The lines had nearly crossed the rice field. "I don't know!"

Kyoshi said. "But I can't stay up here and watch anymore! Drop me off and fly away if you have to!"

A scream came from the house. The occupants had spotted the *daofei* closing in on them. The memory of swordsmen wearing yellow around their necks likely still haunted this region of the Earth Kingdom.

Kirima swore and mashed her fist against the saddle floor. "No," she said. "If you go, we go." She flicked the cap of her water skin open and pulled the cloud vapor inside, condensing it into ammunition.

"Once we hit the ground, we'll follow your lead," Wong said to Kyoshi.

Lek groaned but brought Pengpeng around in a tight turn, descending as fast as it was safe to. The others gripped the edges of the saddle and hung on for dear life.

"*Thank you*," Rangi said to Kirima, the wind whipping her words, forcing her to shout. It was the nicest she'd ever been to the Waterbender. "*You're true companions of the Avatar.*"

"*What good is that if we're dead?*" Kirima yelled back. Though she blushed, just a bit.

Please don't let us be too late, Kyoshi prayed as they sprinted toward the barn. She'd chosen that building over the house, remembering the setup in Hujiang. The tiny hut wouldn't have fit a big enough audience for Xu and Mok's grandstanding tastes.

The contingent of *daofei* stuck outside the doors sprang to their feet in alarm, but relaxed as they drew closer. The paint still caked on their faces made the Flying Opera Company instantly recognizable. The ghosts in red and white were honored guests of their boss. Kyoshi pushed deeper inside. She could see over the heads of the crowd to an empty space in the back where Xu probably was and shoved her way through until she found him.

The leader of the Yellow Necks sat on a bench, calmly reading a book. He must have missed literature in prison and taken it from the house. Against the wall behind him, Mok and Wai stood guard over a woman and her son, who couldn't have been older than seven or eight, cowering and sobbing to themselves, dressed in simple farmers' garb.

They'd been beaten, their faces bruised and bloody. Her anger at Xu laying hands on a child paled before the sight of what he'd done to the boy's father.

The *daofei* had tied the tenant farmer up and hung him by the wrists over the rafters with a long rope, several men holding on to the other end so they could raise and lower him at Xu's command. Underneath, they'd set up a fire and a rendering cauldron full of boiling water. It was big enough that if they dropped him, he'd be fully submerged in the vessel. The farmer's big toes dangled in the liquid, and he screamed through his gag.

Kyoshi ran up and kicked the heavy cauldron over, spilling water in the direction of the *daofei* holding the rope. They let go, and she caught the farmer in her arms. She heard the hiss of blades being drawn as she laid the man on dry ground, twitching in pain but still alive.

Xu didn't look up from his book. "You spilled my tea," he said. He licked his finger and turned another page.

She'd come to the conclusion that Mok's affected noncha-lance was a pale imitation of his elder brother's. Xu had proba-bly learned it from someone else. Like Te, they were all copying their predecessors, in a cycle that went on and on. Kyoshi drew strength from the fact that her own links went back further, among the most righteous in history.

"Xu!" she shouted. "Stop this! Let them go!" She heard shuf-fling behind her and a familiar, reassuring warmth. Rangi and the Flying Opera Company stood at her side.

Xu clapped his book shut and stared at Kyoshi. He'd combed his long hair and cropped his beard as best he could.

"First off, it's Uncle Xu to you," he said. "And second, this man is an abider. He worked for those who imprisoned me. He grew their grain and took their coin, which makes him another weight on the scales I must balance. If you can't handle this, you're not going to like what I do to the town of Zigan."

Kyoshi's fists tightened. If they were playing roles, then she would imitate the strongest, the bravest, the best. "You don't get Zigan," she snarled. "You don't get any town in the Earth Kingdom, nor this farmhouse for that matter. You get the free air you can fit in your lungs, and nothing else."

She heard her friends tense up beside her. Xu preemptively waved off the *daofei* who were ready to hack her to bits.

"Kyoshi, was it?" he said. "Kyoshi, I'm eternally grateful to you and your compatriots for rescuing me. But you're young, and that's why you don't understand. Eight years of my life were stolen from me. Thousands of my followers. At your tender age, what would you know about that kind of injustice?"

They're all the same, Kyoshi thought. *Every single one. Whether they clothe themselves in business or brotherhood or a higher calling only they can see, it doesn't matter. They're one and the same.*

"A lesser man might quit in the face of a setback that large," Xu said. "But not me. I relish the work, not the reward. I will get what I am owed."

They look at themselves like forces of nature, as inevitable ends, but they're not. Their depth is as false as the shoals at low tide. They twist the meaning of justice to absolve themselves of conscience.

Xu smiled benevolently and tried to find his spot in the book again. "The world is on the verge of forgetting my name. Which means I didn't carve the scars deep enough last time. I'll do better with the second chance you've given me, Kyoshi."

He motioned at Wai, who still hovered over the mother and son. Wai shoved the woman onto her hands and knees and yanked her head back by her hair, exposing her throat. She screamed.

They're humans like us, made of skin and guts and pain. They need to be reminded of that fact.

"I SAID STOP!" Kyoshi shouted. There was a backing to her voice that punched through the air. Wai hesitated, remembering the last time he'd drawn his knife in her presence.

Kyoshi pointed at Xu. "Xu Ping An! I challenge you to face me on the *lei tai*, immediately!"

It was the one idea that could have forestalled both him and his army from exploding into a frenzy of violence. Maybe Xu didn't think much of Kyoshi, but he had to respect the challenge. The Code that empowered him in the eyes of his followers demanded it.

There was silence from the crowd as her words sunk in, but

Xu responded as if it were the most normal request in the world. "Challenges are meant to settle grievances," he said, dabbing the pad of his forefinger with his tongue again. "What insult have I given you?"

"Your existence," Kyoshi spat.

She didn't know it was possible for a group of hardened killers to gasp collectively. Now Xu paid her mind. He put the book down and stood up. His men parted to form an aisle between him and the barn door. Only Kyoshi and the Flying Opera Company stood in the middle, barring the way.

"Bending or without?" Xu asked, perfectly at ease.

"Bending," Kyoshi said. It was the only way she'd stand a chance. She remembered her fans in her belt. "Weapons. Anything goes." She felt the flare and turmoil of Rangi's emotions beside her but heard no protest.

"Very well, then." The prospect of a duel registered on Xu about as much as a fly landing on his nose. Perhaps he'd already assessed her abilities and that was the amount of threat she represented. "Let's get this over with."

It was a lopsided arrangement. Six on one side of the rice field, hundreds on the other. In the middle, a team of Yellow Necks used shovels from the barn to pile dirt into a raised platform. With an earthbending *lei tai*, the fighting surface had to be shaped from the element, not made of wood like the one in Hujiang.

Kyoshi had declined to assist with construction in the hope that stalling would create more time for a governor's militia, an Earth Kingdom army, for any help at all to arrive. At this point, she'd take Te and a couple of angry servants armed with brooms.

"This was your plan?" Kirima said as they watched the dirt flinging into the air.

"It wasn't a plan so much as a thing that could have happened and did," she said. "I noticed none of you tried to stop me."

"There's little else you can do," Wong said. "Especially if you want to stop him from razing Zigan to the ground. It's right next door, and the nearest Earth Kingdom army outpost is a five days' march away."

Kyoshi stepped behind Rangi and embraced her, feeling her warmth. None of the others commented on their closeness. "I'm sorry I keep doing this to you," she muttered, her lips close to the Firebender's ear.

Rangi leaned back into her. "Today you get a pass. As the Avatar you would have tangled with horrors like Xu on a regular basis. This might be the first time you've done your duty since we left Yokoya."

It felt good to get a decision right, though it was uncertain how long she'd live to enjoy it.

"Kyoshi, can I speak to you for a moment?" Lao Ge said. "In private?"

The others frowned, slightly confused. As far as they knew, there was no particular relationship between Kyoshi and the old man that warranted a conversation prior to her imminent death. Lao Ge was more likely to give her a few shots of wine for courage than a pep talk.

Kyoshi followed him behind a curtain of rice stalks. "What do you think you're doing?" he snapped once they were alone.

He'd never taken such a tone with her, not even after she'd saved Te's life.

"You think it's wrong to fight Xu?" she said. If Lao Ge was going to argue that the Yellow Necks were good for the health of the Earth Kingdom, then he truly was as loopy as his outward persona.

"No, you fool! What I mean is that if you wanted Xu dead, you should have struck him down without notice! Blindsided him! *That* is the way of the predator!"

He seemed positively disgusted at the notion of an honorable duel. "Facing him on the *lei tai* and hoping for the best is the mentality of an herbivore braying and shaking its antlers to look good in front of the rest of the herd," he said. "I wanted you to drink blood, not chew grass."

Kyoshi took a step back. She bowed deeply before him, fully and formally, holding her angle at length. It wasn't the deference of a student to a teacher, but rather the rarely used apology bow, only trotted out in the Earth Kingdom in moments of true sincerity, and she kept it going until she heard a snort of surprise from Lao Ge.

"I'm sorry, Sifu," she said. "But I'm not doing this as a killer. I'm doing this as the Avatar. Even if the world won't know it."

Lao Ge sighed. "Stop that. You're embarrassing both of us." She straightened to see his wrinkled face arranged into an expression of scorn. It was ruined only by the genuine concern in his eyes. "Figures that the one time I find a pupil I like, she tries to be as mortal as possible," he groused.

"Well ... maybe Xu might suddenly pass away where he stands in the next five minutes?" Kyoshi said to any spirit or legendary creature of death nearby that might overhear and take pity on her.

"Death doesn't work like that," Lao Ge said. He reached up and patted her on the shoulder. "You're on your own."

The *daofei* finished stamping the platform flat. It was smaller than the one in Hujiang. There would be less room to run.

Xu hopped onto the *lei tai* first, swinging his arms to loosen his shoulders. He'd changed into a vest and a pair of pants cinched at the ankles. Mok and Wai stood in his corner, the elevation of the platform hiding them from the chest down.

"If anything happens, take Pengpeng and get out of here," Kyoshi said in an ironic echo of what Rangi had once told her. "Find someone with the power to intervene before the Yellow Necks grow their numbers again."

"What if it's the Gravedigger?" Kirima asked.

Kyoshi paused. She wondered if her hatred would follow her into the afterlife, whether the purity of her revenge was so important that she'd turn away his help in saving lives.

She didn't answer the question. Instead she gave Rangi one last squeeze and hopped onto the platform. She was still geared from last night's battle. The face paint had started to flake off.

Kyoshi steadied her trembling fingers against the handles of her fans. The stagelike nature of the *lei tai* added the tension of a performance to the stakes of a duel. Had Rangi been this scared, elevating herself to fight? Facing Tagaka had been less nerve-wracking than this. The battle on the ice had happened too fast for her to think each step through.

You weren't as afraid back then because Jianzhu was there, on your side. The thought held too much truth for her to swallow. She drew her weapons.

Xu grunted and sighed as he hugged one knee to his chest and then the other. "For the last time, Kyoshi," he said. "Are you sure about this?"

You and your friendliness can go straight to the bottom of the ocean. "You should ask yourself that question," she said. "I think your kind has a little too much certainty."

An unnamed young *daofei*, rather than Mok or Wai, stood nervously in between them with his hand raised. Kyoshi spread her fans and settled into a Sixty-Forty stance that Wong had taught her, equally good for striking or bending. Xu bounced lightly on the balls of his feet, preferring not to signal his approach to earthbending.

"Ready!" the referee shouted.

Kyoshi licked a drop of sweat off her lip. It tasted like grease. She scuffed a little more weight into her front foot. Xu began to inhale through his nose.

"Begin!" the young man shouted, before diving off the platform to safety.

Kyoshi summoned her energy, starting with her connection to the ground and extending it through her weapons. She would overwhelm her opponent with a barrage of earth.

But she was too slow. And she was playing the wrong game entirely. Xu thrust his arms forward, two fingers extended from each hand, and struck her fans with a bolt of lightning.

DUES

HER SPINE nearly snapped itself in two. Each drop of her blood had been stung by a viper bat. Her hands felt numb and tacky. The skin had been burned off them.

There was a thump and a jolt through her body. An eternity later, she realized it was her knees hitting the ground as she collapsed. The rest of her torso followed. Her headdress went tumbling as her jaw impacted against the platform.

With the side of her face pressed against the dirt, sounds were amplified. She heard more than one person screaming. Rangi, for certain. Would the others be that saddened? It was hard to say. She caught a glimpse of them and saw only sheer bewildered horror on their faces, the inability to comprehend what kind of element she'd been struck with.

Xu walked over to the side her face was pointing, blocking her view. She had never heard of bending lightning, never been struck by it, but that was the only explanation for what she'd seen, cold-blue crackling zigzags running from his fingers into her body. She tried to get to her hands and knees but collapsed, her chest flat against the ground.

"Remember," Wong said from the distant past, a blur of hazy recollection. "It's over when the winner says it's over."

Xu planted his feet and shot another bolt of lightning straight into her back.

"It didn't have to be this way," he shouted. He punctuated his sentence by sending a third and a fourth blast of lightning pulsing into her body. He intended to cook her corpse beyond recognition. "You had the greatest gift in the world. My respect. And you threw it away. For what?"

He kicked her in the shoulder, a meaningless act other than to show his disdain. "Don't think I didn't notice how you've looked at me since last night," he said. "Staring at me with condemnation in your eyes. What you don't understand is that men like me are beyond judgment! I do as I will, and the world must bear my discretions with submission and gratitude!" A fifth bolt, for emphasis.

What Xu didn't seem to know was that none of the lightning strikes beyond the first had hurt to the same degree. Kyoshi played dead while she came to her senses. There was still a searing heat that enveloped her upper half, separated by a layer of fabric. Her survival could have had something to do with the chainmail in her jacket, exposed by the tears and scrapes from last night's raid. Better to stay pressed against the ground until she saw an opening.

Xu breathed in again and shot a continuous stream of lightning at a target he thought was surely dead. Kyoshi smelled her clothes smoking as it washed over her body. He was desecrating her.

"Stop!" she heard Rangi cry from far away. "Please stop!"

It was the hopelessness in her voice that set Kyoshi over the edge, the complete surrender of a girl who would have been invincible if not for her love. Kyoshi had put that weakness in Rangi, and Xu had torn it open. He was torturing the person Kyoshi cared about most in the world.

And by every spirit of every star in the night sky, he would pay for that.

She reached out and grabbed Xu's ankle. The sudden course of lightning into his own body made him squeal, an undignified, high-pitched noise that was music to her ears. He stopped the flow in time to be dumped on his back, Kyoshi completely upending him.

Her eyes felt like they were leaking. Not with tears but light. She thought briefly about swinging Xu overhead and dashing him against the ground or twisting him like a wet rag between her bare hands. He was surely more fragile than a solid iron bar.

No. He needed to be shown what a true force of nature looked like. His men had to see him beaten not by strength but by retribution from the elements themselves. She switched her grip on him from his foot to his collar.

She rose into the air, not with dust-stepping but a whirling vortex that sucked her higher into the sky. Xu screamed and dangled from her grip. The tornado she rode blew the *daofei* back. From this distance they were so tiny and pathetic and human.

Kyoshi extended her free hand, palm upward, and the stalks of rice around Xu's men set ablaze. She curled her fingers closer together, and the flames, accelerated by her winds, hemmed them in. Many of the outlaws shrieked and threw themselves on the ground, rolling to put out the fires that had caught on their clothes.

Kyoshi looked down the length of her arm at Xu. He shielded his eyes from hers, her inner light too harsh to take in. His mouth gaped open and shut like a fish. The air was moving too fast for him to breathe.

"**You forget, Xu,**" she said, and a legion of voices synchronized in the eye of the storm. "**There is always someone who stands above you in judgment.**"

It was possible that other, more powerful people spoke through her in this moment. There was a chance she was simply a puppet beholden to their collective will. But an unassailable feeling of control told her that wasn't true. The voices could lend her insight, eloquence, but they couldn't take over. Many of them seemed to disapprove of what she was doing.

Let them, Kyoshi thought. She was in command. She brought Xu's face closer to hers.

"**What will you do now?**" she said. "**Knowing that your every step will have consequences?**"

She needn't have asked. Behind the terror in Xu's eyes there was a stronger, deeper outrage. His soul lacked any porousness, and the chance she so generously provided had washed off like rain on lacquer. *How dare she?* was the only thought running through his head. *How dare she?* Consequences were for his victims! *He* was a man who did whatever his power let him!

Xu mistook her analyzing frown for a lapse in her guard and spat a gout of flame in her face.

So he's a Firebender, she thought as she diverted the flames off to the side with a tilt of her head. A shame for him that he'd given away his intentions so clearly and that dragon's breath was the first act of firebending Kyoshi had ever performed. She wasn't as surprised as he'd expected her to be.

The lightning generation was unique though. A refinement of the art? A singular talent? She had so many questions for Xu about that. Too bad she would never get the chance to ask them.

Both Lao Ge and Jianzhu were right in some measure. Shortsighted men like Te and Xu were parasites who gnawed at the very structures they exploited for power and survival. They were blind to the fact that they existed not through their own merits but due to the warped form of charity the world had decided to give them.

And Xu had exhausted his. Kyoshi was the only thing holding him up. She opened her hand and watched him fall.

By the time she touched back down to the earth, the wall of fire that surrounded the *daofei* had burned itself out. Most of the swordsmen had taken the chance to scatter. Judging by the trails trampled through the crops, they'd fled in every direction, a routed army without a leader. Mok was gone. He and a few others had dragged off Xu's body before disappearing into the rice stalks.

Surprisingly, Wai still remained. He stared at Kyoshi, transfixed, his jaw agape. Reverent. Kyoshi didn't know what to make of the cruel, unusual man. He seemed to constantly need a powerful figure to tell him what to do.

"**Begone,**" she said with the last of the echoes in her throat.

Wai made the fist-over-hand gesture and bowed deeply to

her. He and the remaining *daofei*, mostly survivors of the massacred Kang Shens, faded away into the fields.

Kyoshi looked around for her friends and couldn't see them. "Are you, uh, still possessed?" she heard Lek say, his voice muffled as if speaking through a porthole. "Or are you you again?"

"Will you please just show yourselves?" she snapped.

There was a grinding noise as they rose into view. Wong had bent them a shelter to hide in below the surface, the same way Jianzhu had survived when she'd first lost control and entered the Avatar State. She wanted to tell them that this time, she hadn't gone berserk. She'd been fully aware of her powers heightening with whatever vast reserves of energy the Avatar had access to.

She'd been fully aware of killing Xu.

If Rangi wanted to embrace her, she restrained herself well. She and the others stood before Kyoshi, stiff and hesitant. They'd known her, had gotten accustomed to the idea that their inexperienced friend could bend all four elements, but they hadn't really seen the Avatar before, until now.

"Don't do this," Kyoshi said. "Please. If you act like this, I won't be able to . . ." Her knees buckled.

Not this time, she thought to herself. *Stay awake. Be present for what you have done. Look at your actions instead of turning away.*

"Kyoshi, your hands," Rangi said, aghast.

She held them in front of her face. They were riddled with burns from where the lightning had struck her fans.

"We have to get her to a healer!" Kirima shouted, her sharp face already losing its edges as Kyoshi's vision blurred.

"Kyoshi!" Lek said, suddenly close to her, propping her up as best he could from underneath her arm, the last person among them who should have tried to hold her up physically. "Kyoshi!"

She lasted less than two minutes before succumbing to the pain.

MEMORIES

THEY BROUGHT her back to Zigan. The other details were less clear.

At first Kyoshi had tried to refuse the medication thrust upon her while she writhed on a wooden bed in some dark building. She remembered the heady sweet state that Jianzhu had put her in before summoning a horror from the deep, before murdering Yun, and she resisted any attempts to cloud her awareness.

But then her hands betrayed her by sending waves of blanketing, enveloping agony into the rest of her body. Her resolve broke, and she gulped bitter concoctions from wooden bowls without questioning their source. The medicine split her mind from the pain like she'd cut off Te's palace from the *daofei*. The injury was still there, gnashing its teeth, but she could watch it from a distance.

The images after that came in the acts of a play. Wong fussing over the sunlight and furniture in her room, unable to do anything else. Rangi curled up into a miserable ball. Many times there was an old Earth Kingdom woman Kyoshi didn't recognize, her wrinkled head floating atop a cloud of voluminous skirts. She guided Kirima in her amateurish water healing by referring to medical charts, pointing out where over Kyoshi's scorched hands the cooling water should be directed. The lack of confidence, the worry in Kirima's face, during these sessions was endearing.

After some time had passed, she felt the most recent dose of medicine fade away without feeling the screaming need for more. Clarity infiltrated her skull again. Her thoughts were able to focus on the only person in the room now, the rest of the group taking a rest shift. The wheel had spun and landed on Lek.

"You're here?" she said. Her tongue was fuzzy in her mouth.

"Good to see you too, you giant jerk." He sat in a nice chair that didn't belong. By her best guess, this room was in the abandoned part of town and had been set up as a makeshift hospital. An herbalist's cabinet with many small drawers had been lugged in, drawing tracks of dust on the floor.

"How long as it been?"

"Only three days or so." Lek flipped through a textbook of acupuncture points. Kyoshi had the suspicion he was looking for anatomical illustrations. "You're recovering fast. We got lucky. Mistress Song is one of the best burn doctors in the Earth Kingdom. She lives down the street a couple of blocks."

That must have been the old woman who popped in and out of Kyoshi's waking dreams. "Then what's she doing in a place like Zigan?" Skilled doctors were in high demand, more likely to be held inside the walls of manors like Te's.

It seemed like Kyoshi would never be able to get more than a handful of sentences out without making Lek angry. "Trying to make a home," he said, misinterpreting her surprise as disdain. "Getting caught in place while her village changes and decays around her." He got up in a huff. "I'll go get Rangi. You can have someone worth talking to."

"Lek, wait." They'd gone on too long as misguided rivals. She'd decided not to let her parents have any more hold over her life, and that started by being civil with the boy they'd chosen to spend their last years with instead of her.

He actually listened this time, crossing his arms and waiting.

Wasn't expecting that. Kyoshi found herself at a loss for words. They had nothing to formally apologize to each other over. She ran through a list of things to say.

"You're . . . really good at throwing rocks," she blurted out.

How articulate. If her hands weren't mittened in bandages, she would have bit her nails. She had no choice but to invest further. "What I mean is, you saved me back at Te's palace, and I never had the chance to thank you. You were incredible back then. How did you learn to shoot like that?"

She hoped the flattery, which was completely genuine and deserved as far as she was concerned, would make him smile. Instead his face grew old before her eyes. He tossed the book aside.

"Do you know what a gibbet is?" he said after a hefty pause.

Kyoshi shook her head.

"It's a form of punishment the lawmen use over by the Si Wong Desert," he said. "They hang you in a cage, high up on display as a warning to other criminals. During the dry season, it's a death sentence. You can't last more than a couple of days until thirst takes you."

"Lek, I didn't mean to dig up—"

"No," he said gently, raising his hand. For once he wasn't angry with her. "You should know."

He sank back into the chair, throwing his legs over the armrest, and stared out the window. "I was living in the streets of Date Grove, a settlement near the Misty Palms Oasis. My brother—he wasn't my family by blood. He was my friend. We'd sworn to each other. We were copying the tough guys and swordsmen who came in and out of town looking for work. A regular gang of two, we were, ruling our patch of gutter."

No wonder she and Lek didn't get along. They'd shared too much, had the same stink. "What was his name?" she asked.

"Chen," Lek said. He bounced his foot, the chair squeaking with the motion. "One day Chen got caught stealing some rotting lychee nuts. We'd done it hundreds of times before. Sometimes in broad daylight. The townsfolk never cared. Until one day they did. Enough to put Chen in a gibbet."

The shaking of his foot grew faster. "It might have been a new governor trying to throw his weight around. Or maybe the villagers got sick of us. They clapped him in those bars before he knew what was happening."

"Lek," Kyoshi said. She couldn't offer him anything but the sound of his own name.

"I held out hope though!" he said with a little hiccup. "You see, the gibbet was old and rusty. It had a weak hinge, or so I spotted. I gathered every rock I could find, and I threw them as hard as I could at that weak point, trying to bring the cage down.

"The villagers, the abiders, they laughed at me the whole time. Especially when I missed. I could have knocked a few of their teeth out, but it never occurred to me. I couldn't waste a single stone. After a few days, Jesa and Hark found me passed out under that gibbet. Chen must have died before they got there, because I woke up on Longyan's back as we flew away. I couldn't use my arm for two weeks afterward, my shoulder and elbow were so swollen."

Lek swung his legs off the chair, unable to stay in the same position lest the memory catch up to him. "The funny thing is, Date Grove doesn't exist anymore. It was running out of water, on its last legs while I was there. It's been swallowed by the desert. The people of the town killed my brother to uphold the law, and it meant nothing in the end. If the law was there to protect the village, and the village didn't survive, then what did they gain?

"I always wondered if those people felt satisfied about condemning that one boy, that one time, while they fled the sandstorm that buried their houses," Lek said. "I always hoped Chen's death was worth it to someone."

Kyoshi bit the inside of her cheek until she tasted blood.

"So anyway, Jesa and Hark saved me, I learned how to earthbend, and I swore an oath that I'd never miss a target again," Lek said. "That's how I'm so good at throwing rocks."

There wasn't a right response. The right response was undoing, going back, reweaving fate to arrive at a different outcome than him and her in this room.

Lek smiled halfheartedly at her silence. "Did you ever consider that your parents might have left you where they did so you wouldn't have to live that kind of life?" he asked. "That maybe they were protecting you?"

The notion had crossed her mind, but she'd never given it credence until now. "The way I figure it, Jesa and Hark assumed the abiders could treat you better than they could," Lek said as he wiped his nose. "You were their blood. Priceless. Me, I was useful. As good as the next kid with fast hands, and just as replaceable. I sufficed."

"Lek." She thought about what truth she could tell him in return. "I believe, as usual, you're wrong."

Kyoshi spotted the twitch in the corner of his mouth. "And I'm glad that if my parents couldn't be with me, they were with you," she added.

A long time passed before Lek sighed and got to his feet. "I'll tell Rangi you're up and coherent." He paused by the door. His expression turned hesitant. "Do you think . . . once things settle down, I might have a chance with her?"

Kyoshi stared at him in astonishment.

Lek held her gaze as long as he could. Then he burst into laughter.

"Your face!" he cackled. "You should see your—Oh, that has to be the face you make in your Avatar portrait! Bug-eyed and furious!"

And to think they'd shared a moment. "Go soak your head, Lek," she snapped.

"Sure thing, sister. Or else you'll do it for me?" He waved his hands in mockery of waterbending and made a drowning noise as he left the room.

Kyoshi's cheeks heated in frustration. And then, like a glacier cracking, they slowly melted into a grin. She noticed what he'd called her for the first time.

THE AMBUSH

IN JIANZHU'S opinion, it was good to be home in Yokoya. No matter how many awkward questions the staff had about the team he'd left with. Where were Saiful and the others? What happened to them? Were they okay?

Dead in the line of duty. *Daofei* ambush. And no. By definition, no.

He owed Hei-Ran better answers though. Not only did the lie go a level deeper with her, he needed her input. After shutting the doors of his study on the faces of his troubled servants, he dumped his missed correspondence on his desk while she sat on the couch.

"The trail went cold in Taihua, and we lost a shirshu," he said. He knifed a wax seal off a mail cylinder. "But that's why we have the mated pair, isn't it? Redundancy, the key to success."

"Jianzhu," Hei-Ran said. She seemed a little cold and withdrawn, sitting on his couch.

"Ba Sing Se is near Taihua." The letter was from that brat Te. "I'll bet they're somewhere safe behind the walls. I'll have to round up my contacts in all three rings."

"*Jianzhu!*"

He looked up from the scroll.

"Stop," she said. "It's over."

He looked at her carefully. There were several ways in which it could be over. It depended on what she knew. He waited for her to continue.

"I kept an eye on Hui's movements while you were gone," Hei-Ran said. "A little more than a week ago there was an explosion of activity coming from his offices. Letters, messengers, gold and silver being transferred."

A little more than a week ago. That would have been Saiful's message arriving in Hui's hands. Hui's understanding would be the partial truth, that the Avatar might have been taken by *dao-fei*. But he still thought Yun was the real deal. Hei-Ran knew the girl was the true Avatar but not the results of the tracking mission and the outlaw settlement in the mountains.

One had the latest news, the other more accurate news. He had to mind the asymmetry.

"Hui is acting on the information *you* gave him at the party," Hei-Ran said. "He's building a case with the other sages to take the Avatar away from you. If he's made this much progress based solely on Yun having a falling-out with you, how do you think people will react to learning about Kyoshi?"

So far, that revelation had not gone well for anyone who'd heard it. "How do you think we should respond?"

Hei-Ran curled up on the couch, hugging her knees. She looked so young when she did that.

"I don't want to respond," she said. "I want to tell Hui and the sages the truth so they can help us extend the search. Jianzhu, I don't care about the Avatar anymore. I want my daughter back."

He was surprised at her lack of endurance. As far as she knew, her daughter and the Avatar weren't in any particular danger. Of course, the reality was that they absolutely were, if they were in the hands of outlaws. But Hei-Ran didn't know that.

Jianzhu sighed. Her daughter would never come back without the Avatar, the Avatar would never come back without . . . what, exactly? The wheels spun in his head. This was exhausting.

"Maybe you're right," Jianzhu said. "Maybe it is over. This farce has gone on for too long."

Hei-Ran looked up hopefully.

"You said Hui started his moves a week ago." Jianzhu scratched the underside of his chin. There was a scab there from where Saiful's blade had nicked him. "It'll take him at least another two weeks to send missives and get responses from all the sages who matter in the Earth Kingdom. They'll gather in Gaoling or Omashu and then summon me to answer for my mistakes; that's another week. That's plenty of time to ready a statement of the truth."

He shrugged. "We may even find Kyoshi before then. The facts will come out immediately in that case. I'd lose the Avatar, but you'd be reunited with your daughter."

Hei-Ran was heartened. She got up and placed a hand on Jianzhu's unshaven cheek, stroking him gently with her thumb.

"Thank you," she whispered. "I know what you're sacrificing. Thank you."

He leaned into her hand, pressing it briefly to his face, and smiled at her. "I have a lot of unopened mail to get through."

The smile vanished as the door to his study closed. Alone, he picked up Te's letter again. He'd been right not to give Hei-Ran the full story. He'd always been by himself in this game.

The message from the boy governor was written in a sloppy, rushed hand, devoid of the flourishes that normally came with high-level correspondence. The only authentication was the personal seal, which officials kept on their person at all times. It was as if Te had written it from somewhere other than his palace and while in great distress.

At first, Jianzhu had been against installing such a young governor from a family with a history of corruption, but had eventually found it useful, the way the impressionable child looked up to him. He could pretty much get Te to do anything, including reporting threats to the Earth Kingdom to him first before warning the other sages. Like now.

The scroll crumpled in Jianzhu's hands as he read about Xu Ping An's jailbreak. His veins threatened to burst from his flesh and skitter away.

Against every inclination, Jianzhu had kept the leader of the Yellow Necks alive as a favor to his Fire Nation allies so they could study how the man was capable of bending lightning. It was a skill so rare that some thought it a folktale or a secret that had been lost to the ages. Either way, it made Xu a valuable, dangerous specimen. And Te, who owned one of the most defensible prisons in the region, had managed to let him escape.

Jianzhu furiously scanned Te's account of the events, fully expecting to keel over and die from anger. Instead, farther down the page, he found salvation.

There had also been an attempt on Te's life, the letter went on, as if Te weren't eminently replaceable. Two assassins had almost killed him but at the last minute decided to show mercy. An old man, whose description Jianzhu didn't recognize, and a girl.

The tallest girl that Te had ever seen.

And unless panic had addled his mind, he'd seen her bend earth and air.

Jianzhu leaned back in his chair. He ignored the superfluous details that ended the letter, something about painted faces and how Te needed to end the cycle of grifting that his family had been so deeply ensconced in and could Master Jianzhu spare a few lessons in wiser governance and blah blah blah.

The Avatar was alive. Relief washed over him like ice water.

But what on earth was she *doing*? She had left Taihua and reached Te's palace before the full moon, which meant moving at a reasonable pace. Her actions didn't sound like those of a captive.

Jianzhu let the question go unanswered while he opened another letter. This one was from a prefectural captain in Yousheng, a territory that bordered Te's. The lawman had captured a handful of *daofei*, scared witless, with an unbelievable story. Their leader, Xu Ping An, had been murdered by a spirit with glowing eyes, drenched in blood and white ashes, who had carried Xu into the sky before sucking the life-giving flame out of his body and consuming it for herself. The captain thought that the dreaded Xu Ping An had died years ago at Zhulu Pass. As the esteemed sage who'd defeated the loathsome *daofei* leader, did Jianzhu have any information that might shed light on the situation?

Glowing eyes, Jianzhu thought. He'd seen those eyes close-up before, and nearly lost his life. He made a quick mental map of Yousheng and found that the fleeing bandits could very well have seen the Avatar between Te's palace and Zigan Village.

All right, then. Things were looking up. With some slight adjustments, he'd have the Avatar back under his roof. He didn't understand what she was doing or why, but he didn't care to. He had her location, and he had time.

It wasn't until the next morning that he found he had run fresh out of the latter.

One thing he and Hei-Ran had gotten good at in their younger days was talking to each other through fake smiles and laughter. It came in handy when they had to maintain a front during gatherings of high-ranking officials while Kuruk dozed off the previous night's revelries or made eyes at pretty delegates. Jianzhu stood in front of his gate, his feet wet with morning dew, and waved happily at the approaching caravan that was emblazoned with the Beifong flying boar.

"Did you know about this?" he said to Hei-Ran. He thought his teeth might crack from frustration.

"I swear I did not." Hei-Ran was as angry at him as he was at her. "I thought you said we had weeks."

It should have been that long. How the Earth Avatar was taught was solely up to his or her master. To revoke that bond required a conclave of Earth Kingdom sages. Gathering a sufficient number of them from across the continent should have taken as long as they'd discussed the day before, if not longer.

And yet judging from the size of the caravan and the banners that flew from the tops of the coaches, Hui had pulled together enough heads seemingly overnight. He had to have been preparing this power grab since before the incident in Taihua.

He'd underestimated the chamberlain. Taken the man at face value instead of considering what depths lay beneath.

The lead coach pulled up to the gate of the manor and came to a stop. The boar on the doors split open to reveal Hui, who'd traveled alone.

"Chamberlain!" Jianzhu said with a boisterous smile. "What a delightful surprise!" Jianzhu wanted to reach out and throttle him in full view of the rest of the caravan. He might have been forgiven. Avatar business or no, showing up unannounced was as rude as it was in any other circumstance. "Is Lu Beifong with you?"

"Master Jianzhu," Hui said grimly. "Headmistress. I wish I could say I was here under more pleasant circumstances. Lu Beifong will not be joining us."

Jianzhu noticed Hui didn't say whether or not he had the old man's approval for this action. He watched the other sages step out of their coaches and tallied who had come. Herbalist Pan, from Taku, carrying his pet cat in his arms. General Saiyuk, the lord commander of Do Hwan Fortress, another political appointee like Te who was vastly underqualified to lead that stronghold. Sage Ryong of Pohuai—

Spirits above, Jianzhu thought. Had Hui simply scavenged the entire northwestern coast of the Earth Kingdom for allies?

It might have been the case. There was no one from Omashu or Gaoling or Ba Sing Se, where Jianzhu's support was the strongest. Hui had handpicked the attendees of this surprise conclave, sages he could influence. Promises and vast sums of money must have flowed like water leading up to today.

Zhang Dakou was here too, Jianzhu noted dryly. No Zhang worth his salt would pass up an opportunity to humiliate a Gan Jin.

Their numbers were surprising. He hadn't realized these many sages fell outside his sphere of influence. Perhaps about a fifth of the most important people in the Earth Kingdom had arrived on his doorstep with hostile intent.

"Well!" he said cheerfully, smacking his hands together. "Let's get you all inside and refreshed."

The staff was aflutter. They hadn't had any warning that guests were coming. The dire nature of their short notice was made more apparent by Jianzhu entering the kitchen and personally overseeing the preparations. Nay, *helping* with them.

"Everyone, calm down," he said reassuringly as he hoisted a massive kettle onto the stove himself. "You don't have to pull out your finest work. It's not your fault; there simply isn't time."

"But, Master, so many of your peers at once?" Auntie Mui said, near tears. "It'd be shameful to give lesser service! We have to—we have to line up a midday meal, and dinner, and, oh, there's not nearly enough firewood!"

Jianzhu opened the kettle lid and peered inside to check the water level before turning around and laying his hands on the woman's shoulders. "My dear," he said, looking into her eye. "They're here on business. I doubt you'll have to feed many, or any of them. Concentrate on getting the tea ready. That's all."

Mui turned redder. "Of-of course, Master," she stuttered. "It would be impossible to discuss important matters without tea."

She bustled off to yell at the servants in charge of the tea selection. Jianzhu dusted his hands off carefully and gave a weary sigh.

Jianzhu entered the grand reception hall to a trying sight. The sages had seated themselves across three sides of the room, behind the rows of long tables, and Hui was in the middle where the master of the house would normally be. He was sitting in Jianzhu's chair.

Hei-Ran was off to his left. She traded a wide-eyed glance with him. *What are you going to do?*

What Jianzhu was going to do was sit down, alone, behind the remaining table, and wait. He felt stares burning into him from all directions.

"Master Jianzhu," Hui said. "Could you ask Master Kelsang and the Avatar to join us?"

The servants opened the door and entered with steaming trays of tea. Jianzhu milked the moment for all it was worth, waiting to answer until each sage had a cup placed before them. He made motions of thanks to the maid who gave him his, and took a sip, praising Auntie Mui's choice of the blended oolong.

Only once the staff had left did he speak. "You know as well as I do I cannot. Master Kelsang and the Avatar are still on their spiritual journey."

Hui smiled tightly, a motion that pulled his blocky face to the side. "Yes, their journey. The abbots of the Air Temples haven't seen them once since you made that claim. Is it not strange that Master Kelsang hasn't taken the boy to any of the temples, whether to visit the sacred sites or simply to resupply?"

"I don't wish to speak ill of my friend, but he does have a rocky relationship with some of the more orthodox Air Temple leaders. And places holy to the Air Nomads exist around the world. They're nomads."

"And what holy places are in Taihua?" Hui snapped. "Perhaps the previously unknown settlement of *daofei* there?"

Jianzhu stayed calm. "Chamberlain, what are you saying?"

"I'm saying that the Avatar's last known whereabouts happened to be in a nest of criminals, traitors, and outlaws, and that he hasn't been seen since! I'm saying that we have to assume the worst! That he and his companion are in mortal danger, if not dead already!"

There was the clank of a single dropped cup. Hei-Ran knew he'd tracked the Avatar to Taihua but not that the mountains had been crawling with danger. Nor had any of the letters he'd read last night mentioned a firebending girl. The fate of her daughter was unknown.

Hei-Ran looked at him like he'd stabbed her in the heart. That was the one gaze he couldn't meet. He concentrated on Hui instead, on this usurping little badgerfrog who'd fancied himself a player of games. Strictly speaking, Hui didn't have evidence in hand. But he could get it at his leisure. There was no hiding an entire town, nor the secret tunnels that supplied it.

"You have demonstrated unforgivable negligence at best and cost the Earth Kingdom its portion of the Avatar cycle at worst!" Hui said. *And the people I've bribed to appear today will attest to that.* "You are no longer fit to serve as the Avatar's master!"

He'd chosen to use *those* words. Jianzhu snapped.

"And *you* are?" he shouted at Hui, leaping to his feet. "You who want that power and status for no reason other than it's there!?"

Hui took the time to smell and sip his tea, knowing he'd won. "This gathering has not yet decided whom the Avatar, if still alive, should learn from," he said smugly.

Jianzhu felt queasy. His forehead grew damp. "This *gathering*," he sneered, swaying on his feet. "This isn't a proper conclave of sages. You've identified my enemies among the leadership of the Earth Kingdom and brought them to my doorstep like a bandit gang!"

"What has he promised you, huh?" he yelled at the assembled faces, nearly spinning in place. "Money? Power? For centuries men like Hui have carved up this nation and offered slices to anyone who'll pay! I'm the one trying to make it stronger!"

They blinked slowly, coughed hard, didn't respond.

Hui sniffed, his nose starting to run. "We meet the minimum number required to strip you of your duties. If you're . . . if you're done grandstanding, we'll take the vote."

Jianzhu retched. His insides heaved in and out and his vision went blurry. "What is going on?" he shouted at Hui. "What did you do to me?"

"What do you mean?" Hui tried to stand but collapsed back in his chair. He put his hand to his nose in astonishment. It was covered in blood.

"What's happening?" someone shouted. Sounds of vomiting

filled the hall. A servant opened the door behind Jianzhu to see what the commotion was and screamed.

Jianzhu collapsed forward, his upper body slamming against the table. He couldn't see Hei-Ran. But like the needle of a compass, his hand reached toward her as he blacked out.

FAREWELLS

KYOSHI GAVE a start when Lao Ge walked into the room, alone. She immediately took a defensive posture in her bed on the chance he'd belatedly come to exact a toll for denying him his victim. He didn't help matters by brandishing a small blade as he entered.

"Time to get the bandages off," he said.

"Why are you the one doing it?"

"I can be convincing when I need to be." He sat down next to her bed and gently applied the knife to the cotton wrappings on her left arm.

There was a rasp of the sharp edge on the cloth, of fibers giving way, that made her shiver. "You looked lost in thought when I came in," Lao Ge said. "Are you regretting killing Xu?"

He pierced the first layer and she contemplated screaming for help. "No," she said. "I feel bad about letting Te live."

Lao Ge gave her an exasperated look and wagged the knife. "You know, we can rectify that pretty easily."

"That's not what I mean. I told you I accepted the responsibility of saving him, and I'm not turning back on my choice." She rolled her lips between her teeth. "It's more like I feel . . . inconsistent. Unfair. Like I should have either killed them both or let them both live."

Lao Ge started rolling the severed end of the bandage into a round bale. "A general sends some troops to die in a siege and holds others back in reserve. A king taxes half his lands to support the other. A mother has one dose of medicine and two sick children. I wouldn't call your situation a particularly exalted one."

Her mentor had a way of cutting her down to size. "People of all walks, high and low, choose to hurt some and help others," he said. "I can tell you it'll only get worse the more you embrace your Avatarhood."

"Worse?" she said. "Shouldn't it become easier over time?"

"Oh no, my dear girl. It'll never get easier. If you had a strict rule, maybe, to always show mercy or always punish, you could use it as a shield to protect your spirit. But that would be distancing yourself from your duty. Determining the fates of others on a case-by-case basis, considering the infinite combinations of circumstance, will wear on you like rain on the mountain. Give it enough time, and you'll bear the scars."

He spoke out of kindness and sorrow, perhaps not as immutable as he claimed to be. "You will never be perfectly fair, and you will never be truly correct," Lao Ge said. "This is your burden."

To keep deciding, over and over again. Kyoshi didn't know if she could take the strain.

Lao Ge started on her other arm. "What I'm curious about is what you'll do next," he said. "Do you feel strong enough to take your man now?"

Kyoshi was distracted by the smell coming from her unwashed hand. "What?"

The old man tut-tutted. "Some seeker of vengeance you are. Your quest. Your ultimate goal. You defeated the same enemy Jianzhu did. Do you feel strong enough to take him down now?"

Kyoshi hadn't thought about her fight with Xu in those terms, that the leader of the Yellow Necks might be a yardstick to measure herself against Jianzhu by. It seemed like an oversimplification.

And yet.

She didn't give him an answer. Lao Ge finished unwinding her second arm. She flexed her pale and wrinkled fingers. The pain was gone, but her hands were mottled and shiny, missing their lines and prints in some areas.

"Go," Lao Ge said. "See your friends. I have some business to take care of on my own."

"Don't kill Te," Kyoshi said. She was pretty sure the boy had ridden to safety, out of the reach of Tieguai the Immortal, but it was worth mentioning anyway. "Not after I went through the trouble."

Lao Ge made an innocent face and pocketed the knife he'd been using.

"I mean it!" she yelled.

Kyoshi washed her hands in a basin and went to the next room. The Flying Opera Company had been sleeping there, the bedrolls laid out on the empty floor. Rangi and Lek were the only two members present, playing a game of Pai Sho that Lek scrutinized with intense concentration and Rangi looked bored with. Judging from the layout of the pieces, she'd been toying with him, making blunders on purpose.

She glanced up and gave Kyoshi a smile that could melt the poles. "You're on your feet again."

"I've been off them too long," Kyoshi said. She'd inherited the group's need for safety in motion. "I don't feel right staying in the same town for so many days straight."

"The rest of us agreed we weren't going anywhere until you were a hundred percent better," Lek said. "Kyoshi, you took a lot of . . . lightning bolts? Honestly, I don't know how you're alive."

He turned to Rangi like it was her fault for not knowing what Xu was. "I mean, I've never met a Firebender other than you. Is that some kind of dirty trick you people pull out to win Angi Kois or whatever?"

"No!" Rangi protested. "Bending lightning is a skill so rare that there are barely any living witnesses who can confirm it exists! And the reports don't mention Xu was from the Fire Nation at all! Do you think I'd let Kyoshi walk into a fight without telling her everything I knew about her opponent?"

Kyoshi watched them argue over Xu's secret technique. She hadn't noticed his eye color, but then, not every Firebender had blatantly gold irises. If there was anything she'd learned recently, it was that *daofei* brotherhood didn't require blood ties. Mok and Wai could have sworn to Xu without being related to him.

A Firebender had ended up the leader of a gang of Earth Kingdom outlaws. It was no different than a disgraced Air Nomad doing the same. Perhaps her mixed parentage made her understand such outcomes were less rare than people assumed.

"Oh, Kyoshi," Rangi cried with sudden dismay. "Your hands."

They'd been the first injuries she'd noticed after the duel as well. Kyoshi held them up to show they'd healed. "They feel fine."

"But the scars." Rangi entwined her fingers with Kyoshi's and brought them to her cheek. Kyoshi was glad she'd washed thoroughly.

"You had such beautiful hands," Rangi said, nuzzling at her palm. "Your skin was so smooth and—"

Lek coughed loudly. "I have an idea for that. Come on, love-birds. Let's go shopping."

Zigan hadn't been particularly friendly to strangers the first time they'd entered to buy food. Now in the light of a new day . . . it was worse.

The townsfolk stared at her with fear and hostility rather than the plain rudeness of before. Doors and shutters slammed closed as they walked by. Residents who couldn't afford such nice entrances vigorously shook their hanging rugs and curtains for emphasis.

"Do I still have paint on my face?" Kyoshi said. "Why are they looking at us like that?"

"Well, for starters, a lot of Zigan saw flashes of lightning and a pillar of wind and fire from your duel with Xu," Lek said.

"And then some of the *daofei* passed through town as they fled, telling stories of a giant with eyes of blood who drank the soul of their leader. These idiots haven't necessarily put together that you're the Avatar. I heard one shopkeeper say you were a dragon in human form, which explained why you could fly and breathe fire."

"But I saved them from the Yellow Necks!"

Lek laughed. "Kyoshi, by a strict interpretation of the Code, *you* are now the leader of the Yellow Necks. Dr. Song's no dummy, and it took a lot of begging to get *her* to think about helping you. She saw a *daofei* girl who'd challenged her elder brother for control of their gang and won. Face it, sister. You are dangerous."

Kyoshi was surprised at how much it irked her. The first heroic, selfless feat she'd performed as the Avatar, and it was tainted. The context had already crumbled away, leaving her no better than Tagaka the pirate queen.

But then, hadn't she understood this from the very beginning? Her legacy was part of the cost she'd been willing to pay to bring Jianzhu to justice. It always had been. It was simply . . . a higher price than she'd anticipated.

That was the story she repeated to herself as Lek led them inside a cramped shop. A brush of a hand against her face made her squeak. It was a glove, dangling limply from a hook on the ceiling.

An old man as dried and stretched as the skins he sold sat on the floor. He nodded at each of them, without the fear or disdain of the other villagers.

Kyoshi thought she knew why. Leatherworkers and tanners, peasants who made their living by crafting products from animals, were considered unclean in many portions of the Earth

Kingdom. It was part of the hypocrisy that Kyoshi hated so much. People from all rungs of society depended on and clamored for such goods but despised their neighbors who made them. She remembered the fine boots Yun had worn that day back in the manor, and her heart ached for him.

"We're looking for a pair of gloves for my friend," Lek said. "They'll have to be big, of course."

The shopkeeper gestured at one wall where the largest examples hung. Kyoshi pressed her hand against the glove at the very end of the row and shook her head.

"I got one or two more, bigger, in the back," the old man said unhurriedly. "But they'd be no good for regular wear. Not unless you figure on fighting a battle every day."

"I think . . ." Kyoshi said, "we should give them a shot."

He shuffled around, staying seated, and rummaged in a pile. "The back" of the shop was simply whatever was behind him. He produced a cracked hide bag and pulled apart the drawstring. "Made these for a colonel on the rise in the army a long time ago," he said. "Poor fellow died before he could pick them up."

The gloves were more like gauntlets. The thick, supple leather fastened to gleaming metal bracers that protected the wrists. Kyoshi pulled them on and buckled the straps. The fingers were snug, a second skin, and the armored portions heavy and reassuring.

There was no way these gloves would be acceptable in polite company. Their very appearance was aggressive, a declaration of war.

"They're perfect," Kyoshi said. "What do we owe you?"

"Take 'em," the shopkeeper said. "Consider it a gift for what you did."

He elaborated no further. Kyoshi bowed deeply before they left the shop, grateful to the core.

There was at least one person who saw the truth.

They walked down the street in high spirits. Kyoshi pulled one of her fans out and levitated a pebble. She could bend perfectly with her new gloves.

"If only it were this easy to find shoes that fit," she grumbled.

"It's better than being short and skinny," Lek said morosely. "If I was your size, I'd be ruling my own nation by now."

Rangi laughed and squeezed his arm. "Aw, cheer up, Lek," she said. She prodded his bicep, working her way higher. "You'll fill out soon. You have good bone structure."

Lek turned a deeper red than the face paint they wore on the raid. "Cut it out," he said. "It's not funny when—agh!"

Rangi had suddenly yanked him downward by the arm. Her knees dragged in the dirt. It was as if her entire body had gone limp. "Wha—" she mumbled, her eyelids beating like insect wings.

Lek yelped again and swatted at the small of his back. As he spun in place, Kyoshi saw a tuft of down sticking out of him. The fletching of a dart. She instinctively brought her hands in front of her face and heard sharp metal *plink*s bouncing off her bracers. But the back of her neck was uncovered, and a stinging burn landed on her skin there.

The sensation of liquid spread over her body. *Poison,* her mind screamed as her muscles went slack. Lek tried to ready a stone to hurl at their attackers, but it fell out of his hands and rolled on the ground. He and Kyoshi collapsed on their faces like the *daofei* who'd been lashed by the shirshu.

It was different from the incense Jianzhu had drugged her with. She could still see and think. But the poison was having different reactions in her friends. Rangi seemed barely conscious. And Lek began to gag and choke.

Feet ran over to them. Pairs of hands quickly grabbed Rangi and dragged her away.

Just Rangi.

Kyoshi tried to shout and scream, but the poison had its strongest grip on her neck, where it had first entered her body. Her lungs forced air out, but her voicebox added no sound. She could see Lek. His face turned red and puffy. He clutched at his swelling throat. He was having some kind of reaction. He couldn't breathe.

Tears streamed down Kyoshi's face as she lay inches away, helpless, unable to save another boy from Jianzhu's venoms. The dust turned muddy under her eyes.

It was nearly half an hour before she could crawl over to Lek and check for a heartbeat that wasn't there.

She arrived at their building at the same time as Lao Ge, Wong, and Kirima. They saw Lek's body in her arms and reeled like they'd been struck. Wong crumpled to the ground and began to sob, his low moans shaking the earth. Lao Ge closed his eyes and whispered a blessing over and over without stopping.

Kirima was as pale as the moon. She held something out to Kyoshi, her hand trembling uncontrollably.

"This was stuck on a post in the town square," she said, her voice raw and bleeding.

It was a note. *Avatar. Come find me in Qinchao Village, alone.*

Pinned to the paper it was written on was a silky black topknot of hair, crudely severed from its owner's head.

THE RETURN

JIANZHU SAT by Hei-Ran's bedside in the infirmary. She was alive, but she hadn't woken up yet.

If he were ever to tell his story in the future, to document his journeys and his secrets, this part would stand out as the hardest road he'd traveled yet. Murdering Hui and the other sages in his own home was nothing. Drinking the poison himself to blunt suspicion, trusting in the training that the departed Master Amak had put him through as well as Yun, was nothing. A good number of servants were dead as well, the ones who'd used the leftover boiled water he'd dosed for their own cups.

Nothing. All nothing compared to seeing his last friend in the world laid low. This sacrifice had been the hardest.

There would be aftershocks, ones that altered the landscape of the Earth Kingdom. The western coast had been decimated of its leadership, especially by the Mo Ce Sea. Certainly, some of the sages who'd drank his poisoned tea were corrupt or incompetent, but many others were as invested in bringing strength and prosperity to the nation as he was. It would take time for the effects to be felt by the common populace, but the parts of the country farthest from Ba Sing Se had without a doubt been greatly weakened.

There would be an outcry from the capital. Investigations. Accusations. But Hui had inadvertently laid the foundation for Jianzhu to come out of this mess clean. He'd identified and rounded up the sages who were not fully on Jianzhu's side, including some that were a complete surprise. That had been the whole point of telling Hui he'd lost the Avatar in the first place.

If Hui had felt the remaining sages in the other half of the kingdom were out of his reach for this gathering, even with the damning evidence of the Avatar running with *daofei*, that meant those particular officials were truly loyal to Jianzhu. When the time came to reveal the true Avatar, he'd would be in a better, more secure position, having tested their limits.

The chamberlain had done exactly what Jianzhu had wanted him to. Only, too fast and too aggressively. That miscalculation had forced him to turn his own home into a charnel house. It had cost him Hei-Ran. He would dig up Hui's bones and feed them to bull pigs for it.

He got up, his knees still a little shaky from the lingering effects of the poison, and brushed a long strand of hair out of Hei-Ran's sleeping face. Her constitution, her inner fire, had saved her life, but only just. Once he had the time, he'd devote every resource he possessed to healing her fully.

Though, if she'd been awake the past day or two, she certainly would have killed him for what he'd done to her daughter.

He'd revisit the matter later. Right now he had an important meeting to prepare for.

They buried Lek in a field outside Zigan's cemetery instead of claiming one of the unused plots within its borders. He wouldn't have wanted to rest too close to abiders, Kirima had explained.

The grid of headstones off to the side resembled an orchard, each gray, fruitless tree carved with the name and date of its owner. Kyoshi counted off the rows, burning into her memory the approximate distance so she could come back to this spot in the future. Following the Si Wong tradition, they'd eschewed any markers, taking care to cut the sod in strips that could be replaced and patted back down. The desert folk considered the simple embrace of the land the only honor worthy of the departed, silence the most fitting eulogy.

Standing there over Lek's invisible grave, Kyoshi couldn't have spoken about him anyway. She had the tongue of an animal in her mouth, the howl of a beast in her chest. Lao Ge was right about mercy having its price.

She'd shown Jianzhu mercy with every thought that went through her mind not dedicated to his destruction. Each smile and moment of laughter she'd shared with her friends had been an act of dereliction. *This* was the cost of forgetting Jianzhu, of not whispering his name before every meal, not seeing his shape in every shadow. And Kyoshi would never stop paying for it until she confronted him.

"What are you going to do?"

Kyoshi glanced up from the patch of grass that cloaked her sworn brother. Kirima had asked the question, her eyes red and hard. Wong and Lao Ge waited for an answer as well.

"I'm going to finish this," Kyoshi said, her voice the breaking of branches and rending of cloth. "I'm going to finish *him*."

"What about us?" Wong said. He had the same hunched, plaintive look as when he was waiting to hear whether or not the Avatar would stay with the group after their escape from Hujiang.

Kyoshi had to give him a different answer this time. She held up her hand. "Here is where we have to part ways," she said.

Qinchao Village had an air to it that many visitors found off-putting. Over half the inhabitants belonged to the clan of Chin, making outsiders feel like they were talking to the same person and being watched by the same set of eyes, no matter what part of town they did business in. There was a degree of tightfisted wealth that drew attention away from a set of bizarre customs and holidays that appeared nowhere else in the Earth Kingdom, many of which revolved around dolls and effigies, small ones for the home and great towering ones in the square for public festivals.

Qinchao folk were insular, even compared to Yokoyans. They exalted their status with borderline treasonous statements, like "A citizen of Qinchao and a subject of the Earth Kingdom," where wordplay and order implied their priorities.

A long time ago, Kyoshi and a group of other young maids had been allowed a few days of chaperoned leave to visit Qinchao.

Jianzhu had sternly warned them not to run afoul of the law there, lest bad things happen before he could rescue them. The other maids giggled and proceeded to ditch Kyoshi with Auntie Mui while they ran as a group from street to street, trying wine for the first time and flirting with actors by the outdoor theater.

Nothing out of the ordinary happened. They'd all come home safely.

But Kyoshi remembered the sense of foreboding she'd had back then as she entered the gates through the circular walls and made her way to the teardrop-shaped town center. There'd been a darkness below the clean-swept streets and ghostly hues of the village that she'd sensed would burst through the surface someday.

She must have been looking into the future. That day was today. And that shadow from the deep was her.

She walked down the main street, unconcerned by the stares she drew. With her headdress adding to her height, her makeup done in a fresh coat of red and white, and the heavy armored bracers strapped over her wrists, she looked half a performer who'd lost her troupe, and half a soldier without her battalion. She attracted attention, openly and without hesitation, like she'd never done before in her life.

This was who she was now. This was her skin. This was her face.

The Chin clan's crown jewel was the great stone teahouse in the center of town. Unlike the ramshackle Madam Qiji's with overnight rooms above a common area, the unnamed establishment was a three-story structure devoted entirely to food and drink, in the manner of larger cities like Omashu and Ba Sing Se. Residents of the village would spend all morning there, enjoying tea and gossip. It was the most obvious place for Jianzhu or her to wait for the other.

Kyoshi lowered her head and stepped inside. The restaurant was built with the second and third floors as mezzanines, letting her see the tables filled with boisterous conversation raining down from above. Waiters carried trays of stacked bamboo steamers through the aisles, calling out their contents, pausing when beckoned by a guest to place small dishes of glistening dumplings on the tables.

The man behind the counter gaped at her and waved toward the dining area. Either it was open seating, or he was too taken aback to deny her entrance. She spotted a table on the ground floor that was still being cleared and moved toward it. Chairs squeaked against the floor as people turned in their seats. A server coming the other way down the aisle nearly dropped his tray and backpedaled as fast as he could.

Kyoshi took a position facing the door so she could see who came and went. The dirty dishes in front of her vanished as if she were a shrine spirit who'd be displeased with any used-up offerings that lingered too long. Once the table was clean, she placed a round, smooth stone in front of her. Then she waited.

Eventually, her stillness allowed the other patrons to go back to their business. The chatter around her picked up. The music of songbirds could be heard from the second floor; a gathering of elderly men had brought ornamented cages to show off new specimens in their collections to each other.

Customers filed in through the entrance over the course of the morning. She took note of their builds, gaits, and faces, waiting for one of them to be Jianzhu. It was only a matter of time before he came.

Her former employer walked in and immediately spotted her sitting at the far table. He seemed slightly stooped. His handsome face was wan, haggard, like he hadn't eaten or slept in days. His hair and beard had been combed, but not to his usual impeccable standards. He looked older than she remembered. Much older.

Jianzhu settled into the chair across from Kyoshi. An enterprising waiter, seeing that a normal person had joined her at the table, came over to ask them what they wanted. Jianzhu sent him packing with a glare.

The two of them drank each other in.

"You look terrible," Kyoshi said.

"So do you," he replied. "The shirshu poison hasn't left your system completely. I can tell from the way you're a little slow-blinking."

He put his elbows on the table and leaned on his hands, giving her an exhausted half smile. "Did you ever realize the animals weren't tracking you, personally, to begin with?" he said. "I gave them Rangi's scent, not yours."

"You were hunting her the whole time instead of me," Kyoshi murmured. His ruthlessness was beyond her comprehension by leaps and bounds.

Jianzhu rubbed his face. "Bringing you back without some kind of leverage would have been pointless. You never would have listened to me. You made that perfectly clear before you ran away."

"I should have seen this coming," Kyoshi said. "You traffic in hostages. You're no better than a *daofei*."

Jianzhu frowned at her. "The fact that you think so means

you need proper training and education more than anything. It's time to stop this nonsense, Kyoshi. Come home."

"Where's Rangi?"

"She's . . . *at* . . . HOME!" Jianzhu yelled. "Where *you* should have been this entire time!"

His outburst didn't draw much attention from their nearest neighbors. Father was obviously incensed at Daughter for dressing up and running away. Nothing they hadn't seen a hundred times before.

Kyoshi doubted very much that Rangi was strolling the gardens of the mansion at her leisure, waiting for her. Jianzhu had grievously dishonored the Firebender by shearing her hair. To avoid retribution, he would have had to imprison Rangi. Or worse.

Kyoshi fought back against the anger that ran through her body. In a hostage situation she needed to remain as calm as she could. But her knee shook a little, contacting the table, causing the stone to wobble.

The rattling noise it made caught Jianzhu's attention. He looked at the round rock. "What is this?" he said. "Another child's toy you picked up while you were gone?"

Kyoshi shook her head. "It belonged to someone who should take part in bringing you down."

"We're wasting time here with your games," Jianzhu snapped. "What are you going to do, if not what I say?"

She couldn't speak her revenge out loud. Now that she was close enough to reach out and place her hands on Jianzhu's neck, telling him to his face that she sought his death would have been a reverse incantation that sapped her will. She was afraid that if she gave voice to her hatred, it would turn to dust like medicine that had sat unused for too long.

"See?" Jianzhu said at her silence. "You came here without a plan. Whereas I'll tell you exactly what I'm going to do if you don't stand up, walk out of here, and follow me home." He brought his face closer. "I'm going to collapse this building and kill everyone in it."

Kyoshi's eyes widened. Her mind skipped over debating whether he would and focused on how he might. She knew he wasn't bluffing.

"That's the trouble with these structures made completely of stone," Jianzhu said. "They break instead of flexing. Which makes them horribly vulnerable to earthquakes."

Kyoshi glanced around them. The restaurant was packed with oblivious townsfolk sitting on floors of stone, their backs to walls of stone, a roof of slate over their heads. In the hands of Jianzhu, it was a death trap. A mass grave in the waiting.

The threat was as real as could be. "You'd be living up to your *daofei* name," Kyoshi said.

Jianzhu froze. Kyoshi thought perhaps she'd insulted him to the point where he'd forget he needed the Avatar, that he'd reach across the table and simply end her life. But he clapped his palm over his own mouth and started to shake.

Tears flowed out of his eyes. It took Kyoshi a while to understand he was laughing hysterically. She'd never seen his true laugh before, and it was a quiet, spasmodic attack that claimed his whole body. She flinched as he pounded his fist on the table.

With great difficulty, Jianzhu gathered himself. "You want to know how I earned that name all those years ago?" he whispered, leaning in with a co-conspirator's trust. "It's a funny story. First, I made an example out of the few Earthbenders among the Yellow Necks. I took my time with them. Then I told the rest that whoever dug the deepest trench to hide in by sundown would be spared, free to return to their homes. Only the ones who lagged behind would be killed."

He chuckled in satisfaction. "You should have seen it. They dug as fast as their wretched hands could take them. Some of them killed each other over a shovel. They *jumped* into their holes and looked up with smug little smiles thinking *they'd* be the ones surviving, not their compatriots."

Kyoshi wanted to throw up. There was no word for what Jianzhu was.

"And there you have it," he said. "Five thousand fresh graves dug by their own occupants. I simply swept the earth over the top. Like I once explained to a former pupil, strength is bending people to your will, not the elements."

He sighed as he shelved the good memory back with its neighbors. "You're very hard to bend, Kyoshi. But if you give me no other option, after I kill everyone here, I may have to go home and cut Rangi's throat—"

Lek's last bullet zipped from the table toward Jianzhu's temple. It stopped before making contact. Jianzhu rocked in his chair from the effort of counteracting her bending, one hand crooked in the air. With great effort he lowered the stone back to the table, pushing against her the whole way.

He was greatly interested by this turn of events. "How?" he said as they fought over control of the rock. "When you left, you lacked the precision to bend a piece of earth this small."

Kyoshi's spread fan fluttered under the table, hidden from his sight. The strain was much greater for her. "I fell in with a different crowd," she said.

"Hmph." Jianzhu looked mildly impressed. "Well, I hope you're happy with what you've learned. Because now you've doomed everyone here." He reached up with his other hand and pulled the roof down.

Kyoshi matched him, bringing her second fan above the table. A tremor went through the building and died down before it could register as a problem with the patrons. Perhaps a very heavy wagon had passed by. The slab roof stayed where it was, though a trickle of dust drifted onto a few tables, causing annoyed shouts from the third floor.

By now a few people were looking at them, drawn by their bending poses. *Run*, she wanted to scream at the gawking bystanders. But she couldn't. Her entire body was tensed to the breaking point, her throat frozen. It was taking every ounce of her effort to oppose Jianzhu's strength.

But as her eyes wandered up to his, she saw that he seemed almost as taxed. His shoulders were trembling, like hers.

"I do need to give your—" he said before cutting himself short. He was likely going to say he needed to give Kyoshi's new friends his compliments. But he couldn't manage talking under the strain.

He noticed her noticing his little moment of weakness. With a surge of anger, he pointed his leg to the side and tried to blow out the supporting wall. Kyoshi made a silent scream as the effort to keep it intact tore a muscle within her body along her ribcage.

She fought through the pain and managed to keep the

destruction down to a single crack running from floor to ceiling. The wall held.

Jianzhu's jaw flexed. He bared his teeth. He and Kyoshi warred in stillness, their whole beings locked in opposition, a perversion of neutral *jing* where they only appeared to be doing nothing. Vibrations began to grow through the building again, the slight rattle of cups against saucers. The patrons on the ground floor nearby might have suspected this girl and this man were to blame, but their hesitance to move kept them within the reach of danger.

The sounds of conversation blurred and slowed, as if the air itself had frozen over. Men and women in Kyoshi's peripheral vision turned their heads at a snail's pace. Their sentences drew out like moans.

Kyoshi might have been pushing against Jianzhu so hard that she no longer knew what was real. She heard a footstep echoing in her ear, and then another.

A cloaked figure walked with purpose toward their table. Neither she nor Jianzhu could move. It was as if a third presence had joined their struggle, clasping its hands over their interlocked bending, squeezing them together.

The person who stood over them with all the familiarity in the world threw his hood back.

It was Yun.

Had she the ability to breathe, Kyoshi would have choked. Sobbed. This was a dream and a nightmare, her highest hopes and cruelest torment poured together in some horrific concoction and flung in her face. How had he survived? How had he found them? Why had he come back, now of all times?

Jianzhu's shock at seeing Yun nearly broke the volatile hold he had on the stone around them. Kyoshi could no longer tell who was in control of what, with their bending commingled together, only certain that if she released the tension by moving or speaking or blinking, the whole enterprise would come tumbling down. The three of them were locked in a private delirium, a prison of their own making.

Yun said nothing. He looked at them with a faint, beatific smile. His skin had the glow of a healthy adventurer back from a successful trip, neat stubble lining his jaw. His eyes twinkled with the same warm mischief that Kyoshi remembered so well.

None of this kept a blinding, nauseating sense of wrongness from pouring out of his body. People had always been drawn to Yun like metal to a lodestone, and Kyoshi had been no exception. But he'd changed. There was something essential missing from the otherworldly being in front of her. Something human.

The boy she'd loved had been replaced by a hollow scaffolding, wind blowing through its gaps. The nearby customers who'd so far tolerated her strangeness recoiled away from Yun like he was a rotting corpse, scraping chairs over the floor in their haste to create distance. They couldn't bear to be near him.

Yun noticed the bullet on the table. Its presence filled him with delight and his face lit up as if he'd seen the object before. He reached over and slowly plucked the stone free while Kyoshi and Jianzhu were still fighting for control of it, tearing the rock from the combined bending grip of a great master and the Earth Avatar. To Kyoshi it felt like he'd ripped a hole in the empty space, removed the moon from the sky itself. She could almost hear a sucking noise as the bullet left her and Jianzhu's grasp.

Still without words, Yun held the rock out, making sure Kyoshi and Jianzhu could both see it. Then he cupped that hand to Jianzhu's chest.

Jianzhu's eyes bulged. Kyoshi felt his earthbending flare outward and was forced to compensate. Yun gently put his other hand, still stained with black ink, to Jianzhu's back. After another second passed, he showed them what had traveled between his palms.

The stone, now covered in blood.

Yun didn't wait for Jianzhu to finish dying. He winked at Kyoshi and turned to leave. Jianzhu teetered in his seat, gagging on blood, a dark red patch spreading from the tunnel in his chest. The waiters screamed.

It was everything Kyoshi could do to contain Jianzhu's earthbending death throes. More cracks raced along the walls, big and loud enough to draw the notice of the patrons. At the door Yun paused and looked back at Kyoshi, seeing her duress, how she was barely holding the teahouse together. He grinned.

And then he bumped the table.

The foundations of the building rose and fell at his command. The impact knocked people to the floor. Kyoshi lost her grip on too much of the stone, and the roof began to crumble. Yun vanished.

A sheet of rock the size of a window crashed to the first floor, narrowly missing a waiter. She could feel the makings of a stampede beginning to form. There were too many pieces collapsing around her. The world was falling apart before her eyes.

Lao Ge had insisted.

Despite her protests that she didn't need to unlock the secrets of immortality, he'd made her join him in his daily longevity exercises. She'd told him flat out that she considered the concept bunk.

"This isn't spiritualism," he said. "You don't have to believe. You simply have to practice."

He'd taken her to the same spots that a guru would meditate in, the curves of flowing rivers, the stumps of once-massive trees, caves bored into the cliffside. But he'd also filled her ear with counterintuitive nonsense.

"Instead of blocking everything out like how you would normally meditate, take it all in," he said while they rested in a meadow on their way to Taihua. "Notice each blade of grass in the same moment you would notice a single one."

"I would have to have a thousand eyes to do that!" she'd snapped.

He shrugged. "Or an infinite amount of time. Either would work."

The riddles never ceased while they prepared for Te's assassination.

"Divide your body in two," he said, while she practiced heating and breaking a piece of scrap metal. "Then divide it again, and then again, and again. What would you have left?"

"A bloody mess." She burned her hand and yelped.

"Exactly!" Lao Ge said. "Put the pieces back, and put them back again, and again, and again one more time, and you're whole once more."

"A human being isn't a block of stone," she said, showing him her reddening thumb for emphasis.

"That's where you're wrong. The illusion that the self is separate from the rest of the world is the driving factor that limits our potential. Once you realize there's nothing special about the self, it becomes easier to manipulate."

To Kyoshi that had been the easiest lesson to take in. She was nothing special. She had never been anything special. That was a mantra she believed in.

Her eyes glowed, but only in a brief pulse. She didn't need to express her mastery over multiple elements like she had during her duel with Xu. Just one. The stone was her, and she was the stone.

Her mind was everywhere, dancing along the tips of her fingers. She'd let go of her fans, but for now, it didn't matter. Kyoshi felt the shape of each piece and how one fit into the next, making it so easy to put them back together. She wouldn't have been able to say whether she meant the teahouse or her own being. According to Lao Ge, there was no difference.

There was a stumble of disruption, almost like ants crawling over her arm. The customers on each floor scrambled for the exits. She watched them run along shattered tiles held up by nothing but her earthbending. Each step the panicking crowd took was its own distinct little thump, another weight to catalog. It was no great trouble to her.

When the last of the occupants had fled, Kyoshi got up, maintaining the form of Crowding Bridge with one raised hand while she stuck her fans back into her belt with the other. She looked at Jianzhu, slumped over. Her revenge encompassed within a single body.

It seemed so bounded and finite. How could such a container have held the volume of her anguish, her wrath? If any feeling at all pressed through the numbness of her unity with the earth around her, it was the ire of a hoodwinked child who'd been promised the end of her bedtime story only to see the candlelights snuffed and the door slam shut. She was a girl alone in the dark.

She decided to leave Jianzhu where he was, not out of any remaining spite. The path that led her to him had simply ended.

She exited into the square. There was a half ring of people around her, giving plenty of berth, staring in horror. They didn't know who she was or how she'd saved their lives. She didn't care.

Kyoshi let go of her focus, and the building groaned behind her. The crowd shrieked as the teahouse collapsed, sending a wave of dust over their heads.

The civilian residents of Qinchao began to flee. At the same time, she heard the clash of gongs and saw lawmen shoving their way through the masses. The officers drew their swords as they closed in.

"Don't move!" the captain shouted. "Drop your weapons and get on the ground!"

She looked at the red-faced, nervous men clinging to their steel. Without saying anything, she dust-stepped higher and higher, ignoring their threats and shouts of astonishment, until she flew over their heads, onto the nearest rooftop, and into the sky.

There was a tree at the crossroads leading into Qinchao. It had a single dominant limb that extended sideways, with a length of rusted, forgotten chain that looped around the branch. Kyoshi wondered what had hung from the end of the chain before it snapped.

Pengpeng rolled in the grass while the Flying Opera Company sat in a circle, back from the mission Kyoshi had sent them on. A short-haired figure leaped to her feet and ran over.

Rangi buried her face in Kyoshi's chest. She shuddered and wept, but she was otherwise unharmed.

Kyoshi cheated on the test Jianzhu had put to her. He hadn't counted on a mere servant girl having such steadfast allies so well versed in breaking and entering. While Kyoshi faced Jianzhu in Qinchao, the rest of the Flying Opera Company raided his manor in Yokoya, using the detailed plans she'd given them to rescue Rangi.

But there was one extra body lying in the shade of the tree. She recognized Hei-Ran, wrapped in blankets. The older woman had a ghostly pallor to her face that was hard to look at. With their family resemblance, Kyoshi couldn't think of anything but Rangi in a similar state of helplessness.

"Kyoshi, my mother," Rangi whispered, trembling in her grasp. "We found her in the infirmary like this. I don't know what happened to her. I abandoned my mother! *I left her, and this happened!*"

"She'll be all right," Kyoshi said, trying to pass conviction from her body to Rangi's. "I swear she'll be all right. We'll do whatever it takes to fix her." She let Rangi recover in her embrace, her sobs slowing down until they became a second heartbeat.

Kyoshi stroked the crop of fuzz left behind by the severed topknot. The Firebender flinched as if she'd grazed an open wound. "I should be wearing a sack over my head so you can't see me like this," she said.

There wasn't a good way to explain that Kyoshi didn't care one bit about her hair or her honor, so long as she was alive. In fact, it was easier for Kyoshi to rest her cheek on Rangi's head now, without all the sharp pins in the way.

After giving the two of them time, Kirima, Wong, and Lao Ge came over.

"The operation succeeded, obviously," Kirima said. "Once you've rescued one person from the bowels of a powerful Earth Kingdom official's personal dungeon, you've rescued them all. You were right. Jianzhu didn't seem to expect that you'd have us on your side. Made things a bit easier."

"I may have helped myself to some valuables on the way out," Wong said. His thick fingers were covered in new gold rings and jade seals, including one that allowed him direct, private correspondence with the Earth King.

Kyoshi saw no issue with that. But his knuckles were busted open and bloody. "Was there a struggle?" she asked.

"No one's dead," Wong said quickly. "But I had to get information the old-fashioned way from some mercenaries dressed in guards' clothing. I may have gone a little overboard. I don't regret it."

He looked at Rangi in Kyoshi's arms and gave a rare smile.

"The Gravedigger took one of ours. I wasn't going to let him take another."

"Speaking of which, where is he?" Kirima said. "Is it . . . is it over?"

Jianzhu was dead. But Yun was alive, an uncontrollable strike of lightning. Kyoshi had no idea what had felled Rangi's mother, nor what would happen to Yokoya in the future without its guiding sage.

And despite her best attempts to sully the position, her dedication to committing every possible outrage and act of disqualification, she was still the Avatar.

Was it over? Kyoshi found she had no answer to that question at all.

HAUNTINGS

THE SOUTHERN Air Temple was unlike any place Kyoshi had ever seen. White towers extended past the tops of swirling strands of mist. Long paths wound like meditation mazes up the slopes to the earthbound entrances. Bison calves frolicked in the air, adorable, grunting little clouds of fur and horn. She didn't understand how a people could wish to be nomads when they had a home so full of beauty and peace.

Kyoshi waited in a garden distinguished by its simplicity and open spaces rather than density and expensive details, like the mansions she was accustomed to. The breeze, unhindered by the grass and raked sand, was a crisp bite against her skin. The garden abutted a temple wall with large wooden doors. Each entrance was covered by metal tubing that spiraled into knots and terminated in a wide, open end that resembled a tsungi horn.

She was alone.

Her friends had gone their separate ways. Kirima and Wong wanted to take a break from smuggling and lie low for a while, living off the injection of loot they'd pilfered from Jianzhu's mansion. They promised to keep in touch and show their faces once Kyoshi had established herself. They were the Avatar's companions, after all. No doubt she could pardon them for whatever trouble they got up to.

Lao Ge declined to go with them, claiming he needed to rest his weary bones. In private, he told Kyoshi that as the Avatar and an important world leader, she was now on his watch list. He was only half joking. But she didn't mind. She was pretty sure she could take the old man in a fight to the death now.

Hei-Ran had woken up. Rangi, fighting through each word, told Kyoshi that she needed to take her mother to the North Pole, where the best healers in the world lived. If there was a chance for her to recover fully, it would be found among the experts of the Water Tribe.

That meant saying goodbye for who knew how long. They could and would find each other again in the future. But as Lao Ge had foreboded, they wouldn't be the same people when it happened. As much as Kyoshi wanted to stay with her, in a single, frozen pool of moments, the current carrying them forward was too strong.

Kyoshi had waited until her friends left before making her move, wanting to spare them of the chaos that would ensue after her unveiling. The Air Nomads often accepted pilgrims from the other nations, letting them stay at the monasteries and nunneries on a temporary basis. With Jianzhu no longer darkening her life, she simply joined a group of ragged travelers hiking up the mountain to the Southern Air Temple.

During the orientation for her fellow laypeople, she'd introduced herself by asking everyone to stand back. In front of the monks, she'd summoned a tornado of fire and air. The blazing, dual-element vortex proved her identity beyond a shadow of a doubt—though the fact that she'd nearly burned down a sacred tree reminded her it was still a good idea to rely on her fans for a bit longer.

As she'd expected, there was a commotion. Many of the senior abbots had known Jianzhu and met Yun. Her existence caused an overturning of the agreed-upon order. She was not the vaunted prodigy of the Earth Kingdom, the boy who'd publicly been credited with destroying the menace of the Fifth Nation pirates.

But there was a reason why she'd gone to the Airbenders instead of a sage from her homeland. The isolation and sanctity of the temple provided a measure of protection as the storm of her arrival howled outside its walls. Though she was a native Earthbender, the Air Nomads took her outrageous account of events as simple truth, told by the Avatar. They bore the anger and blustering of Earth sages who saw her as illegitimate, like she'd somehow usurped her position by being born, and relayed messages to her with calmness and grace.

The council of elders at the Southern Air Temple were not interested in profiting from her presence, nor in dictating what she should do next. They seemed content to listen to her and fulfill what requests they could.

Plus, Pengpeng enjoyed being back with a herd. Kyoshi owed the girl some time off with her own kind.

"Avatar Kyoshi!" someone shouted, breaking her reverie. She looked up.

High above her on a balcony, a tall young monk waved. She stepped back to give him space to land, and he vaulted over the railing. A gust of wind slowed his descent, billowing his orange-and-yellow robes. He touched down beside her as lightly as Kirima had in Madam Qiji's, long ago.

"Apologies, Avatar," Monk Jinpa said. "The tower stairs take forever."

"I've used my fair share of architectural shortcuts," Kyoshi said. She and Jinpa began to walk around the garden as they talked. "What's the latest?"

Monk Jinpa had been assigned to her as a chamberlain of sorts. He was the leader of the temple's administrative group, handling logistics and finance when the Air Nomads were forced to deal with the material world. Even monks needed someone to look after what little money ended up in their possession.

"The latest is . . . well, still a mess," Jinpa said. "The tragedy at Yokoya is worse than we feared. Two score of the Earth Kingdom's elite murdered by poison. And some of the household as well."

Kyoshi closed her eyes against the deep ache. She'd only found out by proxy what had happened at the mansion. "Are there more details?"

"The investigators sent by the Earth King believe that it was an act of revenge by a *daofei* group. Somehow they found out about an important gathering of sages and decided to strike with a level of brazenness that has never been seen before."

Rangi's mother had to have fallen by the same means. And Kyoshi didn't know who among her former coworkers was still alive. She didn't know if Auntie Mui was alive. She had to go back to Yokoya as soon as possible.

"What have you heard from Qinchao?" she asked.

Jinpa scrunched his face. The poor monk was taxed by having so much bad news pass through his ears. As a pacifist, he wasn't used to this level of death and mayhem. "The officers found Master Jianzhu's body. A couple of witnesses have corroborated your story, that a young man killed him in cold blood. But many of the townsfolk aren't convinced of your innocence. Nearly all of them maintain that you destroyed the teahouse."

Kyoshi hadn't told anyone that it was Yun who'd avenged his own death. Looking back, she was barely certain of it herself. The encounter had been as surreal as the one in the mining town where she thought he'd perished. In both cases she'd seen an entity she had no hope of understanding.

"That's all right," she said. "I doubt I'll be bothering the Chins again anytime soon. Is that the last of the news?"

"Ah, no. Master Jianzhu's death came with a complication."

Although it would have been entirely inappropriate, she nearly burst out laughing. Sure. What was another complication, added to the pile?

"It seems that several close associates, including the Earth King and the King of Omashu, held copies of his sealed last will and testament to be opened on the event of his death. It named the Avatar as the inheritor of his entire estate."

Kyoshi brushed the revelation off. "He was training Yun to be his successor in protecting the Earth Kingdom. It makes sense."

The monk shook his head. "The will refers to you by name, Avatar Kyoshi. Master Jianzhu sent the copies by messenger hawks only a few weeks ago. In the documents he confesses to his great mistake in wrongly identifying the Avatar and beseeches his colleagues to give you their full support, as he posthumously does. His lands, his riches, his house—they're yours now."

Kyoshi had to stop and marvel at how Jianzhu persisted in his methods from beyond the grave. It was so like him to assume the privilege of a sudden course reversal, to think correcting a mistake was the same thing as making amends. In his will, Jianzhu expected that, at his behest, the world would see events the way he did.

"Let me guess," Kyoshi said. "While those documents completely settled the matter of whether or not I'm the Avatar, now people think I murdered him to inherit his wealth."

Jinpa could only raise his arms in helplessness. "It is unusual that he was with you in Qinchao instead of his home so soon after the poisoning."

The other members of the Flying Opera Company would have found it funny. At least getting bequeathed the mansion didn't violate the *daofei* oaths she'd taken. She had every intention of keeping to the same Code as her sworn family members, living and dead.

She went silent as they resumed their walk. It was said that each Avatar was born in fitting times, to an era that needed them.

Judging by its start, the era of Kyoshi would be marred by uncertainty, fear, and death, the only gifts she seemed capable of producing for the world. The people would never revere her like they did Yangchen or smile at her like they did Kuruk.

Then let it be so, she thought. She would fight her ill fortune, her bad stars, and protect those who might despise her to the very end of her days.

They reached her quarters. Kyoshi had told the monks she'd be perfectly fine sleeping in the same plain cells as the rest of the pilgrims, but they'd insisted on giving her the room reserved for the Avatar's current incarnation. It was more of a vast hall by her standards. Orange columns held the ceiling up, giving it the impression of an indoor grove, and the dark wooden floor was carpeted with fine bison wool, naturally shed and woven into patterns of Air Nomad whorls. There were stations for meditative exercises, including a reflective pool and a blank stone surface surrounded by vials of colored sand.

"Is there anything else you need right now, Avatar Kyoshi?" Jinpa asked.

As a matter of fact, there was. "I noticed Master Kelsang's name in various registers around the temple," she said. "But in a lower place of honor than his experience would suggest."

"Ah, apologies, Avatar, but that's an issue of Air Nomad practices. You see, it's customary to maintain a level of separation between those who've taken a life, directly or indirectly, and those who have remained spiritually pure. It applies to names and records as well."

So it was a matter of Kelsang being unclean. That was how the Air Nomads had interpreted his efforts to save coastal villagers from the depredations of pirates. She wondered where her mother's name would be in the Eastern Air Temple. Perhaps buried in the ground with the refuse.

She looked at Jinpa's round, innocent expression. Her exploits at Zigan hadn't reached here yet. She thought about how fully in control she'd been when she let Xu fall.

"I'd like Master Kelsang's name restored to its regular esteemed status," Kyoshi said. The casual imperiousness came so easy to her. She hated every inch it pushed her toward behaving like Jianzhu. But it was such an effective tool in her arsenal, enhanced by her dreadful reputation.

"The council of elders won't be pleased," Jinpa said, hoping that she'd back down.

"But I would be," Kyoshi replied. "In fact, a statue would be nice."

He was young and savvy enough to understand the level she was operating at. He chuckled in resignation. "As you wish, Avatar Kyoshi. And if you have further requests, let me know. It's the least my compatriots and I can do after failing to come to your assistance for so long. We were unfortunately in the dark, along with the rest of the world."

Kyoshi tilted her head. "The Air Nomads weren't to blame for my troubles."

"I'm, um, referring to a different 'we.'" Jinpa scratched the back of his neck. "Do you play Pai Sho, by any chance?"

Kyoshi frowned at his cryptic statement and sudden tangent. "I do not," she said. "I have no taste for the game."

Jinpa took her declaration as the signal to leave. He bowed and left her to her solitude.

Kyoshi sighed deeply and walked over to the reflective pool, where a cushion lay at the head. She sat down in the pose Lao Ge had taught her and closed her eyes halfway, her lashes forming a curtain over her view. She'd spent much of her time at the Air Temple meditating in this spot.

It seemed wrong to call it her favorite place. "The only one where she could be at relative peace" was more apt. No one had warned her how empty it would feel to have a singular goal and see it achieved. Yun's reappearance, his assistance, his new and utter contempt for innocent life, gnawed at her edges and kept her from sleeping.

It was cooler by the edge of the pool than the rest of the room. She knew it was from the evaporation, but today there was a downright chill. Her skin prickled with goosebumps and she shivered.

"Kyoshi," she heard a man say.

Her eyes flew open. Where she should have seen her reflection in the water, she saw a changing outline, still of a person, but rippling between dozens of shapes, as if she'd dashed the surface of the pool.

"Kyoshi," she heard the voice say again.

A gust of wind sent her hair flying. A shroud of mist rose from the pool. She blinked, and there was a man sitting on top of the water, facing her, mirroring her pose.

He was in his thirties and ruggedly handsome. He wore the regalia of a great Water Tribe chieftain, his dark blue furs offsetting the paleness of his eyes. His body was adorned with the trophies of a mighty hunter, the sharp teeth of beasts laced around his neck and wrists.

"Kyoshi, I need your help," he pleaded.

She stared at the spirit of the man whom she knew was dead. The man who'd been Jianzhu and Hei-Ran and Kelsang's friend. The man who'd been her predecessor in the Avatar cycle.

"Kuruk?"

TO BE CONTINUED . . .